PHARAOHS
OF THE SKY

PHARAOHS
OF THE SKY

ROBERT L. BALLANTYNE

PHARAOHS OF THE SKY

Copyright © 2015 Robert L. Ballantyne.

All rights reserved. No part of this book may be used or reproduced by any means, graphic, electronic, or mechanical, including photocopying, recording, taping or by any information storage retrieval system without the written permission of the publisher except in the case of brief quotations embodied in critical articles and reviews.

This is a work of fiction. All of the characters, names, incidents, organizations, and dialogue in this novel are either the products of the author's imagination or are used fictitiously.

iUniverse books may be ordered through booksellers or by contacting:

iUniverse
1663 Liberty Drive
Bloomington, IN 47403
www.iuniverse.com
1-800-Authors (1-800-288-4677)

Because of the dynamic nature of the Internet, any web addresses or links contained in this book may have changed since publication and may no longer be valid. The views expressed in this work are solely those of the author and do not necessarily reflect the views of the publisher, and the publisher hereby disclaims any responsibility for them.

Any people depicted in stock imagery provided by Thinkstock are models, and such images are being used for illustrative purposes only.
Certain stock imagery © Thinkstock.

ISBN: 978-1-4917-6527-2 (sc)
ISBN: 978-1-4917-6526-5 (hc)
ISBN: 978-1-4917-6525-8 (e)

Library of Congress Control Number: 2015905896

Print information available on the last page.

iUniverse rev. date: 07/15/2015

For Tonia, who stood fast by me on this three and half year journey

All truth passes through three stages. First, it is ridiculed. Second, it is violently opposed. Third, it is accepted as being self-evident.

--Arthur Schopenhauer

PROLOGUE

He gazed reverently into his binoculars one last time. The swiftly retreating sun cast an ominous glare on the triangular structures before him. In his mind, he envisioned them as new, untouched, unspoiled, when the sand was new, when time itself was new. Long before the deceptive hand of the historian, who, since he could not bury them, chose instead to bury the truth and the knowledge they espoused. Here had been the true Trees of Knowledge. And what knowledge they had offered. Tantalising, it was.

A voice was calling to him. A Tourism and Antiquities Police officer, also his personal driver, speaking in the familiar Cairene Arabic that so dominated the region. *Cairene*. The alluring quality of the word. The way it forms itself in the mouth. It epitomised the region's exoticism. Other words of this land, these people, had the same effect. *Akhenaten*, spoken quickly and accompanied by copious phlegm. *Ana bahebak*: I love you. And he did love it, all of it, this most misunderstood place on Earth.

"We should go now, Professor," the officer said to him. Young, hawk-nosed, shadow-eyed, profusely moustached, clad in the traditional collared white shirt and trousers, black boots and beret, of the TAP. A holstered pistol at his hip. "You wanted me to remind you of the time. You wanted to be back at the hotel before evening."

He elected to linger, still transfixed on the pyramids and a proliferation of advancing shadows the time of day secreted. Hurried shadows. But they were only fooling themselves. Soon the floodlights would be engaged, and these colossal structures would beckon once more; darkness never truly showed itself here. The Giza Plateau was the essence of forever. Like the Nile, like sand. Like time, like memories.

"Professor…?"

His desire was to stay, tonight and forever after, here in the desert, curled under the majesty of the pyramids, so that the sun and the sand might preserve his body as it had those who had come before, before there was anything like necessity and loneliness, when there was only a land called *Khemit* and delicious secrets inhaled by an ancient people. He longed to remain, to become a Keeper of these secrets, these traditions, these realities. As one yearns for happiness or fortitude or love, he yearned for this. Secrets lost on today's populace. Most everyone was a non-believer today.

He nodded. Quite right. They should go.

They turned and strode as one, the soles of their feet on the soul of the world. But they were not alone: they were surrounded by tourists—lost souls, he thought of them—gathered as one sinuous throng, awed virginally in the presence of greatness. Sandals and t-shirts and khaki shorts and sunburns and sunglasses and hats. Rhythmically flashing cameras in the rapidly receding light. Flickers of brilliance captured and reduced in significance on a memory card. Gasping and snapping, gasping and snapping. Visual souvenirs, nothing more. Open and closed apertures all at once. Tourists without the need or desire to inhale, appetites that would not really be whetted. Unaware of the inebriated lies they drank in like bottled water, status-quo nonbelief satisfied their cravings. They assumed they were looking at immense tombs, as he had once assumed. But these were not tombs, nor had they ever been. He was sure of that.

He gazed at the crowd with reverence. Thirty years ago, a wide-eyed graduate student, he'd been like them. Capturing celluloid memories. Thirty years? Had it really been? No, more, in fact. More.

They arrived at one of the parking lots east of the complex, where a herd of tour buses grazed patiently on the tarmac. This lot, surrounded by the sands of the Sahara, the same sands which abruptly die at the encroaching vegetation imbued by the Nile. Such is Egypt: a nation of more than 80 000 000 existing compactly along a swath of arable earth, itself constituting no more than five percent of the country's total mass. The vegetation-spawning river meanders northward until it divorces itself into a superfluity of limb-like appendages; it is these limbs which in turn issue an expansive progeny of opulent, fertile fields and forest known as the Nile Delta. The Delta, like an outspread fan, dominates the central portion of Egypt's north coast.

He waited for the officer to open the rear door of a black police SUV, entered appreciatively. But his mind was elsewhere, soaring over valleys and rivers and deserts. Everything was about to change: friendships, research, knowledge. Everything. Soon, he prophesied, he would be the most hated man alive.

Hate. Perhaps too strong a word. One hated heartache and hangovers. One did not hate Egyptologists. Then again, one could hate anything one put one's mind to. One could, and one would.

They headed north past the front gates of the pavilion, travelling onto al Ahram. From here they veered right onto the Cairo-Alexandria Desert Road, which ambled still north past sumptuous hotels and apartment complexes.

It had always amazed him, this sandy nation of plenty. A realm of people refusing to submit to nature, who continued to build, testing the boundaries of logic. Out into the desert they were expanding now, encroaching. Greater Cairo, in its increasing vastness—its skyscrapers and hotels and mosques—had grown so close to the Plateau, it was now mere walking distance from a hotel to the pyramids themselves. And yet, he sneered, tourists and documentarians alike often angled themselves in such a way as to capture the Plateau facing the west, cleverly so as not to include the ever-penetrating metropolis that jealously eyed the real estate upon which these ancient relics rested. Cairo, growing, yet often concealed.

Technically, the urban centre opposite the pyramids isn't Cairo at all, but the city of Giza, the third largest in Egypt, three million strong, also the capital of Giza Governorate, which snakes along the Nile southward, then branches off west into open desert. From the air, Giza and Cairo appear as one, linked by concrete and smog. Greater Cairo.

They continued north on the Cairo-Alex, then angled west. The passenger's eyes gravitated to the road ahead, where he spied his hotel. The regal Le Méridien Pyramids—the original, now that one existed near the airport as well—offering breathtaking views beyond lazy sycamores of the Plateau and its stone occupants. Naturally, such a view amazes foreigners. To Egyptians, it is normalcy.

He beamed transiently as the car approached the front doors of the hotel, offered his many thanks. He jettisoned at once, saw that the officer was also exiting the car.

"I pick you up tomorrow at twelve o'clock to take you to airport." This time the words were spoken in passable English.

Twelve was fine, Khaled. He would see him then.

The young man was still beaming. "When next you come to Egypt, Professor Trent?"

He suppressed a smile, opted for a simple shrug. Soon. He turned and passed through the front entrance of the hotel and disappeared within.

Le Méridien Pyramids boasted one of the more elaborate hotel lobbies he had ever seen. A deluge of marble: a polished, two-toned marble floor, refined and stone-cut marble walls, an extravagant marble staircase that dominated the space beyond. There were stores, a diner, recliners along its outer walls, the entrances of many affectionately flanked by ancient black Egyptian statuettes sporting gold *nemes* headdresses and *shendyt* skirts. This was all beyond the front desk, which he bypassed with barely a look. He moved towards the bank of elevators located along the far wall, a solitary silhouette in a sea of hungry tourists. He smiled indifferently to various passers-by and found an available lift, directed it up to his room.

There were, of course, two basic sets of rooms: those that overlooked the city, and those that overlooked the pyramids. He always reserved a deluxe suite with a king-sized bed that looked westward, out onto the Plateau. The pyramids would gaze back symbiotically. The Great Pyramid, supposedly belonging to the pharaoh Khufu, with Khafre's in the near distance, turbaned in trademark casing stones at its summit.

The room was spacious, coated in a warm earthen tone. Curtains flanked the window, wrinkled like a face, offset by darkened folds. A dark, round table in the far corner, balanced by twin orange chairs. The bed, arrayed in white Egyptian linen, pillows like concealed breasts. Nearby, a desk of dark brown Egyptian sycamore, joined to a wall unit housing a television. His laptop was there, centred between an impressive mountain of books and a reading lamp. Another yellow chair had been inserted under the desk.

It was just past six o'clock. He hadn't eaten in hours, but he was not hungry. He needed instead to shower, to wash off perspiration that had coalesced along his back and under his arms. To wash off the guilt. If only he could be so lucky. The guilt had been self-inflicted. He would have to live with it.

He cast off his khaki trousers and buttoned shirt, tossed them unceremoniously onto the bed, made his way to the bathroom. It was only when he began adjusting the knobs to gain the desired water temperature that he began to tremble.

He let the water from above cascade down over his head, his shoulders, a full two minutes. He turned the tap off and stood there, head hung in penance, staring at the droplets that retreated through the drain. He didn't know how long he stood there—a moment? Five? Ten?

He exited the shower and reached for one of the various white towels at the ready. Rubbed himself dry, secured a bath robe, then walked back into his room. He turned to the desk, peered down at the laptop. Turned it on, then stepped away, towards a safe located nearby. Opening it, he removed something clad in a brown cloth, then returned to the computer and seated himself in the chair, the obscured object still in hand. He typed in his password, then waited several seconds. Opened his picture folder.

Stared.

Stared at the image, at the message below it he had written to himself.

He minimised the image, activated his email messenger, typed in a desired address. Waited. His eyes drifted from the screen to the books nearby. The one on top was his own Bible. He stared at it unrelentingly for several seconds, reached over, caressed its worn leather cover. Then he urgently reformed his outstretched hand into a fist.

Was he really going through with this? He so wanted not to, wanted to turn the computer off, to walk away, to take the elevator down to the diner. But it was too late. He had to do this. He had unconvincingly convinced himself of it. The world had to know. The deniers would have a field day; they would tunnel away at the walls of his theory with pickaxes of disgust. But these walls would hold fast, he had told himself. Because they needed to. Because he had an obligation to circularise the truth. That was what he intended to do.

A message appeared.

Did you enjoy digging in the sand?

How he had enjoyed it! He had felt like a boy again, on a beach somewhere and somewhen distant, peeling back the layers of the Earth, delving into her confidences. This had been part of the agreement. He had dug, delightfully on his own and unobserved by anyone.

Do you have it?

He did. For two days now; it had taken him this long to make contact. They had had an agreement: he would uncover the evidence, hand it off, be paid handsomely. Then the discovery would be leaked to the world without any connection to him. He nodded fearfully as he thought this, gulped for air. Eventually the world would come to know it had been him. But that wasn't it—that wasn't the reason he'd delayed. He had needed time.

He eyed his Bible once again, his breathing uneasy. This was the hardest thing he'd ever had to do. Betrayal is how the Egyptians would come to see it, and the government would expel him forever. Such a betrayal went against every moral fibre of his being. And yet he knew he was willingly complicit. He'd betrayed the people of this land, and he'd destroyed his reputation, which was anything but an idle and false imposition.

We agreed on a rather generous sum for your betrayal. You didn't seem conflicted at the time.

Regardless, there had been other complications. He licked his lips uncomfortably. Things had gotten dangerous. Someone had been on to him. He had known it, had already known trouble even before this return to Egypt. He and his companion Hammond, they'd—

But now was not the time. There was no need to describe his globe-hopping these past several months, the other secrets he'd uncovered.

No one is onto you. No one knows.

That was a lie. Someone always knows.

How could anyone know where he had been, what he'd seen? How could anyone have known about pyramids in Mexico, about ancient cities in Peru and Bolivia and India? About a sunken city off the coast of a Japanese island? About factories in Australia and America, and what was being produced there? How could anyone have known about the secrets buried across Europe, within structures in plain sight? And, of course, how could anyone have known about the secrets here in Egypt, along the banks of the Nile and beyond? But others *had* known. Other forces at work here, besides this pixelated figure and those he worked for.

Besides, he had needed to sort things out. The ardent non-believer, now converted to the truth. But he was not yet done with soul-searching. Egypt had been his life.

No.

The *truth* had been his life. He'd been searching for it for decades. And now he'd found it. Everything else was irrelevant.

With some reluctance, he raised his right hand, the veiled object now visible. He removed the covering, balancing the artefact in his palm, as if to a cybernetic eye of the one with whom he spoke.

When would they make the exchange?

The silence on the other end was deafening. Then: Well done, Professor.

This was just the tip of the iceberg.

All in good time. Someone is on the way.

On the way? Here? Now?

He should be at your door any minute.

He hesitated, ran an anxious hand through his wet hair. This made no sense. Who was coming to his door? He had been led to believe the arrangements would be made by himself and no other.

A sudden knock startled him. Something was wrong. Why hadn't this visitor been announced at the front lobby? How was he already in the building? How did he get in? How did he know the room number? No one knew the number.

Just answer the door.

He rose apprehensively, walked, hesitated momentarily when he gripped the handle. Another knock jolted him out of his temporary stupor. He turned the knob.

It was Khaled of all people, smiling glowingly. He was out of uniform, dressed casually in a stylish black blazer, a pale blue collared shirt beneath. His physical features had changed radically as well. No moustache, the hair cropped.

"Hello, Professor."

He glanced back at the computer screen, hopelessly confused.

When the Egyptian spoke again, he did so in curiously improved English. "I wanted so very much to tell you, but I have my orders, as do you." In his gloved right hand, he was holding a brown box with a buttoned lid. It lacked any ornate design, save for a black stripe that ran across its top and around its circumference. He followed the professor's eyes from the case to his own face, reached up, rubbed his shaven lip with beguiling satisfaction. "Ah, yes. Of course."

The professor had seen him drive off, hadn't he? No, he realised. He'd turned away. He'd had no reason to watch. He gravitated to Khaled's eyes, saw that they were hungrily transfixed on the object in his hand. He nodded, extended the hand with the object still tightly wrapped. Again he noticed the wooden container.

"Your money is here," said the Egyptian.

As if on cue, the professor reached down without looking and unfastened the box. His hand dove in with admitted greed, probing its perimeter. But there was no money. He glinted downward with tepid bewilderment. There was something else, moving within the obfuscating shadows.

And then he felt something terrifyingly painful. Something like a bite. Or a sting. He recoiled at once, staring down at his hand. A large, reddish welt had already appeared.

The Egyptian released the container and stepped dismissively past him, toward the computer. And then tears erupted from his eyes, instantly obscured his vision. His body screamed out in unabashed agony. He dropped to his knees, saw through his tears that something was emerging from the fallen box, was crawling across the carpeted floor. Something black, scuttling rapidly. Something terrifying. He watched the Egyptian reach down with nonchalance and snatch whatever it was up by its enormous spiked tail, return it to the simultaneously retrieved case. He wanted to cry out, but he could not, for his windpipe was closing. He wiped at his face, at saliva pooling at the corners of his mouth.

The assassin seated himself at the terminal, placing the once-again concealed scorpion atop the Bible. He turned and watched with minimal satisfaction the professor's final valiant gasps at life, the spasmodic thrashing. Then the convulsing spectacle went silent, and the professor's head dropped lifelessly to the carpeted floor.

An Egyptian fat tail. Its bite is lethal.

He turned to the screen.

It is done.

You're not finished yet. Open the professor's email account.

He did so, scanned the sent messages; sundry letters of little importance, all more than a day old.

No messages sent in the past twenty-four hours.

You're certain?

But there is something else here.

An image, minimised as if forgotten. He brought it to full screen.

What do you see?

I see...a mountain. And a message.

What does it say?

It contains numbers.

Numbers?

Numbers.

KHEPER

A light ahead in the darkness...
He is gripped with fear...
Two figures are watching him...
They are walking towards him...
He powers up the nerve to open his mouth, to scream in horror...
He can feel hands reaching around his arms, pulling him upward...
No! No! Get away! Get away! Oh, God, get away! Please!—

The first thing he perceived when he awoke was calmed lighting. It made him uncomfortable. He came to understand that he was in a hospital bed, in a room built for four. But he was the only patient.

Had he been awake previously, he would have noticed that the nurse had entered the darkened room again. He would have noticed her run a smooth and delicate hand over his forehead. He might have smelled the roses in the hand sanitizer she was wearing. He could not know how she studied him through the fluttering of curled eyelashes, scrutinised the rhythmic palpitation of his chest as it rose and fell with each breath. How she studied his chart. No change in his breathing. He did not see how, satisfied, she floated across the floor towards the window, pulled the curtain further across. The sun had receded, and he did not see how she gazed out at the adjoining wing of the hospital, then down towards ground illuminated by pale yellow street lights. He could not see how she turned towards the open doorway through which she had just come, lowered the lights, and disappeared. He noticed none of these things; he had been out since before his own arrival.

He glanced down. He was still wearing his baseball clothes. A navy blue shirt, "Silver Bullets" offset in attractive grey lettering and numbers. Grey shorts, lazily blanketing his thighs. He lay back, closed his eyes, tried to remember.

He saw light posts surrounding the baseball diamond, colossal effigies denying aggressively creeping shadows. His Bullets and their opponents, Damaged Goods, orange-trimmed amid prevailing black. His teammates hunkered down at their positions like soldiers of the Ardennes. The score was 12-12. There were bleachers, once vibrant blue, now worn and chipping, sprinkled by a scattering of fans. There was a cantina, now similarly neglected.

The air was dense with unwanted mosquitoes attacking in carefully orchestrated dive patterns. He remembered swatting futility at them, listening to the curses of others. Someone had brought bug spray. What a novel concept, they had joked, each in turn applying it across exposed arms, legs, necks.

Apart from the humidity and the mosquitoes that so dominate southern Ontario this time of year, it had been a perfect night for baseball in the tiny community of Thamesford, encamped along the banks of the Thames River, equidistantly situated between London and Woodstock. Thamesford, the home of Calithumpian, UFC star Mark Hominick, and the Thamesford Trojans. His hometown. Logically, it was also the home of the Thamesford Men's Slow Pitch League. And on this clear evening, he mused now, nothing could have been better.

He remembered the rising action now. Jim, the first batter of the inning, had promptly lined a single up the middle. Kyle had followed with a blooper into shallow right field. Then he had stepped towards the faint chalk-lined rectangle that was the batter's box, long since erased by tonight's action. He had dug in, rubber spikes on the soles of his shoes burrowing into the soft sand. His hands had tensed round the bat's handle. Green-eyed, he had scrutinised the pitcher, awaited the first pitch.

He remembered taking three balls, the rousing from his bench that he might walk and have to buy a case for the team. No one walked in slow pitch. So he prepared to swing on the fourth pitch no matter what. As it turned out, the fourth pitch would have been a strike anyways. He had swatted at it before it had had the chance to land, slamming it far down into the right field corner. It had bounced violently up against the chain-link fence as the nearest fielder hastened to catch up with it.

Jim scored easily, as did Kyle. He, in turn, had churned around first base, fervently sniffing the distinct possibility of a triple. His ears had alerted him to the boisterous urgings of his teammates, voices in waves competing with his own concentration. He had rounded second and gazed at third, perceptively noticing the third baseman on the opposing team suddenly pulling off the bag. An errant throw; third base was his. He had let up ever so slightly. Then everything went wrong.

He hadn't seen the ball coming. For a split second, he had felt no pain, only an immense vibration in the back of his head. And then, as delayed sound hastens after a streaking jet, belated pain had washed over him. He had stumbled, lost his balance, had fallen over into the gravel infield. A cloud of dust had spontaneously risen about him.

It was then, as he had grimaced in expectant agony, both teammates and opposing players hastening to his side, that he had realised he'd been struck in the head by the ball. The pain had been unbearable, a red-hot, throbbing incessancy radiating from the rear of his skull. He had sensed a teammate taking him under each arm, lifting him to his feet.

They were calling to him, his teammates. He could hear their motley voices. There were other voices, too, from those of the opposition, and the spectators.

Tenderly, he had been escorted to the bench. The unmasked umpire stepped closer to have a look. Was he alright?

He would be fine, he had replied, waving away the official, who retreated to home plate to resume the game. But that had been a lie. He had felt anything but fine. The pain was unendurable. Even in this league, where so many once played competitive ball, men can still throw with intensity.

The umpire had roared authoritatively to the bench. Time for a pinch runner. Thus, the game had resumed, and for several seconds, everyone had crowded in on him, asking him the same question: how did he feel? The answer had been obvious.

Someone—he thought it might have been Jim—had suggested he go to the hospital and have his head examined. He had tried to focus on the slim face in front of him.

He had nodded, his eyes glossed over. He was having trouble seeing all of a sudden. He had opened his mouth to speak, but there had been something strange about the deliverance of the words. Trance-like. He remembered what he had said.

2958450631080309. That was what he had said. *2958450631080309.* Nothing else. Random numbers. He remembered the gaping stares.

And now he was being discharged. There was a sizable lump on the back of his head, but no fracture. His teammates were free to take him home. And so home he went, floating first onto Highway 401, then west until they reached the city limits of London. Turning off at the Wellington exit, they moved north, towards his home.

Take it easy. As if. Red Iron Design was the wrought iron company he owned and slaved away at six or sometimes seven days a week. A staff of one. At 27, he was his own boss. He couldn't afford to take it easy.

He was only in the door a minute when he heard his phone ringing. His mother, the only family he had. Could he call her family? What is family—how does one define the word? A family consists of at least one parent for a child. A parent who nurtures, protects, educates, loves. Love. That was the word he was searching for. She had never provided that. She had no concept of the word. Love was about simply being there. She had never *been there*.

How long had it been since they'd last spoken? A few months, maybe? And what had that conversation been like? Like the others before it, for the past several years: a vacant mother forcing questions the answers to which never seemed to matter. What had happened? There had been happy times, years ago. He'd given up questioning how they had gotten to this stage. He suddenly remembered the painful conversations, wherein he'd ask what he'd done wrong, why she'd slowly grown so cold, so remote. There was never an answer: she'd lie and say it was a phase she was in, or there was stress at work. She didn't realise how easy it was to see through her.

He glanced at the phone. It had been him of late, years or so it seemed, initiating all communication. He resisted answering for several seconds. Finally, he brought the merciless ringing to an end.

Mom.

Oh, he was home. That familiar vacant voice on the other end.

He got home early tonight.

From where?

Naturally she had no idea. He told her again how he played ball Wednesdays, how he'd been doing so for the past three years.

Oh, right. She had forgotten.

So, what was the occasion?

She hesitated. Occasion?

She didn't normally call unless there was a real reason. Why was she calling?

She was defensive. Couldn't a mother call her son every now and again?

He smiled. Most sons would like a mother who did that.

And what was that supposed to mean?

She knew what he was talking about. He changed the subject. He'd been hit in the head tonight, playing ball.

Hit in the head? Mild concern.

He had been running to third; the ball had got him on the head. He was alright, though.

That was awful, she verbalised, and for a moment he wondered if she meant it. The absence of emotion in her voice was palpable. She couldn't have. He needed to start taking it a bit easier, she told him. He was going to really hurt himself playing those sports.

He had been playing since he had been a kid. Did she remember? Regardless, he was fine.

Well, she was just calling to see how he was doing. And how was he, besides the bruise?

He considered this. He had a mother he rarely talked to or saw, and a father he'd never met. He was suddenly bitter all over again. How did she think he was doing?

He needed to let that business with his father go, she told him. His father hadn't been there for him, or for her. He had walked out on the both of them, before he'd even been born. They'd been through this. Why bring it up again?

Sometimes it still bothered him, he told her. Everyone else he knew had a father. And a mother that they had a relationship with. This was no relationship. She'd been to this house—what—twice, maybe? Now he was on the offensive again. She lived a half hour or so away, and yet she never came by. She never invited him over, either.

Some things are out of one's control, she replied. Whatever that meant. She then elaborated. Like fathers running out on their sons.

There she was again, pointing fingers at others. He was talking about *her* absenteeism.

She paused, and he wondered if she might hang up. It had happened before. Then she admitted softly that she was aware of her failures as a mother, that she knew she'd let him down. She knew he had questions, wanted answers, but it was so difficult to talk about what had happened.

And then he felt guilty. She did this often, the master manipulator. His tone calmed. In the end, it was very simple. He just missed her.

And she missed him, too, if he could believe it.

Several seconds passed.

How was he sleeping?

He shrugged. The same. It was embarrassing to talk about.

He didn't have to be embarrassed with her.

How could she say that? She was as impersonal as a stranger. How could he feel anything but embarrassment?

It had always been the same with her, she said. Did he still sleep with a light on?

He used a plug-in usually, he said, or he left the bathroom light on. For years and years. He hated discussing it.

And work? All well?

All was well.

He could have done anything, she said just then. The sky had always been the limit for him. She wasn't disappointed in his choice for a career. But that was a lie.

He didn't think it had mattered to her.

Of course it had mattered! How could it not? He was her son, after all.

Yes, that was what the birth certificate said, he responded with a calculated coldness.

He had been a boy genius, she said. He could speed read while others struggled just to finish. Remember the *Lord of the Rings* trilogy she had bought him? He had been how old—six, seven maybe? Didn't he read the whole thing in—

He didn't remember, he lied.

And what about his love of dinosaurs growing up? The little riddles he would make up.

He didn't recall.

That was a lie, too. He remembered combing over volumes on the dinosaurs, memorising names, statistics. Short names, long names. *Micropachycephalosaurus,* the longest of all, for one of the smallest creatures. There's irony. That one he still recalled. The name was a workout in itself. *Micro-pach-y-ceph-a-lo-saurus-wal-king-through-a-deep-dark-for-est.* Then he remembered another. *Xenotarsosaurus* looks like *Carnotaurus. Xen-o-tar-so-saur-us-looks-like Car-no-taur-us.*

She was still at him. Did he remember how he would purposely skip classes and choose not to hand in assignments?

He did not. Lie number three.

Why did he do that?

Because school had done nothing for him. And she knew this. Why was she bringing it up now?

She remembered that when he had tried in school, he had achieved. But mostly he had chosen not to. Why hadn't he?

He thought he had just covered that, he snapped, then calmed himself. He supposed he had never received the support he'd needed. Maybe she knew a little something about that.

She ignored the remark. So, all was good with work?

Yes. He was pretty busy. He glanced at the clock. He had to go. The doctor had said he needed to rest.

He could sense in her voice faint gratitude for ending the conversation she had initiated. Okay, she said without heart. He should call her soon.

He would. He hung up. What was the point, really?

He headed immediately upstairs, showered quickly, popped a Tylenol. He used the two-way mirrors in the bathroom to examine his injury. It was a lump—that was for sure—protruding out from under cropped brown hair at the rear of his head.

Trudging back downstairs, he made for the kitchen and grabbed some ice. He wrapped it in a towel and held it to his head. Then he wandered to the living room and planted himself on his couch in front of the television. He glanced at the black and white Stratocaster and 100 watt Marshall sitting in the corner for a moment, considered playing. He began to channel surf instead.

The Jays were on, and he dropped the converter at once. He eyed the score in the top left corner. The Jays were leading the Rays 5-2, bottom of the eighth. And in Tampa, too. What a surprise. The world must have been out of its cosmic orbit.

Dark blotches suddenly appeared on the screen. There was something wrong with the television. No, that couldn't be it; the thing was only two years old. He squinted. The blemishes were morphing into something else. Numbers. He closed his eyes; obviously he was seeing things. He reopened, but they were still there, staring beguilingly back at him, the game almost entirely blacked out underneath. A pattern of numbers.

He realised he already knew them by heart. 2958450631080309. Over and over.

In frustration, he turned off the television and headed upstairs to bed. He brushed, plugged a night light in on the wall outlet. He hated the dark, and he didn't know why. It was a secret he'd kept guarded. This was something one was supposed to outgrow. He had not; in fact, if anything, this dread of the dark was something that had developed over time, far after he'd passed from toddlerhood to youth.

She was on his mind again just then. He remembered her back when he was so young, how she would always have lights on in the house at night, when she was asleep. He'd awake and find the house illuminated as on Christmas Day. But it had never been Christmas in their home, even when it *had* been Christmas. He'd asked her about the lights, and she'd told him without hesitation how much she hated the dark. And then, years later, when he himself had suddenly begun to hate it as well, she seemed indifferent, unconcerned. What kind of mother acts so? Then he gave up wondering and began accepting. That was when their relationship disintegrated into the fine particles of dust it now was.

He laid down, still overwhelmed by the sequence of numbers. He tossed one way, then the other, but still they were there. He shook his head futilely, sat up, glanced at a pad of paper on the nightstand. Always handy to make sketches or take notes when something work-related came to him in the night, a moment of inspiration in the darkness—or when someone called far too late and he had to scramble to jot down a phone number. He reached for the pad, grasping for the pencil that he knew should be nearby.

He wrote. Over and over again the numbers, cathartically transcribing them to the page. Rhythmically, mechanically, somnambulistically. It wasn't his hand guiding the pencil. And yet, of course it was.

Another thought entered his mind. Without hesitating, he turned over the page and began to draw something even more bizarre: triangles—some large, some small, right side up and upside down. All over the page. Then he was turning the page over and starting anew. Fresh triangles everywhere. He was reminded of the poster at the hospital.

And then, as quickly as it had begun, the drilling of the numbers in his head inexplicably ceased, as did the penchant for the shapes. He dropped the pencil, stared down at paper. How many triangles had he drawn? He shrugged and counted them. 42. He turned the paper over and counted there, too. He paused. 42 again. Without effort, he had accomplished this.

Exhaustion interrupted, and he systematically released the pad, closed his eyes, remembering nothing more.

The computer deactivated, the man slumped back in the chair of his cramped office. He'd just witnessed a murder. A murder he'd sanctioned. He took a second to contemplate the logic of his actions.

Regardless, it was time to report. Time to go see Pharaoh.

He stood, straitened his suit over a bulging stomach, exited the tiny, windowed room. He emerged into a short passageways of sorts, flanked on either side by wooden shelving units, his feet pressing onto hardwood that creaked with character. Above, archaic chandeliers hung, basking the bookstore in antiquated light. A short stairway ran to his left, up into another tier of volumes. An employee was standing there, thin, blonde, clad in khaki pants and a light collared shirt, sporting glasses that did not curl around his ears. To the right was the entrance and cash register. There was a smattering of people in the store, perusing both the inner shelves and those that lined the outer walls.

A man was behind the counter, also large and dressed far less regally in a collared plaid shirt, jeans, and sneakers. He glanced up at the other, wiping longish locks from his face. He nodded. The other nodded back, adding simply, "It's done. Going to see Pharaoh," and strode past.

He reached out and opened the front door, sandwiched as it was between several large, vertical windows. Emerging into a vastly approaching Washington twilight, he glanced up at the store's name, not knowing why. The Colonial Bookstore, emblazoned in traditional gold-lettering against the green-trimmed façade of the shop's front. The grey brick building, conjoined on either side, was more than two hundred years old.

He stepped onto the red and dark grey brick sidewalk of historic M Street and its colonial shops, gazing back and forth at teeming tourists and shoppers. Here, he thought, one would never know they were in Washington at all. This was cozy little Georgetown, the oldest suburb of the city, where colonial buildings hinted at a time before America was yet a nation.

He traversed the busy M and Wisconsin Avenue intersection, emerging on Wisconsin's east side, just past the elegant PNG Bank. There was the bus station. He took his place behind what he assumed were a pair of young newlyweds chattering about where they might go for dinner. Dinner. What time was it? He stole a glance at his watch. Just after eight.

The bus arrived, and he boarded it for the short journey north. He stared blankly at shops and banks and restaurants and hotels that jetted past. Minutes later, he was exiting at the Wisconsin/Hall Place stop. Back onto the sweltering street.

He turned right just past the hardware store onto Observatory Lane. Here, a path, warmly shrouded in streetlights and overhanging trees and occupied by joggers, wandered easterly, then slightly south, then north, in a circular pattern. There, on a rounded stone bench, not far from the main building of the observatory complex, three men awaited his presence. As usual. One of them was important. The man he had sardonically dubbed Pharaoh. Pharaoh., sans *kalasiris*, sans *kohl*, sans *shendyt*, sans *nemes*. Modern Pharaoh, dressed impeccably in a finely tailored suit, hopelessly attractive—grudgingly so: broad shoulders, meticulously attenuated blonde locks, darting sky blue eyes, a deftly cut jawline. Pharaoh, overseer of all things unseen and unknown.

He was motioned to sit. He did so, wiping at a stream of perspiration on his forehead. Should he instead genuflect? No, that is taking the joke too far.

"Seldon."

Sir.

"Well?"

It's done.

"Then he won't bother us anymore. The object?"

We have it.

"And where is it now?"

Taken into hiding. To a lone building on a tiny island in the middle of the desert.

That seemed to satisfy Pharaoh.

The world will thank you one day, sir.

"Perhaps. You've come so far, Seldon. Since that day I found you down on your luck in Singapore. Do you recall that day?"

I do.

"And how do you feel now?"

My first, sir.

Pharaoh stroked his chiselled chin. "It gets easier." He held out a cultivated hand, studied his cuticles. He stood and prepared to leave, but the fat little man was hesitating apprehensively, heaving pathetically in the frustrating heat.

There's just one more thing, sir. Something Trent was looking at just before he died.

"Yes...?"

A set of random numbers.

"Tell me."

He fumbled in his pocket, extracted a folded piece of paper. 2958450631080309.

"That's all?"

Does it mean anything to you, sir?

A shrug suddenly rancid with weariness. "It meant something to Trent. Find out what."

As light streams down from a cloudless sky, the obese detective's dilapidated 1990 burgundy Vectra rambles across Cairo, negotiating endless traffic congestion. The sounds of horns and music unleashed from car stereos fills Inspector Hondo Wasem's eardrums. Melodious Cairo, the city that never sleeps. He watches as rays from above ricochets off the hoods of passing cars, runs a hand over his sandpaper-stubbled face, his podgy nose. He glances sideways with supercilious brown eyes at his partner and somewhat friend, the much slimmer inspector Fadil Nahas. He notes the other's sullen demeanour.

And then Nahas explains why: his daughter Hannah, now sixteen, wants to start wearing miniskirts. Like her friends. It's all his wife's fault. Naima. Far too damned liberal. She encourages this kind of thing with all three of their daughters.

Wasem doesn't really care—fatherhood is as foreign to him as weight loss. He voices an opinion nonetheless: if the girls want to dress more Western, they should be allowed to do so. Ironically, fewer women than ever before do indeed dress this way. Forty years ago, one would have been hard pressed to find Egyptian women covered in significant numbers; today, the opposite is the norm.

Wasem has often wondered if he has made the right decision, staying here. With both parents dead, his brothers left years ago for British Columbia. *Kanadaa*. Why has he remained in a country of crippling poverty, where the population is exploding, where the majority are now under middle-age?

Nahas exhales obvious disgust. His *zooga*—his wife—Naima wanted a job, so he let her get one. But her newfound feminist independence goes too far. Soon he will have to worry about his *banaet*—daughters—coming home abused. In Egypt, sexual assault is part of the culture. Mohamed Diab's *678* made that clear enough.

Nahas should be more open-minded, Wasem tells him. After all, he is a Copt. More formally known as Coptic Christians, "Copts" are the remnants of the once-dominant religious group in Egypt in the wake of the Greek and Roman conquests. Today, Islam dominates Egypt, and has since the tenth century, but a sizable Christian population of anywhere from six to eight million still exists. That despite massive Christian emigration to other parts of the world over the years. The brief rule of Mohamed Morsi and his Muslim Brotherhood would certainly have opened the way for a religious crackdown. But the Muslim Brotherhood were ousted months later, thankfully for the Copts.

"Religious crackdown? On the subject of female modesty, I'd have been in favour," Nahas says. "Just because we're in the minority doesn't mean we need to dress like it. Even Bishop Bishoy says women need to be more discreet. He says Lady Mariam wore a Tarha. Now my Hannah wears miniskirts. She wants to be like the other Meriam. Meriam George."

"Miss Egypt."

"They all want to be like her."

Wasem laughs. "Can you blame her?" Then he adds, "What would Jesus have done about it?"

"He wouldn't have had to do anything. Back in His day, women dressed appropriately."

They pass a group of men standing on a street corner garbed peculiarly in white loin cloths, their heads shaved. They are calling out—chanting—something. A smallish crowd is gathered nearby, some snapping photos, others filming.

Wasem points. "What is that?"

"I can't be sure. They look like Hanuti followers, I think."

"Who?"

"The ancient priests."

"What are they doing dressed like that in this day and age?"

"It isn't illegal. They aren't breaking any laws."

"They look ridiculous."

Nahas smiles, his eyes lingering on the passing demonstrators. "Maybe they have the right idea. Maybe Egypt needs something new, something different."

"Maybe you should join them."

"Maybe I should."

"Anyway, we have something new. It's called democracy. Other countries have had it for years."

Nahas changes the subject. "It's not good being in law enforcement when you're a Copt, I can tell you that."

"Where did that come from?"

"It's getting worse."

"Oh, I don't know. Mubarak made Christmas a nationally recognised holiday."

"Big deal. How many Copts did he hire into government? How many Copts are in *any* positions of importance?"

"I have no idea."

"Why would you? You're not a Copt." Nahas gazes out the window, the city streaking past, illuminating him in rapidly vanishing bars of light. "It's all gotten so out of hand. It's time for change."

"We've had plenty of that in the past few years. What's next: a Coptic takeover?"

"Speaking of which, when was the last time you saw the inside of a mosque?"

"Decades," Wasem scoffs, turning the car into the entrance of Le Méridien Pyramids hotel. A giant, bulbous man, far more so than the average Egyptian, he struggles to clear his impressive gait from his dilapidated Vectra. A beached whale, he suddenly remembers being called once. Funny, he thinks: Egypt has no whales. He sneers at the phalanx of black Tourism and Antiquities Police SUVs already on hand. "What the hell are they doing here?" he curses, slamming his car door to accentuate his frustration. "This is a murder investigation. TAPs hang out at the touristy places. They don't investigate murders."

This is true. The Tourism and Antiquities Police are an ophidian police force designed with the express purpose of assisting the hordes of foreigners who flock to Egypt's various tourist destinations. These white-and-black bereted men are required to speak English but often can't. Bribe-takers, too. *Rashwah*. But *bakshish* is the term they would probably prefer—tip. Serpentine bribes are their most discernable trait: because of their omnipresence at tourist sites and in and around hotels, they harass tourists incessantly far more often than they facilitate. Everything has a price. A tourist has a question? Pay for the fangled answer. A tourist wants a photo of a mosque—which is perfectly free and legal, of course? Pay to take the photo.

But can he blame them, really? The *bakshish* is the way of Egypt. For here, where the vast majority of people live in squalor, where drinking water and electricity are an everyday concern for far too many, the *bakshish* is often all there is. Egypt was once a land of the *fellahin*—poor farmers. Poor because the *pashas*, the Ottoman rulers, owned everything. The *fellahin* worked the land, but they could not own it. And when the world began to visit Egypt, to view its sights—to *rape* it—many of the *fellahin* gravitated to the cites and this new world of tourism, and the *bakshish* was unleashed on the foreigner. And then 1952 came, and the glorious revolution. Funny, though, that so many still suffer. Funny how the *bakshish* is still a way of life.

Are all TAPs corrupt? Certainly not. Is bribery even construed as dishonest in Egypt? No. For many, bribery is survival. In Egypt, one does what one must. Especially now, when there is so little opportunity for the *bakshish*: most of the tourists have stopped coming out of fear. There is little reason to wonder why that is. New, radical political parties are now legally permitted to exist. The once-banned Muslim Brotherhood, for instance. The Salafist Parties, *al-Nour* and *Dawa*. *Al-Nour* wants to rip up the treaty with Israel, to get closer to Iran. Iran is a glowing symbol of independence to *Al-Nour* because it defies America. But the *Dawa* would go one step further: the *Dawa* sees Egypt's ancient past as deplorable. The Sphinx, the statues, the temples, the tombs—everything. All part of the deplorable past. The *Dawa* believe these ancient sites and artefacts should be concealed, hidden from view. Just like their women. The *Dawa*'s spokesman, Abd Al-Mun'in Al-Shahhat, said it best: "The Pharaonic culture is a rotten culture." Interesting way to put it. How much does that rotten culture give back to this country each year, even now?

But they're not all bad. The Muslim Brotherhood is much more practical. They only want tourists to stop wearing bikinis on the beach. And no more alcohol! Never mind that millions of Egyptians themselves drink.

So, yes, the *rashwah/bakshish* is a way of survival to so many. Unless one is friends with the former president. Or the former president's wife. Then things are different. Hosni and Susanna. The Mubaraks. They should have had their own reality show. Egypt's finest. Egypt, land of plenty. Plenty of billions from overseas aid, millions in restoration donations from UNESCO and other organisations. Plenty of millions in international travel shows: King Tut on display for the world, earning a fortune. And then there's that canal. Billions and billions. Where *did* it all go?

The Mubaraks, worth billions, are the Suezes of Cairo. Oh, but that's right. Mubarak was cleared of all corruption charges. Billions in the bank, while so many suffer. But no corruption. Right. And now the rather hefty charge of murder hanging over him has been dropped as well. Must have been someone else who ordered the army to open fire day after day on all those protesters. It couldn't have been him. He loved his people, loved his country.

Rashwah. Bakshish.

And so, the TAPs. Yes, they harass, but they are trying to survive. But enough have overstepped their authority to cement their reputation amongst foreigners. And as Wasem seethes, he sees several of what he considers the slithery bastards, congregated outside the hotel, deceptively feigning importance, problematically mingling with khaki-clad regular city policemen.

His gait facilitates him through the chorus of officers, where he perceives minimal leers of disdain. Disdain is something he has grown accustomed to over the years. Ironically, he has come to regard it as a security blanket, tightly wrapped and comforting. It keeps him happily alone in this world.

As is standard procedure, the officers who have responded to the call have quickly scanned the crime scene and then sectioned the room itself off. David Trent's body had been found lying near the window, in front of a desk where a solitary lap top and wooden box rest undisturbed. Saliva, oozed from his mouth, has pooled under his downturned face, temporarily staining the neutral carpet. His eyes are open, and one hand is clenched into a furiously frozen death grip, a suggestion of a pointless struggle. Oh, how he must have gasped for life. The other petrified hand, a reddish fissure apparent on its backside, is far more mysterious.

Wasem and Nahas gain admittance by the controlling officer. It is then that a young, uniformed paramedic approaches them. "We have the coroner on sight," he reports, though he isn't sure who to look at. Who is in charge?

Wasem spares him a brief, irritated look. "Move."

The paramedic looks him over. Everyone knows Wasem; his reputation has preceded him. Fifty something. Ridiculously overweight. Clad as always in a buttoned shirt, accompanied by dress pants that are belted below the ridge of his enormous, gluttonous belly. Terse, obtuse, argumentative, ignorant, unresponsive, callous. And here and now, as always, it will be Wasem, revelling in his bailiwick, who will command this investigation.

Without warning, the inspector scrapes impatiently past the annoyed paramedic. He approaches the body of the fallen professor, stares down at it for several seconds, then probes the room with his eyes. He spies a nearby coroner, bent at the knees, jotting notes on the position of the body. Voices behind him. Other police officers are entering the scene in random succession. He sighs wearily, muttering to anyone within earshot. "I need this room cleared."

The coroner glares viciously. "It figures they'd call you."

"Relax, Bayoumi."

Bayoumi stands. "I place the death at around 6:30 last night. Looks like he was bitten."

"Bitten?"

"Scorpion bite."

The controlling officer nearby nods and writes the time down on his pad. "I'm turning the investigation over to you, Wasem."

Wasem nods anticipatorily, his flat, bloated face bobbing rhythmically. "Get forensics in here. And get rid of the damned TAPs."

The officer glances beyond the police tape. "Forensics isn't here yet. They're on their way." He seems to ignore the second order.

"I see." Wasem eyes the officer's name badge. Samir Ramzy.

"I called them," Ramzy glowers at him. "What—you don't believe me?"

"Stopped for a coffee on the way, have they?" Wasem is already stepping clear and gazing at an opened safe near the neatly made bed. "That's interesting," he says to no one in particular.

"What is?" Nahas offers, glancing in the same general direction.

"He's been robbed."

"Why's that so unusual? Lots of people get robbed. You know that."

"Yes, but this one's wallet is still here."

Nahas stares uncertainly. Sure enough, there is the wallet. Brown leather, with a clichéd ankh imprinted on its exterior.

"Not the wallet." Wasem is staring in at the safe.

By this time, the forensics team has arrived. Ramzy orders everyone out. The forensics officers step into their protective bunny suits, then they are photographing anything and everything.

Wasem reaches into his pocket and produces a pack of cigarettes. He places one in his mouth and lights it, nodding at Ramzy, who is glares at him.

"You can't smoke in here, Wasem. You know that."

"Uh huh," he replies, barely acknowledging the remark. Emphatically, he blows a large smoke ring into the air near Nahas' enlightened head.

They both turn at the sound of an opening elevator. The scene's primary investigator, Colonel Zaid Deeb, has arrived.

"Figures," Wasem mutters.

Zaid Deeb. Superbly dressed in a dark uniform offset with polished shoulder insignia, polished buttons and boots, and various polished medals of distinction attached ridiculously to his breast. He wears his dark hair stylishly straight back, gelled to perfection. In truth, he is not unattractive, and at forty, maintains a well-chiselled figure. A runway model in his own mind. "Alright," he begins as he arrives at the entrance to the crime scene. He speaks perfunctorily. "What have you got for me?"

"The victim has been identified as Professor David Trent of Toronto," Ramzy replies. "He is sixty-two years old, and he has been staying in this room for the past twelve days conducting research on a new book. He boarded at this hotel several times in the past." Ramzy hesitates. "You probably know him already."

Deeb scowls. "How?"

The officer shrugs, unsure of how to proceed. "Well, he is the same archaeologist David Trent who has been on Egyptian television many times, sir. He spoke fluent Arabic."

"Where's the forensics team?"

"Already inside collecting," Nahas replies, cocking his head to the murder scene. "I took the initiative."

"*You* took the initiative?" Deeb spins aggressively toward him. "I call them in, not you. Don't forget who's in charge here."

"We assumed you were too busy," Wasem burbles casually, his eyes burning into the face of his superior. "After all, it's day time, so there are plenty of golf games and luncheons to attend."

"What the hell are you on about?"

"You know what I mean. You're far more interested in grooming your own reputation than commanding this force."

The fact that others within ear range are aghast is one thing. The fact that no one attempts to counter Wasem's claims is also weighty.

"I have to give you credit, Wasem," Deeb says after a few seconds. "You've got nerve. Part of me wants to suspend you. Besides, what the hell are you doing here in the first place?" He stabs a finger at both inspectors, slicing the air in an outlandish show of bravado all the more evident since his arm is tensed.

"We were assigned the case, Colonel, as is standard procedure. But you already know that, naturally, being in charge and all."

"I don't like you, Wasem. I'll see to it that you're taken off the case."

"No one likes me. Big deal." The inspector stops, his eyes observing the insignia on Deeb's shoulder. "My God, they've promoted you again."

"Brigadier General now."

"You're really moving up the ranks. You must be so proud of yourself."

"You will refer to me as *Brigadier General*," his superior hisses, pointing emphatically to the new insignia.

"Of course. Brigadier General. That makes you second only to the major general, doesn't it, sir? That bodes well for the force."

Deeb wants to hit him, has often thought about it. He relents in the end, clearly choosing the better option. "I can find other work for you, you know. It isn't like you're irreplaceable."

"Tell you what: you start taking a more active role in your job, I'll start paying you the due respect. We both know I'm the best goddamned inspector in the city. You need me." He gestures to the TAPs in the vicinity. "And why the hell are the Tourism and Antiquities idiots hanging around here?"

"What's that problem?"

"Well, sir, they assist tourists. As you can plainly see, this one's dead."

The brigadier is reddening in outright humiliation. Bright tomato red. His face looks like it's ready to explode. He rotates awkwardly to the controlling officer, mumbles something, and the controlling officer turns and says something else to another. It's the telephone game. Within seconds, the TAPs are being ushered from the scene.

The grimace that has these past few seconds adorned Wasem's face fades: the presence of the Antiquities Police is bad enough, but Deeb's utter lack of awareness of their presence unnerves him. He has long-since accepted the new general as an oblivious idiot, but even Deeb should have had the foresight to clear the TAPs himself. This is strange.

The forensics team exits the crime scene, and this is the point in which Deeb showcases another of his inexhaustible abilities: he gives way to his artistic aptitude. Re-entering the room, Wasem and Nahas in tow, he immediately extracts a note pad from under his uniform jacket. How such a pad of paper that large has been concealed under there is anybody's guess. In any event, Deeb initiates a hastened yet still detailed sketch of the room and body.

"Sir, the victim was killed from an apparent scorpion bite," Nahas says. "Wasem here believes the victim was robbed. But not from his wallet—there is an open safe there down to your right, beside the bed."

Deeb sacrifices a few seconds to glance down in the direction the inspector has indicated, nodding nonchalantly. "I see."

Wasem reaches into his pocket and withdraws a pair of clear white gloves, steps over to the nightstand, carefully opens the wallet. Inside it is the usual paraphernalia: driver's license; social insurance card; birth certificate; various credit cards; and some money, in both Canadian and Egyptian currency. He gently closes the wallet and turns to the commanding officer on the scene. He regards the nightstand and bends down to his knees, which crack under the strain. He peers into the open safe. Then he works his way back to his feet, eyes the table by the window and the little brown box resting on a mound of *kutub*—books—next to the laptop. Something in his head tells him to open the box, and as he does, he steps backward nervously. The scorpion within has scuttled into a defensive posture, tail raised threateningly. The inspector refastens the lid. "Found our culprit."

"What, it's still in there?" Deeb wonders.

He ignores the obvious, his eyes settling on the laptop. "We'll need to take a look at that as well." He strides gruffly past Nahas and begins prodding around the room. At length, he moves to the coat closet near the front door, well in view of the scrutinizing commanding officer and his note pad. He examines a few hanging sports jackets, busily searching the pockets of each. Within seconds, he produces a cell phone. "We'll need to look this over also."

Nahas approaches the table and computer. He glazes over the *kutub*. "A book on pharaohs, one on the pyramids…a Bible." He stops, reaching out for the Bible, opens both its covers and allows the pages to spill open in front of him. "Lots of notes in here. Apparently, *Exodus* was a hot topic."

"*Exodus?*"

"The book of *Exodus*." Nahas glances down at the remaining books and continues rifling through them. "Oh, this is interesting."

"What's that?"

"Some travel books. Apparently the professor wanted to see the world. Here's one on Mexico, another on Peru, Bolivia, India, Japan, Denmark."

"Let me see one."

Wasem receives the Mexican guidebook, turns it over in his hands, as if to reveal the answer to this mystery. But none is forthcoming. He sees that some pages are dog-eared. He flips randomly through, pauses at one of these marked pages titled "Durango." There are paragraphs, presumably descriptions on the state. He has no interest in reading. There are photographs, too, of rugged landscapes and villages and festivals. One photo is of an odd-shaped mountain. He studies it. The top of the mountain seems to be missing, as if it's been sheared off by some gargantuan scythe. What is more, the photo has been circled in red pen.

Nahas is shuffling through one of the other books. "He's got notes jotted on random pages."

"Maybe he was travelling before he came here."

"Or maybe he was on his way to one of these places afterwards." He collects the books and the computer under his arm. "Anyway, he must have spent a lot of time down at the museum, like any good foreign Egyptologist. Maybe we should go down there and see if we can talk to someone."

By this, Nahas is referring to the Cairo Museum.

"Good idea. I'll go." Wasem turns to his superior. "What do you say, sir?"

Deeb is still doodling.

The inspector scoffs under his breath and begins to exit the room. As he does, Nahas follows, laptop clearly in hand. Only then does the general take notice. "Hey. Where do you two think you're going?" He is glaring at the laptop under Nahas' arm.

Wasem responds. "We've got a few things to check out. Phone records, emails. I'm heading over to the museum. You can stay and continue drawing, though."

Deeb scratches his chin and continues to stare at the doorway. "You're off the case, Wasem," he mumbles, then returns to his sketching.

The young welder awoke early Thursday morning to an aggressive sun bullying its way through his bedroom curtain. As usual, he'd resisted closing the blinds in the night. He relished the penetrating sun of the early hours; light signifies the transitoriness of darkness.

He suddenly recalled his injury of the night previous. Calloused fingers probed the grasses of hair for the lump. It had contracted, no longer throbbing as before.

He rose from his bed, and his eyes were drawn to the pad and pencil still there on the bed where he'd left them. He remembered the numbers, the triangles. 42 hastily-scribbled shapes on either side of the page. He stared. And then the inexplicable overwhelmed him. Books. He needed books.

It wasn't as if he'd never set foot in a book store before. It was just that he had always avoided such an activity if the possibility presented itself. And yet, even though he was rambling through the front doors and into inebriating air conditioning, he felt something else: he needed to be here, needed to do this.

He perused the shelves, gravitating eventually to the Ancient History and New Age sections. His hands, like mightily enticed hydraulics, reached and drew one volume after another. He balanced the mountain of words on his forearm until the weight was too great and he was forced to find a chair and sit. He inspected the volumes, then paid, disembarked, returned home. And there, on his couch, having decided he would not work today, he began to read.

And he began to learn.

He learned from authors he had never heard of before: Henry Booth, Christopher Dunn, Robert Bauval, Adrian Gilbert, David Hatcher Childress,

Stephen Mehler, Andrew Malkowski, Robert Temple, Michael J. Behe, Robert Wright, Carl Sagan, Zecharia Sitchin, D.S. Allan, J.B. Delair, Graham Hancock, Erich von Däniken.

As he turned the pages, he was reminded of the conversation he'd had with his mother. The speed reading. Yes, he had always been a quick reader. But this was different. The speed at which he was engaged made no sense. And yet he was sustaining this pace, mentally photographing everything. As he closed one volume and embarked on another, previous works would come rushing back to him with super digitised clarity. Cognitive high definition.

And then, as if still possessed, he returned to his truck. On Western Road, he spied the hospital, the extremity of the University of Western Ontario, rising above the maples. He turned left onto Lambton Drive, meandered past the double-pillared entranceway into the university grounds. Straight ahead was Alumni Hall. He turned left again, parked. He spied the university library, D.B. Weldon, one of the largest in Canada, a curiously modernist structure amid others steeped in antiquity.

At first, what he learned was standard historical retelling, of ancient Egypt as it has been taught in history books and classrooms and documentaries. One name in particular stood out.

Amenhotep IV was the son of the pharaoh Amenhotep III. In the fifth year of his reign, he changed his name to Akhenaten. There were various translations of the new name, but it essentially denoted "being in the living service of Aten." He married a woman named Nefertiti, among others, a marriage that spawned Tutankhamun, the youngster who would eventually succeed him. Akhenaten was one of the last pharaohs of the eighteenth dynasty.

In ancient Egypt, a dynasty is a period of time in which one dominant family ruled. One man governs, then his son, and so on. When the next ruling pharaoh was not part of that bloodline, the dynasty was broken and a new begun. Ancient Egypt had over thirty dynasties in all, organised by modern scholars into three kingdoms—the Old, Middle, and New. Akhenaten and his son Tutankhamun ruled during the late New Kingdom, considered the golden age of ancient Egypt.

Akhenaten is famous because he abandoned Egypt's polytheistic religious tradition for that of a single god, Aten. Aten and no other. All other gods were banned. Then he moved the capital from Thebes further south, to a city he called Akhetaten, known today as Amarna.

Soon after his death, Akhenaten's efforts to convert Egypt were undone: the worship of Aten was thrown out, and all attempts were made to eradicate

Akhenaten from memory. It was the General Horemheb who so strove to erase him forever, first as advisor to Tutankhamun, and later as pharaoh himself. Particularly ruthless in his efforts, Horemheb defaced the heretic pharaoh's statues and struck him from the official records. Akhetaten was levelled and abandoned, and the seat of Egyptian authority returned north to Thebes.

Akhenaten was unusual in his appearance. His assumed mummy was discovered in 1907, but even today, its identity is still a matter of speculation. The body was discovered in the Valley of the Kings, a massive gorge that served for over five hundred years as the final resting place for deceased pharaohs. While debate rages on, the mummy's features seem to match the man now reborn in rediscovered wall paintings and statues. These depict a long, thin face, swollen lips, a sunken chest, a bloated stomach. And an unusually misshapen head: the back of his irregularly-sized skull slopes unnaturally backward. Tutankhamun, whose mummy was discovered by Howard Carter in 1922, possesses the same distinctive feature, which is why so many believe the 1907 mummy and Tutankhamun are most certainly related.

This unusual cranium may well be the result of incest, which was the norm among Egyptian royalty. Birth defects were common. It was customary for sons and daughters of the ruling pharaoh to intermarry. Some pharaohs might even have had their own daughters as concubines. The rationale is simple: intermarriage ensured a purely preserved bloodline.

Tutankhamun himself died when he was just eighteen. Speculation abounds as to the cause of this death: Tutankhamun has what appears to be a fracture in the back of his skull, and for decades it was thought maybe he had been murdered by his successor, Horemheb. Nowadays scholars think maybe he just had some serious health problems. But in 2013, new evidence came to light that he probably died as a result of being run over by a chariot. Perhaps even in battle.

The Egyptians possessed sophisticated mummification techniques. They drained the body of all its fluids, then extracted the major organs through various bodily incisions. A type of salt called natron was then used to help preserve the body, which was then wrapped, again and again. Thus, the final result. The mummy. All of this took several days, and the more elaborate the mummification, the more the cost. Some things never change.

*T*iny statues were placed in the tomb of the deceased. Carved beforehand in the appearance of the departed, *shabtis* were meant to take the place of the deceased in the After Life, to carry out menial tasks for the dead. Some tombs might include a *shabti* for each day of the year, accompanied by implements or tools in order to carry out the desired work.

Of the pyramids, many of which at one time contained mummies, he learned that the infamous Giza Plateau complex actually has nine pyramids in all, though only three are ever mentioned in any detail. Giza is only one of six pyramid complexes along the western banks of the Nile; the other locations of pyramids are at Abu Rowash, Abu Garab, Abusir, Saqqara, and Dashour. There are some 22 pyramids along the Nile's banks.

At Giza, the three famous pyramids were built as tombs for three generations of pharaohs: the first, the Great Pyramid, the largest of the three, was built for Khufu; the second, which still contains its original casing stones at its pinnacle, was built for Khufu's son and the next pharaoh in line, Khafre; the third, much smaller than the other two, was built for Menkaure, son of Khafre and grandson of Khufu. Of the Great Pyramid, its summit is curiously flat: the capstone that should be there is missing. There is no explanation as to why the pyramid is flat. Perhaps it was unfinished? Perhaps something else.

All of this knowledge and more he acquired as he breezed through one book after another. He glanced at his watch and saw that he had been here several hours. It was time to leave.

When he returned home, in the early afternoon, he sat at his kitchen table with his purchases and began to read. And read.

He was encountering an alternate version of history. Alien intervention, pyramids built not as tombs but as machines. How the ancient oral traditions that define humankind draw the same conclusions: that humanity is connected to the stars. How modern-day Egyptian protectors of the oral traditions are called Keepers. They can be found inhabiting various tourist sites. Academics dismiss the Keepers' teachings, but there is logic in their words.

The word *Egypt* is a Western interpretation of the Greek word *Aegyptos*. *Aegyptos* in turn is a translation of the Ancient Egyptian term *Hit-Ka-Ptah*. *Hit-Ka-Ptah* means "The place of the projection of Ptah," or words to that effect. *Ptah* was a creator god. *Hit* means "place," and *Ka* means "projection of the soul." The Greeks misinterpreted this term so many centuries ago, a misreading that permeates today: they assumed *Hit-Ka-Ptah* meant *all* of Egypt, but to the locals, *Hit-Ka-Ptah* was just one place within the greater territory of what constituted Egypt. All of Egypt was actually known as *Khemit* by the Egyptians. As vowels were rarely written in ancient Egypt, *Khemit*—K-h-e-m-i-t—is a best guess as to the word's spelling. To the ancients, it was written K-M-T.

Khemit means "black land," which relates to the Nile's rich black soil. Many thousands of years ago, when the geography of Egypt was far more tropical than it is today—it was not a desert at all—black soil abounded far beyond the river's banks. In fact, legend—and modern geology—hints at a much bigger river that used to lie to the west of the Nile, where there is today only desert. German geologist Max Blanckcenhorn called this river Ur-Nil. Tunnels beneath many ancient structures today, with reports of water still flowing through them, are believed to have been built to bring water in from the Ur-Nil.

The word "pyramid" is derived from two Greek terms: *pyramidos* and "pyramis". The latter denotes the three sided form a pyramid resembles. However, *pyramidos* has a much different meaning: "fire in the centre." Of this there is no direct denotation. Or so it is thought.

The Giza Plateau is west of the Nile, just outside modern day Cairo. Some call it the Giza Necropolis, which refers to a large burial area. Technically, there were people buried there, as there is evidence of cemeteries, but historians refer to it as a necropolis because they propose that pharaohs were buried in the three larger pyramids. There is no evidence for this. There were no pharaohs buried there in the pyramids because the pyramids were perhaps already standing centuries before any of these supposed pharaohs existed.

The Giza Plateau was actually part of a complex area known to the Khemitians as *Bu Wizzer (W-Z-R)*, a long chain of pyramids running north to south, several kilometres along the western edge of the Nile. *Bu Wizzer* means "Land of Wizzer," Wizzer being a god the Greeks translated as "Osiris." Today, some refer to this chain as the Band of Peace. In particular, the distance between the pyramids of Giza and Abusir is mathematically equidistant to the distance of the three main pyramids at Giza itself; these three pyramids at Giza are in turn equidistant with each other in comparison to the three stars comprising the belt of Orion in the night sky.

The names attributed to the pharaohs were often not names at all; rather, they were titles. Sneferu, for example, the pharaoh generally attributed with building three pyramids at Dashour, was not named Sneferu at all: "Sneferu," in fact, translates to "double harmony" in Khemitian. The title relates to the energy given off by the pyramids at Dashour. In fact, all of the pyramids were constructed with the idea of energy in mind. The Great Pyramid, for example, was a complex machine, perhaps able to harness energy from the sun and the water that flowed beneath it to create hydrogen. And because the rooms of all the major pyramids in the Band of Peace were tuned to specific frequencies, it is possible that each structure was a centre of harmonic resonance.

The head of ancient Egypt, the pharaoh, depended on bloodlines for his rule, but it was not his own family connections that mattered—it was his royal wife's. Bloodlines ran through the wife, not through the husband. In fact, the Khemitians placed a large emphasis on *mat*rilineal descent. Historians have assumed the male pharaohs dominated society. This is largely through mistranslation of ancient texts, and through misunderstanding generated by the Greeks. An example is the word "pharaoh." The word comes from the Khemitian term *Per-Aa*, which translates to "High House," the house of power. The ancient traditions state that the goddess Isis (Greek translation) was wife to the god Osiris (also Greek translation), but it was Isis who was represented by a throne, not Osiris. That meant that *she* was the real seat of power, not her husband. Since the Greeks based their society on patrilineal descent, they assumed the Khemitians did as well. They did not. And since it was the female who was truly the source of power and property, it would have been up to the male to try and connect with women of successful bloodlines, to align themselves with power and property. Whether these women were the man's own sister was irrelevant.

The Khemitians believed in a cyclical timeline, without a true beginning or end. A cycle, comprised of five distinct stages, endures for many thousands of years. Each stages lasts for perhaps five or six thousand years, so a full cycle could last twenty-five to thirty thousand years. These cycles continue to this day, constantly evolving from one to the next. The five stages of the cycle were grounded on the five positions of the sun, from dawn to sunset. The first stage was *Kheper*, The Driller. It was so named after the scarab beetle, who digs down into the ground and hides, then re-emerges. It was also associated with dawn, birth, or awareness of consciousness. The second stage, when the sun has risen and it at its highest point in the sky, was called *Ra,* The Stubborn, emphasised by the ram. The Khemitians believed the ram to be a stubborn animal, and this obduracy epitomised those first years of life, when adolescents test boundaries. The third stage was known as *Oon*, The Wise. This is when the sun is in the early afternoon point in the sky. This stage was symbolised by a man standing with a staff. This stage represented adulthood, rationality, full consciousness. The fourth stage, however, was perhaps the most important. *Aten*, The Wiser, is when the sun is beginning to set. This is late afternoon, early evening. The term "wiser" was applied because this was when consciousness was at its zenith. The symbol was an old man slightly hunched, holding a staff. The Khemitians believed that all individuals were at their most profound point in life at this moment: well past middle-age, when they had acquired a lifetime of knowledge through experience. The fifth and final stage of the cycle was known as *Amun*, when the sun had set and there was only darkness. *Amun* meant The Hidden, the age of all things darkness: consciousness is lost, nothing is known, one stumbled around in the darkness. To the Khemitians, there was no symbol for this darkness. Humanity was now in the age of *Amun*. This is because approximately five or six thousand years ago, Khemitian society began to devolve. Past knowledge was forgotten. This devolution endures today.

Original Khemitian society lacked gods in the modern sense of the word. They had what they called "neters"—principals or ideals. There were 360 of these principles in all, and according to modern oral traditionalists, we humans are today only in touch with five of them—our five senses. The ancient Khemitians strove to be in touch with *all* of them—or as many as they could—and they therefore lived a much more conscious, spiritual life than we do. Each neter was represented by a symbol, and the Khemitians could visit temples that were meant for spiritual communication with these neters. An example of a neter was wisdom, or consciousness. One does not worship wisdom or consciousness, but one might devote oneself to the enlightened understanding of what that principle or concept is.

Perhaps during the Age of *Amun*, these neters morphed into gods, deities that were worshipped in a modern sense. This religious metamorphosis was accomplished by the spiritual leaders of Khemit, priests known as the Hanuti, who decided that it was no longer permissible for individuals to be able to openly communicate with the neters. The Hanuti realised that if they alone could be made the link between the people and the neters, then they alone would have real power. And began to exert more and more control. They altered Egyptian society and created the religion that is studied today in history books. The temples meant for spiritual communication were transformed to become religious places for deities. The Hanuti soon controlled all aspects of life, and coupled with this control was corruption. For example, mummification became a money-making venture. There were different degrees of mummification, all for different prices. People who could pay did so, but those who couldn't afford the exorbitant prices got the bargain bin version.

By the time the pharaoh Akhenaten assumed power, he could clearly see that his society had been living in the stage of *Amun*—darkness—for some time. He sought to restore Khemitian society to the time before the darkness, a time of enlightenment. A purging was essential to set things right. To accomplish this, he took drastic measures: he outlawed the Hanuti, outlawed religion as it had come to be known. Aten represented this neter of enlightenment, and, therefore, Egyptologists are wrong when they translate Akhenaten's name as meaning "Through the door of Aten," or words to that effect, referring to Aten as a god. In fact, the name does not refer to the worship of Aten as a deity at all. It refers to this return enlightenment or spiritual reawakening, represented metaphorically by the rays of the sun.

And now, a whole new cycle was just about to begin. Kheper would again unfold itself: a new age, a new dawn. A new world.

He moved beyond the study of Khemit to learn that life did not evolve on Earth: it arrived here from beyond. Around 10 000-9500 BCE, catastrophic calamity ensued. A star roared into the solar system and caused irreparable damage while on its way towards Earth. It actually destroyed a planet that was once between Mars and Jupiter, pulling remnants of that planet with it. Those remnants eventually impacted upon Earth, which devastated our planet: huge storms the likes of which ancient ancestors had never known fulminated, the oceans raged. This is known in the Bible as the Deluge. The alignment of the planet actually shifted. Entire continents were devastated, animals became extinct, human life was decimated, new seasons came into being. Earth itself convulsed, causing the mountain ranges we know today. Then everything cooled—a mini ice age. The survivors were left to recreate themselves in this new world.

But the damage was not equivalent across the planet: the pyramids continued to stand, though they no longer functioned for the purpose with which they had been constructed. They were left as dead relics of a long-lost past.

And all this matters because evolution did not occur as historians believe. Humankind did not evolve: we *de*volved. The Khemitian civilisation was at its high point before the catastrophe, and then all was lost. And amid this devastation was when the Hanuti took control.

Of the Great Pyramid, he learned that the construction of the Great Pyramid's King's Chamber defies explanation. The walls, floor, and celling are composed of red granite stones so incredibly aligned that even a human hair cannot pass between any of them. Even more bizarre, the dominant resonant frequency with which the chamber radiates is equivalent to F#. And the empty "sarcophagus" in the centre of the room radiates at a harmony almost identical to perfect A. Sound engineers have tested and proved this theory, and musicians have recorded in the chamber with this information in mind.

The dominant F# frequency of the chamber is also the harmonic frequency ascribed to planet Earth—according to ancient Egyptian sources. F# is also the dominant harmony in DNA, when its basic strands are converted to a musical form. And water molecules, when adapted to music, also form a reoccurring pattern of F#. Pyramids. DNA. Water. What was the connection? He chuckled, remembering the fixation he'd had in his musical days of songs in the key of F#. Why had he so appreciated the key then? He could not have known, except that there was a sort of musical perfection, or harmony when one played in F#.

To the Khemitians, at least once the Hanuti seized control of society, the human body was known as the *khat*. Every *khat* had a soul that was divided into five parts: the *ib*, *sheut*, *ren*, *ba*, and *ka*. The *ib* was the heart, often left in the body during mummification. The *sheut* was a person's shadow. The *ren* was a person's name, and the *ren* would live on long after a person died as long as it was spoken or written down. The *ba* was a person's personality, everything that made one unique to others. The *ka* was a person's essence, and it, too, would live on after a person died, though, like the living, it required food and drink in order to do so. For this reason, food and drink were placed in tombs. The dead would not eat or drink these offerings, however: rather, the deceased essentially absorbed their nutrients.

The object for the deceased was to ensure their *ba* and *ka* reunited in the Afterlife every night. This reunification was known as *akh* and could only be achieved if the proper funerary rites were implemented. The *akh*, then, was the form the deceased took in death, and it could be conjured by living family members through prayer; it could also roam on its own, like a ghost, impacting the lives of living people in either good or evil ways.

Then he learned of Ma'at, the female Egyptian deity personifying truth, morality, law, and justice, as well as the moral and ethical good that Khemitians strove to follow. Ma'at was also the goddess who oversaw 42 commandments, among them *thou shall not kill, thou shall not commit adultery, thou shall not steal*. The intention for all Khemitians was to follow these commandments.

When one died, they would arrive at *Duat*, the home of the gods. They would enter the Hall of Two Truths and stand in front of Anubis, a jackal-headed god of the Afterlife, and confess to any sins related to the 42 commandments. The deceased's heart would be weighed against a feather—the feather of Ma'at. This was known as the weighing of the heart, and it was the reason the heart was left in the body during mummification. A good heart, free of sin in past deeds, was comparable to the weight of the feather. A sinful heart would weigh much more. If the dead rightly confessed to having committed no sin, they could pass on to the *Aaru*, the eternal paradise. Those whose hearts personified sin were devoured by Ammit, a demon whose body was part lion, crocodile, and hippopotamus.

Lastly, he began to understand a larger connection with the number 42. Ancient Khemit, founded by the congregation of 42 distinct tribes, had then been divided into 42 administrative districts along the Nile, and these districts had been known at Nomes. In the Bible, the genealogy of Jesus had 42 generations; in Revelation, it is said that Satan will hold dominion over the Earth for 42 months; in the book of Ezra, 42 360 exiles return from Babylon to Jerusalem; in Kings, when Elisha is mocked for being bald, God sends bears to maul 42 of the mockers.

And then floodgates of awareness were unlocked.

Jackie Robinson, the first African American Major League baseball player, wore 42.

Elvis Presley was 42 when he died.

Titanic was travelling at a speed equivalent to 42 km/hour when it struck the iceberg.

Chuck Yeager broke the sound barrier in his X-1 at 42 000 feet.

In *The Hitchhiker's Guide to the Galaxy*, 42 is the answer to "life, the universe, and everything."

Friar Laurence offers Juliet a potion that will allow her to simulate death for 42 hours.

Thriller, *Back in Black*, and *The Dark Side of the Moon*—the three highest-selling albums in music history—are all approximately 42 minutes in length.

A marathon is 42 kilometres, the distance between Marathon and Athens, an expanse travelled by a Greek messenger to warn of an impending Persian attack.

The original *Alice in Wonderland* has 42 illustrations.

Prince albert died at the age of 42; he and Queen Victoria had 42 grandchildren; their great-grandchild, Edward VIII, abdicated when he was 42.

The world's first printed book, Johannes Gutenberg's Bible, has 42 lines per page.

And on and on.

He wondered if this was all mere coincidence. After all, one could compile such a list for any number, couldn't they? Album lengths, references in literature, the Bible—such were accidental coincidences, no more.

And yet…

Nubar Yaghdjian stared out the twin screen doors of his tiny apartment, onto Mahmoud Bassiony. His view was severely obscured by a thick, grey haze; this little surprised him. Every day the same, except on those rare occasions when it rained. Cairo, the centre of Egypt, a cramped cesspool of smog.

He gaped at the sprawling cornucopia straddling the Nile at the edge of the desert. Incalculable high rise apartments, mosques, skyscrapers, intermingled like some multicultural exhibition. The new Egypt.

He left for the Cairo Museum, his place of work. On his way, he passed a street vendor preparing *ful medames*: fava beans mixed with oils and spices. Early morning succulence. He stopped, eyeing the simmering concoction in a large pot, then his eyes gravitated to stacks of pita bread alongside. He looked up, saw that the vendor was smiling, asking him what he wanted. He gestured to the pot, then the bread. The *ful medames* was dished into a bowl, then offered on an oversized plate, two pieces of bread separated alongside.

Located in downtown Cairo, the Museum of Egyptian Antiquities houses unquestionably the most extensive collection of ancient Egyptian artefacts found anywhere in the world. The building that has been the home to this museum since 1902 is an immaculately-carved, largely square red brick structure. The entrance is curved at its summit, as are the six luminous panes of glass garnishing its front wall. Hidden from view to the average visitor from the ground, a large dome is visible from higher elevations directly behind the main entrance.

Inside, visitors are directed to two levels: the ground floor, and the first floor. The ground floor has plethoric collections of coins, pottery, and other smaller artefacts. There are also sarcophagi and statues. However, it is the first floor that most visitors generally gravitate to, since it is here where the famous mummies of pharaohs such as Akhenaten (presumably); his son, Tutankhamun; Ramses II (or Ra-mesu, as he would have been known as in antiquity), the longest-reigning pharaoh of all; and the only female pharaoh, Hatshepsut, can be found. In particular, it is Tutankhamun, whose unearthing by British Egyptologist Howard Carter in November 1922, that garners the most attention. The tomb Carter found was largely intact. Within, the most dazzling possessions were the pharaoh's brilliant golden sarcophagus, which is actually a series of radiant sarcophagi of varying sizes, placed one on top of the other by the pharaoh's embalmers. The brilliant gold mask, which concealed Tutankhamun's mummified corpse, hanging proudly and ceremoniously on the wall on this floor, is a constant source of fascination by tourists.

It is Tutankhamun's father Akhenaten who is also of particular interest. What visitors find interesting about this pharaoh is his dolichocephalous skull: Akhenaten boasted a remarkably large cranium, which cultivates upwards, then slopes back unnaturally. Did an affliction cause this extraordinarily shaped skull? Perhaps. Theorists have debated for decades just what it was that affected the pharaoh. Did he deliberately modify his skull, a process known as artificial cranial deformation still practiced today in parts of the world? Perhaps. There is also the theory that Akhenaten was born this way, and that his oddly-shaped head is nothing more than a birth defect.

For the young, aspiring tour guide Yaghdjian, questions about the appearance of Akhenaten's skull were always entertaining. He enjoyed pointing out that Tutankhamun's head was also irregularly-shaped, as was that of Akhenaten's other offspring.

It was a good thing he could still point out these differences: in January 2011, severe looting of the museum took place, as young demonstrators lashed out at Mubarak and his Supreme Council of Antiquities. Luckily, these mummies were not taken. At first, the head of SCA, Zahi Hawass, assured the public that all was in order. Eventually, Hawass had to admit that 54 items had been stolen, many from the Tutankhamun and family collection. Across the country, several ancient sites were also vandalised, a blemish on an otherwise productive—and necessary—day of protest.

Zahi Hawass. A symbol of all that had been wrong with Egypt before the uprising. Dubbed Egypt's "Indiana Jones," Hawass was featured in numerous documentaries, uneventful live specials, and his own reality show. Besides his salary with the SCA, he was also paid an annual sum of $200 000 from National Geographic. He had lectured around the world, his fee ranging from $10 000 to $50 000 per appearance. He even had his own clothing line: Egypt's Indiana Jones had long-since taken to dressing the part, often visible in a Stetson hat, khaki pants, denim shirts, and gently worn leather jackets. The proceeds of the clothing sales were meant for charity, he claimed, always the compassionate soul. And his generosity had not gone unnoticed amongst the world's top celebrities. Besides a long-time friendship with the notorious Omar Sharif, Hawass had rubbed shoulders with everyone from Princess Diana to Tony Blair to Bill Clinton to Barack Obama. Laura Bush, wife of the former American president, once introduced him to a crowd of eager onlookers as her friend.

Indiana Hawass. Zahi Jones. Arrogant, fiercely temperamental, impatient, he was no longer a part of things here. Scandals had undone him. There was the case in February 1988 of the Sphinx's conveniently crumbling shoulder, which cost former antiquities head Ahmed Kadri his job and allowed Hawass to move up the ranks. There was the disappearance of a priceless statue in January 1993, during a visit by Muammar Gaddafi. In all, *thirteen* statues mysteriously vanished under Hawass. In 2011, he and Susana Mubarak were accused of pocketing millions to taint DNA results on certain mummies. It is believed by some that these results indicated that Tutankhamun, his father Akhenaten, and grandfather Amenhotep III were of Western European, not Egyptian, descent. Shocking to say the least. *Rashwah*! Then there was the time when Hawass turned 63, the mandatory age of retirement for Egyptian government officials, but was somehow given a new post: Deputy Minister of Culture for life. And, of course, there was the about-face, in which Hawass initially supported the Mubaraks during the opening days of the revolution, then changed his mind, condemning Mubarak and giving full support to the uprising. Finally, in July 2011, he left the Ministry building for the last time. Hundreds of police were on hand to ensure he was not injured. To the sound of *harami*!—thief!—he was swarmed as he was ushered into a waiting taxi.

But during those good years, when Hawass was pocketing untold vast sums, thousands of young and aspiring home-grown Egyptologists were forced to scramble for employment upon graduation. Most could not find work even on their own country's archaeological digs. The lucky ones gravitated to Hawass' offices, albeit for meagre salaries. Others, like Yaghdjian, became tour guides. Many found no work at all.

He adjusted his khaki uniform in the bathroom of the worker's cafeteria. A tender, unadulterated face gawked back at him. Beyond, mouse-like chatter from other guides instigated his ears. At length, someone must have said something humorous, as they all burst out laughing. Yaghdjian glanced over, said nothing.

Images flooded in. It was a year ago suddenly, and he remembered Trent befriending him innocently enough. The conversation eventually morphed into fast friendship. At times, Trent had seemed preoccupied with Akhenaten, and the two would visit that pharaoh's artefacts and speculate on one theory or another. He was fascinated with the pharaoh's skull, apparently source material for a future book. A book that was unlikely to see the light of day now.

Yaghdjian wandered to his locker, where his eyes lapsed into free fall, lingered on the locker's floor, beyond his shoes. There was something protruding underneath. Something smallish and colourful. He reached for it. What he collected made no sense. A photo of an unusual mountain he did not recognise. Rock and sand gushed from surrounding terrain and then congregated into a conspicuously smooth peak. A shaved peak, like a face. No, not a face: a field, or a large plain. A table top. Table Mountain reincarnated. The top was shrouded in a darkened hue, in stark contrast to its paler base. At this base, he spied sparse snippets of vegetation.

His brows furrowed as he turned the photo over. There was nothing on the other side. He studied the image again. Was it Egypt? It didn't look like it, regardless of the hordes of mountains east of the Nile.

But who had put the picture here? And why?

Someone was entering the change room. He turned, and there stood an imposing round man in casual attire, drooping like overweighed tree ornaments. His face, a forest of thick stubble, sported a deadpanned stare. There was a book under his arm.

Can I help you?

Wasem nodded at him and strode reservedly past, glancing casually about. "You're not in any trouble, if that's what you mean."

A relief.

"I'm sure you've heard about Professor Trent?"

I have.

"I'm Inspector Hondo Wasem. I understand you were close with Trent. I need to ask you some questions."

Certainly, sir.

"How do you say your name?"

With copious phlegm, accent on the first syllable. The tourists have a hard time saying it. They always pronounce it "Yaw-Gin."

"What nationality is that?"

Armenian.

"A *khawaga*." An Egyptian-born son of immigrants. "You're not from Cairo. What accent is that?"

I'm from Idku.

"Ah. Coastal boy."

Yes. Born and raised on the Mediterranean.

"Anyway. How well did you know him—really?"

I've only been at the museum a little over a year, and Professor Trent would fly in for research. We would talk every time he came in, and we got to know one another well. We used to converse in Spanish from time to time.

"Spanish? What the hell for?"

The professor spoke several languages, and I have some training in Spanish. Did you know that there's a wonderful little connection between Spanish and Arabic? Arabs dominated Spain for centuries, and Spanish is inundated with our lang—.

"Ask me if I care."

Yaghdjian averted his eyes from the detective. He did that sometimes—spoke on trivial matters. A nervous habit.

I can't believe he's dead.

"He was murdered," Wasem suddenly barked with emphasis. "The papers have it right. We're still working on the who and the why."

I see.

"I need to know if you ever noticed anything strange about Trent, particularly towards the end."

Actually, I'm glad you asked. I have some things I need to tell you.

"Like what?"

The last time I saw Professor Trent, he seemed a bit…

He searched for the right word.

Preoccupied. Stressed.

"Stressed?"

Yes, stressed. Like he was up against a deadline or something.

The inspector was unimpressed. "Anything else?"

Yes. He asked me about Amarna.

"Amarna?"

Amarna, yes. Akhetaten.

"What's so special about Amarna?"

Yaghdjian hesitated. Was the inspector serious?

Well, it's where the ruins of Akhenaten's capital are located.

"You mean the pharaoh?"

Yes, sir.

"Why was Trent interested in that particular pharaoh?"

He was writing a book on him. The last time I saw him, he asked if I'd ever been down there, to Amarna, and I said yes. He told me he'd just come back from there.

Wasem remained hardened. "Did he ever talk to you about other countries? Mexico, perhaps?"

Mexico?

"You've heard of it?"

Of course, but I don't see the connection. We were just talking about Amarna.

"Right, and now I want to talk about the professor's travel habits. Did he ever mention anything to you about travelling?"

He did, in fact. Mexico, Greece, Denmark, India, Peru, Bolivia—

"Tell me."

Well, it's funny. A month or so ago, Professor Trent came in to the museum. He had just arrived from Copenhagen, he told me. He was very excited. I was confused, because as far as I knew, he only visited Egypt. Anyway, I asked him about Denmark, and he told me about Copenhagen. He'd been there with someone named Hammond.

"Hammond?"

Yes. Hammond. That was the gentleman's name. Anyway, the professor told me how he loved Copenhagen—the people, the museums, the history. He asked if I'd ever been, and naturally, I told him no.

"Uh huh."

He told me about how the Danes had such a rich Viking history, and they had these things called trelleborgs. Viking settlements. He said if you drew a line on a slant, starting from the north of Denmark, you would pass straight through four of these settlements, through Delphi in Greece, then Giza. Remarkable.

"Really?" Unfeigned interest. "Is that true?"

Apparently. He said that most people weren't aware of this phenomenon, but those who did were intent on disproving it. That seemed to annoy him.

"Perhaps it's just mere coincidence."

Perhaps. The critics annoyed him, at any rate.

"Annoyed him?"

He seemed agitated. This marvel was very important to him. I could see he was quite passionate about it. So I asked him what sparked his interest in Denmark, since he seemed normally preoccupied with Egypt. He told me he had lots of interests, and he started mentioning all these other places he'd been to.

"What other places?"

He'd been to some countries in Asia—Japan and India, and then he'd been to Lebanon and South America and some other places like Mexico. Australia. He definitely mentioned Australia. He said he was doing some research from time to time in these countries.

The inspector swung the book into view. Yaghdjian could see "Mexico" written on it. The burly man was rifling through pages, then he stopped.

"Does this mean anything to you?"

He was holding up a page. A mountain. Yaghdjian stared, said nothing, reached for his pocket. Blood filled his anxious cheeks.

The strangest thing. I've got one just like it.

A light ahead in the darkness...
He is gripped with fear...
Two figures are watching him...
They are walking towards him...
He powers up the nerve to open his mouth, to scream in horror...
He can feel hands reaching around his arms, pulling him upward...
No! Get away! Oh, God, please!—

Again. The second time he's dreamt it. Dreamt what? What memory is this? Is it a memory at all?

It is Friday morning. He dresses—white t-shirt, old jeans—heads downstairs, devours a bowl of cereal. He needs to get to work, to his small Red Iron Design shop not far away, where he toils with wrought iron, producing wondrous results: railings, signs, garden and driveway gates, home and garden decorations, security bars, kitchen cabinet frames, awnings, curtain rods, shelving, furniture. He is an artist more than anything else, a da Vinci in his own right.

He arrives at the shop. Inside is a fridge, work bench, table, lathe, a wall of tools. Two windows. His other home. He immediately sets to work. He has to install a set of railings for a front porch in Wortley Village. Beautiful, old cast iron railings, which he had bought and then powder-coated in black. The supports he built himself.

He loads his red Ranger, sets off. He drives purposely, seeking distraction from recent events. Injuries, numbers, triangles. Books and more books. Ridiculous.

The client's house gazes out onto the land of the Monsignor Feeney Centre across the street, the old teacher's college. Still an imposing structure, a landmark in Wortley Village, the building has sat empty for years now. Its yard now acts as a park, surrounded by gaping elms, maples, and spruces, as well as century homes.

He sits back, opens a Coke, wipes at sweat on the side of his face. He stares at the roaming Feeney yard, swaths of shade cast against an interminable blue sky. There is a girl on the grass, in shorts with her shirt hiked up, face down, brownish hair spread about her like spilled coffee. Not far away, an athletic-looking man probably in his twenties, in gym shorts and a black t-shirt, walks his dog, staring intently. He can't be blamed. The little pug sniffs busily at something. The air is alive with vivacious cicadas, droning hypnotically.

Something flutters past him. A butterfly has perched itself on a flower. A Monarch, clinging to the stem. Orange wings, black veins, yellowish-white orbs. Its antennae point curiously downward. Inquisitive proboscis rummage the ground. He watches it for some time. It is everything that is right with this world.

Back to work. He realises he's drilled the holes too small in the railings; he will need to make those bigger. He sets about re-boring. Then he positions the railings, screwing them into place. At length, he reaches for his paint can. It is criminal to install black railings and leave the silver screws exposed. He dips the brush in, begins tinting the heads.

The customer is not home; they'd arranged for the rest of the instalment tomorrow. He packs up his things, glances once more at the girl in the park, then leaves for the confines of his shop.

Noon promptly approaches. *So soon?* he wonders. In the fridge is a sandwich from Quiznos, saved from the day before, along with a bottle of water. Lunch will encompass a mere ten minutes; he doesn't have time to linger. From six in the morning to usually at least that time again at night, this is his only break. These precious ten minutes.

He inhales the Barbeque Smokehouse Chicken sandwich while sitting at the table and matching chairs, his own creations. He flips the television channels until he finds the local news. He's missed most of the big stories.

Immediately the newscaster, an attractive dark-haired woman, dives into the next story.

And now a story we've been telling you about all week. World famous alien astronaut theorist Henry Booth arrives in town tomorrow for a lecture at Alumni Hall.

A photo of a somewhat elderly intellectual appears above her right shoulder: intense eyes, a strong jawline, a perfectly-shaped head devoid of hair—what was it a Korean friend had once told him "bald" was in *Hangul? Tae mori. Tae mori, buk buk-i! Dead head! Nothing grows on your head!* Yes, that was it. He'd always liked the way it sounded. But the photo—an imposing figure.

It's the first time Booth has visited London, and his imminent lecture has ruffled more than a few feathers throughout the city. John Phelps has more.

The woman and image morph into a reporter standing in front of Western's Alumni Hall. Young, a dark suit, blonde.

Thanks, Maria. I'm here outside Alumni Hall, where most of the tickets for tomorrow have been sold. I've spoken to several people here on the campus, as well as in the area, for their take. As many know, Dr. Booth is a strong proponent of the alien astronaut theory, as you mentioned, Maria, which he has promulgated worldwide.

He freezes. One of the many books he read yesterday belongs to this professor.

Dr. Booth believes that historians have been seriously erroneous, that what we read in history books is in fact false. He posits that we humans were either created by, or at the very least visited by, extraterrestrials thousands of years ago, and that we continue to be visited by them today. He claims that famous architectural structures, such as the Great Pyramids in Egypt, were created with the help of extraterrestrials. He also makes it clear that all organised religion is flawed, in that "gods" were in fact aliens, not spiritual deities. This sentiment has made him a few enemies over the years. He strives for a re-evaluation of human history. Now, I should mention that although many scholars have dismissed these concepts, I can tell you that the ancient astronaut theory is growing: you can visit any New Age section in a bookstore to see evidence of that.

That is interesting, John. What can we expect from Dr. Booth tomorrow evening?

I expect things to get heated. Protestors are planning a demonstration, but campus security here tells me they will be monitoring the situation to ensure that nothing gets out of hand.

I assume this is nothing new for Dr. Booth—protestors, I mean.

Not at all. Over the years, Dr. Booth has been called—I have a list here—"vainglorious," "arrogant," "shrewd," "dishonest," "a quack," "immoral," "obtuse," "shameless," and on and on.

The newscaster is laughing. *That's quite the list.*

I spoke to Dr. Booth just a few days ago, and he joked he would actually be disappointed if no one showed up to protest. He says as long as there's controversy, then at least people are talking.

John shrugs embarrassingly. *I must confess, I find this subject fascinating, so I'll be here tomorrow. It should be lots of fun.*

John, great talking to you. Have fun tomorrow night.

Thanks, Maria. Talk to you soon.

That's John Phelps on location at Alumni Hall. In other news...

He turns off the television, remains in silence. Part of him wants to laugh. The other part cries out for joy. Perhaps this Henry Booth can help him.

And then it is there again, a voice in his head, the same presence that told him to read all those books. He stands, makes his way to the office computer, stares at the screen.

Google Earth.

Why?

He drags the mouse across the table, clicks on the icon. The world envelops before him, a little blue and brown and green ball in the blackness of space. He rolls the mouse to the right, and Africa revolves into view. He zooms in on Egypt, and the single blue streak that is the Nile, snaking its way down the length of the nation. And then Cairo. And just to the left of the city, on the edge of the desert…

He sits back and his jaw drops.

RA

The Great Pyramid. That is where he must go. He can only wonder why. And then the professor, the one named Henry Booth he has just seen on the news, emerges in his mind. He minimises Google Earth, moves on to Youtube. There, Henry Booth is ubiquitous. Lectures, videos, interviews. Where to begin? And then he spots a particular video, a few years old. The professor on George Stroumboulopoulos' old show, *The Hour*, before Strombo moved on to *Hockey Night in Canada*. He clicks on the image.

Stroumboulopoulos is introducing the professor to the show, and bottled-up applause is released, immediately filling the air. It splits and crackles the computer speakers like firecrackers.

Stroumboulopoulos is dressed in jeans and a dark collared top, earrings jingling reflectively in his ears, hair cropped short and jelled stylishly forward. He stands from his customary red chair, offers his hand to a man making his way across the stage. The tall, head-shaved professor takes the interviewer's hand in his, glances back at the bluish background of the stage set here among the Toronto CBC studios, beholds his image and name scrawled across in a somewhat gaudy form. Nonetheless, he smiles gingerly, finds his own red leather chair across from Stroumboulopoulos.

Straightaway, it is obvious the professor is unsure how to position himself in that chair. To the welder, the chair is tantalisingly appealing; he imagines how one could sink luxuriantly into it. Perhaps the professor can, too; because of this, he is wary, has probably been so for decades. One must be in his line of work: he has likely learned that there are always seductions out there. They were once high school history texts, then they were university texts; then he, too, was one of them himself, inviting and enticing others with alluring red leather fictions. But not anymore.

Apparently, he is the first UFO expert on this show. He is urged to divulge some of his life to date, and he does so. He was a university professor and a prominent historian, but over time, his thinking evolved, as he puts it. There was no sudden epiphany; rather, his conversion was gradual. As a professor at the University of Toronto, he began to question the persistent, axiomatic human acceptance of history. He wondered how humanity went from primitive cave men fighting over and hoarding fire to constructing massive pyramids that correspond precisely with the belt of Orion's Star up in the night sky. He thought to himself: how did we do that?

And how is it, for example, that the Great Pyramid in Egypt is almost precisely twice as tall as the Temple of the Sun in Mexico, and almost precisely the same diameter? How is it that this Great Pyramid and its nearby cousin, the pyramid of Khafre, appear almost precisely the same height, with Khafre's pyramid on a slight incline, when, conversely, the Temple of the Sun and the Temple of the Moon in Mexico appear almost precisely the same height, whereas it is the Temple of the Moon that is on the incline? And why are the Temple of the Sun, Moon, and the Citadel—also known as the Pyramid of Quetzalcoatl—mirrors of those at Giza in how they are aligned precisely in the formation of Orion's Belt? How is it that two distinct civilisations thousands of kilometres apart, thousands of years apart, can have so many similarities? Mere coincidence?

He asks why it is that massive pictographs in the Peruvian desert, known as the Nazca Lines, display animals that weren't from anywhere near the area. How did people in Peru thousands of years ago know about these animals? But it isn't just Egypt and South America that so impress him. He wonders how an apparently submerged city off the Japanese island of Yonaguni can exist, if civilisation is supposedly only five thousand years old.

And it has to be a city off Yonaguni; it cannot be a natural formation, as some scholars say, because there are far too many square and straight edges. I am aware that straight lines can be naturally created in stones along fault lines, but Yonaguni is extreme. It had to have been built in a time when the surrounding water levels were radically different than they are now. This would be thousands of years earlier than what the experts believe is the oldest civilisation.

And so, because of examples like these, he began to face the facts: there is far more to history than we know or have been taught. And that was when he started looking skyward.

He then explains briefly what the ancient astronaut theory is. The theory has been with us for quite some time, but it gained international attention in the '60s when Erich von Däniken published his *Chariots of the Gods?*. A mega-bestseller, the book poses questions: Däniken asks how certain historical sites around the world could have been built the way historians or archaeologists have proposed. The answer: we had help.

The human race could not have built these awesome structures using the simple methods or tools they are purported to have used. At least in Egypt, where the pyramids were supposedly built in a strict time frame corresponding to the rule of each pharaoh. It's impossible.

Like Däniken says, we had help. We had help because we are in fact direct descendants of extraterrestrials. They made us, gave us far superior cognitive abilities, and left the primitive cave men in the dust. That's how we suddenly went from hoarding fire to constructing pyramids overnight.

But doesn't that completely refute Darwin's theory of evolution?

Not necessarily. If we look at the fossilised remains of primitive humanoids, we can see that indeed there was an evolutionary process. However, somewhere around 200 to 250 000 years ago, a far more advanced form of humanity suddenly materialised: Homo Sapiens. What's strange is that Homo Sapiens was on the Earth at the exact same time other more primitive humans were. The experts agree on this. Where is the evolution here? This was sudden, unexplained. Interbreeding between Neanderthals and Homo Sapiens has been evidenced in our modern DNA, albeit minimally, but what I find interesting is how some prehistoric humans remained completely primitive, while others began building vast civilisations. Not right away, I grant you, but much sooner than archaeologists prefer to say. Where did this sudden mutation, this injection in brain power, come from?

And so, he does endorse evolution, believes it is silly not to. Yes, primitive humans undoubtedly did evolve, interbred with one another, then went extinct. But Homo Sapiens simply materialised from thin air, and unlike the Neanderthal, stuck around. It is on this point of intelligence that has him convinced that something else was at play here. Something beyond evolution.

He accepts that these theories are still radical today. Othello demanded of Iago the ocular proof; so, too, do people want proof to satisfy their doubts. But when one takes the time to travel to these places, to study them in depth, one begins to see things one did not see before. The ocular proof *is* there, right before humanity's very eyes.

Egyptologists deride the notion that the Egyptians built the Great Pyramid and other structures with sophisticated techniques, but it is obvious that copper chisels and hammers could not have been used solely. How do copper chisels and hammers cut stone with a precision that most modern machinery cannot match? For example, the Grand Gallery of the Great Pyramid is a large tunnel-like space just under nine metres high and 46.5 metres long, on an incline of almost exactly 26.5 degrees from beginning to end. The incline is precisely the same throughout. The measurement is astounding. A modern house is not so precise. And yet this precision was accomplished through solid stone thousands of years ago. Think about those numbers: a precise incline of 26.5 degrees for a distance of 46.5 metres through solid stone weighing several tonnes each. That is hundreds of thousands of pounds. Egyptologists and archaeologists out there want to believe that such an advanced people as the ancient Egyptians, who built colossal structures to within millimetres of precision, accomplished as much with simplistic means. But just because there isn't evidence of a higher level of machining lying around in ancient Egypt doesn't prove anything. Any expert in the field of engineering—even an experienced constructionist—can easily contradict traditional Egyptian building theories. Clearly the Egyptians used machines to cut their stones. Powered somehow, perhaps by the Earth itself.

 The professor uses a modern analogy to prove his point.

 Why it is that soldiers today, when marching in unison, suddenly break step when they're about to walk across a bridge? Basic physics. Marching creates an amplified frequency of sound. When the soldiers cross a bridge, if they remain in marching formation, there is the possibility that the rhythmic frequency created by their steps will interact with the bridge's own resonant frequency. Such an interaction could potentially cause the bridge to break apart. This is exactly what happened to the Broughton Suspension Bridge in England in 1831. The soldiers marched across, the bridge began to vibrate, and then forty or so of them fell in. No one died, but there were injuries. Nineteen years after that, the Angers Bridge in France collapsed during a storm, during which hundreds of soldiers were walking across it. Over two hundred people died during this event. These French soldiers had in fact tapped into the resonant frequency of the bridge, which precipitated its collapse. Since then, British and French soldiers break step when crossing a bridge. The collapsing of bridges relates directly to the construction of the pyramids in Egypt. To everything, in fact. Everything on this Earth has a resonant frequency. It has been proven that certain structures can amplify sound in such a way that the sound waves can be harnessed as energy. Solar power. Wind turbines. Niagara Falls. Rub your feet on carpet and you produce an electric charge. The machines the Egyptians used to build the pyramids and other structures no doubt employed this very basic rule of physics. I'm talking about manipulating the resonant frequency of objects to move them into a certain place. Gravitational manipulation. It's not at all unrealistic.

There is suspicion with believing in such talk. Part of the reason, again, is what we've all been taught. Theories about carving stones and hoisting them up using ropes or ramps have been accepted because they are plausible. In actuality, the ancient tools on display in the Cairo Museum are hopelessly inefficient. It is insulting to the ancient Egyptians for us to assume these were what they used to build their structures. In 1883, British archaeologist Flinders Petrie undertook what was then the most comprehensive study of ancient Egyptian culture. He maintained that the Egyptian craftsmanship was so precise, only saws could have been used in ancient Egypt. Straight saws and circular saws. And tubular drills, and lathes. And this was in 1883! And it isn't just Petrie who believes in this conclusion: much more recently, Christopher Dunn, a highly-respected machinist and designer, with no prior schooling in ancient Egypt, carried out another comprehensive study of the Great Pyramid, and his conclusions were the same: that the Egyptians were utilising far more advanced technology than simple hammers and chisels. Machine technology in a time devoid of machines. If one truly and definitively wants to analyse Egyptian construction technique, doesn't it make sense to listen to people who know a thing or two about construction?

Dunn proposes that the Great Pyramid at Giza was designed not as a tomb. He's right about that—there's no way the pyramid was ever built as a tomb. He postulates the pyramid was a perfectly designed engine that combined hydrogen and water with the Earth's harmonic frequencies to create power: the pyramid itself took in the Earth's vibrations, then channelled these vibrations, together with hydrogen, to produce the equivalent of a power plant. An ancient reactor in a sense. As for why the pyramid isn't used as a power plant today, the solution might be rather simple. Petrie offered a suggestion, unbeknownst to him, that Dunn capitalised on. Petrie noticed some damage in the King's Chamber, and he speculated that an earthquake sometime in the past must have caused the pyramid to shift ever so slightly. Dunn went further: he speculates the King's Chamber shows damage reminiscent of an explosion. He believes there must have been some kind of event in that chamber—an energy build-up that the Egyptians couldn't handle, for example—and the chamber was therefore damaged. He cites burn marks as possible evidence. Once irreversibly destroyed, the pyramid could no longer be used for its intended purpose. It sat dormant, and as the centuries passed, ancient Egyptians lost track of its original purpose.

And as more evidence of a civilisation far older than most currently realise, there is also the Great Sphinx at the Giza Plateau, Egyptologists have had quite the debate over its age for several decades now. Traditionally, it was assumed the Sphinx was built around the same time as the second big pyramid at Giza, by the pharaoh Khafre. That would be sometime around the year 2500 B.C.E. However, in the 1950s, a French Egyptologist proposed the Sphinx demonstrated clear evidence of water erosion. New experts have weighed in on the theory, and it is now believed by many that the erosion on the Sphinx makes it thousands of years older than Khafre, during a time when Egypt looked much different than it does today, when it was far more fertile, not just along the Nile, but far and wide. When Egypt was a lush, green place. The funny thing is, this isn't anything new: in 1904, a British Egyptologist named E.A. Wallis Budge said, "This marvellous object was in existence in the days of Khafre [...] and it is probable that it is a very great deal older than his reign and that it dates from the end of the archaic period." *Much more recently, Egyptologist John Anthony West asked geologist Robert Schoch to weigh in on the debate. Schoch confirmed that water erosion is apparent on the Sphinx. Thousands of geologists all around the world agree with the water erosion theory.*

The professor then proposes a test: they will talk their way through the building of the Great Pyramid as it is currently accepted.

The first thing one needs to do is go grab a copper hammer and chisel. Then one needs to find a piece of stone weighing, let's say, about fifty tonnes. The stone needs to be chiselled into a rectangular block. But we'll need more of these blocks. In fact, we'll need two and a half million of them. Now, it isn't just about cutting stone with chisels: Egyptians cut with precision. Each stone must be cut to within one tenth of an inch of accuracy. Modern builders are happy if they can cut something to within a twentieth of an inch using the latest in modern technology, but we will strive to do better—with copper chisels. Thousands will be needed. We'll have to create a quarry somewhere, naturally, to cut the stone blocks. Then—and here's the best part of all—we'll have to lift them out of the quarry and transport them about five hundred kilometres away. And we only have twenty years to do it.

Stroumboulopoulos questions if twenty years is indeed impossible. The professor turns, and behind them, his face has been replaced with a calculator. He begins to conduct an experiment with numbers.

There are approximately 2.5 million stones in the Great Pyramid itself, and the experts believe that the pyramid was built during the reign of the Pharaoh Khufu, who ruled for approximately twenty-three years. He takes a year, 365 days, and multiplies that by twenty years. The result: 7300 days to build the Great Pyramid. He then mentions that it is likely the Egyptians weren't even working every day—they weren't slaves building this pyramid, after all, and so would have naturally had days off to rest, as well as religious days afforded them. *So, therefore, the 365 day work model is inaccurate. However, the accepted theory is twenty years, and so, how many stones a day, on average, were added to the pyramid over that time? 2.5 million divided by 7300 is 342.4657534246575.* He reduces the number to 342. *Approximately 342 stones a day were added to the pyramid to complete it during the reign of Khufu. How many stones per hour would that be, on average? 342 hours divided by 24 is 14.25 stones per hour. That is a stone every 4.3 minutes. If one assumes ramps were used, which is the most accepted theory, imagine what that would have looked like: stones several tonnes in weight being dragged up, with workers on their way down at the same time—a logistical nightmare considering the sheer size and scope of the construction project they were building. And let's keep in mind the weights of these stones. A single stone weighing, say, two and a half metric tonnes is 2268 kilograms. That's almost 5000 pounds! And there are over two and half million stones on the Great Pyramid. Within the inner chambers of the pyramid, the weight of the stones is even more impressive. The ceiling of the King's chamber is composed of nine stones weighing an estimated 362 tonnes. That's an average of just over 40 tonnes per stone. 40 tonnes is over 36 000 kilograms. That's almost 80 000 pounds per stone. 80 000!*

Twenty-four hours a day for twenty years uninterrupted. *I stress again that modern evidence indicates these workers were not slaves, and so wouldn't have worked uninterrupted. The Greek historian Herodotus tells us 100 000 men were worked for three months, then replaced with another 100 000. And so on. But we have to remember that they would have been segregated, as Herodotus tells us, at the pyramid work site, at the quarry far away, and on the river tending the boats. The timing isn't impossible, as the math shows. Just highly, highly unlikely.*

And what about this ramp the experts say they used? The Great Pyramid is over 146 metres in height, or 480 feet. Believe it or not, it remained the tallest structure in the world until the Eiffel tower was completed in 1889. A ramp would in itself have been a major undertaking, perhaps similarly as time consuming as the pyramid. Thousands of workers would have had to constantly raise it accordingly as each row of the pyramid was completed.

He then tackles the tomb theory, which he hinted at earlier.

The Great Pyramid, in particular, was apparently a tomb for the Pharaoh Khufu. But there's no credible evidence to support that theory. Herodotus wrote of the pyramid as a tomb, and because in one tiny corner of the King's Chamber there's an inscription that bears Khufu's name, many attribute this as evidence. Also because of something called the Westcar Papyrus, which identifies Khufu as the builder of the pyramid. The Westcar Papyrus is decent evidence, except that it dates from several centuries after Khufu's death. And the Egyptians speaking to Herodotus were living so long after the building of the pyramids, it's just as conceivable they were no longer sure of its purpose. Perhaps they were lying—or speculating. The truth is, nothing, let alone a body, has ever been found in there. Therefore, we can't believe anything, especially anything Herodotus tell us. For example, he says Khufu was not like his father in that he was cruel and wicked, and that he shut up all the temples and forced his people to build the pyramid for him. I have already addressed the notion of slaves at Giza. But if one truly wants evidence that no pharaoh was buried in the Great Pyramid, look to a man named Al Mamun, the caliph—governor—of Egypt long after the world of ancient Egypt had vanished, long after Greek, then Roman rule, long after Islam had replaced Christianity as the dominant religion. Al Mamun ruled in the ninth century C.E. He had heard stories of buried treasure within the Great Pyramid, of riches beyond compare. So, in the year 820 C.E., he ordered his men to find a way in. There was and remains an entrance to the pyramid, but Al Mamun's men were not able to penetrate it. This barricaded entrance is noticeable from the ground by the angled blocks that adorn its crown, and in Al Mamun's day, casing stones on the pyramid would likely have covered this entrance. Casing stones which are no longer there today, of course. Many were used to build Cairo. Perhaps an earthquake loosened them from the main structure, and they thus became available building material. Either way, unsatisfied and undeterred, Al Mamun ordered his men up the pyramid to carve out a new entrance, which in fact they did do, along the pyramid's north face. Their efforts paid off: this new and crudely tunnelled corridor eventually conjoined with what has been coined the Descending Passage, a long service way running south into the bowels of the pyramid. When one enters today, always through the Caliph's entrance, they arrive at this Descending Passage. They will also notice another tunnel. This is what is known as the Ascending Passage. This intestinal passageway leads one into the structure's more fascinating organs: the Grand Gallery, the Queen's chamber, and lastly, the King's Chamber. When Al Mamun's men finally entered the King's Chamber, they found nothing. Odd. They created the only workable entrance into the pyramid, the entrance still in use today, and yet the pyramid was empty. Grave robbers from past centuries could not have beaten these men to the treasure; the only known entrance was impenetrable. Al Mamun's men were the first to break in. Perhaps while its construction is still underway, before the entrance was sealed forever, the pyramid was looted. But wouldn't that have been noticeable?

All that could be found in the pyramid was a large box believed to be a damaged sarcophagus. But there is no credible evidence that this box is in fact a sarcophagus. And so, perhaps the Egyptians told Herodotus and other Greeks what they themselves presumed was true. At the same time, it's entirely possible they might have been lying to protect their own culture's secrets. Perhaps this is ongoing even today. There are allegations of corruption in Egypt, of, for example, doctoring DNA samples on mummies to hide ancestral truths. Some Egyptians are very protective of their past; the same might have been true thousands of years ago. The priests and only a select few others were privy to the inner workings and history of the region.

But where is the proof for all of this? Why, it is before our very eyes. All we need do is look.

And, so, you're saying the Egyptians must have had help.

They had to have. But where did these helpers come from? Why is it that the three largest pyramids at the Giza Plateau and those found along the Avenue of the Dead in Mexico—both mathematically similar in precision—are aligned precisely to match Orion's Belt? Robert Bauval and Adrian Gilbert pointed this out to us. Why Orion? What's up there that was so important to these people?

There is so much out there we should be questioning. We need to revise our teaching of human history. We've only known about dinosaurs for a few hundred years, and look at how their discovery changed our perception on the age of our planet. Columbus turned right and sailed across the Atlantic looking for Asia. He was supposedly crazy to think he could find China. And far more recently, in March of 1997, thousands of eyewitnesses saw something over the city of Phoenix. Even the former governor of the state of Arizona, Fife Symington, admits today that it was a UFO.

We are not alone. We have never been.

It was a radiant Saturday morning: a cloudless sky, an inescapable blazing sun. There were several cars on the 401 West, sweltering under its oppressive glow. It was under this canvas that two vans plunged along the tributarian 401, a stark contrast to the surrounding traffic of sedans and transports, for one of these vehicles was anything but ordinary. It was a customised 2010 dark grey Dodge Caravan, elongated and expanded to become the very epitome of practicality and luxury on the road. Rotating leather seats along the sides, a coffee table and couch in the rear. An isle running down the middle. A mini-television hanging like a chandelier behind the front two seats. A tour bus more than a van, really. And Professor Henry Booth had taken it from one side of the continent to the other.

Within the customised van, besides the professor at the wheel, was one other person. A young woman, shockingly attractive: brunette, tall, seductively athletic, fiercely intelligent. She was mastered in five languages. She was dressed casually, but that would change before the lecture. Lauren Haaksma was Aphrodite in all sense of the word.

A silence had descended within the van, precipitated largely by the absence of the professor. He was there, but he was not there, his mind elsewhere. Thoughts of a murdered friend, dead on the floor of his hotel, blood oozing, vacant eyes in death, clasped hands in death. He was thinking too, of tears he had conceded, and—

His cell phone was ringing, a ringtone for the antiquated. But this was no antiquated man. It awakened him from his stupor. He reached into his khaki pants pocket and extracted the device, put it on speaker. He did not recognise the number but accepted the call all the same. "Hello, who is this?" he said impatiently.

The voice on the other end was muffled and ambiguous. A poor connection.

Am I speaking to Professor Henry Booth? someone was asking in an immediately decipherable accent.

"You are. With whom do I have the pleasure?"

My name is Inspector Hondo Wasem of the Cairo Police Department. I am calling in regards to the recent death of Professor Trent.

Wasem waited several seconds, uncertain of how to proceed.

Professor? Are you still there?

"I'm still here. I'm just surprised you're calling me."

I understand he was your close friend?

"Best friend, yes. I need you to cut to the chase, Inspector."

The culprit was a scorpion.

"A scorpion?"

A fat-tailed scorpion. The little devils are natives of Egypt. Their venom is extremely potent.

"Inspector, I've been to Egypt countless times. Since when do scorpions enter hotel rooms and murder people?"

When they are invited in, Professor.

"Come again?"

Trent had discovered something very important. He was murdered for this, I believe. I was hoping you might have some insight.

"Sorry to disappoint. I can tell you David flew to Egypt a few weeks ago to do some research on his latest book. We spoke a few times via email. I have nothing else to offer."

Regardless, someone came in and robbed your friend—there was a safe left open. There was something in that safe. They killed him for it.

"What was in there that David had to die for?"

I wish I knew. I wish *you* knew. But there is a catch: there were no signs of forced entry. Whoever the murderer was, your friend knew him. He let him in.

"And then unleashed a scorpion on him?"

Something like that. We found the scorpion still there, in a box.

There is a long drawn breath, and the professor imagined Wasem shrugging helplessly on the other end.

The professor gazed out the window of the van. The scenery blurred past, a washed out painting. "That's rather chilling, Inspector."

We're working on suspects. This is one of the reasons I was calling you: do you know of anyone who might have wanted to kill Professor Trent?

"Who goes around killing Egyptologists?"

Granted.

"David and I know many people in Cairo. People all over the world, really. I couldn't even begin to guess."

I understand. Just something to think about. There was a computer in Trent's room. Our men gave it a thorough search. There was a picture he had been looking at just before he died.

"What of?"

A picture of a mountain. And words: "Seek out 2958450631080309."

"I have no idea what that means."

Nothing?

"Nothing. It's very strange. It's like he was writing in code or something. He was looking at it just before…?"

Perhaps he was in a hurry to decipher the code. Before it was too late. Professor, there is something else. Something that may amount to nothing in the end, but I want to tell you regardless.

"Go on."

There is a young man here who works at the Cairo Museum. He befriended Professor Trent in the past year, and apparently the two had become somewhat close.

"Yes. Nubar Yaghdjian."

Ah, you knew this?

"David and I both know—knew—Yaghdjian."

Anyway, the professor was murdered on the Wednesday night, but this Yaghdjian remembers Trent arriving at the museum only the day before, on Tuesday, and acting rather unusual.

"How so?"

Well, he was asking the Egyptian man about Amarna. Does *that* mean anything to you?

"Of course. The ruins of Akhetaten. David had been there many times. He was an expert on Amarna."

Yes, but Yaghdjian says the professor seemed nervous. "Stressed" was the word he used. This was the day before the murder.

"What else did he tell you?"

That's it. Trent came in, spoke to him apprehensively about Amarna, and that was the end of it. Trent was very excited about all the archaeological work going on there. But there's more: he had in his possession several travel books. Mexico, Denmark, India, Japan, Bolivia—

"Travel books? You're sure they were his?"

They were in his room. And Yaghdjian confirmed the professor had been travelling extensively of late. Do you know anyone named Hammond?

"Hammond?" The professor paused. "Yes, of course. Brent Hammond. A young archaeologist. His father was one, too, before he died. He, David, and I were all very close. I keep in touch with Brent from time to time. He's always off somewhere, looking for something."

Apparently he and Professor Trent had travelled to Denmark.

"That's not likely. David and Brent barely knew each other."

You said you were all very close, yes?

"With the senior Hammond. And I know Brent, but he and David were only acquaintances."

Yes, but Yaghdjian confirmed this trip to Denmark.

The professor gaped out the nearby window. How—?

Was the professor religious?

"Not particularly. Why?"

There was a Bible with his things in the hotel room.

"David studied the Bible on occasion when his work justified it. But he wasn't especially religious. It's not unusual for us to carry one around."

Maybe so. But then it gets interesting.

"Yes?"

On the Thursday morning, only hours after the murder, this Yaghdjian found something unusual in his locker, something he knows for certain he did not place there.

"I see."

In his locker was a picture of a mountain in the desert. The same mountain Trent had on his computer with the words and numbers I asked you about.

The deflated professor sighed. "You just lost me."

I'm just wondering if this might mean anything to you.

"A mountain in a desert? No, it means nothing to me."

Perhaps it has something to do with Amarna.

The professor pondered the statement, could find no logical conclusion to draw from it. "There are highlands around Amarna. Maybe that's what the photo shows."

No. This is very distinctly a mountain. And it is peculiar: the peak is completely flat. Shaved off, like Table Mountain. But this is not Table Mountain. It means nothing?

"I'd have to see it, Inspector. But off hand, no, nothing. I can't be expected to know the physical appearance of every individual mountain in Egypt—"

Of course not. I only—

"—but I can tell you that nothing like that exists in or around Amarna."

You're sure of that?

"I'm sure. You think David planted that photo in this man's locker?"

It's possible. I think he was trying to tell Yaghdjian something.

"I see."

Really, we have so little to go on.

There was an uncomfortable pause. The inspector continued.

So, if anything comes to you, I would appreciate it if you contacted me.

The professor sensed that the conversation was coming to an end. "Of course. I assume this is the number I can reach you at?"

Yes, this is my cell number. Please don't hesitate to call if you think of anything.

"We will speak again soon, Inspector."

Friday was difficult: an attempt to work despite an exasperating preoccupation with all that had been learned the previous day. As well, he was still drawing triangles and writing down numbers. It had become an obsession, and he found it discouraging, hopeless. But today was Saturday; Henry Booth was in town. Perhaps today would offer hope.

And now Saturday afternoon beckons. The young welder retreats from his shop back to his home. Now he begins to worry. What if there are no tickets available? After all, the news story made it out that Booth is exceedingly famous. And what of the stigma, the one he will surely endure from his friends when it is eventually leaked that he has sought out this professor for answers to a problem no one can comprehend?

Is he buying into the theory, aliens travelling to Earth thousands of years ago and affecting the human race? Aliens helping us build pyramids? He cannot be sure where he stands. And yet, he finds himself irrevocably drawn to the lecture.

Seven o'clock. When he pulls in to Western's campus and drives past Alumni Hall an hour early, he is not surprised to see people already mingling outside. There are the banners from the religious groups the news cast had mentioned. One reads, *"God is not an alien."* Another: *"Even Satan doesn't want you."* The people holding them and lingering nearby are of a kaleidoscopic variety: young and old, some with an erudite allure, others lacking. He chuckles as he seeks out a place to park.

As luck would have it, there are a handful of tickets available. He purchases one and finds his way into a newly-formed line. And at half past seven, the doors finally open. Twenty-three hundred or so stifling patrons eagerly pour into the welcoming air conditioned venue.

He takes his seat and surveys the settling crowd, smells what he can only describe as anticipation in the air. It is an euphoric atmosphere, like it is before an entertainer hits the stage. He notices some attendees are carrying books the professor has written. Autograph seekers, he muses, or keeners who will be thumbing through pages of subjects the professor will assumedly discuss. They are here to find answers, to be reassured. Those who ridicule have remained outside, or so it seems. They will not spend money on something they do not respect. But of those here inside this auditorium, of them he wonders. Wonders if any of them are like him. Do any of them possess the same unique penchant for drawing triangles, for copying mathematical numbers across a page?

A man is making his way through the isle, towards the young welder. The man is elderly, paper-hair white and a weathered face that has seen a great deal of sun. It is summer, but this man looks as though he is in the sun all year around. Perhaps a snow bird. He is clad in a navy blazer and grey slacks, a white collared shirt unbuttoned at the top, stark against his bronzed neck, his exposed clavicle. The clavicle itself, like the man's hands, shows the look of age: freckles or sun spots dot skin stretched thin. The man seems emaciated. Those hands. Bones are visible beneath, and blue veins like tree vines. He walks with a sort of limp, the left leg dragging ever so slightly. He is polite as he makes his way through the seated crowd, and a Bible is now visible in his right hand, tucked under the armpit. A red ribbon hangs from it, serving as a bookmark, no doubt.

The gentleman sits, nods to the young welder, opens his Bible and begins scrolling with a gnarled finger down a page. The welder cannot help but look—such is the way with people and curiosity. The man is studying the Book of Exodus. Interesting. But why bring a Bible to this lecture? And why Exodus, of all things? Perhaps Genesis; that might make sense, if Henry Booth is to discuss an alternate theory on the creation of humanity. He wonders if the gentleman knows something he does not.

He looks up from the pages, realises the man has noticed him, smiles in embarrassment. The gentleman seems nonplussed, however; he nods cordially and says with a European accent, Do you read the Bible?

No, he replies, perhaps too quickly, he does not.

Much we can learn from the teachings of the scriptures, the gentleman tells him, then the two fall into awkward silence. The gentleman is again studying his page, and the young welder looks away uncomfortably. What accent is that? Dutch, perhaps? German?

Unsatisfied, he regards the stage. A large screen, carefully positioned along its rear. In front, a laptop and projector ready to display who knows what.

At precisely eight, the lights dim. There is a concert feel, that sudden burst of anticipation with the reduction of illumination. From below, amongst the darkness, a solitary beam of light discharges from the projector. All eyes remain fixated on the screen.

At first, there is nothing to see but the cosmos, a million miniature orbs twinkling against a black backdrop. Then there is the Earth in all its splendour, quickly drawing near. The audience is being invited closer and still closer, through the clouds, then plummeting down into a jungle of lush foliage and rivers. The sounds of nature emanate from the loudspeakers, invading eardrums: birds, mammals, the tranquil swish of water. Cicadas or crickets or both. And then people appear. They are of a long-lost era, prehistoric. Naked, hairy, their foreheads protrude disproportionately, and they converse with one another in muted grunts. They are passing by the clearing, and one in their number has stopped to glance skyward. He begins to pant and then yell capriciously, cajoling his companions to follow with their eyes that which he now observes. The others do as he bids, tilting their heads. All around there is a sound, steadily increasing, as of a descending airplane. But this is no airplane. In fact, the sound is not of the Earth: something is descending towards the group of humanoids.

It is a vessel, a spaceship, though those below fail to comprehend it as such. To them, it is an oversized bird perhaps, a cloud, some form of demon. A dragon. It is large, as large as a football field, with undulating lights along its sides and undercarriage. Lights that ululate ferociously. It is rectangular in shape, protracted from its domed bow through to a pair of immense engines in its rear. It appears unconcerned with the inhabitants below, all of whom are now scattering, racing for the protection of the trees.

It lowers to the ground, resting majestically on the soft ground. And then, as quickly as it has begun, the ship grows mute, and familiar sounds of nature return to the ears of the audience.

Some of the inhabitants step timidly towards the edge of the foliage; others refuse and retreat further into the protective confines of the fauna. Those who remain can see something happening to the ship: a ladder is being extended downward, and almost immediately, humanoid life forms clad prominently in navy blue helmeted suits appear, stepping down. They are wearing backpacks, assumedly for purposes of oxygen. They move purposefully, as if they have done this before. And perhaps they have, here on Earth or elsewhere throughout the universe.

They now stand shoulder to shoulder, five of them, glancing at one another through semi-transparent visors, surveying the environment around them. Then one of them reaches up and removes his helmet. The audience braces itself, as do the Earthlings, but the result is surprisingly anticlimactic: it is a man, his features somewhat exaggerated by human standards, but a man nonetheless. To the inhabitants of the jungle, however, some of whom are already stepping clear of the flora, he is so much more than that.

The other aliens remove their helmets as well, each displaying slightly varying features: the pigment of their skin ranges from grey to pink, and their ears are much larger than an Earthling's, drooping slightly. Although the size of their eyes vary from one to the next, all are much larger than the Earthlings'. Their noses are smaller, almost slits on their faces. Their mouths are far larger, lipless, stretching from one cheek to the other.

But the Earthlings view them as something else, and one after another bows benevolently before them. The aliens exchange tentative looks, but it is evident to them that the Earthlings mean them no harm. The first of the group raises his right arm high overhead and emits a series of sounds that can only be construed as dialogue. Then the others follow suit, a cohesive diatribe.

And then the screen goes dark and begins to rise, and a solitary spotlight grows in intensity, illuminating both the stage and a rather imposing man. He walks across the platform from the right side. A black suit, tieless. Intimidating in stature: thick, bare headed, goateed, yet there emanates from him a benign quality—a trusting man. He reaches up to activate a headset microphone he happens to be wearing. His voice and the chilling words that accompany it reverberate ominously throughout the auditorium.

"Imagine that everything you know is wrong."

ROBERT L. BALLANTYNE

Partial Transcript: Professor Henry Booth lecture, Alumni Hall, University of Western Ontario
London, Ontario
Saturday, July 7, 2015

Welcome, one and all. Welcome to a new way of looking at things. Welcome to the world of the alien astronaut theory, dismissed by academics around the world, professionals who will tell you that people like me are delusional. I'm here to tell you that we're not delusional; I'm here to tell you that what we have to say is sound, logical, and, ultimately, irrefutable. I'm here to tell you that everything you know is wrong.

For thousands and thousands of years, including today, we have been and continue to be visited by extraterrestrials from other worlds.

I think before I go any further, I should introduce myself. My name is Henry Booth. I'm sixty-two years young, and I have a doctorate in Ancient Civilisations. I love the ancient world: it's what I live for. Egypt, Easter Island, Peru, Mexico, Bolivia, Italy, Greece, Lebanon, Israel, Iraq, Iran, Turkey, Malta, India, Thailand, Vietnam, Cambodia, Japan—places I have been to on more than one occasion. Places with historic ruins that have stood the test of time.

But long before I was globe-hopping, I was being brought up in a stanchly religious home. We went to our United Church every Sunday, and I became intimately familiar with the Bible. As a high school student, I was intrigued with how certain passages could be traced to historic sites in places like Egypt, Israel, and Iraq, and I became obsessed with seeing these places for myself. But I must say that even when I was young, I constantly thought, "Wait a minute. That sounds a bit unbelievable." Consider the following scenario: "A man went to talk to a crowd of thousands, and he made food for everyone with only a single loaf of bread and a few fish." "What? You must be kidding." "Hey, it's written in the Bible." "It's in the Bible? Well, why didn't you say so? It must have happened, then."

This is how I was raised, and how I perceived the world: that everything in the Bible must be believed. I would relay my concerns to my parents, explaining to them how portions of the Bible seemed unrealistic, fantastical, even. Their answer was simple—too simple in fact: "These stories contain miracles. Miracles are supposed to be unbelievable. That's why they're miracles." Maybe so. But maybe, when it comes to God, blind faith isn't enough.

But I am not here to espouse religious intolerance. The religious texts so many hold so dear to their hearts are extremely valuable. We just need to decipher what is written on the pages. That's all.

It was years later, while teaching at the University of Toronto, that I began to seriously doubt what I knew. By that time, I'd travelled and had seen plenty, and I'd written extensively. But I was frustrated: I wasn't getting the whole picture; the facts weren't always adding up. Too much was far too often unexplained. Miracles in the Bible. Ancient ruins whose construction still bear the imprint of implausibility. Our own human history. These axioms began to wear way at me, a nagging suspicion that we as humans had it all wrong. I wondered for a while if I was going crazy. Imagine standing in a lecture hall and talking about one thing, while all these contradictory thoughts are running through your head at the same time. Eventually, I resigned my post.

Then I stumbled onto Erich von Däniken's Chariots of the Gods?, and the rest is history. As many of you likely know, von Däniken was one of the first authors to state in clear, everyday language that we do have our history all wrong, and his explanation as to why was surprisingly simple: that ancient peoples of this Earth were visited by extraterrestrials. He went on to claim that there is abundant evidence suggesting these extraterrestrial visits took place, and that these visitors gave everything to humanity: mathematics, medicine, architecture. Since then, other authors have included our very origins as humans on this planet to that list, that we are the result of human and extraterrestrial hybrid DNA. Pretty heavy stuff, yes? That's what I first thought, but over time, thousands like me have come to the conclusion that, on the whole, von Däniken is right.

This is not to say that von Däniken hasn't come under criticism. One can turn to his Wikipedia page and see a list of his errors and omissions. It's quite a list. People love to tear his theories apart. But, as he himself says, he is simply asking questions, and his proposed answers are, at times, admittedly, conjecture. That's where it all starts, people: we need to ask questions, perhaps questions without definitive answers. But if we don't ask the questions, we won't get anywhere. And von Däniken has sold millions of books, which means people are interested in what he has to say. People like you out there tonight. That's a start: interest generates questions, questions generate research, and research ultimately generates answers.

...

So what answers can I give? What's the real truth? Look at our evolution: we went from primitive to sophisticated almost overnight. And we're still evolving. Look at what we were doing just a hundred years ago compared to today. The past hundred years alone has seen tremendous technological sophistication across the Earth. What will the next hundred years offer?

...

Now, this is not to say that everything in the ancient world can be attributed to extraterrestrials. That would be presumptuous. I think we can assume with relative certainty that much was created without the help of extraterrestrial technology. But there are also times when the improbable is the only answer.

I have to laugh when people say to me, "Don't you think these theories are a bit far-fetched?" First of all, the basic pretences of the ancient astronaut theory have already been out there for decades, even centuries. People hundreds of years ago began suspecting there was something strange going on. Consider the Bible: God creating the world in seven days; God producing Adam, then Eve from Adam; God instructing Noah to build a ship and then collect two of every animal in the entire world. Unbelievable? But it's in the Bible, so for centuries, it was accepted as the truth. So I say to people who ask me why I believe in theories that sound far-fetched, "Well, aren't some of the stories in the Bible far-fetched?"

And then there's another one of my favourite arguments: I've had several discussions with religious representatives over the years, and I hear the same thing over and over again: that some parts of these religious texts should not be taken literally, that they are metaphorical, allegorical, more than anything else. Perhaps. Or perhaps eyewitnesses to extraterrestrial phenomenon didn't understand what they were seeing, and so they tried their best to explain their observations using the only words available to them. They saw things—extraterrestrials—coming out of the sky, so they assumed they were seeing gods. It was easy to see something appear in the sky and shrug and call it a god.

...

There is a theory I've studied over the years known as Xenoglossy. Xenoglossy is the ability by someone to suddenly recall foreign languages they believe they have never been exposed to before. As if this foreign tongue has been locked away over time and then is suddenly released through some sort of major, traumatic event. Something physical, such as a near-death experience, or an emergency operation. The death of a loved one. A divorce. Something powerful, impactful.

How is this possible? How can someone with no prior knowledge of a language suddenly speak whole words of it, complete sentences? There must have been exposure, even though there is no memory of such. What implants this ability in people? And for what purpose?

I think we can go beyond language recall. Sometimes it's a person with limited mathematical ability that can suddenly solve incomprehensible equations; sometimes it's someone suddenly drawing meaningless images in a compulsive manner. I once met a man who had never studied airplanes but woke up one morning and, within a matter of minutes, drew a fully detailed schematic of a jet engine. How does this happen?

After countless interviews regarding this phenomenon, the conclusion I've come to is that extraterrestrials have in some way implanted this information into the minds of these people. Now, why would extraterrestrials want to do this? I've asked myself, too. After all, a man in Vancouver who speaks English and only English, but then wakes up one day speaking fluent Tok Pisin, is certainly unusual. By the way, Tok Pisin is a language that is spoken in Papua New Guinea. But why would extraterrestrials want this man to speak another language? Can we ever truly know? Perhaps they received this information through abduction. And the information they are carrying, whatever abilities they suddenly possess, such as the mastery of new languages, may not even make itself known to them for years, decades, even.

But there is some good news on the subject of extraterrestrial abductions. Contrary to what Hollywood wants us to believe, not all of these kidnappings are horrific experiences. In fact, the vast majority of the people I've met have had no ill effects from their abductions at all. These people have continued to live normal lives, despite a nagging suspicion that they know something, that someone—something—is calling on them. And sometimes it gets even more interesting: sometimes abductees and their children have the same visions, dreams, language mastery, what have you. Coincidence? I think not.

There is simply no rational way to explain such phenomena. People suddenly can't do these things without the aid of some higher power. The same higher power that has been coming to and going from this planet for thousands of years. They have an agenda. We can speculate, but we can't ever truly know.

...

We live in an age in which we can fly to the moon, halt the effects of cancer, and so on. Every day brings new breakthroughs. But why has the human race's mental capacities evolved so rapidly in the past few thousand years to accomplish so much so quickly? After all, we went from cave men to builders of pyramids almost overnight, didn't we? Why is this? What I want to say to you all is to ask questions, to never be satisfied with what you learned in a textbook. Stop allowing yourselves to accept the same antediluvian explanations for everything. Be more than that. As human beings, we have the cognitive ability to question. And it's okay to question. Just think, that at one time, it was impossible to seriously consider going to the moon. Well, we did that way back in 1969. What's next? One day the answers will become clear to the human race. I just hope we are all alive when that happens.

Excerpt ends here.

The lecture over, the beleaguered young welder remained in his seat. He'd been blind, all his life. But it was not too late, for here and now, it was splayed out for him like a map on a medical gurney—forceps and needle holders and retractors for roads and rivers and mountains. Like an unearthed tomb now exposed. It was all so clear now.

He rose, gathered his thoughts, turned and nodded with finality to the gentleman beside him, then stepped towards the professor. Out of the corner of his eye he saw a young woman, an assistant of the professor's, it appeared, also walking towards the professor. Late twenties, dressed in a navy skirt and blazer. Beautiful. She was sweeping the auditorium with her eyes, catching him insouciantly in her sights. Embarrassingly, he turned away, then back. She was no longer looking at him, was instead engaged with an audience member. Smiling.

He approached. Excuse me, he said meekly.

The other audience member was moving on to the professor. Perfect timing. He saw that she was smiling at him expectantly. His mouth searched for the words.

I think I need to speak to the professor.

She gestured to a line forming. "By all means."

No, no, you don't understand. I'm not looking for an autograph.

A quizzical look spread across her face. "What, then…?"

She was right. What, then, did he mean? And then it was out of him, vomited past the point of no return.

I don't think David Trent was killed by accident.

She gaped at him, eyebrows narrowing.

He noticed the professor had suddenly glanced his way, reading the look of concern on the young woman's face. He heard the professor ask his assistant what was wrong, saw her turn to him and say something. Then he turned to the professor himself and spoke far more plainly.

29-58-45-06-31-08-03-09. Do these numbers mean anything to you:?

He saw how the professor recoiled, stepping back as though in fear. "My God…What did you say? How did you know about that?"

He was noncommittal.

I don't have a logical explanation. But for the past few days, I haven't been able to think about anything else. I read, I draw triangles. And I don't know why.

"Triangles?"

David Trent wasn't killed accidentally. He was murdered. I'm sure of it.

The professor stroked his jaw menacingly. "And why do you think that?"

I don't know. I only know that somehow it has something to do with the numbers I quoted you.

"The numbers," the professor gasped. "How...how do..."

They're geographic coordinates, Professor. They're the location of the Giza Plateau, specifically the Great Pyramid itself.

Lauren was trying to make sense of what she was hearing. "Professor, I don't understand. What numbers?"

He waved her off. "The Egyptian detective...He read them out to me. my god. How is that possible?"

Your friend—he was killed because of something to do with the Great Pyramid. And then someone—

He hesitated.

—some*thing* drew me to you. As if we needed to meet.

The professor stared down at the ground. "The numbers..." He lifted his head. "I thought it was a place. It *is* a place! But it's more. It's you."

It's me.

The night air is dead, stagnant. Time has passed. Stage hands are dismantling the professor's rock star-like stage theatrics.

Alumni Hall's parking lot is somewhat deserted, except for an extravagant Caravan and another much more average-looking alongside it. This second vehicle is open, a few of the professor's personnel loading black boxes within. The equipment.

The professor offers a business card to the welder. "I'll give you my phone number and email. We will need to talk."

I'd like that very much.

"Call me. Tomorrow."

They part, he to his Ranger, the professor and assistant to their Caravan. He trudges across the empty parking lot where his truck rests under the streaming luminance of a light standard. He delves into his pocket, finds his keys, fumbles with the fob.

And then something completely illogical happens.

The little truck explodes violently. Multitudinous pieces of debris are ejected, Vesuvius-like, into the air. Like rain, these mini projectiles plummet downward. The startled welder leaps to what he assumes is a safe distance, stands and backs away accordingly. He watches as tumbling debris continues to pelt the tarmac, impacting everywhere around him.

There is the squealing of tyres, and he turns defensively. It is the professor's Caravan, racing across the parking lot, directly for him. He turns to run, trusting nothing and no one, but he sees that the van is slowing. The side window has been lowered, and it is the professor's beautiful assistant, calling to him.

"Get in!"

What can she mean, get in? He has no reason to join these people. They've only just met. "I need to call the police," he responds, shaking uncontrollably.

"You need to come with us!" she hollers. "Now!"

She doesn't understand. Clearly, she doesn't understand. This is a police matter. She is panicking, behaving as if his life is somehow in danger. And he must admit, while this looks terrible, it has all been some sort of horrible accident. That is the only logical explanation. He's never heard of fobs causing explosions, but anything is possible, he assumes. Besides, he is the farthest thing from a target. Who would want to kill him?

He shudders and turns back to the fiery wreckage.

No, I think you're mistaken. We need to call the police.

"The only mistake someone's made is that you're still alive!"

Unbelievable. She thinks this has been intentional. But how could it have been? Who could he have angered to cause this? And then something impacts the tarmac nearby his foot, burying itself into the surface. A bullet. *A bullet?* Someone has just fired a bullet.

At him.

He races to the van. Lauren has opened the sliding side door, and he is inside at once, breathing profusely. She closes the door, and the professor revs the engine. They race from the lot, dangerously fast, which should unnerve the welder. But not now. Now all he can ask for is more speed.

He stammers in between uncontrollable breaths.

Someone just tried to kill me. Why would anyone want to do that? What have I done?

Indeed. What has he done?

The professor glances over his shoulder. "I'll take you back home with me. From there, we can talk this thing through."

Back home? Don't you live in Toronto?

"Much safer for you there than here. You can't go home. Not now."

The professor peels off down Lambton Drive, then right onto Western Road, away from the university. He is heading south, towards the 401. The other van is following.

Why? Why me? What have I got to do with anything?

"Maybe everything," the professor offers.

What does that mean?

"David was murdered in Cairo, and now someone has tried to kill you. Those numbers. It can't be a coincidence."

Perhaps the professor is right. He recognises how he has suddenly become preoccupied—is that the right word? Obsessed?—with Egypt. The coordinates of the Great Pyramid. This has been no accident.

The assistant contemplates the situation. "We need to get to Egypt as soon as possible."

Egypt? I can't go to Egypt! I have a business here! Responsibilities! I don't even have my passport with me!

The professor slows. He reaches for his cell phone, calls someone. It is the driver behind them. He tells the other to go on ahead. Then he pockets the device, glances over his shoulder. "Where do you live?"

Are you serious?

But he is serious. Deadly serious.

Turn right at the intersection.

They meander onto Sarnia Road.

But you said I shouldn't go to my house. You said it wasn't safe.

"We'll have to take our chances."

Shouldn't we call the police?

They seem disinterested in the prospect.

Lauren speaks. "It's time to find some answers. But we won't find them here."

Hence, you want to take me to Egypt.

Hence, they do. And so risking a short stop at his home is worth it. Unless, of course, no one is following, no one is aware of where they are going. Unless no one cares and this is all some ridiculous misunderstanding.

But that can't be. Cars do not explode like that. They simply do not.

He instructs them through an elaborate series of turns into subdivision-laden west London, along streets they have never seen and will never remember: Thistledown Way, Sherbourne Road, Lawson, Blanchard, Brunswick Crescent, Brunswick Road, and finally, Inverary.

Strange, arriving home without his Ranger. Or at the very least not seeing it in the driveway. He hastens from the van, keys in hand, jumps the tiny porch and opens the door. He leaves the lights off: there is enough illumination from the street lights for him to see where he's going. It also feels like the right thing to do. The right thing? Chances are if someone knows which vehicle he drives, they also know where he lives. He flicks on a light, heads upstairs.

His passport has been little used. A few jaunts across the border. Last year, a bunch of them went to Detroit for a stag party. What a time that was. What a ballpark. But he has never flown, never been outside North America. He's barely seen any of his own country. And now he's agreed to let them take him to Egypt. Egypt, of all places.

He packs the passport and some clothes, races back downstairs. He will have to make some calls. He feels awful leaving. Surely he'll be back by the end of the week? How can he predict this? He can't.

Once he's back inside the van, he feels somehow calmer. He shouldn't; enough time hasn't passed. Adrenaline. Soon, it'll hit him full throttle.

The professor backs out, and they are off. There is silence. He breaks the ice.

And to think this all started at baseball.

"Baseball?" the professor prompts.

I was playing a few nights ago. I took a ball to the head—an outfielder tried to throw me out, and he missed. When they took me back to the bench, all I could think about was those numbers. I kept repeating them. I went to the hospital, they sent me home. That's when I started drawing. Then I went crazy with the reading.

"Xenoglossy," the professor breathes.

"Strange the way it all happened," Lauren says from up front. "It's as if that ball was meant to hit you."

I guess so.

"It exposed some repressed thoughts."

Repressed thoughts? He hadn't considered that before.

"You've been contacted. That much is certain."

He supposes he has. And then he thinks. With the mention of the numbers, he realises this had been the first morning since he'd been struck in the head by the ball that he hadn't woken up with that same obsession of drawing, of writing equations. In his mind, he can see the pages lying on his bed, his couch, the floor, the kitchen table. The same numerical pattern, the same number of triangles on each. But today had been different.

Today *has* been different. He will remember today for the rest of his life.

Professor, when do we leave?

Sunday. It was early afternoon in the museum. Yaghdjian surveyed the tourists who entered through the front doors and into the non-air conditioned gallery. Not the hordes that had once invaded the museum. Recent violence had stemmed that flow. He listened. Some of them were complaining with immediacy: there was no air conditioning in here. Yes, it was true. Not everywhere, but here in the entrance, yes. Other rooms had had units installed over the years. But why complain? This was a desert nation, with stifling heat in the summer, even for Egyptians. Still the tourists droned on. What were these Egyptians thinking? Wasn't this the 21st century? Who had museums without air in this day and age? He wanted to shrug. Bring bottled water, then. Don't stay as long and look on the bright side: you're not likely to find better historical artefacts anywhere else in the world.

He saw the phalanx of informal tour guides standing at the entrance, birds of prey about to be unleashed. This, too, was not as it had once been. Until so recently, tourists would pour through the doors like easy prey. The birds would descend. Nowadays, with far less game, their numbers had dwindled accordingly. Some were still successful, aligning themselves with a married German couple here, a busload of Japanese women there. All for the mighty *bakshish*. Others were not so lucky. These would dart off, perch themselves anew, wait for the next unsuspecting game to come along.

He checked his clipboard. Koreans, not scheduled here for another half hour or so. He'd been practicing for them, having had so many in the past. *Anyong haseyo*: peace be with you. *Pan gap sub ni da*: nice to meet you. He grabbed his bottled water, replenished himself, wiped his brow.

A sudden commotion mercifully silenced him. Relieved, he turned and beheld a throng of Egyptians, men in suits flanked by navy-clad TAPs, darting amongst the crowd of tourists. Among them, the centre of the retinue, in fact, was Helmy Mokhtar, the Deputy Minister of the MSA. In his late fifties, silver-foxed, bulging but not obese. Always sweating, a forever-gleaming forehead. And often angry. He represented the new, untainted, incorrupt version of the old SCA.

Today, Mokhtar was in fine form, gently brushing tourists aside with a feigned smile, then turning and barking something at one of his aides. Or at a TAP. Always at someone. And what did he have to be so incessantly angry for?

After all, he still made his money, both here at the museum, from the government, and from television appearances. What did he have to shout for? And yet he was always shouting, always angry. But today, he was more animated than usual.

The group was brushing towards the elegant marble staircase that led to the upper floor of the museum. Curious onlookers stepped aside, stared. Some began to follow. The TAPs were attempting unsuccessfully to curb their enthusiasm. Yaghdjian eased past them.

Something big was happening. This was the case here every so often. Mokhtar rushing to an exhibit, hoping to make a discovery. Mokhtar rushing with a precession of aides carrying a new exhibit into the museum. Mokhtar enthusiastic. Sometimes television cameras travelled alongside, hoping to catch a piece of history in the making. But there were no crews today. This was spontaneous.

He traversed the staircase, and he saw that Mokhtar was making for one of the side rooms, the one housing artefacts from the eighteenth dynasty. A large room, lined with busts of pharaohs on podiums. Other TAPs were already there, ushering him their way. This was curious.

And then, as he entered, he saw the TAPs and other regular policemen already there sealing the area off. Tourists had already been escorted out, but now more were trying to enter, or at least see what was happening. The police were pushing back. And Mokhtar was sidling past, a Red Sea parting of all. And he was disappearing beyond them, into the room.

When the TAPs beheld Yaghdjian, distinguishing his credentials, they gestured for him to follow.

At first glance, it appeared the museum had been robbed. There was glass everywhere, atop a now empty podium, as well as on the floor. It was strange that someone had chosen this hour, in broad daylight. Strange, too, that the alarm had not sounded. A malfunction? That was certainly not out of the norm. Whoever it was, they had nerve.

He knew the bust that should be there. Of course he knew; he knew every inch of this place.

Akhenaten.

And then Mokhtar saw him, and he was making for him, striding so purposefully that Yaghdjian stepped back intimidatingly. Mokhtar was pointing a finger at him.

"What are you doing here?"

He stumbled with his response.

I am curious is all, sir.

"Don't you have a tour to deliver or something?"

He ignored the comment, despite the fear he held for his job.

How does something like this happen?

Spittle flew from Mokhtar's mouth. "I don't know how something like this happens. But it has happened. No one seems to know anything."

Really? There's glass all over the floor. No one saw anything?

"If you really must know, there was no sound."

No sound?

"The glass suddenly exploded, all over the floor and everywhere else. A tourist happened to see it. There was no warning. We just watched the tank exploding again on the cameras. Very strange."

Someone must have seen the perpetrator.

Mokhtar squinted skyward, his eyeballs rolling with precision. "Of course someone should have. But there was no one."

No one?

"No one. One moment, the case was fine. The next, it was like so."

As if it smashed on its own?

"Really, haven't you some place to be?"

He ignored the man a second time, peered at the object. What was it? something was wrong. Something that hadn't been there before. A stain. Exactly where Akhenaten once rested. He stepped forward.

Mokhtar was suddenly buzzing in his ear. What did he see? What was he doing?

I have a hunch

He turned to the nearest police officer.

Sir, can I enter the scene to have a look?

The Assistant Head of Antiquities glanced from him to the empty case. "What do you mean—what are you looking at?"

The bust has been taken, but there's something else there now.

Mokhtar wasn't comprehending.

He pointed emphatically.

The bust. I can tell you with complete confidence that something's wrong here. That stain never used to be here.

"Stain?" The words stumbled clumsily from Mokhtar's mouth.

You need to let me get closer, sir.

"Go ahead."

It was clear at once that the stain was actually several small, somewhat lighter-hued numbered hieroglyphics. Numbered hieroglyphics? A combination, a code? What sort of code? He raised his eyebrows accordingly.

That's odd.

"What is?"

It's a series of hieroglyphics.

Mokhtar was the first to answer. What did he mean? Hieroglyphics where?

The bust is gone, but in its place is this...this...I can make out a series of hieroglyphics. Numbers.

Numbers?

Numbers.

"Read them to me."

Yaghdjian did so.

Does it mean anything to you?

"Of course it doesn't. What could this mean to anyone?"

And then a curious thought came to the Egyptologist, darted in and out of his mind as if not fully committed to exposing itself. He grasped at his cell phone, paused, turned away. Somehow, all he could think of now was the one person who might be able to offer something of an explanation.

The professor picked up right away, and Yaghdjian could sense by the tone of his voice that there was tension on the other end.

I am so sorry to call you, Professor Booth. It's Nubar Yaghdjian.

The tension seemed to ease. "Nubar? Good to hear from you. You must be feeling awful about what's happened to David. I spoke to the detective."

Detective?

"Wasem."

Oh, yes. Actually, the reason I'm calling may have something to do with that. Or maybe not. I don't really know.

He was fumbling again.

Anyway, I'm here in the Cairo Museum. Something strange has happened. For whatever reason, I just had to call you.

"Things have happened here, too."

Yes. A bust of Akhenaten's gone missing here in the museum.

"I see."

Not like that. Not a typical burglary in any way. Mr. Mokhtar's going bananas. Apparently the cameras didn't pick anyone up.

"This sounds more like the paranormal than what I'm in to."

They're all investigating away here. It's quite a scene. But there's something puzzling.

"What's that?"

In the place of the bust, there is a rather long-winded set of numbers.

He felt suddenly stupid.

I don't know why I called you, Professor. This is ridiculous.

The voice on the other end had changed again. Concern. Unadulterated concern. "Read them to me, please."

He stepped closer to the scene of the crime again, peered down at the stain.

29584—

"29584150631080309."

The phone dropped from his hands, the voice still mechanically resonant on the other end.

My God.

OON

The professor's house rose like a gothic palace from the road, a gargantuan stone structure of flying buttresses and arched windows. Pot lights, hidden among indentations, tiled upward, illuminating outer walls, detailing intricate angled masonry. The house was only one of several buildings: the main house, a guest house, a separate car garage, a shed. All in corresponding stone. The cost must have been exorbitant. All of this was shrouded behind a soaring black wrought iron gate engrossed in an intricate formation of sharpened spears.

The welder studied the installation. His eyes wandered. Pine trees had been placed like sentries every few metres, age forcing them shoulder to shoulder. An ancient oak was festooned to the centre of the yard, multitudinous branches emanating from its broad trunk, flourishing outward, a horde of tentacles clad in rich greenery. A collection of cherry blossoms straddled the broad, slithering laneway, vibrant pinkish leaves overhanging curiously. And the air, ripe with noise: an orchestral choral of cicadas, comingling tymbals like stadium noisemakers.

The main gate swung open automatically.

Soon enough, the young welder followed the professor and his assistant through an enormous set of twin oak doors and into a foyer. Here he saw at once the antediluvian impression of the exterior persist yet within: huge ceilings offset by oak panelling, overhead beams traversing and dissecting, oak pillars, an oak staircase at the far end of the foyer leading to an upper level. The floor was of Macassar ebony, a darkened tessellation of lines and grooves. He scanned the walls of the foyer and its paintings and photographed images, all further framed in black wood. The Great Sphinx, crop circles, Stonehenge, the Great Pyramid, lines in the Nazca Desert. Upstairs, through the spindles of the oak railing, more images.

He was shown to a guest room, fell asleep almost immediately. And hours passed, he knew, because he awoke to the sun beaming in on him.

He wandered through the labyrinthine-like structure that was the professor's home, awed consistently like Rainsford in Zaroff's baronial hall of feudal times. He gazed on various figurines and statues, tall and magnificent. Knights in brilliant armour. Dark-skinned Egyptian guards, staffs in hand, clad in *shendyts* and *nemes*. Busts of assumedly important figures from ancient Greece and Rome.

He eventually found his way into what he could only assume was a library. Two-storied, with panes of glass several feet high dominating the far wall. Two tiers of shelving, with a ladder at each end. In all, there must have been hundreds, if not thousands, of volumes contained here. He perused further into the room's interior. A large table in the centre, upon it a handful of reposing books. Six chairs delicately arranged around its circumference. All in all, an impressive display of literate authority.

As he was about to enter, he noticed a sign above the entrance.
We are like butterflies who flutter for a day and think it is forever.
Carl Sagan.

He let his eyes wander the room some more. He spotted a bust. Wild, curly hair, bearded, bedecked in a *chiton*. Surely a Greek; that much he knew. But no eyes: the sculptor had covered them over with a cloth.

King Oedipus. He with eyes who could not see.

He wondered if such words were applicable to today. Eyes that could not see. Most of humanity was this way. But not all. In the past, there had been some who had seen. Some of America's founding fathers. George Washington. Benjamin Franklin. Thomas Jefferson. Writing about the extraterrestrials before and after the revolution. Thomas Jefferson was told of a UFO sighting in the year 1800. Clearly intrigued, he presented his findings to the American Philosophical Society.

He considered more recent history.

The Nazis supposedly utilised alien technology in prototype weaponry. There exists evidence, including admissions by Nazi physicists who later emigrated to the U.S. to work for NASA. NASA, once composed of several high-ranking Nazi scientists. Some of the most despicable people in history, men who performed experiments on concentration camp inmates, had had their records wiped clean to come to America. The British, French, and Soviets had shared in the spoils, too. It is difficult to believe that men who should have been tried for war crimes were instead helping put people on the moon. Joseph Mengele, probably the worst of the lot, a man who repeatedly performed horrific experiments on men, women, and children, was offered a place in the Soviet Union. In the end, Stalin reneged on the offer, and eventually Mengele fled to South America. Werner von Braun, an eminent rocket engineer who later worked at NASA, used inmates from Buchenwald to help build and test his V-2 rocket. He admitted the prisoners were in deplorable condition, but he exploited them nonetheless. He would later claim the Nazis acquired many of their ideas from extraterrestrials. Today, many speculate the Nazis were indeed obsessed with alien contact.

Other interesting claims of UFO contact came from Zecharia Sitchin. Startlingly influential, Sitchin supplied what he perceived as facts for Däniken's proposed alien-human DNA hybrid theory by studying Sumerian mythology and adapting his theories based on these stories. The Sumerians are regarded as one of the oldest civilisations on Earth. They settled in Mesopotamia, today known as Iraq. From their legends, Sitchin theorised that long, long ago, the Earth was visited by aliens from a planet in our solar system which remains hidden to this very day. A twelfth planet, known as Nibiru. Nibiru is so very far away, that only every 3600 years does its orbital pattern bring it into close proximity with others, namely Earth. Many modern scientists and astronomers have speculated on the possibility of such a planet.

The citizens of Nibiru were known as the Anunnaki, and they were ruled by King Anu. Nibiru was a troubled planet in that its atmosphere had become damaged, and somehow the Anunnaki were able to use gold as a solution. The process by which gold was used has never been understood, but what is clear is that the precious metal had become scarce on Nibiru, and so more was needed. Hence, approximately 450 000 years ago, the Annunaki journeyed to Earth during that short window when their world passes closely by. They came when the animals of the Earth were much different than they are today, when humans were primitive hairy beasts who had no notion of civilisation.

The Anunnaki—the gods, as humanity's primitive ancestors came to regard them—arrived in ships, and they set up spaceports and colonies. They landed near the Tigris and Euphrates rivers, but they also established a mine near the Zambezi in southern Africa. This was where the modern human would eventually be created. The fact that humans originated in southern Africa and then migrated elsewhere has been confirmed by palaeontologists.

As they migrated, over time their appearance changed to suit their new environments. But 450 000 years ago, they were still in the Homo Erectus stage: bi-pedal, with large ape-like craniums.

The Anunnaki set up gold mines, and it was they who toiled in these mines. But a rift developed between the miners and their superiors. The working conditions in the mines were poor, even with the advanced technology one can assume they brought with them. The workers rebelled, refusing the drudgery of the mines, and a compromise was struck: a new "worker" of sorts would be created. The Anunnaki called on their offspring, known as the Nefilim, and it was through the Nefilim that Homo Erectus DNA was surgically implanted. At first, fourteen Nefilim females were recruited, and between them they produced seven males and seven females. Over time, the Anunnaki Enki and a human woman produced another type of offspring, which today is known as Homo Sapiens Sapiens, the modern human.

Much later, a descendant of Enki, a god named Marduk, craved and fought for control of the Earth, and the other Anunnaki eventually left the planet, allowing Marduk to have his way with humanity. Humans, for their part, had multiplied beyond control over the centuries. More troubling still was the acquisition by humans of cognitive powers, to act and think for themselves. A man named Adam—Adamu in Sumerian mythology—the original of a new group of genetically-enhanced offspring, was the first original thinker.

Problems ensued: the humans continued to multiply, and they began to spread far and wide across the world. There was also the problem of Nefilim males mating with human females. Eventually, a decision was put forward by the god Enlil: the experimental human must be eradicated. It just so happened that a window of opportunity was at hand, as Nibiru was approaching once again. It had been evidenced that every time Nibiru did so, Earth was effected in some way; there were rumblings that something catastrophic might occur with the next passing. Enki disagreed with the decision to obliterate the humans, so he warned one of them of the impending danger. This human built an ark and brought his family and friends on board, and as many animals as he could find. Ziusudra, or Utnapithtim—Noah—built an ark in seven days.

The Deluge is believed to have occurred something like eleven and a half thousand years ago. A massive tidal wave wiped out anything and everything in its path around the world. Those who survived did so with the continued intervention of the Anunnaki., but those who endured eventually created new civilisations.

Home Erectus. Home Sapiens. In 1859, Charles Darwin published *The Origin of Species*. His theory that humans and other creatures of the Earth did not simply materialise via the hand of God, that they tended to evolve over millions of years, was a shocking revelation. Over time, though, Darwin's views came to be accepted as fact. Today, there is plenty of debate over evolution: many experts now question how organisms can evolve naturally. And more and more experts also give credibility to the notion of life elsewhere creating life here. Sagan believed everything on Earth originated elsewhere in the form of its DNA. This was accomplished through meteorites impacting on the Earth, carrying foreign genes from other worlds. What grew from that DNA was a replication of what had previously grown elsewhere. Everything here came from somewhere else. Known more formally as panspermia, the theory was first posited by Greek philosopher Anaxagoras. In the 1970s, two British astronomers, Fred Hoyle and Chandra Wickramasinghe, reintroduced the notion that all life on this planet originated elsewhere. At first they were ridiculed, but in time, others began to accept their theory. People like Sagan. Every day, asteroids, comets, and meteors either impact on Earth or in our atmosphere. Earth is inundated by these foreign invaders perhaps thousands of times each year. These invaders originate from somewhere far away, and as they travel through space, they acquire space dust containing imbedded bacteria. This bacteria either lands on our planet, or is absorbed into the atmosphere and slowly percolates down into the air. And bacteria cannot be destroyed: even though it is travelling on the back of a meteor that collides with our atmosphere at several thousand degrees, it will live on. It doesn't require a heat shield like a space shuttle.

"Something's happened," said a voice behind him, and he turned and saw that the professor was standing there. Arms stoically at his side, a passive expression across his face. "An acquaintance of mine called me from Cairo. We need to talk."

Dawn breaks over Toronto, red and grey flecks splattered on the sky.

The professor opens the doors to his mansion. Humidity massages his face. He gazes out on his front lawn: the golf green, the oak trees, the lilacs and hostas nudging one another for supremacy. He turns and ushers the others outside. They parade across the mansion's driveway to a waiting vehicle: an emerald green GMC Sierra. Within seconds, they vacate the driveway.

In the front seat, next to the professor, Lauren points casually at a parked white Suburban just out of reach. They are being watched, she surmises with calmness.

The Sierra responds immediately, opening up on the Suburban, which appears caught off guard. But this does not last; within seconds, their assailants are properly engaged.

The standard route from the professor's home to the airport is to turn onto the Don Valley Parkway, head north, then merge when the DVP becomes Highway 404. Then exit on 16th Avenue, turn onto Cachet Woods Court, and then into Buttonville Airport's main entrance. But not this morning. From Beaumont Road where the professor lives, the Sierra hooks left on Glen Road, then right on South Drive. The professor will try and lose the Suburban in Rosedale.

The airport. This is where they must go, to board the professor's private jet for Cairo. The conversation between the professor and the welder the night previous discussed as much. For the welder is too engaged to stop now. He *must* go.

In the rear, he ponders the trailing vehicle, the bomb in the parking lot. The implication is all too clear. And while the two up front appear calm enough, he surmises they must be as scared as he.

They meander down South Drive until it forks south and then west. They progress onto busier Mount Pleasant Drive, and here they continue north. At length, the professor turns right onto Whitehall Road, and they begin winding again, down one street and up another.

The mini-convoy works its way throughout Rosedale: Gregory, MacLennon, and Edgar Avenues, then back south onto Glen Road, east on Maple Avenue, east again onto Dale Avenue, south on Castle Frank Road, and finally on McKenzie Avenue, which snakes north and eventually morphs into the Don Valley Parkway. No more subdivisions to hide in now. They are in the open. Toronto is momentarily lost behind walls of foliage on either side of the road, save for intermittent condominiums that peer over the tree line.

The welder spots the Highway 404 sign. Soon, they will be on the highway, then north for some fifteen minutes to the airport. He assumes the professor will open up when they merge onto the highway. There is a chance they can still elude their pursuers before they get to Buttonville.

The professor seems to be reading his mind, and he espouses aloud. What if, for some reason, their pursuers have already assumed where they are headed? They cannot drive straight to Buttonville; they must lose these assailants first.

They race along McKenzie, then at the last possible instant, angle south to merge with the DVP. The Suburban too late scrambles to make the exit, overshoots the ramp, breaks immediately. Within seconds, they, too, are headed south, well behind the Sierra and its occupants.

Downtown Toronto appears abruptly in intervals. On the right, skyscrapers and the CN Tower materialise and then vanish in an elaborate disappearing act. Finally, as the road angles to the west and straightens, the skyline becomes unobstructed with finality, unfolding with each passing moment. The tower, once the tallest structure on Earth, now dwarfed by Dubai's awe-inspiring Burj Khalifa, is still king here, arching upwards past the office buildings and condos with a proud grace.

They increase in speed, zipping in and out amongst cars. The Suburban, lagging behind, roars to keep pace. At times, it will pull directly in behind the Sierra. Then the professor applies the gas again, and the two are separated once more.

Past the Jarvis exit, the DVP twists north, where the downtown continues to divulge itself. The CN Tower and several of its cousins are now on the left, while other skyscrapers remain fixed on the right. And then the two clusters merge, before separating again. Finally, they divide irrevocably as the Sierra and Suburban race towards them.

Flanked by condominiums, the Air Canada Centre jets past on the right. Still in the distance, the Tower squints curiously from behind buildings. Cranes are visible now, cranes everywhere. Scores of condos in various conditions of completeness, a growing city unparalleled on the continent. It has been said that no city on Earth, in fact, has more building projects underway at present than Toronto.

Further ahead, the white-domed Rogers Centre looms. By this time, the Sierra is merging onto Lakeshore Boulevard. And then, as the truck ramps downward and under the sudden Gardiner overpass, it slows at the first traffic light in some time.

But the Suburban has chosen not to slow, and it slams into the rear of the truck with enough force to launch the Sierra into the intersection. The truck escapes right on Dan Locke Way, and the chase is renewed.

The young welder gapes at the efforts of their pursuers. Where are the police? How long can two vehicles carry on in such a way down the streets of the largest city in the country? Surely someone has called in to report the erratically-driven vehicles. Being pulled over would be a blessing.

They persist past Bathurst and the old Loblaws building, at which point the Sierra skids across lanes and veers towards Front Street. Again, the Suburban cannot make the turn in time, and it sails past, lurches across the median and banks at a steep angle, turning back towards the intersection.

The Sierra passes under the Gardiner again, roars across the bridge that overlooks railway tracks dissecting the city's downtown. It angles onto Front Street and again increases speed. The Suburban has slowed at the intersection, so as not to overshoot the street again, but the loss of speed allows the Sierra to open a wide girth between the two.

They are now approaching the downtown from the opposite direction, and a green GO train scoots by on the right. The professor glances into his rear view mirror. Like an emerging predator, there is the Suburban all of a sudden, materialising from behind a delivery truck, swiftly gaining.

They race past Union Station on their right and the elegant Royal York on their left, approaching the glittering Royal Bank Plaza and TD Towers that indicate the corner of Bay and Front Streets. They chance north again, speeding through a red light. The Suburban stays with them, weaving around an angrily honking red Audi.

They persist north, soaring office towers dominating the skyline, thousands of panes of shimmering glass co-reflecting like mirrors. Brookfield Place Tower, Design Exchange, Commerce Court West, First Canadian Place, Scotia Plaza, Trump Tower, Bay Adelaide Centre. One after another, yearning skyward, casting ominous shadows upon the largely deserted street. Ahead, as if parting the sea of concrete, the bell tower of Old City Hall is visible. The professor endures in this direction, watches as the lights at Bay and Wellington turn, holds his breath, presses the gas and screams through the intersection.

The Suburban flies through as well without stopping, and a small convoy of vehicles screech to a stop to avoid impact. One of the cars, a yellow taxi, sails across the intersection, braking all the way, spasms sideways, and crashes into the side of a black Smart car. The impact propels both vehicles across the intersection and into the empty patio at the ground floor of the Merrill Lynch building.

The Sierra passes through the intersection at Bay and King, past the white Bank of Montreal building, once the tallest in Canada. It jets right on to one-way Adelaide, pausing only slightly, even though the light is red. A blue Sunfire is cruising through and then slamming on its brakes.

Next is the Temperance and Richmond intersection, and then there is old City Hall, majestic as ever, once a visual landmark that overlooked the harbour front. But Toronto has grown like ivy around it, and it has been left to wallow amongst the skyscrapers.

The professor turns right, and they head down Queen Street, a red TTC streetcar shuffling past. An orange and green taxi is parked ahead, and the professor times the weave in and around it and the streetcar. The Suburban is not so lucky, sideswiping the taxi and knocking the driver's mirror to the asphalt.

They crook south onto Yonge Street and make for Front once again. From there, they hope to go east along Front, to where it becomes Eastern Avenue and then merges finally onto the DVP. They race through the lights at Richmond and Adelaide, and the young welder sees that the battered Suburban, its front bumper crumpled, its right side smashed and streaked with taxi green, is now slowing at each intersection.

They pass through the Wellington intersection again, past a sprinkle of red and grey-bricked buildings that speak of an older Toronto. Then, as Front approaches and the Sierra turns, the Hockey Hall of Fame glides past. Joe Nieuwendyk and Ed Belfour are staring down from two of the large rectangular panes along its outer eastern wall, their best impression of that bill-boarded oculist T.J. Eckleburg. From here, as Front becomes one-way, the skyscrapers largely fade into the rear, and front-iron, brick-laden coffee shops and stores ornament the road.

The welder notes the Suburban unexpectedly moving to the inside lane of the street. Its driver must be taking advantage of the one-way flow. The implications of the Suburban's movements are obvious, and he warns the others to brace for impact.

He is wrong. When the Suburban pulls alongside, its front passenger window is lowered. There are several men inside, all clad in black balaclavas. The front passenger is toting a pistol. He fires, and a bullet rips through the Sierra's back window, exactly where the welder's head had been only seconds before. The professor banks to the right in an attempt to evade another shot, and the Sierra begins to weave erratically across all three lanes. The Suburban strives to keep pace, but the sudden flow of traffic is an effective barrier.

At Front and Church Streets, the road splits again into two-way traffic. A green and orange taxi is ahead, as well as a red delivery truck stopped along the side. The Sierra meanders in between the two, and the Suburban is forced to slow to avoid the delivery truck. The Sierra accelerates, speeding down Front and seemingly out of range.

At length, the attractive partition along Front disappears. When it does so, the Suburban moves to the opposite side of the street, in the face of minimal oncoming traffic, and soars past the few cars that would have slowed it in its rightful lane. The Sierra's lead dwindles with each second. At length, the Suburban again crosses back over, and, pulling alongside, the masked passenger takes aim a second time. The shot rings out, but the Sierra maintains its trek along the highway.

Enough of this. They are larger, stronger; they have that advantage. It is time to use it. The professor cranks the wheel to the left. Stomachs twist unpleasantly as the truck careens across into the left lane. Within seconds, there is a sickening crash as they impact with the enemy SUV.

The Sierra retreats, then smashes into its pursuers a second time. Fresh damage is evident on the Suburban's front quarter panel. Then the professor slams on the brakes, and the Suburban shoots ahead of them. He positions in behind, and without delay, rams the truck from behind. The Suburban buckles, veering to the right and colliding with a parked Federal Express truck. Its entire front end crumples under the impact, though the Fed Ex truck barely moves. Finally, it has come to a stop.

And then Front is weaving and morphing with Eastern Avenue. The DVP will follow soon enough, a larger, open highway that becomes Highway 404. The 404 runs north-south along the eastern edge of the greater Toronto area, bisecting the cities of Scarborough, Markham, Aurora, Newmarket, and beyond. It is one of the busiest highways in the country, and along with Highway 400 on the western edge of the city, is a major lifeline for motorists navigating the metropolis.

As soon as they enter the highway, breathing sighs of relief, two more white Suburbans appear, as though they had been lurking behind all along. But that has not been the case; they would have been spotted. No, these two others must have been called in by the felled pursuers. They dash onto the DVP and immediately pull alongside the Sierra, which now finds itself sandwiched between them. They begin to close in.

The first collision comes from the left, then the right. The Sierra bows under the strain, but the professor maintains control. He veers left and impacts with the vehicle on that side, pushing the Suburban into the median. The Suburban gives way, and the Sierra is free, just as the assailant on the right nears for another strike. They jet to freedom.

Behind them, the welder watches as the two predators align themselves briefly, then peel off. They are making for the flanks again, but the professor is applying the gas pedal to maintain distance. A group of vehicles are ahead. All three lanes appear to be busy, but as they narrow the gap between this group, there is space in between the many vehicles.

Some space, anyway.

The Sierra moves right, passing a lagging silver Caravan, then angles left and into the middle lane, directly behind a transport and in front of a black Topaz. The Suburbans, both of them frustrated by the manoeuvre, are wedged in behind. The Sierra darts left, blows past the transport, and then right again and past a jeep in the left lane.

Several minutes pass. The Sierra distances itself from its assailants, but in time, both Suburbans appear again, and as the traffic begins to space itself out, once more the gap dwindles. At length, the two pursuers separate again, and the professor, aware of what they are re-intending, veers to the right lane.

One of the Suburbans slows, moves right, rams them from behind. The other, appearing now to the right, intends the same. The Sierra snakes once again to the left and bulldozes into the Suburban with terrifying force. The other's driver momentarily loses control of the wheel long enough for the left side of the vehicle to scrape the guard rail. An appalling screech fills the morning air, and a shower of sparks wash over the front of the vehicle.

Then a break. Ahead is a construction site on the left-hand side. The professor times it perfectly, swerving left and forcing the damaged pursuer into the temporary barriers that have been erected. The Suburban flips over, sailing high into the air, and lands upside down on the highway with a thunderous crash, debris ejecting in all directions. The traffic slows, an action which in turn halts the final Suburban.

And then, finally, the sound of sirens.

The Sierra carries on.

The assassin had watched them ply mechanically into the truck. It was obvious they were unaware of him, huddled as he was just past the wrought ironed gates of the professor's property. He'd remained there in that silver Civic for hours, having barely slept the previous night, watching, listening. A steadfast vigil of the professor's mansion. He had long since self-cultivated to ignore the unrelenting supplicant of sleep.

The bugs had worked perfectly. Bugs he'd planted with delicate ease the day previous, when the professor had been in London. House alarms no longer worked against him; they were a simplistic barrier, nothing more. He had honed his craft to evade any system. And so he'd bugged the professor's home: chairs, clothing, tables, counter tops, toilets—everywhere. And then he'd listened. And he learned.

Learned some, but not enough. It was the professor who initially concerned him, because Henry Booth was Trent's friend, and perhaps he would understand the code Trent had left on his computer. But then this other had appeared. And the code had become a someone.

As he had prepared to follow the professor, a tinted white Suburban had suddenly wheeled out from behind him. He had turned and watched it pass, observed as it raced after the Sierra. This was no coincidence.

But there was more on his mind this morning. Two preoccupations. The first was that a headache the past few days was still prevalent: it had begun innocently enough, as soon as he had arrived in this country. Lack of hydration, perhaps; however, this was the third day now, and although his pain threshold was extraordinary, he was not unaware of its persistent aggravating presence.

The second preoccupation was more unusual. His mind was rambling through streets and alleyways of memories, to a long-forgotten incident he hadn't thought of in years. Faded like old leather, but still there, still tangible. A young boy, a wretched homeless creature like himself, who had witnessed firsthand something of sheer illogic. Even now, after the passage of so much time, he could still smell the repugnant aroma of burning wreckage and charred bodies blazing in the sand. How these smells infiltrated his nostrils! And he could yet remember the sound of it coming down all around him, a literal firestorm from the sky. He could recall how it had impacted so close to the wretched boy—too close, for the boy should never have survived.

He'd been young, perhaps ten or so, and he remembered seeing it streaking across the fountain blue sky, just west of Cairo. He'd been there with friends, homeless friends who, like him, had never known a civilised life. That wasn't exactly true: he had known a mother at some point, but she had given him up or been killed or run off or something—he no longer recalled. He had learned to live on the streets, had learned how to beg foreigners—*'ajnabiy*—for money. "*Geeb Fuluus!*" he'd cry, and they would offer money in kind. He'd learned how to steal, too, from foreigners and locals alike. How to exist on his own. And later in life, he would acquire the ability to read, to speak foreign tongues.

But this was not what he was suddenly remembering. He was remembering the airplane.

It had been a large commercial liner, travelling on a southerly trajectory. He had watched it with the other boys, including the wretched little creature he happened to be running with at the time, watched as its white underbelly arced gracefully across the enveloping blue sea overhead. They had all pointed excitedly. What was it like to fly, to look down on a world of deserts, forests, oceans, mountains? What was it like to view the pyramids from above? What was it like to watch the Bedouin, the people of the desert, trekking like ants across a golden landscape? What was all of this like?

And then something curious happened. He remembered the wretched boy on the ground pointing upward presciently, mouthing something, his words lost amid a roar overhead. The plane was teetering portentously, its wings oscillating like some children's toy replica thrown into the wind. Back and forth. The pilot must have lost control—that was the only logical explanation. It suddenly sputtered and arced east, away from its unknown destination, back towards Cairo. It was losing altitude swiftly.

People had run then, he remembered, for the safety of nearby buildings, where Cairo met the desert. And he had turned too, fearful as the plane descended ominously. He saw his friends ahead of him, screaming frantically as they raced across the hot sand in a self-manufactured veil of grimy dust. And he was screaming, too, his hands out in front of him in a helpless gesture, running past and deserting the wretched boy. He was yelling to his fleeing companions. *Don't leave me. Don't forget me.* And behind him, the wretch was yelling, too.

Then something terrible. The plane had crashed, that much was certain. He ran on, imagining with eyes in the back of his head what it must look like, matching sounds to images of the unfolding situation on the desert floor. He looked. The nose of the craft had barrelled into the sand, disintegrating upon impact but still ploughing forward. Like an avalanche towards those watching. The wings slicing the air like twin javelins. And there were explosions, too. Debris was landing all around him as he ran—pieces of fuselage, a chair with someone still strapped into it, a door. He saw things rain down from behind and above all at once, and he saw the people who had been there, adults and his friends, running and being struck. They were collapsing under the debris, falling and not moving again. He was screaming at where they were now buried, where they had been. He could no longer see them. And then he turned, and he saw what was left of the plane, a massive burning meteor, carving a trench through the desert towards him. He shrieked again, raised his hands, dropped to his stomach, closed his eyes.

He remembered now the sensation of fear as debris and body parts catapulted over and past him, how he had been miraculously spared when so many had not. More people were disappearing into the searing mass. And he realised that everyone was gone, everyone who had been there. Everyone except that one boy and himself.

How long had he lay there before he rose? How long had it taken him to realise that he had not been injured? No fire had singed his flesh, no piece had cut his skin. Nothing. Not a single contusion.

He had fled the scene just as the ambulances had arrived, had heard their haunting cries in the distance as he ran. After a time, he had stopped, turned to view the destruction form higher ground. He remembered the crater and then the snake-like path the plane had created in the landscape. There were small burning fires everywhere, debris everywhere, and the bonfire that was the main body of the plane that had spared him.

For some time afterward, he had wondered why he had been spared. Days, months, years. And then, like a healed wound, in time his memories faded, and he moved on with life. And now he was remembering again. Strange.

And as he snapped back to reality, lagging somewhat far behind in his rented Honda, one hand pressed to his throbbing forehead, he sensed impatience. Impatience led to poor judgement. He would need to suppress that state of mind. Yes, this seemed a ridiculous route to the airport. Yes, someone else was after the Sierra. At least he had not been identified.

When the second and third Suburbans appeared, he telephoned Garrett Seldon. It took Seldon several rings to pick up. His voice had that peculiar early morning gravelly feel to it, like sandpaper, digitally processed over the phone. The assassin activated the phone's speaker, then dropped the device onto the seat next to him.

We have a problem.

He imagined Seldon fidgeting uncomfortably. Sitting on a cushioned chair, perhaps, studying a laptop, useless folds of skin spilling slightly over the chair's edges. Or perhaps sitting up in bed, a cramped single, amid a cluttered bedroom, clothes strewn across the carpeted floor. Either way, the same folds of skin. That much he knew for certain: they'd met in person, and even the oversized collared shirt Seldon had worn that day had done little to conceal what was underneath.

Who is Mark Brydges?

"Who?"

Who is Mark Brydges?

"I've never heard the name before in my life. I thought you were following Booth!"

Exasperated, he hung up. Seldon had seemed in such control all those months ago when they'd first met, when the contract on David Trent had been offered. Calm, cool, collective—he had appeared all these things then. Appearances could be so deceiving.

His mind flickered to that meeting. He'd been on assignment in London. Seldon had contacted him through a mutual acquaintance. Was acquaintance the right word? Perhaps it was. It had been winter, and London had been cold and wet. Foggy, too. Cold, wet and foggy. He had shivered like he never had before.

They'd met in a pub. Ironic meeting there, seeing as he didn't drink. Seldon had suggested it. Had been there before, apparently. He had shown up dressed professionally in a beige trench coat, dark hair brushed to one side. Hair that should have been shaved, or at least severely trimmed; Seldon was balding, though he possessed not the courage to so drastically alter his appearance for the better. He'd sat down, looked the Egyptian in the eye, had glanced down to the ice water being lapped up by a straw into smallish pinkish lips. He had studied the eyes, hauntingly passive, the hawk-like nose, the goatee that shrouded a chin in mystery. A false goatee. His eyes had floated to the broad, square shoulders under the navy sweater. He'd noticed the arms, packed and chiselled, under the sleeves. All this the assassin imagined. As for himself, he'd noted the hanging jowls, the slumped shoulders, the rounded waist. A knock-off Rolex on one wrist. Poorly-manicured fingernails, the skin drawn over the cuticles like window coverings. A loose and sagging belly.

There would be no pleasantries: they'd discussed nothing but the job. This was how these things were done. Seldon had gotten right down to it, had offered photographs of Trent. He'd studied them, had memorised the face within seconds. A handsome facade with slightly protruding cheekbones. Deeply-set eyes. A protuberant ski-sloped nose. An English nose. Whitish hair, neatly combed to one side.

Then the price. Half now, half later. Seldon had slid an envelope across the table. They had discussed a timeline: he would want to introduce and engender himself to the professor. That would take time. Which was fine, Seldon had said. He had nodded, said he'd be in touch. Then he left.

All of this in full view, in a semi-crowded pub in London. That was how so much of his work was finalised. In the eye of the public, there is little reason for anyone to be suspicious. People offer money to others all the time in public. In public, people show photographs. Nothing unusual.

Back to the present. A sign rushed past advertising Buttonville Airport. *We are headed to the airport after all.*

From his vantage point, he saw the Suburban pull alongside, saw its passenger window suddenly lower, saw the pistol. It was now emphatically clear what was happening.

He perceived one of the Suburbans suddenly banking dangerously close to the left side barrier in a futile effort to avoid the now offensive-laden truck. Then the flip, the shattered truck careening through the sky and onto the road ahead. He slowed with the rest of the traffic, far away from the accident. Now something else. He watched as two police cruisers attempted to streak past, their lights blazing, their sirens cutting the air. And then the remaining Suburban was being forced over to the side of the highway.

He passed by the stopped vehicle and the police cruisers. The damage from the guard rail was impressive: the white paint had been stripped away to a ghastly grey, and the frame of the SUV had been forcefully warped and ripped inward. He gazed ahead and saw the Sierra, but he knew where they were going. Curiosity was on his mind now:

He steered the car along the shoulder, slowing perceptively, staring into his rear-view mirror. A third police cruiser had arrived on the scene. It had pulled alongside the Suburban. The traffic was slowing, greedy motorists gawking at the unfolding scene. Two officers were out of their vehicles, standing intimidatingly at the driver's side door of the SUV. An active conversation transpired. What were they discussing? And why weren't these officers drawing on a vehicle that, it could be logically deduced, had been reported as firing shots at another moving car? His eyes moved to the rear of the third police cruiser. Someone was inside, looking on with what appeared to be consternation. Light streamed in through both windows, elucidating an elderly face, white hair, a navy blazer, a lightly collared shirt. He did not appear to be a police officer.

Of course. It all made sense. The police weren't going to arrest these men. The fact that they had forced the Suburban to a stop while the Sierra escaped had all been by design.

Within several seconds, the police officers had waved the Suburban through. He waited several seconds, then started up his own engine. He kept his distance.

The Suburban was making for the airport. He followed.

Buttonville's elongated entranceway belied the fact that this was a relatively small airport. A smattering of cars in the parking lot, a smattering of planes on the runway, a smattering of people.

The dilapidated Suburban was cycling through the parking lot, clearly probing for the Sierra. At length, it slowed; the truck was easy to locate in such a smallish lot. The assassin decelerated accordingly, parked nearby, exited immediately. The driver of the Suburban also withdrew. No longer masked, the man was tall, dark-haired, of European descent. He made for the terminal entrance, striding purposefully. The Egyptian remained stealthily in tow, spying the Suburban as he passed, the occupants within similarly unmasked. He turned back. The driver entered the terminal, and he waited several seconds before following suit.

Now within, he stopped, observed. The driver was scanning the lobby, was making himself rather conspicuous. A lost little boy, turning round and round.

The assassin stepped forward. He touched the man lightly on the arm.

Excuse me.

The man, obviously shocked out of a stupor, turned to him.

I have to talk to you.

"I'm sorry?"

It's regarding Mark Brydges.

The driver's piercing green eyes suddenly come to life. "How...? I don't understand."

Quickly. But not here.

He tightened his grip on the man's elbow. He gestured with his nose to the washroom.

They walked. The Egyptian opened the bathroom door, held it for the other to enter. He let it close on its own, locked it surreptitiously. He quickly surveyed the room and saw that they were alone.

"What is this about?" the man said as the door clicked closed. English was not his first language.

The assassin turned to him. Without warning, he grabbed the man and forced him into a headlock. Rushing forward, he rammed the head against a stall door. The door swung inward, and the man slumped within. The assassin leaned in close.

Who are you? Who sent you?

The driver glanced up at him. A gash was already forming on his forehead. He sprang forward, catching the Egyptian unawares, and the two crashed against the stall's partition.

The assassin stood and closed his first, lashed out at the unknown assailant, catching him squarely in the jaw. The man shook it off, planted an elbow in his ribs. He doubled over, and the driver rammed him a second time. This time, however, he was prepared. Even before he was thrust backwards against the barrier, he already had his arm around the man's neck. He tried to apply the necessary pressure, but the angle would not allow it. He felt another elbow in his ribs, and two more after that. He released his grip, staggered, grabbing at his side.

He glanced up, saw that the driver was making for something. A pistol. He dove, catching the man in the stomach. The assailant toppled over, the pistol falling from his hand. He kicked it away, crouched defensively, allowing himself a breath. The man was also hesitating.

And then the two of them leapt forward. The Egyptian had the momentum, however, and he backed the man onto the toilet. The driver kicked at him, thrusting him back out of the stall. He eyed the pistol some ways away, realised he couldn't make it. He lunged at the assassin, an anticipated move: the Egyptian stepped aside, catching him in a headlock, turned, spied a sink nearby. He rocketed the man's head against it once, and the body went limp, collapsed. He grabbed the man by his hair, now bathed in sweat.

Who are you?

The man shook his head. He swung out wildly, a half-closed fist. The assassin easily sidestepped him, reached down, grabbed him by the face with both hands. Then he snapped the neck, quickly, painlessly. The man dropped lifelessly.

Satisfied, he dragged the driver brusquely to the stall, positioned the dead man on the toilet, pulled and crossed the legs so that they were invisible from below. Then he closed the door, turned and collected the pistol. He noticed an attached silencer. Perfect. He retreated from the washroom, then the terminal itself.

The Suburban was still parked in the same space. As the Egyptian stepped towards it, he could see there were three occupants in all. They were actively engaged in conversation. He listened for a moment. Was it German? Dutch? No, Scandinavian, perhaps? He couldn't be sure.

He leaned into the open driver's side window, pistol in hand. He killed them in succession, one bullet each, before they even saw him, then dropped the pistol and retreated to his own car.

Something caught his attention. He turned and saw a private jet streaking into the sky. He could not have guessed why, but something told him that this was Mark Brydges. He turned and wandered back into the terminal, his phone in hand. He began to text Garrett Seldon.

※

When the phone rang again, Seldon was prepared. "I don't have anything for you."

Then I have something for you. I am going after Brydges. And I will ascertain for myself the identity of his assailants.

"I told you I needed time for that."

Take your time, then. They aren't going anywhere.

He could hear Seldon gulping apprehensively. "Booth's cell phone remains bugged, yes?"

So far.

"I've looked into Mark Brydges. He's clean."

That does not explain why someone wants him dead.

"I told you. I'm on it. This will take time. Everything's getting so out of hand. Car bombs, chases, and now leaving the country for Egypt. Why are they going there?"

I don't really understand it myself. Something to do with a break-in at the Cairo Museum.

"I need to call my superior. We have agents in Egypt, but I need his authorisation."

I think you misunderstand me, Seldon. I do not seek permission. I am going.

"Not yet."

You contracted me to decipher the code. Brydges *is* the code. He knows something, and I intend to fulfill my obligation.

"If you think that means killing this Brydges—"

Decipher the code, you told me. I have done so. *Eliminate all threats*, you told me. Clearly, Brydges is such.

"But we don't even know why these others are after him. Really, I think it best you wait for me to call you back."

I will contact from you from Egypt.

"That's not the way this works." Yet he surrendered nonetheless, exasperated, he. "Text me your flight number and estimated time of arrival. I'll have an agent meet you at the airport."

I prefer to handle this alone.

"Not a chance."

He relented.

Have it your way. I will contact you.

"I will also need the flight number of Booth's plane. You can take charge of things when you arrive, but it makes perfect sense for someone to monitor their arrival and follow them to wherever they're going."

Yes, that did make sense.

The number is BD177 from Buttonville to Cairo.

He hung up.

The phone conversation had only ended a few seconds before Seldon turned to his list of contacts and tentatively dialled the number of Vannevar Denison, whom, he predicted, would be displeased. Pharaoh had most likely been awake for hours, probably up at dawn to run a small marathon. Then a massage and bath provided by the servants.

The phone clicked on the second ring.

Seldon, what the hell is going on? A car bomb? Then a chase? Who the hell is this you hired?

And hello to you, Exalted One.

"There has been a change of plans, sir."

Explain.

"We know what the code means, sir. It isn't anything to do with Henry Booth."

You're sure?

"It's someone named Mark Brydges."

Never heard of him.

"Regardless, they've boarded Booth's private jet for Egypt."

He imagined Denison, lying in his tailored bathrobe on his king-sized bed, glancing out at his parted curtains. Only recently finished showering, the scent of body wash still potent in the air.

What the hell for?

"No idea. Something to do with this Brydges."

If he's that important to someone else, he's important to me.

Silence. Wheels must be turning, Pharaoh thinking fast.

Seldon, I don't need you to make any more calls whatsoever.

"I'm sorry?"

Pack your bags.

"You're sending me to Cairo, sir? Now?"

Now.

"Sir, the Scorpion is on his way to Cairo. He expects to be met there. He also intends to finish the job once he gets there."

What—to kill Brydges?

"We may not be able to stop him. He is rather committed."

Then we may have another problem.

There was rustling on the other end of the phone. Pharaoh must have opened his walk-in closet and was searching for clothes to pack.

But we'll deal with that in time. Get packing, Seldon. Meet me at the airport as soon as you can.

"Meet you, sir?"

I'm taking charge of things.

The inspector pulls himself from his bed, his belly drooping gravitationally. He glances at his clock. It is hours before daylight will appear. It doesn't matter: he can't sleep, and when he has hunches, he has long since learned to act on them.

He bends over for the clothes lying nearby on the floor. White collared shirt, grey trousers. Dirty. Smelly. Perfect.

Now dressed, he steps out of the front door of his apartment and down the short flight of stairs to his parked car. His smallish three story walk-up faces Ahmed Amin Street, in the heart of Dokki district. A dirty grey building surrounded by similar dirty grey buildings. It isn't exactly where he wants to be, but it is affordable. The Nile is just down to the east, and the posh Gezira Island and its glittering lights can be seen in between the condo towers on nearby Mohammed Faheem. The city's tallest structure, Cairo Tower, is fastened to the island and is visible most of the time, day or night. Like tonight.

He lunges for the door handle of his Vectra, but a sudden commotion across the street gives him pause. There, on the sidewalk, a small mob of people have gathered, pointing excitedly to the sky. He follows their gesticulations, gazing upward. The clouds have rolled in during the night, dimly illuminated from the city's glow, but there are no visible stars. And yet, as he stands there, staring, his eyes settle on a single inimitable light. It isn't an airplane—it isn't moving. Square in shape, it simply hovers. Floating, rotating, transmogrifying from white to red and then back again, a consistent dual-hued pattern.

He glances back to the crowd, his ears drinking in their words. Mostly youngsters, many echo the same refrain. *Il samaa! Il samaa!* they shout. *The sky! The sky!*

UFO.

He smirks, offers one last look, shakes off the ridiculous notion, approaches the Vectra. Within seconds, he is jetting across slumbering Cairo to the police headquarters. In spite of his scepticism, every so often, he regards the sky, searching for the object orbiting the city. Then, privately embarrassed, he shrugs it off. Ridiculous. What is he doing? He is acting delusional. And why? Perhaps an undigested bit of beef, a blot of mustard, a crumb of cheese, a fragment of underdone potato. Yes, something like that. Thank you, Dickens.

The station is mostly deserted, unsurprising given the time. He sees a lone non-commissioned officer at the front desk look up and perceive him hobbling past. He nods absentmindedly, turns into the seemingly abandoned main room, a large space dissected into numerous cubicles. It is still, eerily silent. These cubicles are offices for the grunts. He makes for his own and sits at his desk.

Deeb's office is at the end of the corridor. He's been in there several times. An opulent office. During the day, brilliant sunshine streams through a pair of large windows flanked by dark curtains. On the walls, framed drawings, the brigadier's handiwork on display for all to behold. A series of plaques hang strategically on around the brigadier's desk. They are awards and degrees.

Of late, even before the murder scene, Wasem has noted vexation in Deeb. This despite his recent promotion. Vexed, as if he's continuously straining to repress a bad bout of gas. A face tomato-red, cheeks puffed like a blow fish. Admittedly, it is an attractive face. People in power must have some attractive qualities. Deeb looks like a model: his head is neither round nor square, but that perfect in-between. Like an oval. A football. Yes, Deeb has an attractive football-shaped head. His eyes are shielded by long lashes, and his cheeks, clean-shaven as always, do not protrude. He is fit: to accentuate as much, he purposely wears tight-fitting shirts.

The inspector turns back to his own office and desk. He gazes at Trent's collection of books, opens the one on Mexico again, turns to the image of the mountain. Something falls out as he does so, and he stoops to pick up a piece of paper. It is a scribbled note, handwritten, presumably by Trent. It discusses a place in Florida known as Coral Castle.

Coral Castle is an unusual stone complex that was built in the early twentieth century by a Latvian immigrant named Edward Leedskalnin. He constructed the castle using massive limestone rocks, some weighing several tonnes. He began the project in the 1920s, then moved it to its present location near Homestead. He refused to allow anyone to watch him work, and apparently he only worked at night. He never used any cranes or other machinery, which would have been heard by outsiders—no one ever heard a sound. There is a legend that two boys spied on him one night and saw him manipulating the rocks as if they were balloons. Regardless, the castle became a tourist attraction: Leedskalnin used to charge admission. He lived there alone, and he would conduct the tours himself. He was routinely asked how he built the castle, but he refused to divulge his methods, instead implying vaguely that everything he knew was derived from the ancient Egyptians, and that everyone has the ability to manipulate the magnetic possibilities of objects if they only take the time to learn. He died in 1951, and though he left behind various writings, nothing on the construction of the Castle has been found. There's been endless speculation ever since.

He rolls his eyes, turns on his computer and waits, then types in his password.

He turns to INTERPOL's main page. In the Search at the top right, he types in "fugitive." The results are overwhelming. He minimises his search to "Egyptian fugitives." He reads through the reduced list of names for several seconds, unimpressed. He clicks on the News link. Here are scores of news releases regarding unsolved crimes, updates on the apprehension of fugitives, and more.

This search is still too general. He types in "murder." Then he sits back and waits. He is greeted by a horde of news dispatches. He refines the search to "scorpion," and this search provides a more manageable number of leads. His eyes light up when he spies the first headline: *"June 22, 2014. Global alert for Marseilles murder suspect issued by INTERPOL."* He clicks on the page.

Lyon, France—The French government have confirmed the murder of a Belgian businessman on vacation in Marseilles as Gaston Provost, 48, of Antwerp. Mr. Gaston was found on Sunday morning in his hotel room, dead from an apparent scorpion bite to the hand. This is the third time this year that a man has been killed from scorpion bites, and this gruesome discovery follows a string of similarly apparent attacks in recent years.

The *third* time?

On February 3, Libyan businessman Ashraf Shamekh was found in a hotel room in Leningrad, and on April 19, German politician Günther Rihm was found in a hotel room in Barcelona. In May of 2013, two more such attacks were reported: American professor John Forrest was found in a hotel room in Lima, and in December, politician Alexander Viskovatov was found in a hotel room in Dubai. In every case thus far, a scorpion bite has been confirmed as the cause. The particular type of scorpion is what is known as a fat-tail, a native of northern Africa and much of the Middle East.

That's interesting.

For a list of all similar murders, click on the link below.

He does so.
My, you've been busy.

Gaston Provost, Belgium. Murdered: Marseilles, June 22, 2014
Günther Rihm, Germany. Murdered: Barcelona, April 19, 2014
Ashraf Shamekh, Libya. Murdered: Leningrad, February 3, 2014
Alexander Viskovatov, Russia. Murdered: Dubai, May 7, 2013
John Forrest, USA. Murdered: Lima, December 17, 2012
Luis Zulueta, Spain. Murdered: Paris, April 4, 2012
Spyridon Hatzipanagis, Greece. Murdered: Rome, March 23, 2011
Nino Castiglioni, Italy. Murdered: Mexico City, June 15, 2010

Anyone with information on this or any of these other possibly related crimes are asked to contact their local crime enforcement detachment.

Eight men. And David Booth's name will soon be added to this list. In succession, he studies the mini-profiles that accompany each victim. The same details every time: a fat-tail in a brown wooden box left at the crime scene. None of the men had been robbed. Nor had the murderer forced his way into any of the rooms. Interestingly enough, each of these men had either been businessmen, politicians, or professors. Booth seems to fit in nicely.

He gently massages his stubbled chin. What is the connection? Were they all separate contract hits, or were they related? This information will not be found here; he'll have to do what he does best: investigate.

There is something else. His phone is buzzing. He reaches for it, is stunned by the message.

Henry Booth has changed continents.

It was a pleasant Saharan morning. Bloated marshmallow clouds peppered the sky, the retreating sun probing through inquisitively.

They had abandoned Cairo Airport, the only real choice for private and charter flights. They were in a taxi, east of Cairo, in what was the newest experiment: New Cairo, a city fashioned completely in the desert. The taxi propelled them onto Airport Road, a straight thoroughfare that leads to El-Orouba, one of the many arteries that traverse Cairo.

The welder was in awe of this new land. Highways lined with palm trees, visible desert immediately beyond. Nothing like home. He gawped at the passing Cairo Military Academy Stadium on the right, in the heart of the district of Heliopolis. There was the gaping curvature of Heliopolis Fairmont Towers on the left, an enormous wall of glass reflecting shards of morning light. And then another stadium on the right, and what appeared to be empty space on the left. No, not empty: some airplanes, some helicopters. Runways. Al Maza Airport. Not so much used anymore, with the big new strip operating now.

And then, Cairo began to build around them. Not as Toronto does, with high rises and skyscrapers, but with minor apartments of white and red and grey, perceptible through the palms that dotted the road and skimmed past like waiting pedestrians. The majestic al Galaa theatre on the left, a rectangular, marbled frontispiece with a pyramidal rooftop, four robust columns safeguarding its entrance. And then a statue of Ramses II dissecting El-Orouba briefly. Tall, erect, arms resigned at his sides, eyes gazing at the metropolis before him.

They were ascending slightly, now onto El-Galaa Bridge. The overpass facilitated glimpses of the winding Abou Bakr El-Sedeek and El-Nozha highways below. Grey asphalt intersected by ranges of greenery, of palms and sycamores. The oil palms themselves were irregular: shorter, thick trunks, leaves sprouting from apexes like residual hairs on a balding head.

Above, forever outstretched was the radiant blue sky. But still no high rises.

Suddenly, out of nowhere, as El-Galaa lowered and became El-Orouba again, Cairo was unfolding like a map. The posh Le Méridien Heliopolis was there, and white-drabbed mosques and apartment buildings rose above the swaying palms on either side. Further along was the conspicuous Baron Palace, its Hindu-inspired steeples arching to the sky. Abandoned, now home to thousands of bats, the palace a distant reminder of when Europe's fascination with Egypt was at its height, when Heliopolis, the city that once surrounded the structure, was several kilometres from downtown Cairo.

Minutes later, fourteen nearly identical condo towers emerged on the right. The Omarat El Oubor complex, with building number fifteen straddling the corner of the boulevard, which was now Salah Salem. Convenient towers, lacking the allure of the Baron Palace. Stark exteriors peppered with patio-curtained colours.

To the left was the hulking Cairo International Stadium, dated but still relevant in a land that had made a living out of such monuments. And then a maze of overpasses and winding and twisting and bending and intersecting highways. Modern Cairo. It was here that they were veering off to the north, onto 6 October Bridge, which looped to the west. Immense minarets bared themselves amongst the scattered condo towers and hotels.

Ahead, the road was sloping back to the south. And with its higher elevation, for the first time, the river was now visible. *The* river. Like mountaineer's hooks, bridges spanned the water. The broad river stretched far into the horizon, a circuitous sinew zigzagging gently through outstretched urban sprawl. And beyond, on the opposite bank, more skyscrapers and condos and mosques and towers and highways.

But they would not be crossing the river. They were turning south, to the west of an impressive reddish building with large, rounded windows. It was an especially large structure, somewhat deficient in charm again to the Baron's Palace or some of the mosques they had passed. The Cairo Museum. The Egyptian Museum, officially.

Then he was walking with the others towards its beautifully sculpted entrance of pathways and statues, of palms and sycamores and sphinxes and pharaohs. A red brick edifice equipoised by a curvaceous white marble entranceway.

It was after nine in the morning now. The museum opened at nine. Tourists were sprinkled throughout the lobby; birds of prey perched close by.

Perhaps he'd set his expectations high. Perhaps he was being unfair. But he had pictured something more elaborate than this. Besides the large columns that dominated the lobby, and the remarkable glass specimens on display, he had imagined something like the British Museum. He'd seen that one in pictures. That lobby boasted a massive, rounded and windowed structure, basked all in white. The Rotunda. There, several soaring windows persisted in around the edifice, beguiling all who stood below, each tessellated with darkened double panes refracting light from the lobby back onto itself. Each of these sheets was exceedingly large, far bigger than an average adult human. However, it was the ceiling that was the real attraction: a massive, unremitting confluence of glass spliced together and further intersected by an innumerable expanse of translucent triangles via steel girders.

Someone was striding purposefully towards them. The welder watched the professor extend his hand. Nubar, he was saying. Nubar Yaghdjian. Young Yaghdjian spoke next. The investigation was ongoing, but the decision had been not to close the museum: tourist dollars, money needed in these times.

When they reached the upper level, it was noticeably stickier. The welder wiped his forehead, already thick with sweat. Ahead, the scene of the crime, cordoned off. A man was there—Helmy Mokhtar, he was told—alongside several suited big wigs, directing traffic. Police officers and reporters dominated the remainder of those present.

Shattered glass splayed across the floor, and nearby was an empty wooden base, its transparency evident by these fallen shards.

Mokhtar, now aware of their presence, began barking in their direction.

He paid little mind, continuing to stare beyond the yellow police tape into the room. He heard the professor enter the conversation, Yaghdjian too, and at length Mokhtar agreed to let them pass. He stepped forward, under the tape, avoiding the glass, a safe distance from the display stand. The conversation continued: the professor suggesting possibilities, Mokhtar refuting all.

And then, mouths continued to form, but he was no longer aware of any sound. All he thought of was the empty stand in front of him. It seemed to be mutating, melting and running outward like wet paint, like ice cream in the burning sun. He closed his eyes, reopened them. It was no good. The entire room was changing: the walls were vanishing, replaced by stark blue sky; the base was itself now a shadowy mountain, rising above a mostly flat, barren landscape of washed-out browns and greens, weedy Ocotillo fauna. And as his eyes focused on the mountain itself, he perceived an exotically level summit, sheared flat by time, wind, and rain. Something told him this was not Egypt. And he knew at once, somehow, that one day he would go there.

✻

What is so appealing to Egyptologists is the quantity of history Egypt offers away from places like Giza, or Karnak, or Thebes. In truth, ancient Egypt resonates fully from north to south. An example of this is the ancient ruins of Tanis, northeast of Cairo in the heart of the Nile Delta. Most tourists dismiss it as a point of interest, but those who make the trek are treated to a different part of Egyptian history: conquered Egypt.

Long before Indiana Jones was searching for a very unrealistic Tanis in *Raiders of the Lost Ark*, the city was a Khemitian capital during the 21st and 22nd dynasties, a period of Libyans rule. Then known as *Djanet*, and later renamed by the Greeks, it is today known at San El Hagar.

For those that do choose to journey north from Cairo, Tanis is a breathtaking archaeological site devoid of the teeming crowds that populate Giza. Surrounded by palm trees and papyrus fields, the massive dig itself is vegetation-sparse, and with the surrounding hills, Tanis appears more arid than fertile. From the sky, the land is an arbitrary swath of differing greens and browns.

On this particular Monday afternoon, under a sweltering Egyptian sun, tour buses draw close to the site. Tourists stand in two distinct groups, milling about the fallen pillars of temples and the remaining stone walls of tombs. Some of the more aggressive sightseers have broken off from their groups. Among these is a family of t-shirt and shorts-clad blond Norwegians: a father, mother, and two rather plump young boys. They have wandered over to a series of these walls—or, rather, the sons have wandered over, and the parents ineffectively impede their progress. The two boys take to climbing the walls, shouting excitedly to one another, re-enacting some episode that is lost on all but themselves.

An Egyptian tour guide stands nearby, conversing with the main group until he realises what has happened. Climbing on the ruins is frowned upon, and the guide, middle aged, bearded and imperfectly polite, knows he must enforce the rule. He momentarily excuses himself, steps over to the walls.

He watches the grossly overweight boys spring up and down, bouncing like balls. Their parents seem oblivious, chomping down on popcorn and taking pictures.

"Madame," he pleads with the mother after several seconds, "these ruins are very old. Could you please tell the children to stay off them?"

She turns and opens her mouth as if on cue. "Stay off the ruins!" or something to that effect: she is speaking Norsk, and so the tour guide can only assume. Then she impolitely reverts her attention to her popcorn, unwilling to take the matter any further.

As the guide has already predicted, her words do little to alleviate the situation. The boys, now aware of his displeasure, continue to climb the ramparts, and eventually one of them loses his footing and topples over and out of visible range. The boy shrieks with a carefully orchestrated shrill lacking in substance. He waits on the other side of the wall, rubbing an uninjured knee, waiting for someone to take notice. Time passes; no one appears. After all, the rampart is a shadow of its original height, and so it poses little danger.

Furious, the boy barks something, and he scampers off beyond the ruins, towards one of the outlying hills and minimal vegetation. He moves into long grass. Palm trees rise elegantly in the distance. He freezes, stares down into a lowered part of land—not so much a valley; a slight dip in elevation. He continues to gape for several seconds before he turns and again calls frantically to his family. Something there, he says.

The tour guide sees that the boy is at least in a safe place, away from ruins that he can ransack. He observes the parents calling casually to the lad, who refuses to vacate his current position. And the manner in which the lad regards raises suspicion that perhaps there is indeed something there to behold. He will have a look; the parents seem content with the suggestion, speaking to one another and then calling to the other boy, perhaps inviting him to come and have some food. Always eating, these foreigners.

The guide steps through the long grasses. The boy seems appreciative that he is coming—that anyone is coming—and the guide momentarily warms to the lad. The annoying little brute intent on destroying history and then feigning injury a short time ago has been replaced with one too often ignored. Is that not why children act out, after all? Who cares. This could be something important: new discoveries are made by casual observers all the time in Egypt. It would be exhilarating to be a part of one.

He stops, and fervent shouts from the boy, now in English, fade from his ears. So, too, do the sounds from other suddenly approaching tourists. He can only stare. For what he sees is impossible.

For several metres in all directions, the grass has been flattened. There are circles everywhere, imprinted by crushed stalks. The circles seemingly concentric, are of varying sizes: some are huge, others quite small. And each and every one of them is connected by a corresponding pathway. These circles and conduits are too numerous to count. The whole thing is dazzlingly intricate, marvellously beautiful to behold.

What is most impressive is the way the circles seem to have been crafted: from the centre out, judging by the way the grass has been flattened. And that is what is so impossible: how could someone—or some people, certainly—have done this? The precision seems unrealistic, unachievable. Why would anyone want to do this? And why here? Why not in a farmer's field, to charge admission? Isn't what they do in England? He remembers reading something about this in his past. England is the place where they are most common. They are known as Crop Circles in English. So far as he is aware, Egypt has never seen their likes before. England has. 90% of all crop circles are found in England.

He begins to see the circles in a new way: their interconnected pattern gains familiarity. There is an outline of a head, arms outstretched, a belt around the torso, legs separated and pointing to the west. Yes, he knows this, is not imagining it. In particular, he knows the belt, the three circles there in close proximity. But what is it called? He wracks his brain, but nothing comes.

But there is more, he realises, as he reaches for his cell phone to call in what he presumes will make him famous. Below the portrait, there are inscriptions of sorts. Not inscriptions: he knows these symbols well enough. Straight lines, others rounded like bent tree trunks. Like all good tour guides, he recognises hieroglyphics. These are the symbols for numbers. And so on. He begins to mouth the sequence.

29-58-45-06-31-08-03-09.

In Arabic, his name meant *Aqrab*. Al Aqrab. The Scorpion. Al Aqrab from *masr omm al donya*, the mother of the world. That is what Egyptians once said. And proudly, too. Did they still say it? Perhaps they did. The older generation, at least. His *walda*.. Mother. Strange that he should think of that. Strange that he should think of something so foreign to him. Foreign like the desert to so many, outstretched below him now. Like a mother. An anticipatory embrace. *Walda*. There it was again.

He gazed out the plane's side viewport. Cairo was unfolding like a table napkin. Office towers and steeples and minarets and condominiums spewed upwards. These he could see through the cloud of smog that blanketed the city, a sickly cough refusing to dissipate.

Odd that the memory should come back to him so recently, the one of the plane crash. And then again now. The second time today he'd thought about it. The only thing then and now had in common was an airplane—sometimes the slightest tangible link is all a memory needs to resurface, he conceded. He stared out past Cairo, the plane angling downward in his direction, facilitating an expansive view of the outlying desert beyond the city's borders. There. That was where it had happened. Where he should have died, but hadn't. He should have died numerous times since then. But yet he lived.

It was long in the prime heat of midday when his plane touched down at Cairo International Airport. Brydges would have already arrived a few hours ago. He would have to move fast; he had work to do.

It was no surprise that no one was there to greet him. He had become a loose end. It was a sixth sense he had acquired over the years: the ability to detect betrayal. Seldon would betray him—this he had assumed early on. Only, it would not be Seldon per se who would commit the act: no, Seldon lacked the confident polish to double-cross. It would be his superior who would force the issue. In fact, he had even alluded to it with Seldon over a conversation they'd had some time ago. He with his deadpanned tone, Seldon the bumbling fool.

I believe one day, when I have served my purpose, you will tire of me, Seldon.
Why would you say that?
Because I have seen it before.
Before? What—with other contracts?
Betrayal is common in this business. Just as I betrayed Trent, you will betray me.
You're saying this as if you expect it.
I do. I do expect it.
Nonsense. We have an agreement here—a contract. I have no intentions of throwing you over. I wouldn't even know how to go about it.
That doesn't surprise me. It will not be you, then, but some other.
Doubtful. This was my operation from the very beginning.
Do not be so naive, Seldon.

Then he imagined another scenario he had forgotten about. What was this, this sudden series of flashbacks? His vision clouded, then reformed on the streets of Athens. Athens, a city he felt almost as much at home in as here in Cairo. Family connections, apparently. But also where he had been contracted before, where he had returned to collect from one whose name he no longer recalled, for the life of someone that no longer mattered. A gungy hotel on a warm spring day, outer walls spray painted, inner walls crusted and flaking. Up the stairs he travelled now just as he had then. He had suspected trouble: a knife had been in his palm, concealed under the cuff that dangled flirtingly over his wrist. The contact had set up the rendezvous. Third floor, some room or another. They would make the final payment, then they would separate once and for all. And as he entered the room, he saw his contact, briefcase in hand. He spied, too, two other men there, hovering threateningly in the shadows. They had moved quickly, but he had been faster. Punches, headlocks, muted grunts. The blade cut their throats in unison. Like sliced vegetables. They had dropped just as quickly as they had sprung from the protective darkness which had so recently enveloped them. Then he had turned on his contact, who was backing nervously away, knocking a lamp from the bedside table. Hands up in protestation, something about doubling the money. And then he had killed this man, too. A third throat slashed, blood coupling with that already spilled, darkening a drab grey carpet a sickly crimson. Then he had departed, briefcase in hand—the briefcase that he been denied in the first place—back on the Athenian streets, along the boardwalk and under the ancient allure and probing eyes of the heightened Acropolis.

That had been the first time. Since then, he had learned to trust his intuition. A nervous contact was an ill omen. Seldon had been nervous. Nervous and unprofessional. Often, things had been satisfactory with Seldon's predecessors: the payoff had been made, he had turned and disappeared. A few of the contacts had called him again to arrange additional hits, even. But men like Seldon—these he had learned how to spot from a distance. One must always be careful.

One contractor had been pleasant enough to work for. He'd been hired by this man several times, sent to several exotic locales: Marseilles, Barcelona, Leningrad, Dubai, Lima, Paris, Rome, Mexico City. The first job had been in Mexico City. An Italian archaeologist. His first archaeologist. Nino Castiglioni. He'd befriended the archaeologist in La Merced Market, dressed as a local, wearing a sombrero he'd wondered might have been tacky. But Castiglioni had not seemed to mind. He'd told the Italian he was a visiting professor from Morocco, conducting Mayan research. Castiglioni wondered how and why he'd approached him. Ah, he had responded, the leather shoulder bag you're carrying: I have one of my own. Only we field experts carry them. I can tell you're one. That had seemed to work, and the two had then gone for lunch. It was during a meal of *mixiote* that he had explained he had something to show, was so excited for his discovery. It was in a box in his hotel. Castiglioni, several Coronas already wasted, invited himself up. In truth, the assassin had already stolen the key to an unoccupied room of some random hotel. When they'd entered, the box had been there, on the nightstand. Castiglioni had opened it, and the scorpion had done its work. Then he'd fled.

The man who had contracted this hit, and the several afterwards, was an elderly gentlemen, dressed professionally in what appeared to be a blue blazer and grey slacks. Sometimes he wore a turtle neck; on other occasions, when the weather begged for less—as Mexico had—he wore a white collared dress shirt. But it wasn't the clothing the assassin remembered; rather, it was the man's impressively tanned skin. Worn, weathered, freckled with sun spots. He was a northern European, evident by his accent, yet he looked like one of those sun-worshippers who crave vacations south during the winter months, or who buy homes in places where winter is a consistent non entity. He wondered just then if perhaps this man was he who had been sitting in the rear of that police cruiser along the 404. What a strange coincidence if that were the case.

The ancient European had been professional, had paid well. And then he'd disappeared. Perhaps there was no one left to liquidate. Ridiculous. There was always someone.

And then he'd met Seldon.

He exited the airport, his eyes shielded from the world beneath a pair of shadowy sunglasses. He'd donned the fake hair, the moustache. Recognising him would be difficult.

There were hundreds of people milling about, wandering to and fro like spilled marbles. Someone in that crowd was waiting for him.

He carried on to a row of parked taxis and toktoks just outside the main entrance. A potbellied driver, standing casually nearby his vehicle, smoking a menthol cigarette, gestured to him excitedly. The back passenger side door was opened for him, and he entered with a nod.

The Cairo Museum, please.

As soon as they jetted away from the curb, he glanced around casually. Indeed, there was a black car, an Audi, by the looks of it, also departing. Coincidence? A few turns later, the Audi was still with them, his suspicion confirmed. But how? How could Seldon have known what he'd be dressed as? No, it was impossible. And yet, the Audi was most certainly following.

Regardless, it was to be a lengthy ride. The assassin calmly opened his solitary travel bag and produced a magazine. *Maclean's*. The new mayor of Toronto on the front cover. What about that other one, the troubled one? he wondered.

From time to time he would glance back. Still there.

He wondered if the occupants within—two men, a driver and passenger—were new to surveillance; they were painfully deliberate in their actions.

At length, his cab turned onto Meret Basha and neared the museum. He leaned forward.

Stop now.

Recklessly, the driver did so, and the ensuing confusion produced a minor logjam. How perfect. The Audi had been inadvertently cut off several cars behind.

He overpaid for his ride, exited the cab, bag in his hand.

He had chosen a perfect place to stop: a busy street surrounded by large buildings. Hordes of pedestrians, ox cart wagons, motorbikes chugging along, street vendors. The smell of meat grilling in the open, of pollution. The smell of home.

The black Audi appeared again. It ground to a halt along the side of the street, in full view of him. He stared back at the two occupants now emerging. It was here that he would elude them once and for all. If not in amongst the volumes of humans, then down by the river, perhaps. Yes, down there, by the infused concrete and tethered boats and trees.

The men were jacketed, jeaned, t-shirts visible beneath. The appearance of nonchalance, but he could sense their apprehension. They stared silently at him. Clean-shaven. European. American? Canadian, even? One seemed to be itching for his jacket pocket. Small wonder what might be in there.

Imperturbably, the assassin spun and moved east, the short distance to the corner of Meret Basha and Wasim Hasan. Here he turned along this new road, crossing the street to the south side, flanked by the towering Cairo 7 on one side and Cairo 15 on the other. Cairo 7, the former National Party building, still sporting the scarred evidence of burning. He remembered briefly that summer of 2011. The fires, the protests, the confusion. So long ago now. Mubarek's last days in power.

His pursuers quickened their pace in silence. They made no motion to overtake him. He stepped around the walled perimeter that separated the city from the water's edge. Here, sycamores and scores of moored ferries toyed with the ghostly breeze. An entire population of fishing boats, taxis, private entertainment yachts, up and down both sides of the river. They stared languidly back at him, rocking rhythmically with the ebb and flow. He remembered being much younger, coming down here and staring jealously at them for hours at a time.

The quantity of pedestrians thinned considerably here, down by the water's edge. Not crowds; rather, bits and pieces of crowds. Some were hand in hand—young couples out for a stroll in the blazing heat—others vessel owners preparing for a day out on the water. At night, the Nile is like a Christmas tree, a dazzling myriad of floating ornaments swaying to its pulse. Christmas in a land where so few celebrate it.

Behind him, his pursuers stepped haphazardly around the wall. They scurried after him, into the line of trees dotting the river. They stopped short when they realised he was no longer intending to escape, fondled in their jackets, extracted knives. This was how it was to be done.

He walked further, stopped when the foliage thickened, dropped his bag, assumed a defensive position. They pressed forward, circling apprehensively. One was considerably larger than the other. He concentrated on the smaller of the two, waited for him to make his move. He didn't have to wait long.

The assailant lunged at him, and he caught the man around the neck and brought his knee up. One smack and the man was down, mumbling in pain. The knife had fallen from his hands. He saw it, but the second man was attacking now. The second pursuer lashed out, his own motion carrying him slightly past the sidestepping assassin, who grabbed him by the back of his hair and thrust him forward into a nearby tree. The man dropped and moved only slightly.

The first assailant was on his feet, scanning the ground for his knife. The assassin lurched forward, and the attacker realised his weapon was there, just beyond either's reach. He, too, sprung forward, and they found themselves caught in one another's grasp, hands around each other's throat, twisting and turning for control of the situation. By this time, the second attacker had recovered, had stepped forward, blade in hand, waiting for a clear shot.

The assassin elbowed his assailant in the head, found himself conveniently free, reached for the knife. It was then that he saw the second man rushing around towards him. He grasped the knife just in time, spun while still on his back, and plunged it deep into the upper chest of the armed aggressor. The man wheezed, blood sputtering from his mouth. Then he dropped, the blade still imbedded. The assassin withdrew it and turned to the first attacker, who was now retreating timidly.

The man twirled and tried to run, and the Egyptian raced across the expanse of ground between them and leapt outward, catching him around his midsection. They toppled, and he steadied the man in a headlock, drew the knife across his jugular, staring ahead into a gently wafting sycamore. The man convulsed, then slumped; he held firm. It was over.

They'd sent amateurs, but more would be on the way. If he intended to stay in Cairo, he would have to do so in disguise. Camouflaged in his own city. But he did intend to stay: fee or no fee, Mark Brydges was still alive, and the thought of an uncompleted contract rankled him deeply. But there was other unfinished business with which to first attend. Then he would find Seldon, and the real fun would begin.

The headache had returned. It had vanished in the recent hours, but it was back now. Strange how it persisted. He grabbed painfully for his travel bag and moved further along the river. The bodies were concealed enough for now; in time, they would be spotted. He would be long gone by then.

He stared out at the oscillating pendulums of boats one last time, watched the water lap upon the concrete barrier of the shoreline. Slurping intermingled with the occasional bump of a bow. He thought back to his youth once again, of reclining here by the water. Then he fled, depositing the memory like refuse along the bank.

It is fascinating to meet someone in person after having been introduced solely by phone. One builds impressions that are often far removed from reality. So it was must when the professor beheld Hondo Wasem for the first time. At least from the perspective of the young welder. Wasem was a giant of a man, sweating in khaki trousers and a sky-blue collared top, hair slightly tussled, face shadowed in stubble.

The professor introduced the inspector to his assistant and the young welder, offered Wasem coffee, which the inspector politely refused.

"I trust you'll be staying put for a few days?"

Wasem's tone was sarcastically acerbic, and the welder liked him immediately. He studied the two of them as they spoke. The professor explained their reasons for leaving Canada: the code on Trent's computer corresponded to the Great Pyramid. He then described the two attempts on their lives, and an incredulous Wasem strained to comprehend how this could be. Then he changed the subject.

"Are you hungry? You must be very hungry. Leave it to me. I know a place not far that delivers the best shawarma in the city."

Several minutes later, they were reclining in the living room of the apartment. It was clear the bloated inspector was just as hungry as the others, downing his packaged take-out in mere seconds. He glanced around the room. Suede furniture, of a brownish hue. The walls were far lighter. There was an original oil painting along the wall where the couch was positioned. A scene of a balcony overlooking sparkling waters. The Greek islands, perhaps.

Wasem had news of his own to report. David Trent had been keeping secrets: he most certainly had been travelling of late. He'd recently returned from Denmark, but he'd been elsewhere all within the year. And there had been another minor breakthrough. Yaghdjian had remembered a prior conversation between the two regarding Denmark.

The welder listened a moment longer, heard that Wasem was leaving the young officer Ramzy to watch the villa for the evening. Ramzy was clearly not impressed, but the inspector was in charge, and the decision had been made. The welder smiled again at the detective. A man to trust. And then he wandered into the living room of the spacious abode, planted himself on the couch. He eyed the television remote, turned on the TV, began surfing.

It took a moment or two to find a news channel. Al Jazeera. Carrying a live feed, presumably from somewhere in the country. Split screen. There was a suit-and-tie reporter on the left, microphone in hand. On the right was what appeared to be footage from earlier in the day. A helicopter angle of a field.

He strained.

And then he understood.

The metallic blue Škoda Yeti roared through lush Egyptian countryside, a playful shadow on a greenish landscape. This was Al Sharqia Governorate, northeast of Cairo, home to the ancient city of Tanis and Mohammed Morsi. And as far as the young welder was aware, it was now home to Egypt's first ever crop circle. At least, that was what the professor had told him.

He was behind the professor, who was in turn behind the wheel. Lauren was also up front, while Yaghdjian sat next to him in the rear. Behind them, Ramzy followed in his cruiser, maintaining a comfortable distance.

They were approximately 140 kilometres from the heart of Cairo, travelling along the slowly winding San Al Hagar-Al Husseineya highway into the tourist-neglected Delta. In truth, the Delta stretches across a vast distance along Egypt's north and is home to millions of citizens. Here, there was barely a trace of desert. Flatland reigned, lush plantations dominating. All around was a panorama of field after field after field. And always palm trees, attenuating in size as the horizon and ground converged. A different world mere kilometres from the land of the pyramids.

Their position on higher elevation allowed them to easily identify both the ruins of ancient Tanis on a ridge, as well as the crop circle to its immediate east. The interstellar blueprint was simply huge. An expansive constellation; flawless artistic symmetry.

As they parked, they could see, resonating outwards like a web, undulating and meandering spider legs that regularly broke into great corpulent patches. Though not all of these patches were connected by the sinew; many orbs hung in a completely uninhibited orbit around the main mass. Stars. The stars of Orion.

Congregated around the pattern were dozens of people, curious onlookers and enthusiasts alike, snapping photos, chatting intently. Police officers were also present, maintaining all a safe distance from the formation.

The welder glanced at the professor as they neared the formation.

Is there any chance this might be a hoax? You mentioned most are hoaxes.

"A design patterned after Orion, in a field in Egypt, with a line of numbered hieroglyphics that correspond to you, to those on David's computer?"

Understood.

The professor immediately signalled to Ramzy. "We're just going to have a walk around."

Someone was yelling towards them in Arabic. The welder saw what he assumed to be the lead police officer on the site, evidently warning them not to move any closer. As the welder watched, Ramzy approached the officer, speaking muted Arabic and pointing to the professor. Perhaps it had been the mention of Wasem; perhaps Ramzy had gone higher than that. In any event, after a lengthy exchange, the lead officer stepped away and gestured for the visitors to move forward.

"Smart man," the professor quipped. "They're out of their league here anyway. They have no idea what they're looking at."

Ramzy provided a translation. "He says his men are looking for evidence to find the perpetrators of the hoax."

"This is no hoax."

The welder studied the field. Each formation had been groomed precisely in that collapsed stalks were laid between standing stems. To crop circle enthusiasts, this is called combing. The stalks inside each shape had been brushed downward in one massive stroke. How could one accomplish such a feat? A crop circle hoax is difficult to spot. Hoaxers wear boards on their shoes, concealing any trample marks within the perimeters of their patterns. As they walk in a preconceived pattern, the boards flatten the stalks equally, conveying the impression the work was done by otherworldly beings. However, one still needs to enter the field without disturbing any stalks outside the pattern. This is often the easiest way to spot a hoax. Here, the execution was exceptional. Nothing suggested human intervention. No discernible trample marks. If this was a hoax, how could someone have gotten from one circle to another?

He stepped slightly forward, crunching on downed mature wild grassland. The leaves had been forced into the earth, their frayed ends now extended failingly along the ground. He moved away from the others, the sounds of audience members—for that was what they had become—now audible. He moved east, further into the field, then south, in the direction where the hieroglyphics had been etched into the soil. Overhead, against a soft blue backdrop, a helicopter hovered, its propellers a steady, rhythmic chronometer.

He sensed something. Something ethereal emitting from the field. Did the others feel it? He glanced over, wondering. Apparently not. And yet, he was not imagining it. Pure energy, generating within him a sensation of harmony. Yes, that was it. He was in harmony with the field.

The professor gravitated nearby.

Do you feel that?

"Feel what?"

That—that…

What was it, exactly?

I can't explain it. I feel…strange.

He stared at his hands, outstretched like paws.

I feel…

He hunted for the right word.

Alive. It's like I'm in tune with the harmony of the ground or something. I am literally humming with energy.

The professor stared at him. "I don't feel anything."

He closed his eyes, grazed his palms along the tops of the stalks, all of a sudden dizzy and agitated. He rubbed at his eyes.

"Are you alright?"

He glanced down through still-blurred eyes. His balance—he needed to sit. His entire body gave way vertiginously, and he toppled over. Now on his back, he squinted up at a sun-drenched sky and churning propeller blades. Then his eyes closed completely, and he eased into a seeming cataleptic state.

✱

He is no longer there on that grassy plain. Instead, he is standing in the centre of a dimly lit room. An incredibly vacuous room—more a warehouse than anything else. But this is no warehouse: the walls are emblazoned with multitudinous Egyptian hieroglyphics. The main floor space is dominated by tables and stools and huge, elongated shelves in methodically and competently arranged rows. Passable light emanates from holstered torches fastened along the walls. He peers at the shelves. What is on them? Scrolls of paper? Yes. Thousands of them. Hundreds of thousands. Stacked with care on each shelf, trolled up neatly, wound with wool or rope or something. And there is something else.

He is not alone.

A man is here.

The man is no giant, perhaps five and a half feet tall. An unusual appearance: voluptuous reddish lips, black kohl-*enhanced eyes, mascara that dominates to the cheeks and extends, as if straining, towards the sides of the face. Cheeks enriched with red dye. All this offset by an olive complexion, the result of generations under the Egyptian sun. He is bare chested, his stomach protruding unnaturally outward, his chest sunken oddly in. His head is festooned in a black and gold-striped* nemes *that dangles onto each shoulder. Atop the* nemes *is the red and white* pschent, *the double crown that Egyptologists believe signifies domain over both Upper and Lower Egypt. The lower, or red, portion of the* pschent *is hollow in its centre, in which the white crown reposes, propelled upwards at the back like a bowling pin. Enfolded round the* pschent *is a golden* uraeus, *the upright cobra that all pharaohs wear to signify dominion. The* uraeus' *eyes gaze forward above that of the pharaoh, alive and not alive, surveying and not surveying. Alongside the* uraeus *is the second emblem of the* pschent: *the golden vulture. It, too, reclines in mute surveillance. Elsewhere, everywhere, he is clad in scores of jewels, wrist and ankle bracelets, necklaces. About his waist is the ceremonial* shendyt, *a white cloth skirt that circumvents the torso, extending to mid-thigh, drawn to on the right with a golden brooch. The legs are bare. His feet are sheathed in intricately woven sandals interlaced with jewels of gold.*

Here is the perfect specimen of hybrid fusion, a body preserved for all time. Undoubtedly concealed under the pschent *is the overly large, sloping cranium, the same skull that has puzzled Egyptologists for decades. For there has been no disease to spawn the abnormal manifestation. It is simple genetics.*

The welder knows this figure. The sunken chest and bulbous stomach, the overly-developed lips, the skull.

The pharaoh, standing, stares emotionlessly, as if he is not alive. But his chest stirs rhythmically, indicating that he does indeed live.

And then a curious thing happens. Through seemingly padlocked lips, he begins to speak. Words emanate from somewhere within, piercing the young welder's cerebral cortex in such a way that he telepathically understands everything that is being said. Telepathy. A summons. He is being summoned.

To something called the Hall of Records.

He has heard of it. The Hall of Records was first described by Plato in his Timaeus. *In this dialogue, Critias tells a story of the infamous Solon who, years ago while in Egypt, was told of a place named Atlantis. Believers today speculate that Solon's Atlanteans must have had contact with the Khemitians thousands of years ago. The world's most famous psychic, Edgar Cayce, predicted just that. Cayce had the apparent ability to contact past lives while in a trance. Atlantis came up often during these trances. Cayce said that thousands of years ago, the Atlanteans came to Giza and built a massive repository—a library—of their knowledge of the world and its history from time immemorial. He called this repository the Hall of Records. So far, after several attempts, this Hall has eluded Cayce's followers. And certainly not everyone agrees that it's even there. But some of the excavations detected evidence that there are unexplored tunnels or chambers under the Sphinx. Something is down there. An underground library, built by the Atlanteans. They stored thousands upon thousands of written accounts of the Earth's history, materials they'd collected. Oh, the secrets buried down there! Not there—here. For he is here.*

It is made clear that this is all simply a reincarnation: a representation of a long-dead pharaoh, a representation of that ancient library. This is not Akhenaten, but a simple vessel, so designed to deliver a message. A number of messages, actually. The first of which confirms the Hall of Records, sealed far below the unrelenting sands of time. It is here that the secrets of planet Earth are contained: the dawn of humankind, the coming of the pharaohs from the sky, the convergence of two races, the evolution of humankind from cave dweller to engineer. The germination and diffusion of the hybrid race across the continent, across all continents. It is here that all myths became truths.

But there is more: he has been chosen. Because he was chosen once before.

Before?

Yes, that is what the figure says.

And when these words puncture the contours of the welder's mind, each and every hair on his body regimentally prostrates. The words shock him to his very core. What does the pharaoh mean? But stubbornly, the words to form that question do not come.

No matter: the answer is on its way.

Everything dissolves—the pharaoh, the shelves, the scrolls, the Hall—and it is suddenly night. He is outside now, in a forest of evergreens and maples. There is a gravel road, faintly illuminated by a full moon.

He knows this place, can remember it now. For several summers, he and his mother, along with the Alcock family, would journey from their homes north along Lake Huron to what was then Ipperwash Provincial Park. Land stolen from the aboriginals of the area. A carefully concealed secret. He'd loved this place. Glittering beaches and trails, elaborate sand dunes atop a bluff that overlooked the water's edge. Like peering eyes. It is rumoured soldiers engaged in beach storming exercises here during the Second World War. He and the others had used the dunes for a much more practical reason: to build forts.

The trees sway with a breeze that hadn't existed a moment before: maple, pine, ash, spruce, all moving rhythmically in a natural tempo. Besides the scant light from the moon, there is no other illumination. The darkness is pervasive, eerie. Everywhere. Dreaded darkness.

He looks down and discerns that he is riding his bicycle. He must have been returning to his camper, back at the campground. He recollects now these rare occasions, when his mother had attempted a sense of normalcy, of happiness, substance.

Again, he is not alone: there are the silhouettes of the two Alcock boys, Chris and Brian. Chris is two years older, Brian a single year. Constant companions in these early years of his life.

They turn a corner. Branches from prickly ash trees lunge greedily at them. The brothers have pulled ahead, and now he is entirely on his own. But he's been here before, so many times, and he knows the way. So there is no concern.

And then, almost imperceptibly at first, then growing in illuminated crescendo: a light ahead in the darkness. A pale blue light. Where is it coming from? From amidst the trees, or beyond the forest itself? He can't tell. All he knows is that his eyes are hardened on its bizarre appearance.

He slows, considers briefly a course of action. But there is only one choice. The illogical choice, the choice that anyone would make. He continues on, towards the light. Damn humanity's magnetism to curiosity.

At length, the road dissects into two. He leans left, the direction from which the light emanates.

It is strange: it is the heart of summer, when the palpable heat presses itself so against one's body. But now, the intensity of that heat has dissipated. The temperature has plummeted ominously. It is as if the seasons have reversed themselves. And the breeze has increased to a forceful gale, gaining momentum, intensifying still for no apparent reason.

The light continues to propagate from its strategically concealed position behind the army of foliage. He sees that if he continues on this road, he will pass it by. He decelerates, dismounts, lays the bike along the roadside, out of the way of any passing cars. Then he reaches forward, brushes back a handful of greenery, and plunges into the unknown.

There is no longer any shrouded mystery: the light flaunts the way. He is shaking now, a profusion of fear and the natural elements. He curses again his curiosity, but still he will not turn back. Not now.

It's more than that: he can't. Something is calling out to him.

Amid the now overwhelming blue light, he spots a clearing ahead. As well, a steady droning has become apparent, likewise developing. As he nears, the hum increases in crescendo, a cacophonous assault on his ears. It is something else as well. Numbing. He turns his head away, closes his eyes to block it out, stumbles forward. He is breaking through the last of the vegetation.

He comes to an abrupt halt, looks up and stares. Then he begins to panic. Out here in the unobstructed clearing is the source of the vibrant blue hue.

It is a ship.

A spaceship.

The immediate appearance of the ship is simultaneously awe inspiring and terrifying. It is massive, encompassing the majority of the clearing. It is not round; rather, it is rectangular, winged, with a viewport like a face that gapes back down at him. A bird of prey. Its true colour is obscured in the blue light, and along its fuselage are viewports. Antennae are visible, everywhere, a thousand curious proboscises. Underneath, squat, powerful legs for landing gears support the hull. Three legs in all, a tripod of stability. The drone emanates from within the interplanetary traveller, perhaps some hidden engine.

He is gripped with fear. He wants to leave, needs to leave. Back to the suddenly inviting comfort of the darkness and away from the ship, the light, the danger. But he can't: his feet are frozen in place. This is his Mount Cithaeron, he pinioned and helpless. And apart from blinking, his upper body is similarly immobile. Yes, he can still do that at least. But what good is blinking except as an intermittent blockage of fear?

He watches. The ship is alive. In the viewports, he can discern tiny figures, staring back out at him. Their individual features are obscured with distance, but they are there. That is enough. They are there, and they are watching him. And it scares the living hell out of him.

From somewhere underneath the ship, yellowish light is suddenly spilling outward, like a bowl full of water, fraternising with the effervescent blue. A door is opening, and what appears to be a platform is being lowered down to the ground.

There are two figures on that platform.

And he knows they are coming for him.

The platform impacts with the forest floor and ceases, resting comfortably. The two figures step down, clad in white—uniforms or spacesuits, he cannot be sure. Their faces are concealed by the fact that the only light originates from behind them. Flawless Gregg Toland backlighting here in the forest. They are helmeted, though he can imagine strikingly elongated skulls that arch backwards. What he can see clearly enough is that they are humanoid.

They are walking towards him, and he powers up the nerve to open his mouth, to scream in horror. Again no sound will come. And then he suddenly feels faint on his feet, as if his numbed legs can no longer support his frame. He pitches forward onto the surrounding leaves and grass and dirt.

And then everything comes in bits and pieces. He can feel hands reaching around his arms, pulling him upward; he can see that he is being conveyed towards the ship. Not dragged—there is no sense of aggression. He is simply being transported. Then he is on the platform. He is ascending. He can see the forest beyond slowing being shut out by the cold, metallic interior of the ship.

Now he is on what appears to be a gurney, in what is a sick bay of some sort. There is excessive white light, overpowering, originating directly from above. He closes his eyes. He will sneak glimpses: other beds alongside, and other people. Humans. Humans! He is not alone. Men and women of varying colours, ethnicities, ages. How many are there? He counts, his head bobbing in both directions. But something tells him he already knows the answer. 41. And he makes 42. Of course. But none of these others are screaming for help. None of them even speaks. They are not in pain. Yet they are lucid, all of them. And then one of them, lifelessly occupied by the light above, now turns to him. And he looks into this young man's eyes, and he sees…what does he see?

The creatures are all around, these humanoid things in white uniforms, scurrying like little children. Snubbed noses; elongated ears; bloated, protruding stomachs; beady little black eyes; pale lips. He closes his eyes again. In fear? No. Not now.

This mass abduction is not like he has seen in the movies and on television. The evil intent is absent. These are not hostile creatures, probing, vivisecting, pilfering from terrified captives what they will. He remembers Fire in the Sky *and how the scenes aboard that spacecraft horrified him when he and friends rented it in their youth. This is not* Fire in the Sky. *And yet, the very notion that he should not be frightened is absurd. He has been taken, after all—he is a captive. They are all captives, brought against their will. But that thought is meaningless now, in a scene that resembles more of a group inspection than anything else. Or like it was when he once gave blood at school with all his friends. They walked to the community centre and the nurses there probed them and drained them. Giving blood, a noble venture. He cannot help but feel this is something similar. But what is he giving? What do the little beings want from him?*

He can feel their hands on his skin. Cold, yet gentle. One rests against his neck, soothingly, reassuring. He regards its owner, peers into those tiny blackened orbs. There is no eyeball, at least none that he can discern. His own eyes float beyond, to the being's face. He thinks he can see wrinkles forming alongside the mouth. Is the being smiling at him? Yes, that is what he sees. The creature is smiling. And reassuringly caressing the back of his neck. There is nothing to fear. This is what he imagines the being says to him.

He can feel, too, the cold impersonality of inquisitive medical equipment on his now naked body. Inquiring, investigating. Where have his clothes gone to? They have been discarded, yet with such tenderness that he did not take notice. Elongated fingers caress his ribs, his chest, his quadriceps. One being has a tiny flute-like instrument in his hand, a bluish light oozing from the lowered end. He drags it painlessly across the chest, then down each leg. Another larger device, lowered from above, round and blinking in a similar blue hue, is being guided across him as well. Again, there is no discomfort.

What are they doing to him? What do they want?

At length, he is turned over. Now on his stomach, hands on his back, he feels inquisitive protracted fingers. And more equipment, cold but caressing. They mean him no harm. That much is clear. And yet it is terrifying nonetheless. He is the wild beast, tranquilised, who watches them through dilated petrified pupils. The beast always awakens and remembers nothing more, is none the worse for wear. So will it be with him.

He can feel an odd, tingling sensation on his back. What is happening? The machine from the ceiling, he imagines, with a pencil-like apparatus at its extremity, it is detailing something onto his lower back. Like a machine on an assembly line, in a car plant. An automated tattoo. And it feels like a tattoo, he assumes, though he has never had a tattoo before. But tattoos are painful, are they not? This is but a tickle, a feather on his back...

...He must have blacked out again, for he finds himself back outside, fully clothed, lying on the ground in the same clearing, this time in darkness. Darkness again. There is no ship, no creatures, no other humans. Only darkness. Terrifying darkness.

He shivers fearfully, rises to his feet. He can perceive in wan moonlight three large imprints in the ground where the landing gears had been. It has all been real.

But he is only remembering this all now. Here in this insentient state, in a field, in a country he's never been to before. Only now can he remember that on that night, he'd awakened in the pervasive pitch blackness of night, alone and terrified, and that he had observed these indentations in the ground. But he had not known what they were, had not known why or how he had found himself there. He had not remembered at the time that there had been nothing to fear; how his brain, unable either by sheer trauma or by some unseen, unknown alien force, had compensated by instituting this now obvious artificial fear of the dark. He had awakened alone to darkness, he was terrified. That was all. There had been a time when he had enjoyed, appreciated even, the stealth of night. Tenting out with friends, watching the stars. Storms at night, those intense, powerful tempests that appear from out of nowhere and down power lines. There had been a time when he had found himself completely at ease with situations like these. And then suddenly no longer. For some unknown reason, never again did he embrace darkness, never again did he find in it any sort of gratification. They had stolen that from him, had replaced it with fear. Fear of the dark. Henceforth, of darkness he would dread.

He discovers that he is able to stand easily enough. Without delay, he locates his way back through the foliage to the edge of the road where he has left his bicycle. He climbs aboard, heads for the campsite.

And then that memory is gone, dissolved as the Hall and pharaoh have before. And now he is back—back where? Where is he? He can't be sure. Darkness surrounds him, nothing more.

This is to be his mission, then: to discover why he has been chosen. The Hall of Records? Is it for this reason? Perhaps. For there, within its confines, is the proof humankind has been waiting for.

He has been summoned. He must not fail.

ATEN

It is dusk across Egypt. Wasem hunkers down in front of several television screens of the Le Méridien Pyramids hotel security room, reviewing video. Again. And still nothing. He scans the room for a respite. The walls are sky bluish, undecorated except for a bank of screens. How many screens? He refuses to count, guesses forty. A multitude of forty. And nothing at all on them. How is that possible? How can so many little faces have so little to say on the matter? How can it be that none of them captured anything of note? It's a miracle. Like Jesus and his loaves of bread and fish. Or so Nahas had once told him. Miracles do happen. Now he is a believer.

Exasperated, he dials Nahas.

"Hondo. Did you see that thing on TV? They're calling it a crop circle."

Yeah, heard all about it.

"Anything?"

Trent outside at the entrance, Trent in the lobby, Trent at the front desk, Trent in his hallway. I'm losing my mind. What about you?

"We ran the license plate of the SUV Trent had been driving around in. Guess what? It doesn't exist. The TAP assured me they have no vehicles with that plate. And what's even more interesting is the fact that they never had anyone assigned to Trent."

Then who is this person in uniform driving one of their vehicles?

"Beats me. They don't usually cater to foreign professors."

Wasem runs a hand over his plump belly, glances over and sees that one of the uniformed security men is suddenly staring at him. He is instantly exasperated.

Can I help you?

The security guard shrugs, turns nervously away.

The inspector returns to his conversation.

Why don't you get on over here and give me a hand with this surveillance video? I have a long night ahead of me.

"On my way. See you shortly."

He hangs up, sees someone entering the room. He rolls his eyes discontentedly.

Ramzy, what the hell are you doing here?

"Don't worry," Ramzy snaps, slumping down beside him. He smells of cologne. Egyptian Musk. Body oil, it's officially known as. He is wearing a black suit and white collared top. Tieless. He slings his jacket over a nearby chair. "I called in a few of the boys to watch them. They're fine."

I need you there, not here.

"That's not your call."

What—Deeb?

"He told me to keep an eye on you."

An eye on me? What for?

The youngster does not respond, and, resigned to this fate, the inspector returns to the wall of screens. What does it matter anyway? At least Deeb hasn't removed him from the case. And this isn't unusual—the brigadier has done it before. No doubt to spite him. *Gaaz*. Yes, he is angry all the same.

Play the lobby video again. But I want it played it back double time—is that possible?

The controller nods. "We can play it on fast forward, if you want."

I want. So it won't take all night.

He turns to Ramzy.

Having fun yet?

The officer yawns, again preferring silence.

"Sir."

One of the guards behind him fiddles with a box of digital tapes. The man has a curious look on his face, as if he's proud of himself, has found something important.

What the hell's the matter with you?

"It's strange, Inspector. The tape for the ninth floor is missing."

What do you mean?

"Just what I said. It isn't here."

It isn't here?

He springs to his feet.

It *was* there. I saw it myself the first time I came down here. Where did it go?

The man shrugs. "I don't know, Inspector. It isn't here."

"Maybe it got placed in the wrong box," Ramzy suggests calmly.

"Not likely," the head of security counters. He has been hovering nearby the whole time. His name plate reads Tarek Abdel-Rahim. Taller than the other men, he fills out his uniform in a more imposing manner. He wears his hair shaved short. He has a large, distractingly gruesome chin. He speaks resolutely. "I double checked all the boxes myself. I don't miss anything."

I don't care. I demand to see that tape.

Abdel-Rahim gapes at him. "Inspector, you already watched it once, and you didn't see anything out of the ordinary before. Is this really necessary?"

He imagines reaching up and squeezing the man's throat. Instead, he flexes his fingers, rolls them into fists.

You ignorant son of a bitch. Find that tape, now!

"You need to show a little damned respect."

Are you trying to stymie this investigation?

The head of security cocks his head quizzically. "Come again?"

It seems like you're working against me. If that's the case, and you were trying to hide something, perhaps you'd enjoy going downtown for questioning.

"I think we both know I'm not trying to do anything of the sort."

Nearby, another security guard grows pale all of a sudden, a bead of sweat trickling down his forehead and onto his nose. He wipes frantically at it. The inspector notices, misses nothing. He gestures to this other man, still maintaining eye contact with the Abdel-Rahim.

What's with him?

"Him?"

He points belligerently at the young man, now sweating more noticeably, shaking like a sycamore in a strong breeze.

This guy. He looks a bit uncomfortable.

He turned to the man in question.

What's the problem? The air conditioning's on in here, so why the sweating?

"Problem?" the young man breaths, wiping his brow.

Yeah, the problem. What's with the sudden panic attack?

"I don't know anything," the man gulps, and before he can say another word, Wasem's hand has closed deliciously around his throat.

Abdel-Rahim reaches over to pry the detective's hands loose. He discovers, much to his displeasure, that the inspector is far stronger than he looks. He steps back exasperatingly. "This isn't necessary. Let him go."

He does so, but his eyes remain fixated on the terrified guard.

Talk. Or we go for a drive.

The youngster straightens, wheezing and gripping his strained neck. "There was a man who came in here. TAP, but in civvies."

A TAP in civvies? They don't exist.

"Regardless, he told me he needed to borrow some of the video for the investigation. I assumed he knew what he was doing. He took a whole box full."

You let this person just walk out of here with a box full of video?

"He was a cop!"

A TAP is no cop.

The youngster speaks shakily. "He said his name was Yusef. I don't know his full name. He wasn't wearing a name badge."

There are only about twenty million Yusefs here in Egypt. Are you sure of the name?

"That's what he said."

It is a start. He nods, savouring the breakthrough.

I assume it was that prick that was taxiing the professor around.

"He brought the box back not long after," the man protests. "Early the next morning, I guess. I didn't check to make sure all the tapes were in there."

I suggest in the future you not give any tapes to TAPs, especially ones without badges.

"Deal."

Might you recognise him if you saw him?

"Maybe."

Wasem barks at the two men sitting in front of him.

Get me some video of that police SUV again, the one Trent had been driving around in the night he died.

Within seconds, the front door camera is cued. There is David Trent exiting the Tourism and Antiquities Police vehicle. And there the driver. About thirty, maybe thirty-five, ethnically Egyptian, tall and athletic. He sports a moustache and masquerades effectively in the white uniform and black beret of the TAP. There they are shaking hands, saying goodbye.

The youngster nods almost immediately. "That is the man who spoke with me."

Freeze the frame.

The screen grinds to a halt.

Zoom in on the driver's face. There—I need that image printed. Then I want you to go back over the other tapes. Every time you see this man on camera with Trent, I want you to zoom in and print as clear and detailed an image as you can. Can you do that for me?

The men bow.

Within seconds, Wasem hears a printer spitting something out. He grabs the paper, regards the image. The face is large and clearly visible; black and white, but a good photo nonetheless. He acknowledges the men in the room.

Nicely done, boys.

He grabs the youngster by the collar.

The man staggers for balance. "Are you arresting me? Where are we going?"

If you were arresting someone, where might you take them?

"But you said if I talked, you wouldn't take me downtown!"

Wasem makes for the door, the guard still in his clutches. An unimpressed Ramzy hovers nearby. "Wasem, what the—?"

What's your name?

"Ayman," the man replies. "Please don't hurt me."

The inspector flips out his cell phone, dials Nahas' number, waits for the inspector to pick up.

"Hondo," Nahas says seconds later. Noise pilfers through the line. "I'm almost there."

Change of plan.

"What?"

We just hit pay day.

"What does that mean?"

It means a face, and it means a name. We are finally onto something.

The summoned passed into the living room, the voices of others wafting in his ears like the breeze. He stepped through the French doors that led to the back yard and the in-ground swimming pool—*hammaem sibaeha*, he'd heard it called earlier by the police. Nothing like hot air. But something about the fact that there was a swimming pool seemed to have a calming effect on him:

heat was tolerable when water was near. He threw off his t-shirt, waded into the shallow end of the pool, his navy swimming shorts instantly blackened by the darkening water.

None of this villa should be here; none of this was Egypt. Not his notion of Egypt, at any rate. Here, palm trees towered over tranquil waters. Where was the violence he had seen on the news? Where were the armed protests, the brutal army repressing the voices of the masses? Where were the rival political parties vying for control of the country? He'd seen none of that. And yet he knew it must be here, somewhere, in this land, even somewhere within Cairo. All he'd witnessed were cell phones and bill boards and women exposed in skirts and sleeveless blouses; BMWs and lavish villas intermingled with rickshaws and donkeys and gas-spewing cars with hanging bumpers; smashed windows and towering condominiums; the ever-present fragrance of petroleum. The good and the bad. But not the terrible. The terrible didn't seem to exist.

Waist deep, his hand floated gently along the surface of the water, heated daily via the burning sun. He joined this hand with his other. Even here in the water, he could still feel the energy from Tanis within. A constant vibrato, like a gently purring cat. Egypt had made him alive.

He reached for his lower back. There. He'd had it for years, and he had always assumed it was a birthmark, something that had gradually appeared while he was younger. A small area of colouration on his lower back. He remembered asking his mother about it. Now he knew how he'd acquired it.

His mother.

She had known. Somehow, someway, she'd always known. It was impossibly ridiculous to think it, but he couldn't help it.

She'd known because it must have happened to her, too. That was why she was also afraid of the dark, had been for years, before his own dread had cultivated itself. Now it all made sense. Why in her consistent melancholy she'd drifted away from him. What had happened to her had also happened to him, and she'd been powerless to prevent it. Shame: that was what she'd been feeling all these years. He'd been so wrong to misinterpret it. The guilt, the inability to protect him. Instead of overcompensating to gain his forgiveness, lavishing him with attention, she'd instead withdrawn, melted away, become a shadow. She'd left him to wonder why. All these years.

But there would be no forgiveness. He could not hate her for what had happened. But the silence, the deafening silence she'd bestowed upon him ever since—that was unforgiveable. A mother should know better.

You knew. And you said nothing. Why?

Lauren was suddenly there, wearing a red bathing suit that was not a two-piece. He glanced consciously down at his own body, abruptly aware while in the presence of such a perfect specimen of imperfections in his stomach and sides. He crouched embarrassingly low in the water.

She was wading out to him, two glasses in her hands.

He thanked her, drinking a mouthful of the darkened liquid.

What is it? Vodka?

"It's called Edge. Egyptian alcohol. Lime flavoured."

It was in the villa?

"Stocked in the living room."

I never thought I'd be drinking alcohol in Egypt.

"Make no mistake: Egyptians drink." She deflected the conversation. "How are you holding up?"

I'm okay.

"You're not the same person you were a few days ago."

At times, I feel overwhelmed. I still have that same sensation running through my body. It's been there since we visited the crop circle. It hasn't left. I'm beginning to wonder if it ever will.

"I have to admit, I'm a little jealous."

Why?

"I guess I always sort of hoped it might be me they'd contact. Or the professor."

I'm not all that thrilled about it.

"I know."

A few days ago, I was out with friends playing ball. It's amazing what a knock to the head can do to a person.

He smiled, and she smiled back at him.

"It's strange."

What's that?

"How little we know about each other."

What do you want to know?

"Everything."

And so he told her. He told her of how he had been born in Stratford, had grown up in nearby Thamesford, but now lived in London, how he had attended Fanshawe College, how he now owned a wrought iron business. He told her how he played guitar, how he'd been in a band called Stand Up For Bastards, how they thought they'd go places, but stardom never materialised.

They'd cut a demo, played some shows, things had petered out. And then they all grew up, became responsible.

She told him how she had lived here before. As a graduate student, studying ancient Egypt. He could see her sifting through memories. Before the Arab Spring. A beautiful, modern campus, away from the hustle and bustle of Cairo. A wealth of relationships with other students from all around the world.

Was he serious when he said he'd read all those books in a day?

He was. It was an odd quirk he'd always had, the ability to speed read. But even that had increased ever since the incident.

Had he read any of the professor's books?

And Then There Were Humans. Yes. Very interesting.

And then he thought about something far more private, and he decided to tell her. Normally he would never have discussed the dark shadows of his personal life, that he was afraid to tell people the truth about himself, but there was something about her that thawed all fear. He trusted her. He explained that his childhood had been anything but normal, that he had never known his father, who had apparently run off before he had even been born. His mother and father had been married only a short time, and he assumed his father must not have been ready for a baby. His mother had never remarried. He had no siblings, and he and his mother had drifted apart these last several years. They rarely spoke nowadays. She had called the other day, but it had been the same old.

He had asked himself why a thousand times, had assumed it had never been anything specific. He could remember his mother in his youth, waterlogged by perpetual melancholy. She had often been depressed, and as for parenthood, he had intuitively surmised from an early enough age that, like his father, it had not been for her. The joy his friends had experienced at home had always been elusive for him. At times, she would offer respites—appear happier, rejuvenated. They would spend time together: baseball games, museums, reading together. Camping trips to Ipperwash.

Micropachycephalosaurus walking through a deep dark forest.

Then, once more, she would become the depressed soul he knew much more intimately.

But there had been an even more apparent shift in her behaviour at some point: her general malaise became permanently pronounced, so that, by the time he had entered high school, their relationship had deteriorated past the point of repair. His vision at Tanis now suggested why—this he kept to himself. Her disinterest in all things had percolated down to him. School became an afterthought. He had turned to the trades, even though she told him he was an academic and that university was where he belonged. But it wasn't a deliberate change: he did enjoy working with his hands, always had. He'd moved to London, created his own business, which was small, but growing.

There was something unusual about him, he suddenly uttered. Curious, she had urged him to tell. He intimated that he was afraid of the dark, that he never slept in total darkness if he could help it, how a night light was always on in his bedroom. When he had been much younger, the dark had never been a problem. He supposed somewhere along the way he had developed this fear—again, he refrained from telling her what he now knew. He remembered that his mother always hated the dark as well. Even before it had begun to disturb him, he could remember her sleeping with a light on. He supposed it still bothered her.

She moved towards the side of the pool, resting her drink on the stone patio. Her toned arms reposed over the pool's edge. She was staring out and up, into the darkening sky. He appeared close by, mimicking her actions.

"Did you ever wonder about where they came from when you were young?"

As a kid? Sure. You watch *E.T.*, you wonder. As of today, I wonder more than ever. I wonder what their world looks like. I wonder if they have music, sports. I wonder if they dream.

They were so terrifying when they came for me, and all those people I saw on the ship seemed prisoners. But they didn't hurt us. They were exactly what we never hear about. Benevolent. They wanted to study me, to give me this mark on my back. They had a purpose for me. For all of us on that ship, I assume. And that one young man turning and looking at me. He was scared, but there was nothing to be afraid of.

"And now they've led you here."

They have.

Tomorrow we can find out why.

They had indeed discussed it. He needed to go to Giza. He thought of the pyramids and their apparent mystical properties, the same sort of thing that can be found in other historic sites around the world. This is part of the World Grid Theory: the world can actually be thought of as a collection of energy zones. Along the intersecting lines of these zones, "hot spots," where energy readings are noticeably more acute, are found. Energy in the form of radio wave frequency, part of something known as radio propagation. The

Earth naturally transmits at a specific frequency, but one can harness this propagation and use it for further purposes. Humans do this all the time. Everything around that works with electricity operates on this principle: radio energy from the Earth is harnessed and redistributed. Was the Great Pyramid once used in the same way, as a conductor of electric energy, as some would suggest? Perhaps tomorrow he would know for sure.

She was regarding him strangely just now, as if working through a theory. He studied the features of her face, the furrowed brows, the tightened lips.

"What are you thinking?"

He was thinking about electrical current, how the pyramid emitted a frequency that perhaps was now reflected in him. Pyramids. DNA. Water. F# running through his head. All beyond coincidence.

"It's calling to you. It's always been calling. You've only just been able to hear it."

She had finished her drink. Laughing with embarrassment, she exited the pool, announced she was going to the washroom, that she'd be back with the whole bottle.

He watched her go for only a second, then forced his eyes away, towards the rear of the villa and the stone fence, where guarded palms and sycamores drooped exhaustedly. Or seemed to. He studied the interlacing pattern of stone that encompassed the fence.

He heard something. A whistle. Not a toy whistle—of human invention. He cocked his head to one side. Beyond the stone fence.

He stepped clear of the water, suddenly refreshed, grabbed his fallen shirt, pulled it back over his head. His feet sensed patterns engraved in the stone below. He made his way onto the grass towards the rear of the house. The whistling was still audible. He gazed out over the fence, into a mini forest of palms and the community park that was the centre of Newmerryland. Playground equipment, swings, more trees. And whistling. He made to call to Lauren, did not see her, shrugged, pulled himself over the fence.

The grass, now heavily shaded, was cool and tender under his feet as he made his way into the interior of the housing complex. He could hear other voices now, home owners on their patios barbequing or swimming, sitting and drinking. He followed the whistling further and further into the forest. Ahead, he thought he saw someone, and he squinted. Yes, definitely someone, apparently staring back at him and whistling.

Someone else appeared from out of nowhere, behind one of the palms, dressed in black and built of powerful stuff, arms enfolding about him, clutching and forcing him to the ground. His vision turned sideways, and he could see the whistler running towards him. He could hear Lauren's voice faintly back in the yard, calling for him, discerned her change in tone, from confused to alarmed. He imagined her running back into the house, and the professor rushing out and not seeing him, then the police officers scurrying.

And then someone was pushing something onto his mouth. A damp cloth, and an odour he'd never smelled before. He tried to call out, but the cloth and the hand prevented him. And the smell, the odour—it was doing something to him. He was being drugged.

He was being kidnapped.

He struggled as best he could, but the figure held fast, like crazy glue at inopportune moments. He could already feel his legs buckling, freezing beneath him. His arms dropped uselessly to his sides, his eyes began to cloud, and he imagined them sagging senselessly downwards. Like the palms and sycamores.

But he wasn't passing out. His entire body had become prostrate, just as it had all those years ago in that forest in the darkness of night. Then, too, he'd been unable to move, but had not lost consciousness.

He was being lifted, his arms in one man's hands and his legs in another's, and he was being rushed effortlessly across the grassy floor. Towards one of the houses, presumably. And as he neared the wall of stone that was the perimeter fence of this new property, he could hear more voices on the other side. Speaking in English. And he could see hands outstretched above the fence, reaching out to him. Then he was being lifted, up and over, and as his eyes turned skyward and stared into an obscured night, he finally lost all consciousness and plunged into his own blackness.

The advantage to having money and power, Garrett Seldon surmised, was that everything was made to seem too easy. Hours earlier, he, Denison, and a horde of followers—agents? What should one call them? Soldiers?—had boarded a private jet for Cairo International. Now here they were, at the lavish 27-storie Sofitel Cairo El Gezira, a tubular edifice overlooking the Nile from the south bank of Gezira Island. Dinner had been excellent at the Le Deck restaurant, where they observed a picturesque skyline scented with a fusion of exhaust and breezy, warm air. They reclined on darkened thatch chairs, engaged in conversation. But Seldon remained silent, staring out at the array of boats that meandered up and down the mighty Nile. He was sweating. All he had been told about Cairo, of its dreadfully hot days and refreshing nights—all this he was now questioning. He could feel the sweat leaking through his semi-casual attire. It didn't really matter to him; he was consumed with the conversation he'd had with Pharaoh on the flight over. Words that still bothered him.

Your man will not have been met by anyone at the airport, Pharaoh had said from the first-class seat next to him.

Seldon had stared puzzlingly back at him.

You heard me just fine. We've had a change of plan.

A change of plan? He hadn't understood.

It's not your job to understand. We won't be needing your Scorpion's services anymore.

But he would have already landed ahead of us, sir. He would have been at the airport waiting for someone to meet him, as I instructed him.

He wouldn't have waited long.

Pharaoh had spoken with a frustratingly simplistic finality. An alternate plan was already in the works, covertly preconceived. His busy little bees, the many who toiled behind the scenes, had been engaged. All without Seldon's knowing.

But, he'd warned, *he's a professional. He won't be easy to—. And he expects the remainder of his payment.*

Pharaoh had not cared to elaborate. He'd reminded Seldon that he had done his job well, and that this had been a decision he had made on his own. He had suggested Seldon sit back and enjoy the flight.

Back to the present. Pharaoh flanked by his bookend bodyguards. The same two men from the park back in Washington. He was off the phone. Regaled in a tailored suit and staring at a laptop, he didn't look very happy. But he wasn't sweating. How was that possible in this climate?

"Do you know what I'm doing, Seldon?"

No, sir.

"I'm staring at a picture of the Great Pyramid, trying to understand how its coordinates have anything to do with Mark Brydges."

It's baffling, sir.

Pharaoh was stroking his fine jawline. "We'll have to bring him in."

Bring him in?

Pharaoh feigned a smile. "Your Scorpion is a difficult target. The men I sent after him didn't succeed."

So he's still at large?

"He could ruin everything."

But you wanted all threats contained, sir.

Pharaoh's brows furrowed. "Seldon, haven't you been following? Brydges isn't a threat. He's why we're here."

Sir, how did he escape?

"Your Scorpion? Two men dead down by the Nile. He could be anywhere now."

He's not going to leave the country. He plans to kill Brydges. He made this clear to me.

Then it dawned on him.

Sir, we need him.

"I know."

No, sir. The assassin.

"Whatever for?"

He's the only one who knows where Trent's evidence is buried, sir.

Pharaoh appeared nonplussed. "No, he isn't. You and he agreed on the location."

We did, sir, but—

"What's the problem, then?"

Sir, I've obviously never been to the location before. It's a large enough area and it could take some time to find the artefact. I...

"You what?"

I trusted him to take care of it, sir. I thought it of no concern. He knows this country better than any of us, naturally.

"Naturally."

I verified the general location, but—

"*The general location.* So you don't know *exactly* where it is. This is what you're telling me."

Sir, I had no idea you were planning to kill him.

"It would have been good to have known this beforehand, Seldon."

You never asked, bastard.

I'm sorry, sir.

"If he told you where he buried it, I'm sure that's where it is. An island, right?"

Golden Horn Island, in the middle of Lake Qarum.

"Golden Horn Island?"

Yes, sir.

It was obvious Pharaoh was making a mental note.

There is only one building on the island, sir. It's hidden in there.

"I see. So, there. You do have a good idea of its whereabouts. Nothing to worry about."

Perhaps Pharaoh understood his role in this mess. Perhaps. "Of course, if we can't find it, what does it matter?" He said it with sudden dismissiveness.

Sir?

"The thing stays buried. Hidden from the public. That's all that matters. No real loss."

It stays hidden? No real loss? Wasn't the whole point to come and retrieve the evidence?

Unless the Scorpion is on his way to get it.

Denison vacillated. "What does that matter?"

He could go public with it one way or another, sir, as a form of payback. This could go very badly for us.

"How?"

He could anonymously leave it somewhere, like the Cairo Museum. It would make the news, people would start to talk…

Pharaoh stroked his jawline a second time. "I don't think we have anything to worry about there."

Sir?

"An artefact that completely rewrites human history? I think, in that event, the government here will be rather quick to dispose of it. In fact, I'll make certain of that."

How?

"I have my ways, Seldon."

This is all in his mind. She is not here and he is not here, either. It is a dream, but all is genuine, plausible. And in this plausibility, here they are in his home, in his living room. Seated on his couch, she is deadpanned as always, blank eyes staring lifelessly down at a dark laminate floor that doubles for hardwood. She is clothed in jeans, faded like memories, a red Roots sweater. Her moonishly pale orbed face is exposed by brownish hair pulled taut to mask dishevelment. But some of it has already come undone, dangling like broken guitar string down one side of her face. Like spaghetti noodles over the edge of a bowl. Spaghetti. He remembers they used to eat it together when he was young. Everything when he was young.

Xenotarsosaurus looks like Carnotaurus.

He is standing over her. He can hear his own voice as it resonates outward.
You knew. All this time.
She remains stoic.
Knew what?
You've always known.
I don't know what you're talking about.
How she exacerbates him!
You knew I'd been abducted. All these years.
She looks up for the first time, and he stares into those live, dead eyes.
Abducted? By who? You're starting to worry me.
Worry? As if. He wants to laugh.
That's why we've grown apart: you felt guilty for letting it happen.
She shakes her head. Her hair quivers like the branches of a decaying elm.
You lost me. Something happened to you, yes? And you blame me. Is this why you invited me over here? To talk about this?
It's the only logical answer. All those early years, growing up with a mother who hated the dark. I always thought it was so unusual. Who else has a parent as odd as you? Who else has to lie about that sort of thing to his friends?
That's hurtful.
Her remark is characteristically devoid of emotion. And it is hurtful, he supposes. But it is the truth. The truth! Ma'at should weigh her truthful heart. Let Ma'at have her way. The truth. As if. What does she know of honesty?
You always hated going anywhere at night—driving at night, going for walks.
It is such a powerful emotion, hate. Hate. Hatred. "H8Red," he once saw it spelled on an Anthrax album. He inhales its intoxicating potency. Hatred, which stems from madness. Yes, madness initiates hatred. Hatred is *madness. What was it that hated Norman Bates once said? "We all go a little mad sometimes."*
In the house, we always had lights on at night. Always.
She shakes her head again, the elm trembling as before.
We've been over this.
And you were never truly happy. Why was that?
That's complicated.
I used to think so, too. But now it's all so clear. It's actually quite simple. When I started hating the dark, you became even less happy. Imagine that? You were sad enough, depressed, no doubt, when I was young. But when I started to develop the same sort of behaviour, you turned on me.
Suddenly she is as a lamp, brought to life in the darkness. Or one of those deep sea fish that can instantly generate its own illumination. She is full of energy.

I turned on you? How could you say a such a thing? I never turned on you!

You knew, and you did nothing.

Colour is returning to her face. Incredible! He has to see it to believe it. The cheeks are blushing, still paler than her sweater, but the blush is there, noticeably growing in intensity. But she won't fully redden—this he can predict. No, that would be too much. Too much emotion, too much of anything. And yet, her words are razors to his wounded heart.

I knew? Knew what?

Is her reaction genuine? Now he can't be sure.

I never understood it until now.

He says it with some delay, a note of regret in a minor key.

You'd better start making sense, or I'll leave.

She points menacingly to his front door, and that is enough to burst his bubble of regret.

You'll leave? There's a shock. No, stay. So we can clarify a few things.

Yes, staying would be a welcome change. All she does is flee.

Like what?

Like how it had happened to you, too.

What had happened?

That's why it all makes sense now. They took you, too, didn't they? Long before me—way, way before me.

He shrugs as he espouses the possibilities.

Maybe even before I was even born. But maybe later, when I was still young. What difference does it make?

She is staring down at the floor once again.

I have never been "taken," whatever you mean by that. No one has ever "taken" me anywhere.

He ignores her. Hah! How does she like that? The shoe on the other foot for a change.

And when you realised that it had happened to me, too, you weren't able to cope. You just shut down. That's why our relationship deteriorated. All this time I'd just assumed you hadn't wanted anything to do with me anymore, as if I'd become a burden to you. As if I reminded you of your failed marriage, of a husband who ran out on you before I had even been born. But that wasn't it at all.

Redness is flourishing on her face after all.

What has gotten into you? How could you say such cruel things?

You should have said something.

You should be ashamed of yourself. Calling me here, knowing how fragile I've been all these years. Such ridiculous things, abductions and what not.

Her voice is rising, a barometer ready to blow. Has he ever seen her like this before? Perhaps. It's been so long since he's seen anything from her.

Why have you become so callous? Why? Because we drifted apart? Yes, we did that—how can I deny what's so obvious to everyone?

He cannot back down now. He is in too deep.

I just want you to know that I was angry for so long, but I'm not anymore, because now I understand.

She scoffs as only a mother can do.

Oh, you understand? You really think you know what it's been like for me? You don't understand a damned thing. It breaks my heart to hear you talk this way, to know that all these years you felt so guilty about… The truth is that none of it ever had anything to do with you.

Half of him wants to believe her. It's that half about being a son, trusting in everything your mother tells you. But the other half is urging him, too, tugging urgently on the sleeves of his mind. Telling him to trust his intuition. That she is lying.

You need to stop pretending. We both hate the dark for a reason. And I have this birthmark. I got it when I was twelve years old, in the forest at Ipperwash. When we were on vacation with the Alcocks. They gave it to me.

What birthmark?

Feigned bewilderment. Or so he assumes.

It's okay. You can stop now. I know. They took you too, long before they took me. I don't know why, and maybe you don't know either, but maybe we can look for the answers together.

She is standing all of a sudden, making for the door. He turns as she brushes past, watches her fumble for her shoes. His eyes linger on the laces.

I'm leaving. I should never have come.

He suddenly regrets everything.

Don't go!

But it's too late; he knows it. She will walk out that door, just as she has done so many times before. One door is as good as any other. She must wish for revolving doors: so much faster to get away.

She is pushing through, stepping down onto the driveway.

I should never have come.

He appears at the doorway, slides through, bare feet on the cool cement of the step.

Don't you leave me!

This he hollers at her, the family roles reversed.

Not again!

But he cannot dominate her. No one can. And she is past listening.

And then she is gone. In and out of his life again. Like a lost book rediscovered years later, the front cover dusty, worn. But the words within are the same they've always been. Words as lies. Words lie. She lies. She has always lied. And now he's lost her again.

He opens his eyes. The dream is over, but it was real enough. One day, they will have that very conversation.

He is in a limousine, moving, across Cairo. Fly-by streetlights cast ominous shadows across his body. Night has fallen. He glances around, sees that he is not alone. Several men, conversing with one another, insect-like voices filtering in and out. One of them, dressed in a suit without a tie, reclines just to his right, speaking on a cell phone. The words are indecipherable, but he recognises the language. German. Tall, broad-shouldered, clean-shaven. Blonde. Good looking.

"It's good to see you're finally awake," the man suddenly says to him, bowing to eye level and smiling generously. "I can appreciate what you might be thinking. Don't worry: it'll make sense soon enough. How do you feel?"

Where are we going?

"Where do you think we're going?"

How could I know that?

"Oh, I think you know." The man grins. His teeth are perfect. They sparkle, like silly little diamonds in the dim light. "I'm Vannevar Denison. Pleasure to finally make your acquaintance."

He appraises his kidnapper, the long lashes, the athletic build, the vibrant confidence. A man used to success. Then he regards another close by, a man with none of these qualities. And there is an expression on this other's face rather like frustration. Is he angry? About what?

Clearly you're not going to kill me. You would have done that already.

"Kill you?" the man laughs. "Surely not. You're far more important to me alive."

Then why those other attempts?

"What other attempts?"

He scoffs.

Let's see. First there was the car bomb. Then there was the car chase. I don't think much of your batting average.

A clarifying finger wafts into the air. "Those attempts had nothing to do with me. It's someone else who wants you dead."

Someone else views us as serious threats?

"Not 'us.' You and you alone."

And what am I to you, then?

"Funny, but I didn't realise it in the beginning. I just assumed you were some crazed fan asking for the professor's autograph."

The summoned looks away in disgust.

You've been watching us the whole time.

"Watching, listening."

You're pathetic.

"No. I'm persistent. And if we're talking batting averages, I'd say I've redeemed myself."

The summoned says nothing to this, elects to stare out at the passing city.

"We aren't positive who blew up the professor's van, or who was following you on the highway. Isn't that right, Seldon?" Denison turns to his sullen companion.

"That's correct," Seldon mumbles, caught by surprise, attempting to delete an obvious scowl from his face. "We don't know who they are. We only know what they want."

And what do *you* want?

"You."

He frowns.

Obviously you don't want to tell me.

"Like I said, it will all make sense."

Who are you?

Denison ignores him. "There's a lot at stake, Mark. For everyone."

I can't imagine why.

"Don't be so modest. You're the ankh, you see: the key. With you, I can unlock any secret. And you hold the balance between world peace and anarchy."

The summoned stares in disillusionment at the carpeted floor. He thinks of the baseball field, the screaming ball. So long ago, yet mere days. And now, he is being whisked across Cairo, for a purpose he doesn't fully understand. But one thing is suddenly clear.

You're taking me to the Great Pyramid.

Denison refuses to commit. "And to think this all started when you were twelve years old."

How could you know that?

Of course. Someone must have talked. But this man won't tell him. No, of that he is certain. He plies a different tact.

Denison isn't German. But your German is very good.

"My minor in university," his captor shrugs noncommittally. "But you, you..." His voice tails off, finds itself again. "What was it like?"

What was what like?

"You know. The abduction. The forest, at night, the lights through the trees. The way they exited their ship and came for you. The bringing of you on board, the exam. What was it all like?"

Who was it?

"Who was what?"

Who told you?

"Please. Humour me."

He chokes back a laugh.

Are you serious?

"I assume you were scared out of your mind."

He relents.

That's about it.

"And there were others on that ship, too. I'm curious about them. Whatever happened to them? Were they released? Killed? Still on board all these years later?" And then he stares the summoned cold in the eye. "I wonder if they have the same birth mark as you."

I wonder, too.

That part is true.

"They did something to you. What, exactly? That's the big question."

Who are you?

"I'm whatever you want me to be. Let me say this much. I represent the most powerful people on the face of the planet."

Powerful enough to kill those who want to expose truths?

"Ah. David Trent."

He found something, and it must have scared you. It would have changed the way we perceive our own existence. And you shut him up forever because of it.

"Oh, I'm talking about a lot more power than that. David Trent was but a drop. I'm the ocean, you see."

He pauses.

I'm a threat, too, aren't I?

"A threat? Not to me. To me, you're a revelation."

You plan on using me, harnessing me.

"*Harnessing*. Interesting choice of words. But don't get ahead of yourself. We don't even fully understand all that you are yet."

Why did you have to kill Trent?

"Think mass panic and then world anarchy. Think Orson Welles and *The War of the Worlds*. On a global scale. Imagine if you were able to prove to the world that everything we think we know is mere myth. How do you think that'd go over? Admittedly, you'd generate plenty of interest; you'd find your face on the cover of *Time*. But there would also be those who'd resent you. Many who depend on tourism for their survival. And tourism is accepted history. Financially, whole economies could be ruined. And when people are financially ruined, or at the very least threatened with ruin, they don't think straight. They get desperate. We became a little desperate with Trent."

I think you're wrong. Trent's discovery, whatever it was, would have done so much good. We would all have been better off. It's always better knowing.

"Is it?" Denison is noticeably irritated all of a sudden. "Think about it. 'Don't visit Egypt anymore: everything there's a fraud.' How about Italy? India? Vietnam? China? And why stop there? After you've successfully debunked x number of historical sites around the world, why not start in on religion? Because, in the end, there is a common link between history and religion, isn't there? Imagine: 'Christianity is all wrong. *Islam* is all wrong.' Proving Muhammad a sham would go over real well, wouldn't it? WMDs in the Middle East would increase overnight. ISIS on steroids. There'd be war. Unless you'd want that, of course. Shakespeare claimed some people prefer war as a destroyer of men to the apoplexy of peace. Perhaps that's you."

Do you not hear your own hypocrisy? You're not concerned with religion and civil strife. It's technology. Alien technology. That's what this is all about. That's how this all relates to me. By harnessing me, you create a weapon. *You'll* create the war.

"No. By harnessing you, I will *end* all war."

You'll bring me to the pyramid, see what happens; then you'll whisk me away to Area 51 or somewhere and study me, see if you can exploit the energy that's been rushing through my veins.

"Something like that," Denison answers evasively. "The good news is, the people that view you as a threat and want you dead won't be able to get their hands on you. Now, what's worse?"

A great choice. Murder or an existence as a lab rat.

"At least you'll be alive. I know which I'd prefer."

And with me, you'll build weapons for your government. Then sell the technology.

"Sell it? Why would I want to do that?"

Others will come looking for me.

"I'd think less of them if they didn't."

You won't be able to keep the truth hidden forever. Regardless of what happens to me, one day the Egyptian government will open up the Giza Plateau to major excavation. Then the world will know the truth.

"What makes you so sure? What on Earth would possess the Egyptian government to want to dig for the Hall of Records?"

Curiosity. Human nature. The desire to know for sure what's down there.

"Curiosity? Let's talk reality. An excavation that big would effectively shut down tourism at Giza. Do you know how many tourists visit there every year, even with the turmoil that's been going on here of late? Do you have any idea how much money we're talking? It'll never happen. And not just for financial reasons. If the world was indeed shown what's buried under that sand, it would create all the panic I just described. And there's one other thing." He pauses. "Consider how much financial aid my government gives to Egypt every year. How many billions. And that's just America. Think about the other countries that also pitch in." He shrugs. "What is so easily given can just as easily be taken away."

You'll blackmail them. Cut their aid if they dare expose the truth.

Denison is politically vague. "A fail-safe, you might say. But ask yourself why Egypt would want to expose what's under there, anyway? Egyptians are a proud people, proud of their history. They will never allow anyone to unearth the Hall of Records. And there are plenty of other countries that will back them one hundred percent."

You'll never succeed.

"I already have. I have you."

I won't cooperate. You'll have to kill me.

"We shall see."

The reassurance has suddenly vanished from the voice of his abductor, replaced by these obsidian words. The summoned says nothing more, stares out into the night, wonders, hopes.

Dreads.

Wasem smoked his cigarette nonchalantly. At length, he gazed into the night sky. Seven o'clock, the hour of the setting sun in July. He'd heard his brothers tell him how it set so much later during a Canadian summer. Still light out at nine? Incredible.

And then he saw it again: the revolving object from before. He'd almost forgotten about it. Turning and turning, red and then white. He made to say something, thought better of it.

It was Ramzy who spoke. "You see it, too, yeah?"

See what? he feigned.

"I saw it two nights ago for the first time. It made the news. No one seems to know what it is."

Don't start getting any wild ideas.

He said it as much for himself as for the other. For he wanted to believe it was nothing, some figment of the imagination. Or a satellite, maybe. Yes, that was a tidy little theory. Safe and tidy. Safe from the ridicule of others. But the truth was he knew better. This rotary object, Mark Brydges, David Trent—they were all connected. And something was going to happen. What was that line from 2010? *Something wonderful.* Would it be wonderful? He couldn't say.

"I think it's a sign," Ramzy was saying with skyward eyes.

A sign? For what? From whom?

"Who can know? But it's a sign. I know this like I know a well-made *aish merahrah*. I believe all those stories you see in documentaries. There is life out there, beyond our planet."

Really.

"Really. They've been watching us. Dr. Booth is right about that. And this thing—it's a sign from them. They want us to see it. Maybe it means they're coming."

For what reason, Ramzy? What do we have here they would want or need?

"I don't know. Maybe it's not about that. Maybe it's just about simple contact."

You get all that from some thing up there in the sky?

Wasem was moving on, the cuffed Ayman securely in his grip.

"You need to be open minded, Wasem."

Ayman fidgeted uncomfortably as he was led by the big man away from the hotel to the inspector's Vectra. "I believe it, too," he was saying.

You think that's a spaceship up there?

"Maybe."

You would.

"Is it really necessary to cuff him?" Ramzy intoned.

Ayman nodded vigorously in agreement. "I promise I am not going to try to escape."

Why promise that? That's not what I'd do if I were you. Hell, I'd bolt the first chance I had. And this is a big city to hide in.

"I'm not you. Besides, you'd find me. That's what you do for a living."

True enough.

Wasem gestured to the parking lot at the north end of the hotel.

"I thought we were going to meet someone out here."

Right you are. Another inspector is on his way.

A pair of headlights in the distance turned onto the Cairo-Alex road.

I bet that's him now.

And as the car advanced, he thought of another question.

Tell me something, Ayman.

"I'll tell you anything you want if you can keep me out of jail."

It was too easy to toy with him.

I can't guarantee that, but I can try and get the charge lessened if you help me out.

There was, of course, no charge to lay.

I'm wondering about your friend Yusef. Any idea where he lives?

"No."

No?

"We didn't talk about anything except the videos." Ayman shrugged. "Why would I want to know where he lives?"

Just a question.

"But I can tell you that he shops in Zamalik."

Ramzy hesitated. "Zamalik?" The most famous cultural district in Cairo. "You sure?"

"I'm sure. The day he came to the hotel, he was wearing designer clothes that had Zamalik written all over them."

"How can you be sure?"

"My wife's brother is a tailor at a store over there. Sometimes he gets us deals on clothes. He knows everybody in the neighbourhood. One time he was telling me about this one guy, Charobim, who does high-end suits and what not, for all the richest people in the country. You get a little crest on your clothes. I saw that crest on the inner neck line of Yusef's jacket. And I know the boots he was wearing, too: they were from a store close to my brother-in-law's shop."

Wasem was impressed.

Not bad. What's the name of this Charobim's store?

"Ghali of Zamalik. Seriously top-end."

I'll keep it in mind.

The car was turning into the parking lot, obscured by night and streetlights. But there was something amiss. It was a red Geely SC5. Nahas did not drive a Geely SC5.

And it was going much too fast.

And it appeared to be heading right for them.

He drew his side arm from his breast pocket. The car continued to advance, and he fired once, a warning shot purposely meant to miss. But the driver was undeterred. He fired a second time, burying a bullet into the front right tyre. The Geely slowed, screeching painfully across the tarmac of the parking lot as it streaked past. The driver, clearly contemplating his options, hit the accelerator again. The vehicle rushed forward undaunted.

From his knee, Ramzy released his own shot, wounding the car along its right side. The driver now angled away from the officers, piloting instead for the momentarily unprotected Ayman. Wasem screamed a warning and saw the youngster struggling futility to his feet without the use of his hands. His eyes were wide with fear as he staggered across the lot, searching for somewhere to hide. But there was nowhere to go; there were far too many empty parking spaces, too few cars.

The car struck him with an appalling thud, and his body sailed uselessly through the air.

The inspector fired twice more. The first shot hit the rear left taillight. The second was far more potent: it shattered the rear glass altogether, though it clearly missed the driver's head. The Geely sped off into the night.

Wasem struggled over to the fallen security guard, who was lying awkwardly on the ground. He knew before he reached Ayman that he was surely dead. He turned the body over. Lifeless eyes staring blankly upward confirmed as much.

He had only a minute or so before he saw hotel staffers running towards him. As well, a car was turning into the parking lot. He recognised Nahas in his maroon Renault Logan, leaning out the driver's side door, inhaling insouciantly on a cigarette.

He barked for an ambulance, though he knew it was too late. He stood and stepped forcefully past the gathering throng. Amongst them, a woman was screaming. Ramzy was on his phone, and someone else was racing, panicked, for the hotel lobby.

As Nahas approached, he saw Wasem's gun was trained on him. He froze. "Hondo, what are you doing?"

I might ask you the same damned thing!

"What are you talking about?"

Cut the shit, Nahas. The timing's too coincidental.

If Nahas knew anything, he was clearly adept at playing coy. He stared incomprehensibly at his fellow detective. "I don't what you're referring to, Hondo. Lower the gun so we can talk."

The inspector gestured over his left shoulder.

I call you, then someone shows up and tries to kill us. Ayman here wasn't so lucky.

"Hondo, what the hell…?"

You expected to come here and find me dead.

Nahas blew out hot air. "I expected to find you here in this parking lot with that man!" he bellowed. "Dead, Hondo? Really?"

There was the sound of sirens in the distance.

"Hondo, listen to reason!" Nahas protested, now fully realising that Wasem might indeed shoot him. "How long have we known each other?"

Years.

"Right. Doesn't that stand for something?"

Wasem wilted slightly.

A man's dead here, Nahas.

"So, let's figure out why."

I called you from my cell phone in the lobby. There was plenty of noise going on in there. No one would have been able to overhear me.

"Then maybe your phone's bugged."

Bugged? My phone? What for?

But there was severe logic in this suggestion. Wasem froze; the words resonated in him. He glanced down at his waist, pulled the phone from his pants pocket, stared at it.

"We'll take it over to the station and have it analysed," Nahas told him. "We'll go together, in my car, Hondo." He grabbed his own phone. "Let me call this in."

"I've already done that," Ramzy reported.

Wasem continued to gape at his phone, a bead of sweat dripping down the side of his face. Something was rising deep within him, something of which he had precious little experience.

Fear.

He climbed into the Logan's passenger seat, Ramzy scuttling in behind him, and the car rocketed from the parking lot and the unfolding scene. He gazed out at the kaleidoscope of lights racing past, merging, separating. No one spoke. It was an uncomfortable silence, but his phone beeping brought a welcome respite. He glanced down. It was one of the officers Ramzy had left back at the professor's villa in his stead.

Go.

"We've had some trouble down here at the villa, sir."

Tell me.

"Brydges has gone missing."

He hung up, glanced at Nahas. "More problems. Newmerryland. Quick."

They jetted across the city, east along Al Ahram, then onto Al Rawda and the bridge there, across the Nile and onto Gezira Island. Then across El Makel El Saleh Bridge and north on Salah Salem. Then off the major highways and onto local roads and into the city of Al Abajiyyah, past one condominium complex after another, so many that they eventually merged. Then south onto Kobri Al Ebageah until it intersected with Ring Road. It was here, as they banked east once again, that civilisation largely began to fall away, replaced with the cold emptiness of the desert at night. They shifted into New Cairo, where everything was enviously modern and clean and expensive, followed Ring Road until it veered north. They redeployed east onto more suburban-like streets, past condominiums and houses and golf courses and mosques. Eventually, they found their way into Newmerryland and slowed when they saw the professor's villa.

Only a few years ago, the Newmerryland neighbourhood didn't exist. Charmed by an unseen *pungi*, it had materialised, laying down concrete roots in the sand. It was part of New Cairo, which was similarly non-existent before 2001. This is the new Egypt, the innovative Egypt, building into the desert. An Egypt these men could only dream of. An Egypt of cleaner air, posh new dwellings, and the proximity to several international universities.

There were several police cruisers already on hand, and officers were everywhere, some with dogs, flashlights in hand. There, too, were the professors, out on the lawn conversing with an officer. Wasem stepped forward and literally elbowed the man out of his way.

Professor. We got here as quickly as we could.

"They've taken him."

Who?

"The ones who plant car bombs." The ubiquitous ones. "Whoever they are."

No matter. You'll have your friend back.

"If I were a betting man, there's only one place they would be taking him."

The pyramids.

"We need to get to Giza right away. At least have it blocked off by the police."

Wasem raised his walkie talkie. He was about to call in the request when he heard his name filtering through the chorus of voices in the vicinity. He glanced over his shoulder and swore under his breath. Deeb.

The brigadier's voice was surprisingly tranquil, as though perhaps he'd had time to think through what he would say to the inspector. Time to prepare.

"Wasem, we need to talk."

Yes, sir. I was about to inform you—

"I've placed you on suspension, Wasem."

He stared back at his superior, stupefied. "Sir, I don't think—"

"That's the problem. You've been taken off the case. Off all cases, effective immediately."

The inspector glanced downward, anger rising within. He forced composure on himself as he spoke again.

May I ask what it was in particular, sir?

"I assigned Ramzy to you for your own protection."

My own protection?

"You then *reassigned him*. An obvious breach of protocol, Wasem. And had you informed me here of this situation—" he gestured irritably at the villa "—I would have assigned officers. But you chose not to do that. And for that, after all this time, I am free of you. Your suspension is pending final review, but it will come to pass, Wasem, that you are simply too unfit for duty ever again."

Over something like this?

"Something like this? You arrogant, abusive, incompetent—." The brigadier stopped, breathed deeply, calmed himself. "Nahas is now in control of this operation for the missing Canadian. And the dead Canadian, too." He extended his hand. "I'll take your badge and sidearm."

Wasem vacillated.

"This is exactly what I'm talking about. Your badge and gun—now."

Again he dithered. Deeb instead turned and called for Nahas, who had been watching from a distance. "See that he goes home and stays there. All of this I leave to you to sort out." Then once more he confronted the inspector. "I'm waiting." He paused, hand outstretched. "Deny me again and I'll place you under arrest."

Reluctantly, and with calculated resistance, Wasem handed over the articles.

I think you will come to regret this.

"The only thing I regret, Wasem, is that I didn't do it sooner."

Nahas swallowed uncomfortably. "Sir, I think we need to discuss this further. I need Inspector Wa—"

"If you're not up to the challenge, Nahas, I will find someone else. Regardless, Trent's murderer will be found. This other young man who has gone missing will also be found. And that will be the end of it." He glanced at an officer hovering nearby, snapped his fingers royally. "I'm leaving now."

He shuffled off, and the two inspectors stared uncomfortably at one another. Then Nahas made to speak, but Wasem silenced him.

It's not your fault. He may have my badge, but I have my honour.

"Agreed."

We have a lead in Zamalik. I'm going there now. I'll bring Ramzy. He's been privy to everything, anyway. You do what you can here.

Ramzy was immediately uncomfortable. "Wasem, I don't think that's such a good idea. Deeb will have my badge, too."

The inspector glared resolutely at him, and the young officer shrugged helplessly.

"Let's go."

They are stopping. There, now to the right, a lighthouse at the edge of the island overlooking the vast river, is the cylindrical Sofitel Hotel. Gardens and Al Hurriyah Park dominate much of the surroundings. The Sofitel is lit prettily in the evening sky: deep maroon beams shoot skyward from its base like little lasers. The hotel's name is awash in fluorescent green. To the left sits the sprawling Cairo Opera House. Beyond, in the distance, the purplish-hued Cairo tower can be seen, the tallest structure in the city.

Then the back door opens, and Denison watches the summoned emerge.

"Are we staying here tonight?"

We are.

"I don't understand."

I'm confident the pyramid's not going anywhere any time soon. Something else I have to take care of first.

At once, they enter into a grand lobby, bathed in something between yellow and brown by lamplight, maroon by day. A colossal chandelier hangs majestically, like a rich jewel, towards one end of the spacious room, illuminating couches and chairs and tables. The wall nearby is mostly glass and flanking curtains. Through this is visible the night lights of Cairo.

They enter an elevator. The lift doors open several seconds later.

It is an attractive suite. Large, spacious. A king-sized bed, a desk under a set of windows, a bathroom, a balcony.

The summoned steps towards the window, gazes through parted curtains. Denison senses the anticipation in him, follows his gaze like a giddy school boy. The Plateau is alive with a mix of blues, reds, oranges, greens.

They put on a light show every night. Rest up. You've got a busy day ahead of you tomorrow.

He knows the summoned wants to say something, and he waits, offering the floor. But no words come. It appears the summoned has resigned himself to his fate. He closes the door with satisfaction, nods to Bowles, who is already grabbing a chair and positioning himself in the hallway. Seldon's unattractive form hovers nearby.

"We need to talk, sir."

There is something different in the man's voice. A hardened, authoritative tone. Is Seldon developing a demeanour? Impressive.

About what?

"I just want you to know I don't agree with what you're doing."

So that's what's been eating at you. I didn't see it coming.

"He *will* be a lab rat."

It's a bit late in the game to be developing a conscience, Seldon.

"It's not right."

We'll all know for sure tomorrow.

"And after you've used him, then what? What will you do with the most sophisticated weapon on this planet? Who will you attack?"

Attack? Who do you take me for?

"He deserves to be given the choice."

Given the choice? He didn't have the choice when he was abducted in a forest at age twelve, did he? Sometimes life isn't fair, Seldon. He's been given a gift, as far as I'm concerned. I'm not about to let *that* go back to building wrought iron fences for little old ladies.

"You bastard."

His body doesn't belong to him anymore. It belongs to me.

Seldon's voice is rising. "Don't you care about anyone?"

I'm not paid to care, Seldon. I'm paid to produce.

He gestures to the hallway beyond.

You should go. Take some time, calm yourself. Think things through.

Seldon shuffles off, and Denison watches him go. Seldon has just seen his last sunset. So it must be. There can be no opposition. Not now, when they are so close. He motions to Sanderson, speaks economically.

Another loose end. Take care of it.

Gezira Island is grappled to the mainland via three bridges: the 15th of May, the 6th of October, and the Al Galaa/Qasr Al-Nile. Several characteristics offset it from the rest of the city. Besides the Cairo Tower and the massive Cairo Sporting club that dominates the centre of the island, there is also the district of Zamalik, one of Cairo's most affluent. Comprising much of northern Gezira Island, Zamalik is rich in culture and architecture. It teems with restaurants, nightclubs, coffee houses, and the country's premier performing arts centres: the El Sawy Culturewheel Centre and the Egyptian Opera House. Some of Cairo's more famous personalities can be found here, as well as many of the finest hotels.

Hondo Wasem rarely ventures out to Zamalik, mostly because he knows he can afford very little of what it has to offer. He is unsurprised by the number of wealthy foreigners he glimpses in and around the bustling cafes, bars, and restaurants; similarly, he is unsurprised by the number of wealthy Egyptian nationals present. Egyptians in bars. Egypt is one of the few Muslim countries in the world in which there is no ban on the production, purchase, or consumption of alcohol—except during Ramadan.

It is closing in on nine, and the air is predictably scalding. He envisions sweat pooling under his armpits and back, discolouring his white collared shirt. His body has never acclimatised, even though he was born here. Beside him, young Ramzy, still sharp in his dark suit, is cradling his jacket over his shoulder. There is a casual, billboard sort of appeal to the way he conducts himself just now. He looks attractive enough—Wasem has to give him credit.

Several smells assault him, and he sniffs the air like an attentive canine. Egyptian entrees, Cairo at its finest. *Koshari* is being served everywhere—tomato sauce and onion are potent in the air. Further on, *Mulukhiyah* with its garlic and coriander. Is that lamb someone is serving with it? No, rabbit.

The better choice. *Shawerma*, too, with Tahina sauce, garlic with lemon juice. Lebanese *Tahina*. His mouth waters. He loves Lebanese *Tahina* sauce. But there is no time to savour these Zamalin scents today.

Ramzy's patience is running thin. "Can't we call it a day? Look into this tomorrow?"

Not enjoying yourself, Ramzy?

The inspector's attention is diverted to the shops on the opposite side of the street.

"There is that concern for my career."

We're solving a crime, Ramzy. We need to be here. Ah.

He points at last across the street.

There it is. Ghali of Zamalek.

From the safe confines of the sidewalk, he strides impatiently onto the avenue. A sleek, new Nissan Sunny has to slam on its brakes to avoid running him down. He hears the driver yelling something at him, gives it no thought. *Ya gazma yibn ig-gazma! You son of a shoe!* He loves that one. Egyptians love to throw this one around. Shoes denote dirt, so it's degrading to say this to someone. His mother used to love saying that one.

Behind him, Ramzy is waving to the driver in a gesture of apology. They step onto the sidewalk on the opposite side of the street.

"You're going to get yourself killed."

Wasem opens the door and enters the shop, luxuriates in the intoxicating immediacy of air conditioning. He glances around. The shop is two-levelled. The prices he see confirm what Ayman had said. He scans the clientele. Absolutely. He scuttles over to the counter. Two cash registers greet him in front of a tall, well-dressed, clean-shaven young man.

"Can I help you, sir?" the man asks cordially.

He opens his wallet and produces his badge.

You can get me your sales records.

The man is immediately unnerved. "Is there a problem, sir?"

Only if you dawdle, *behiima*.

"I'm sorry?"

Behiima—livestock. That's one he prefers. Stupid animal. Yes. That one really gets the insult meter on the rise.

Ramzy translates. "We're investigating a murder. We're looking for a name. Please be prompt." He turns to Wasem as the man scurries away, likely to find his manager. "You see? Sometimes just speaking a bit more politely gets the job done."

The sales clerk returns with a much older moustached man in a collared shirt. *Bahaayim!* Plural livestock! Hilarious!

"May I be of service?" the man asks cordially.

Wasem stares ahead in confusion. It is just like those new ridiculous phone systems companies use: you are prompted to punch in various bits of information, and when a living human finally comes on the line, they ask for the same information all over again. He has had his share of cellular blow ups.

We just said why we're here.

He glares at the original sales clerk.

I need to see your sales records. We're looking for a name.

The manager nods. "I see. You're the police?"

No words in reply. Only a perfectly timed scowl.

Now both men scurry away. Wasem wipes a hand over his perspiring face, leans his repugnant right side on the counter, stares out the front store windows. He watches incoherently as pedestrians march past.

The older gentleman returns. He is carrying a large book with a faded blue cover. As soon as he approaches, the inspector dips an eyebrow in amazement.

You keep your records *there*?

"That's right. We have computerised records as well, but these are the receipts."

You Charobim?

The man smiles. "I am. I own this store."

I need to know about a man named Yusef.

The inspector reaches into his jacket and produces a number of the photos from the hotel security cameras.

I need you to look hard at these photos. Then I need you to look for a man by the name of Yusef.

"Yusef?" Charobim repeats. "That's not going to be easy. It's a very common name."

Just look at the photos. Is he familiar to you?

He offers more prompts.

He bought a jacket from here, maybe other clothes as well. Tall, athletic, likely in his early to mid-thirties.

Charobim gawks long and hard, and the inspector isn't about to break his concentration. Finally the man's eyes light ever so slightly. "You know, he is familiar. I have seen this man, I believe. But the moustache does not seem to match."

Then imagine him without it.

Ramzy has another idea. "How about a man named David Trent?"

Charobim glances up. "David Trent? The professor?"

You know him?

"Why, yes, of course," the store owner grins proudly. "Professor Trent came in here many times over the years. I tailored several items for him."

The inspector and police officer stare at one another. Charobim understands immediately he's said something important.

"Why, Inspector? I thought you were asking about this man here in the photo."

This man here was assigned to Trent here in Cairo when the professor last came to visit. I suspect they were inseparable.

"Oh, that's right," Charobim nods. "There was an officer with him at all times." His eyes suddenly discharge on the photo as if for the first time. "Yes. That *is* the man."

Now think very hard. Does he look like someone who came in here on another occasion, by himself maybe, without the moustache? Maybe a man who went by the name of Yusef?

"Perhaps. I have many Yusefs, but I can pinpoint when I made a sale to one. And, gentlemen, I have security video. Would you like to see it?"

Wasem glares.

Why didn't we just start with that?

"Splendid." Charobim turns to the young clerk. "We'll be in the back. Do not disturb us."

The three make their way along the counter and past various tourists. They pass rows and displays of affluent suits. Wasem eyes several of the jackets. Lovely.

The old man reaches for a door at the far end of the store, opens it, flicks on a light. They enter.

Inside is an office, small and smelling something foul. A computer rests on the only desk. Charobim seats himself instantly, unwilling or suddenly unaware that the officers are left to stand. He works the console with surprising precision.

"I am going to cue up the camera video. I will also look into our records. We always keep the names of our clients on record when we make a sale. David Tent will no doubt be in here. This other man you are looking for should be here as well."

Take your time.

Wasem turns to the nearby wall. There is a chalk board and scribbles, assumedly in Charobim's hand, of an unintelligible language. Arabic, yes, but the words are short form for something. Clothing terms? Perhaps. There are plenty of numbers as well.

"Aha. Got it," the owner announces after a moment. "David Trent was here on June 25. He purchased pants. He returned two days later to pick them up and pay for them. So…" He minimises a screen that shows the names and dates of purchases. "We will cue up the video for the 25th. I bet this officer will be on there."

Sure enough, the video, which is in colour, taken from a high angle of the store behind the cash registers, reveals Trent easily enough. The dead walks again. He is smiling and talking with Charobim. And sure enough, just behind him, but clearly in sight is the uniformed police officer, tall and muscular and moustached.

Wasem leans in close.

Can you zoom in on that man?

"Certainly."

The TAP swells accordingly in size, and as Charobim continues to re-centre his face, the image does not blur. Yusef seems to come alive: the hooked nose, groomed eyebrows, black eyes, the hair.

At length, Charobim stops. "I'm afraid any further, and we'll distort the image."

That's fine.

The owner reaches over and places a finger across the man's lip on the photo in Wasem's hand, obscuring the moustache. "Yes. He has come in here many times. Strange that I didn't recognise him at first. It must have been the moustache. And his hair is longer than I remember."

Falsies.

"Why on Earth would he want to do that?"

So people like you wouldn't recognise him. But you do recognise him, don't you?

"Yes, yes, I do."

Now we just need you to give us his full name. And when he came in.

Charobim wipes his face with his hand. "I do remember him. A jacket, you said? And the name—Yusef?" He is shaking his head. "I don't think that was the name he used." He gazes down at the wooden desk, as if it offers him some explanation. "No, he did not use that name." Then he returns to the computer. "No, he called himself Alexander…" He pauses. "Alexander Kalvos. Yes. A Greek descendant."

Alexander Kalvos?

Wasem repeats the name, but the man is already scanning through his records.

"Yes. He is a good customer. I have had him in here many times. Here. I will minimise this first screen, of the police man. Now I will look at a day when Alexander Kalvos was in here. May 12. He was here to have a jacket made."

"A jacket?" Ramzy smiles. "Perfect."

Within seconds, the video of the day is cued. "He was here on that day," Charobim says, fast forwarding through the video. "We will just watch for him."

The other two stand helplessly behind him, but they don't have to wait long. Within seconds, Charobim has found the image they have been waiting for. A tall, athletic, clean-shaven man, in his early thirties, well dressed in a dark tailored suit, conversing with Charobim. There is no mistake. And they know it.

"That's it," Charobim grins excitedly. "That's the man. The police officer. His hair is shorter, his moustache gone, you see, and I think he even changed his eye colour. Contacts, perhaps? But that's him. Look! The cheekbones, the shoulders."

"Oh, we're looking," Ramzy breaths excitedly.

Wasem stares contentedly down at the elderly man.

Now, have you got an address?

"Certainly. Has he done anything wrong?"

Maybe not today. But then again, the day's not over.

Emphatic pounding at the door startles Yaghdjian from his stupor. He realises that he has fallen asleep on the couch in front of the television, for the evening news is on. Protests in Tahrir Square. One unpopular government ousted, another unpopular government now securely in place. New arrests. Which political party sympathisers are these? He glances at the clock hanging on the wall beside the television. It is late for visitors.

His first assumption is that Inspector Wasem has returned for more questions; however, he opens the door to three dark-clothed police officers instead. They stampede in, drilling him against the far wall. He slumps instantly, in obvious discomfort. One of the them turns him over, grabbing at his wrists. He can feel the sudden, cold, metallic repugnance of cufflinks.

"Not a word," the man mouths close to his ears.

Mahmoud Bassiony is a congested street at most hours of the day, and as Yaghdjian is dragged down the steps and into the main lobby, then through the front doors and towards two waiting police SUVs, he perceives that the glut of traffic has decelerated to a crawl, passers-by straining to catch a glimpse of his arrest. Imagine that—he's suddenly famous.

He is pushed headlong into the first cruiser. An anticipatory driver waits up front. The first officer closes the door behind him, then settles into the passenger's seat. The other two, though Yaghdjian can't see them, are no doubt climbing into the second cruiser. And then, as he settles in, he sees that they are off, speeding south on Mahmoud Bassiony, their emergency lights flashing to expedite perceived gridlock. They approach Talaat Harb Square, then southwest onto Talaat Harb itself, a wide avenue predictably jammed with cars. Amid furiously moaning sirens, they journey southwest past the hulking Lotus Hotel, the Canadian Hostel, and the elegant Sun Hotel, then into Tahrir Square. He can see protesters marching haphazardly, surrounded by onlookers and police officers, bearing signs in a mix of Arabic and English. A peaceful demonstration. Democracy at last?

From here they continue due west across El-Tahrir and onto the Kasr Al-Nile Bridge. He notes the twin stone solitary lions that flank either side as they pass. West it is, across Gezira Island along El-Tahrir, then onto Al-Galaa Bridge and off the island. There is the enormous Sheraton Hotel complex on both sides of what is Al-Galaa Square, and the Faisal Islamic Bank further ahead.

They maintain west onto busy Al-Behous, which he knows will eventually end. What then? Within minutes, he has his answer: south onto Sudan, then west again for an extended period on Al-Malek Faisal. From here, amid roaring traffic, endless skyscrapers, and millions of lights, the unmistakably hulking presence of the Pyramids of Giza are visible.

Al Faisal ends at Al Remaia. They veer right into an onslaught of cars heading north, and turn west, still on Al Remaia. He peers to his left and sees the hotel just then. *The* hotel, the one where it had happened a week ago. Yes, one week tomorrow. Le Méridien. The pyramids themselves loom just beyond. And then he can feel the vehicle leaning right again.

They steer north onto the Cairo-Alex Road, leaving the bloated forms of the pyramids behind. He turns to stare in the rear view window at the retreating icons until they gradually give way to other buildings and trees. On their right, they pass the engaging Mövenpick Resort and its various separate bungalows. To the left is an assortment of sparse trees and desert. Further civilisation looms further off.

They continue north, passing the equally impressive Pyramids Park Resort. Abruptly, however, the last vestiges of development begin to fade. Desert and palms creep menacingly in from both sides.

Then an awe-inspiring sight rises above the treeline on the east side of the road. One of many opulent palaces surrounding Cairo. The house is simply enormous. Completely white, a complex series of steeples, rounded rooftops, and balconies. On several of the rooftops, antennae-like appendages surge skyward. A private villa.

They pass an intermingling of trees, more opulent mansions and hotels, and desert. Always more desert. The architecture fades, and they suddenly bank sharply to the left. There, ahead, is what appears to be a single building, a tree farm on the north side of the road. And then a gravel laneway appears, obstructive trees lining both sides, the smooth transference of pavement now a distant memory. Ahead is another building. A warehouse? There are several cars here already, but within the building itself, evident from the windows, there is little light. Curious.

They pull into an opening amongst the other vehicles. The ignition is killed, the men exit the car. His door is opened. He is told to move. He begins to sweat anew. They mean to kill him—this is where he will die. He knows it.

They enter the warehouse, and he immediately beholds several men, sitting on an odd assortment of chairs and couches in what seems to have been a lobby at one point. There are lamps lit on TV tables, turned low. None of the men are in uniform. Are they even police officers? One of them, white-haired with age and wearing a dark suit, stands, back turned, gazing out one of the windows. Silent, patient. He is not an Egyptian. This is odd.

Yaghdjian studies this and the other men. A curious sort. Five in total, only some of whom are nationals. The others are unmistakably European. Or continental Americans. The man at the window is significantly older than the others. Yaghdjian perceives his tanned complexion and flaccid skin. Well-dressed. The others, much younger, are dressed more casually in shorts and golf shirts. One of them sports a goatee.

And then he notices something interesting. None of the Egyptians have any hair. They are a collection of perfectly groomed craniums. One of them is motioning out past the lobby to an open door.

He is forced through that door. He notices a window that peers into the warehouse itself, but all is dark beyond. Through the darkness, he perceives a narrow corridor. There are a few closed doors, and he is being ushered towards one of them just as it is being opened. He is thrust through. The door slams closed, and he observes a tiny office complete with a desk and chair. Nothing hangs on the sterile walls. The desk and chair smell of withered age. It has been some time since anyone has used either.

He can hear the door locking. At least there is light in here. He sighs and sits down. All he can do is wait. He begins to whimper.

A parade of black police SUVs—sporadic flashing lights and a ceaseless blazing of sirens—race through upper class Zamalik. This is indeed a rare occasion; understandably, the streets begin to overcrowd with curious onlookers. No one has seen anything like this since the Uprising.

Wasem, Nahas, and Ramzy are in the third car, passengers of a young, inexperienced officer who is clearly uneasy about his role. In truth, the driver's apprehension is justified: the whole operation has been hastily assembled with few details. Only Wasem and Ramzy seem to know exactly what is transpiring, and why.

It is also an operation being conducted without the knowledge of Brigadier General Deeb. The chief inspector on duty warned Nahas, now in control of the case, that Deeb would never have given authorisation for such a raid. It's too late now—they are committed. There will be plenty to answer for that later. Hopefully they can alleviate the inevitable with armfuls of evidence.

Artificial light from street lanterns filters through the car windows. Wasem stares down at several papers in his hands, and the light dances across the pages, little ballerina poses in the evening gloom. He now has in his possession several photos of Alexander Kalvos. He also has an address. And close to twenty officers. If Kalvos is in the area, this is his last night of freedom.

The young driver wipes a sweaty brow. Can the inspector tell him anything else about this man, he wonders, apart from the fact that he is wanted in connection with Trent's murder?

Wasem shrugs. There isn't much else known to tell. Yet. In fact, he is only now beginning to piece together several clues. Among the obvious is that Kalvos is the executor of those other murders on INTERPOL. The scorpion killer.

They cross onto Gezira at the 15th of May Bridge, then turn north onto Shagaret al Dor, towards the northern tip of the island. The ultra-modern Nile City Towers glitter on the horizon to the right. Twin pylons, a send up to the ancients' at the entrances to their cities. Ahead, the elegant President Hotel looms, then scurries close by. It is here that the vehicles slow en masse, across from a set of stylish walk-up apartments.

In unison, doors open, officers exit, keys and equipment jingle. Inquisitive onlookers gawk. Some of the officers, already assigned to crowd control, take to clearing the area. The rest of the men, inspectors included, head for their destination.

Wasem is the first to master a short flight of stairs to the outside door. His men anxiously align themselves behind him. His heart is racing; he can feel it surging beneath his ribcage. He's been in this position many times before, and he revels in the accompanying rush.

He scans the abode. The *shu'a*. Nice place. There are no lights on; Kalvos is likely not here. Regardless, they are going in. He fingers a pistol he has had to borrow from another, on account of Deeb now in possession of his own.

It is Ramzy who shouts out their intentions. They are the police; they have the home surrounded. They are carrying a search warrant to inspect the premises, as well as an arrest warrant. They will enter with force if necessary.

They wait. After several seconds, it is clear they are not going to be admitted. Wasem gives a nod, and a rather large officer steps by him, reaches back, and kicks the door with such force that it almost immediately caves in. The men teem through like a horde of rats, fan out, flashlights perusing the darkness—until someone flips on the lights.

They are in the middle of an attractive foyer: the kitchen off to the left, a living room on the right, a hallway directly in front. There is a staircase at the end of that hall, and some men are already racing towards it, pistols drawn and at the ready. There is a redolent scent in the air: the aromatic smell of recently cleaned carpet.

It is a meticulously rehearsed operation: a room-by-room inspection, first for occupants, next for clues.

Wasem holsters his pistol, Nahas drawing alongside. The large detective spits on the carpet below, whitish saliva on darkened plush velvet. Wiping his mouth with the back of his hand, he mutters, He's not here.

It is hardly a surprise, Nahas replies. They have him on the run, then.

Officers brushed past with assumed evidence: an address book, photos, trophy pistols in cases, clothing, even the garbage. Wasem stops a man carrying a photo album. He opens it and gruffly turns the pages. There are plenty of images, all conveniently devoid of people, snapshots of seemingly inconsequential sights: beaches, hotels, streets, churches. He rolls his eyes. They are not going to find any photos of him here. He has been too clever for that.

They can collect his prints, then. They can run a search with INTERPOL to see if they have any that match. Fair enough. But this case is priority number one. Certainly that is why they are here, first and foremost.

He saunters off, first into the living room, then to the end of the hall and the staircase: he is going to have his own look around.

It is clear the assassin possesses money. While the apartment itself is modest, the furniture and artwork on the walls are expensive tastes. Custom manufactured in Damietta and then shipped down here.

Upstairs. Two bedrooms and a bathroom. Wasem peers into what he assumes is the master. A king-sized bed and bookend-flanking nightstands, an oak dresser. More from Damietta. He looks down and watches his foot sink into the carpet, lifts it, watches the flooring rebound. New, fresh.

Officers are already conducting forensics up here, as well as ripping the bed sheets off the mattress. The walk-in closet is open, men inside as well. Wasem nods approvingly to the little worker ants and moves on. Ahead is the second bedroom, which he perceives Kalvos has employed as an office. He peers in. A computer at a desk, a single bed, a book shelf. Flowers on the shelf. Vased daisies. He dips a finger into the earth surrounding the stem. Dry. Kalvos has not been here recently. He steps in and inspects the area near the computer. Footsteps behind inform him others are following his lead. There are postcards, bills, other scraps of paper. Nothing looks out of the ordinary. Kalvos has been prepared.

He turns to one of the men. They will need the neighbours. Go and collect them. They will need witnesses to flesh out Kalvos' lifestyle: when he comes home, where he works, who his friends are. That sort of thing.

The man nods and is gone.

The inspector re-enters the main hallway, calls out to anyone who is listening. He wants the men to start looking in the most improbable places. Behind the frames of pictures, under the carpets—even under the floor boards. Search everywhere.

Everywhere? Nahas repeats, striding up to him, a lap top in his hands.

Everywhere. Rip the place apart.

His men are only too happy to oblige.

Time passes. Crawls by interminably. Seconds, then minutes, an hour. It is methodical work, but it is slow going.

A shorter officer taps him on the shoulder. He turns roughly, and the man gestures to the front door. They have some neighbours.

Good, he answers. Find out what they know.

The man departs, another already taking his place, racing up out of breath, his forehead swathed in sweat. He has found something.

A number of officers are gathered around the stairs, flashlights in hand. What is it? Wasem asks them all at once. The man who has brought him gestures to a small storage compartment at the foot of the stairs. The compartment has been covered with flooring and latched, but all this has been removed now. A carpet lays close by; evidently Kalvos had hoped to further conceal the cubicle with it. The opening is large enough for a man to enter and seems to be only a few feet deep.

So what? Wasem barks. A tiny storage compartment. So?

No, sir, the sweating officer replies. It is much more. Look.

He reaches down and knocks on the floor of the compartment. A surprisingly unhealthy sound is produced. It is a hollow floor. There's something under it.

They need to get down there and have a look, he growls. He signals to the man to climb down.

The officer, young, agile, and thin, has little difficultly manoeuvring himself into the cavity. He slides the floor board aside with his foot, spreads his legs, reaches down into the black pit beneath, one hand above to keep his balance. Several flashlights gloss the walls beyond him, and he spies a hidden staircase. He glances up. He is going down to see where it leads to.

He moves down without awaiting Wasem's orders, and within seconds, the entire space lights up: he's found a light on the ceiling. Wasem and the others peer down, and they can see a small room with shelves filled with boxes. The officer pulls one off and skims through it. It doesn't take him long before he proudly confirms the words Wasem has been waiting hours to hear.

Jackpot.

And then Wasem is a ravenous carnivore eyeing morsels of evidence. Everything is here: photos of contract hits, phone numbers, email addresses, off shore account information, passports, disguises.

Wasem watches Nahas shuffle through a series of passports in his hands. Egyptian, Emirati, Spanish, French, Algerian, British.

He gets around.

Look at all these aliases, Nahas says. And look: pictures inserted within some of these.

Wasem gazes at the photos within. Men. He knows who they are. His victims.

He's more careless than I imagined.

He turns his attention to dozens of cardboard boxes judiciously arranged along one wall. David Trent's name has been clearly scribbled on the surface of one. Other names on other boxes. More and more evidence. It is almost too easy, as if Kalvos wants to be caught. He orders the boxes airlifted from the basement. A number of cold cases are about to be solved. He glances back and sees Nahas probing the Trent file.

Garrett Seldon, Nahas muses, staring at what appears to be a detailed list of phone conversations. This must be the one who hired Kalvos. Here's his phone number. Look: he's scratched some notes here in the margin. Months of pre-assassination contact. Killing Trent was important.

Wasem brushes a few more papers aside, lingers on a set of photos below them. They appear to be of ancient ruins somewhere.

What have you got there?

More snapshots of Kalvos' journeys, I suppose. He holds them up. The remnants of a structure long-since destroyed by time and sand. Do you know what this is?

Nahas studies the photos closely for a number of seconds. He nods. I think it's the Amarna ruins.

Of what, specifically?

Beats me. Let's ask our recent university grad.

Ramzy springs eagerly to his feet, and Wasem shoves the photos in his face.

We need your insight.

Within seconds, Ramzy recognises the location. They're right. This is Akhetaten, specifically the ruins of the Temple of Aten. He studies the other photos. All from the same sight.

Wasem sorts through another series of snapshots. These are different. Not victims, not sites. Kalvos in his youth, Kalvos playing soccer, Kalvos selling souvenirs in front of the Great Pyramid.

And then a certain photo catches his attention. Faded in colour, scuffed at the edges. Kalvos and another man standing side by side, posing, neither smiling. An older Kalvos, likely in his twenties. Behind them is the unmistakable Cairo Opera House. For whatever reason, he suddenly remembers that famous building's inauguration. 1988. A big deal when it opened. One of Gezira Island's star tourist attractions. He has always been good with dates.

He stares at the two young men.

And then he understands everything.

Headlights disrupt the darkness of the pre-dawn desert highway, beady little beams in a blizzard of dust and grime. Although the Egyptian drivers can see little, clearly they know the way. And they know how to handle desert driving. That is good enough for Vannevar Denison, who observes the car's rays slicing through the blanketing dust. With one hand on his cell phone, he speaks to Bowles on the other end.

How's our guest?

"Very quiet in there. Sleeping like a baby, I suspect."

Good.

Contented, he hangs up.

Although Egypt is a land of endless desert, lakes do materialise, oasis-like, from the midst of nowhere. One of these, located less than a hundred kilometres south of Cairo, is Lake Qarun. Qarun is part of the fertile Faiyum Oasis. The city of Faiyum, with a population of over 300 000, is just south of the 42 kilometre-long, 9 kilometre-wide lake. Several other towns are located on the south shore of Qarun, as it is here alone that life flourishes; to the north is undisturbed desert. The tiny, shallow lake, while itself an anomaly in a sea of sand, contains a single island, Golden Horn Island. Completely uninhabited, this tiny patch of sand is more an enclosed sandbar than anything else. It is this island that Denison intends to see.

As his driver persists on the Cairo-El-Faroum Desert Road, he spots intermittent light from various settlements on the south shore of the lake. These habitations swell as the car nears. The driver then veers east onto Zawyet Al Kerdaseya. Here the road snakes to the west, water on one side, lush plantations and palm trees on the other. Denison observes houses, boats, weeds. Beyond that, the shallow waters of Qarun, and further still, to the north, the desert. The Egypt few foreigners ever see. Likely that is why it had been chosen.

They pass several houses. Even in the lateness of the hour, locals are out, lounging on lawn chairs or front steps, chatting incoherently. Ahead, two men squat near the water's edge, nonchalant discussion audible between them. A single light post illumines them. The convoy of brand new black Toyota Sequoias stops here.

Denison surveys the two men. They are garbed in shorts and t-shirts; local fishermen, he guesses. There were several boats close by, arranged, of course, for his benefit. These men are hired guides to the island.

Sanderson emerges from the Sequoia's rear seat. He motions to his driver, who also withdraws from the car, immediately engaging in discussion with the two locals. He then drifts to his superior. "This has been arranged by Egyptian Homeland Security?" he mumbles.

Denison nods.

They'll ferry us across the lake to the island.

"I don't like the looks of them."

It doesn't really matter.

"And can we expect the same cooperation at Giza?"

Absolutely.

At length, the driver gestures to a metallic red motorboat. "They will take you now, sir."

They pile in, and the pilot heaves the motor to life. Within seconds, they are jetting across the darkened waters to Golden Horn Island. All is darkness save for the tiny light on the bow of the little boat, a single eye peering into obscurity. Denison squints as water deflects into his eyes. He can hear a second boat behind them. In the minimal light, it is clear they are arching westward around the island. The shadow of the north shore looms beyond, shrouded in mystery. There, yonder, is the epitome of every adventure film or book he's ever come across: unmolested desert, travelling Bedouins, a host of scorpions. And no water.

The boats slow and gallop onto the shoreline a short distance, and he and his men eject themselves at once, simultaneously withdrawing flashlights. Within seconds, several separate beams carve mosaics into the sand. Not far ahead, is a boat house. *The* boat house. The one the assassin had suggested to Garrett Seldon. Before everything had gone to hell. Denison gazes out at the forbidding north shore. The Egyptian had been right to suggest such a place. Away from prying eyes.

It is just as the assassin had said: dilapidated from prolonged abandonment. And yet it has remained within full view of the south shore, all these apparent years. Strange how one takes such things for granted: whoever could have guessed what treasure is buried within its walls?

The abode contains two windows, one on either side of the main entrance. A welcoming little face. Denison opens what barely passes as the front door, notices that it scarcely clings to the wall from which it is screwed. He shines his light inside, soon joined by the others. A single room, complete with an uncovered bed frame and mattress, a table with two chairs, an old oven, shelves fastened into the panelled walls. The bare mattress sags in the centre. The table teeters to one side. The shelves are largely bare, save for old newspapers and a box of fishing lines and hooks. Other than that, the house is deserted.

Let's find what we came for.

Someone translates, and several accompanying Egyptians begin stripping the lodge down: the legs from the table are ripped clear, the mattress on the bed tossed away and shredded, the shelves torn away. The dissection produces instant chaos.

Disinclined to lend a hand, he steps out into the desert night, places his hands in his pockets, breathes out. He can see his breath: desert at night.

Minutes pass, and a sickening groan echoes from within. Someone has turned to the floor boards and is suddenly rupturing them from their fastenings. Sledgehammers are tearing into the building's walls. One thing has become transparent with each passing moment: the assassin did his job well.

Then all grows quiet inside. Denison turns, halts at Sanderson's emerging form. There is no longer any door, it having been wrenched from its hinges.

I don't like that expression.

"You're going to like what I have to say even less. It isn't here."

For a moment, Denison is speechless, motionless. Then he begins to nod calmly, composing himself against the rage that is building within.

Are you sure?

"There's no way we missed it. This cabin isn't big enough to hide anything. It isn't here."

He steps past, preferring his own visual. Within is nothing short of a war zone. The panelling has been hewn from the walls, exhibiting only the foundation. The Egyptians saunter past him. He glances skyward and wants to bellow at the top of his lungs, wants to act out of character for just a few precious seconds. Because he is a character, he thinks, one simple character in an unfolding story. One can never truly know what awaits on the other side of a page. And this page been turned. The great beyond has been more than he could have predicted.

He composes himself, draws in several deep breaths. Appreciative oxygen gushing to his brain calms his nerves. He straightens his tailored blazer, adjusts his open collar.

I suppose this wasn't completely unexpected. There was always a chance this might happen.

The Egyptians are murmuring amongst themselves, and he glances at the one who had translated before, the same man who has driven him here.

What are they saying?

The man shrugs, a cigarette in hand. "They are saying that no one come to this island today. They are out here fishing during the day, and they live along the shore, so they tell me they know if someone come here. No one come here today."

Denison guffaws. Surely plenty of people come to this island every day.

"I think not. No one comes here."

And why is that?

The man takes a drag of his cigarette and gestures to the enveloping darkness. "Look. There is here nothing."

Agreed. Are they certain?

"They are."

And what about yesterday?

The driver shakes his head. "You do not understand. No one comes to this island *ever*. Years, I think."

That's impossible. He could have come in the night, for God's sake.

He sees that the translator disagrees.

No? How do you know? What, do you people just sit around staring out here all day and night? He hid the thing here. He told Seldon. Seldon made sure of it.

Sanderson apprises him anxiously. "Did he, sir? I mean, without Seldon actually being here to witness it, how could he be really sure?"

Denison can feel the rage again.

No. If there's one thing I can say about that prick, he was thorough. He said he took the necessary steps to ensure the artefact was buried here.

"Well, clearly that wasn't the case."

He pauses. What exactly have those necessary steps been? Then it becomes clear: Seldon had simply taken the assassin's word for it. This is what that idiot was trying to tell him. Now he understands. And while he was able to shrug off the possibility of a double-cross at the time, now he seethes. Now he realises how much he hates to lose.

All this time, the thing has been in some other location.

"I think it's a more probable explanation. Sir, these men are locals. They say nobody comes here. You've been deceived."

That son of a bitch lied to me.

He fails to grasp the irony of his own words. He begins to pace, his shoes mining miniature craters in the sand.

It could be anywhere.

Silence permeates for several seconds. Then Sanderson speaks.

"What now?"

He's still here.

"In Egypt?"

And I can tell you why: because I'm here.

"I don't understand."

He knew I'd come down here. He's toying with me.

He pulls out his cell phone, dials a number. And then a curious thing happens. Vannevar Denison begins speaking to someone in fluent German.

The summoned lays on the bed, surfing the waves of useless television for anything in his language. There are few options. He settles on CNN for a while. Within minutes, there is a story of new protests in Cairo. Massive demonstrations in a city square somewhere. He shrugs, stands to stretch his legs. He ambles over to the window, parts the dark blinds. Opens the sliding door, steps onto his balcony.

He is very high up; both a cool breeze and lights from neighbouring buildings below confirm this. The Nile is a black chasm, almost invisible between the city's banks. But there are boats upon it, flickering beacons that validate its existence. He gazes below. There is an elegant swimming pool, elegantly illuminated for those who choose to swim at night. The monstrous Cairo Sporting Club and its much larger twin pools is just beyond. Further still are the illuminated domes of the Opera House. Much closer is the Le Deck restaurant, anchored slightly away from the island. The pyramids are out there, too. Even at this hour, their strobe-lit façades are visible. He assumes they are easier to spot at night than during the day, when the smog conceals their identity.

He should be angry, forced here against his will, away from his companions. He should be, but he is not. He is calm. Strangely so. It is as if he knows all will turn out well, that he will see those others again. That he will learn the secret of the pyramid.

He studies the other balconies. Each room is situated directly under the one above via these enclosures. One could, if one so wished, climb down. He has had some limited experience with rock climbing before, but here he would have no equipment. Yet it might be done, as absurdly dangerous as that would be.

He retreats, closes the blinds, returns to the bed, turns off the television, the lamps. Nothing to do but sleep. If he can.

He cannot. He re-emerges on the balcony.

It is largely suicidal, he assumes, to climb. There is a reason people don't scale the outer walls of hotels. He estimates he is on the 25th floor, only two levels from the top. Further evidence that this is bad idea. He could so easily fall and die. But that nagging suspicion takes hold once again, the one that intuitively hints that all will be well.

Climb.

It is like a voice he hears, yet no one and no thing has spoken. And yet, he has heard it. In his mind. Something has spoken to him. Something oozing with confidence.

He breathes once, twice, full invigorating breaths. Yes, he is going to do this. He gazes over at the balcony immediately opposite to gauge the distance between it and its cousin directly below. If he stays calm, plants his feet carefully, this is not impossible. People jump from outer space, tightrope walk over Niagara Falls. Surely he can do this.

But those people are professionals.

It doesn't matter.

He tests the distance between the railing's concrete spindles. There is enough space to wedge his toes through, but not his whole foot. What he will have to do is lower himself, then hang from the concrete podium of his balcony and direct his feet onto the railing of the one below. Then jump down onto concrete. How hard can that be? He won't have to worry about wedging his feet.

He dangles one leg out over the concrete fencing, retracts it, breathing emphatically. Ridiculous, ridiculous, ridiculous. He swings the leg over again, looks down, shudders. In the future, it is best not to look down. He lowers his leg, sandwiches his toes themselves between two bars. He cannot touch the balcony floor. He will have to hurdle his other leg over, slide his other toes down.

He brings his second leg over, and his hands grasp the top of the railing with all his strength. He is hanging off the 25th floor of the Sofitel Hotel balcony, overlooking the southern tip of Gezira Island. The breeze is uncomfortably strong. He breathes in, reaches down with his foot. It is like entering a swimming pool backwards. If only it were that easy. He moves his hands from the top of the railing, grasps the bars, untucks his toes, gently begins to lower himself. He feels himself slipping. Adrenaline gushes through his veins as he clutches the spindles. Slowly. His balcony floor is at his thighs, then his waist, then his chest. Then he can go little further. He reaches out with his feet, blindly searching for the railing underneath. Finally, he finds it. He sighs. He has done it.

He stops and thinks. How is he going to do this? He will not have anything to hold onto once he lowers himself to the next balcony. He will surely fall.

Maybe not. If he angles his legs inward and inside the railing below, then he will simply have to let go and slide onto the balcony below. He cannot fall if his legs are already inside the balcony's enclosure. Logic dictates this.

He inches down, breathes once again, and releases his hands. He is in free fall, but only for a millisecond. He lands with a thud onto the balcony below. He glances immediately at the doors of the room and sees that the blinds are drawn—he has not disturbed the visitors within. Something else he should have considered. What time is it, anyway? Late, but he didn't bother to check before he left. Hopefully most people are asleep.

He prepares for his next descent. Legs draped over, toes between spindles, hands on the bars, then the gentle lowering. This isn't so hard. He finds the railing beneath, angles his feet inside, lowers his hands onto the bars, slides down, releases. He has done it again.

Something is happening. Internally, he should be panicking, but he feels reassured. It is as if something is watching out for him, protecting him, guaranteeing this maniacal descent is logical.

Something flutters nearby. He pauses. Here, beside him as he scales the outer wall of the hotel, is a butterfly. Through the dim light, he can see little. He cannot know that it is a Plain Tiger, coloured and patterned similarly to the Monarch that he watched only days ago back in London. It rests on the nearby railing, seemingly watching him, curious by his movements. He regards it for a moment, then he must move on. The creature remains where it is, shrouded in shadow, undisturbed by the sights and sounds of Cairo by night.

He starts planning ahead: how will he get himself down to street level? After all, the hotel's cylindrical body is not attached to the ground; it is fastened to a collection of large, rectangular buildings. As he moves lower, however, he sees that it might be possible to jump into the pool from the top of the nearest building. At least from this vantage point. Once he gets closer, he may reconsider the action. He may hurt himself. Hurt himself? Why does that worry him? He's scaling the side of a hotel!

By the time he conquers his tenth floor, he has gained supreme confidence. What a story he will have to tell people back home. He continues, contemplating his next action. He will have to make his way back to the Newmerryland Villa. From there, he can reunite with Lauren and the professor. And yet, he senses something. He has felt it before. Back home, in his house, when all was numbers and triangles. And just now, too, when he was meandering down the wall of the hotel. That voice, if he can call it that. It beckons to him now. He turns and gazes at the pyramids.

Why go there? It's ridiculous to go there. I need to get to Newmerryland.
Why did you come, then?
Come? To Egypt?
You came for answers. You must go west. West to the pyramid.

Minutes fly by. He reaches the final balcony, leaps the short distance onto the roof of the building below, creeps towards the pool. From this vantage point, the pool appears as an extension of the river. Albeit of a different hue, it is elegantly T-shaped and seductively lit. It appears deserted.

He jumps, lands in what he hopes is the deep end. He immediately sinks to the bottom, and his buttocks impact on concrete. It stings, but he ignores the pain and propels himself upward. He breaks the water, rubs his eyes, searches for a ladder. There are several to choose from. He climbs, now blackening the deck with dripping water. He has done it: he is on ground level. He stares up the tubular hotel tower. There is his room. Up there. *Way* up there. He can't believe he climbed all that way.

He steps to the edge of the pool patio. There is a short hedge. Beyond that, a smallish patch of grass and trees. Then a drop to a sort of concrete trim that spans the entire complex. Beyond that is the mighty Nile. But the concrete doesn't run the full length of the river; it concludes further up. He will have to inch his way along a narrow precipice connected to one of the buildings further along. He cannot see much beyond this.

He moves purposefully, confidently. Again the voice calls to him, compelling him to the pyramids. He wants to block it out, but he knows he cannot. He knows the Giza Plateau is where his journey will end this night.

He arrives at the termination of the ledge, sees that he is in luck. Of sorts. The precipice ends, but he can jump down into what appears to be a restaurant patio. But first, he must circumnavigate a fence.

The patio is deserted, unlit. Apparently bar hours are over. He steps onto the railing, drops down, recomposes himself amongst rounded tables, moves past, down to the opposite end of the patio. Another fence. He scales it, lowers himself onto pavement. There is a short flight of stairs upward, and he climbs them to freedom.

He strides past the building to which the patio is attached. Here is Montazah Al Giza, the road his limousine travelled hours ago. It will wind to the north, pass under the Al Galaa Bridge. How does he know this? Regardless, somehow he knows. That bridge is where he's going.

He travels along the road, continuing to drip. Cars drive past intermittently. The road is exceedingly well lit. Locals and tourists pass by, and he can smell alcohol. The air is also heavy with cigarette smoke and exhaust. At times, the steady pulsing rhythm of bass pounds against his chest; Middle Eastern house and techno music. He surmises that such is no better here than back home.

He lingers when the bridge is almost directly above him. There is a ramp that leads up. He takes it, his legs immediately weighted down by the abrupt climb. He can see the Cairo Tower far ahead, a myriad of bluish light in ascending rows, then a short horizontal white light, then the vertical luminance of its spire. Beautiful here at night with so much of it given way to darkness.

It takes only a few minutes to traverse the bridge, and he is back onto level ground again. He is now on the west side of the river, and he knows he has an interminable distance to go. This city is massive.

But luck is on his side. A horn blows behind him, and he turns and sees a yellow and black bumblebee-like toktok buzzing his way. The vehicle slows, and a young man behind the wheel is smiling, white teeth glaring out in the night.

Hello, sir. Where you heading?

West.

Where west?

All the way west.

To the pyramids? They are closed now; you can't see them at this hour.

In that direction anyway.

Would you like a ride?

I'd love one. But I have a small problem: I have no money.

The driver vacillates. Then he grins.

No problem. I on my way home. I live that way. I take you as far as my house. Alright?

Providence has smiled on him again. Or something else.

He settles into the toktok's rear bench, and the driver handles the tiny wheel. The vehicle has no doors, and its little motor spews something awful out an exhaust pipe.

They travel along King Faisal Street, notoriously busy during the day. Traffic at this hour is sporadic. So is their conversation. Time passes, and the summoned finds himself lulled to sleep.

He awakens several minutes later as the toktok abruptly halts. They are surrounded by hotels and apartments. The pyramids loom. He has made it.

This is Al Remaia, the driver explains. Follow this road down and around. You will come to a beautiful hotel. Across from it are the pyramids. Good luck.

Such generosity. How can he repay the man, who is not wealthy but has given his time and energy to help a traveller for free? He cannot, he tells himself. All he can do is appreciate a simple ride.

He has traversed several kilometres to be here. Here, where he is so close.

He takes his time navigating around the hotel the driver mentioned. As he passes its front entrance, he reads the name: Le Méridien Pyramids. The driver was right: it is beautiful. He wonders what it must be like to stay here, essentially across the street from the most heavenly structures on Earth.

Although the Great Pyramid looms in all its early-morning lustre, getting to it will not be easy. There are fences and roads. And guards, he notices as he approaches. Men in uniform: white pants, black tops and berets. These are the Tourism and Antiquities Police. The Plateau is thick with them. Many stride on camelback. He is surprised to see that they are armed: machine guns slung over shoulders or hung from mounts. This makes him uncomfortable. But the Plateau is simply staggering in size, and they rhythmically disappear into the night. There must be gaps in their patrols.

He waits until a camel disappears, then saunters forward. He is entering the desert of the Giza Plateau. The instant his first foot touches the soft sand, he is overcome by a pulsating sensation similar to what he felt at Tanis. He cannot explain it except to say that he feels *alive*. Completely alive, for the first time in his life, perhaps.

The Great Pyramid looms ahead. Its sheer size eradicates everything in its vicinity. Except the night. Had he the time, he would simply stop and stare.

Another rider approaches, and he sprints forward. Soon he is up against a massive stone that once belonged to the pyramid but now lies discarded a short distance away. He touches it. He is touching the pyramid. His body palpitates again, reassurance that he is in the right place. He gallops and comes up against the first row of stones. Casing stones, evident by their smooth sides. He tilts his head back. He cannot even see to the top of the structure. Absolutely breathtaking. He runs his hand over the stone. Amazingly smooth after all these centuries.

He will climb a short distance, creep into the shadows, then sleep the remainder of the night away. Then morning will come. What will it bring? He cannot know. Regardless, he has been drawn here. Let fate decide his future.

He grips the first casing stone, heaves himself upward. Not so long ago, he was dropping down; in any event, rising is much easier and far less stressful, and he ascends a short distance with minimal exertion. He glances back and sees a handful of officers in his vicinity, some on camel back, some on foot. Flashlights scan vacuous shadows spawned by the pavilion's artificial light. He moves along a row of stones, into further darkness, and he begins to shiver. He is uncomfortable. Some things never change.

There is a rustling not far ahead. Someone else is there. He contemplates his next action. Move on? Yes, that is surely wise. But he can't go back, as the officers on the ground will spot him. He can climb, he supposes, and prepares to do so. Then he hears something he cannot believe: his name. He peers out into the darkness, glimpses the form of a figure but nothing more. Who is this that knows him? Out here?

Yet sure enough, the man is calling to him.

"Over here."

Against his better judgement, he moves toward the voice. In a matter of seconds, he realises he does know this man. The plump chap from the limousine. Pouty face.

"I can't believe it," the man is saying. "How did you do it?"

I climbed.

You *climbed*?

Why are you here? Shouldn't you be back at the hotel?

"I have much to answer for. Tomorrow, I plan to give myself up."

Why not do it now? The place is crawling with cops.

"Those aren't cops."

They sure look like cops.

"No, tomorrow there will be more official personnel here. I plan to surrender to them."

More official personnel? How do you know?

"I know."

Just like you all knew everything else. How?

"The professor's clothes were bugged."

When? Where?

"Before you even left Canada. The man we sent—he's very good. We've been listening in on your conversations. Every time you spoke in the professor's company, we heard you."

What will Denison do if he finds you?

Seldon does not answer.

I could wring your pudgy little neck right here and save you the trouble. He says this in spite of himself; he has never wrung anyone's neck before.

"Well I deserve it."

So, what—you've had a change of heart?

"This wasn't what I signed up for. Denison has plans for you."

I am aware.

"How did you do it?"

I climbed.

"So you said. Climbed what?"

The wall of the hotel.

"You climbed *down*?"

Yes. Went out on the balcony, climbed down.

He says it as though it is old hat. And Seldon, clearly in shock, delays before speaking again.

"I see. But why come here? This is the last place you should want to go."

I know. But something…I can't explain it, but I just had to come here; I *need* to be here.

"He will seal off the city. Highways, the airport—he has the power to do it. He will tear this city apart looking for you."

That doesn't concern me. I'm where I need to be.

He extends his hands, views them in the dim light, imagines them pulsating.

That's all there is to it.

✱

Wasem is able to pocket the photo easily enough. The investigation still underway, he excuses himself, retreats outside, ponders the exigencies of the situation. He hears someone behind him, and he knows it is Ramzy. He looks to see if anyone else is with the officer, mumbles under his breath before Ramzy has a chance.

I'm getting out of here.

"You're what?"

I need to leave.

Ramzy regards him with incredulity. "The investigation's still going on. They're uncovering so much in there."

He pats his jacket.

I have evidence, too.

The youngster struggles to understand. He turns and stares at the house for several seconds, then oscillates back to the inspector. "I don't get it. This was your big moment. You should be happy."

Certainly. But if I stay here, I'm dead.

"Dead?"

I don't have time to explain. Either you're with me, or you're not.

"Are you in trouble? From who?"

Nahas appears angelically at the doorway. The illumination from within mimics his outline. "Hondo?" he says from afar. "Everything okay?"

Wasem has taken to sitting on the front steps, and he waves his fellow inspector away without looking up.

Something I ate.

Ramzy glances back at Nahas, wondering if he understands. But his words indicate otherwise. "You need to be in there."

I'm gonna turn in for the night. You can take it from here.

He stands, prepares to depart.

What surprises him is what happens next. Inspector Nahas turns and simply walks back into the house. Through the doorway, Wasem can see him pull out his cell phone, and within seconds, he is speaking to someone on the other end. There is something markedly irregular about his reaction.

That same irregularity satisfies Ramzy. He scampers off after Wasem.

The big man is moving as quickly as his gait will allow. One leg drags awkwardly. He looks to be in such pain. He half turns as he traipses.

"What was that all about?" Ramzy wants to know as he keeps pace. He watches the streetlights playfully reveal part, and then all, of Wasem's bloated face. Part, and then all.

Anyone following us?

"I don't see anyone. What's this all about?"

Without stopping, Wasem reaches into his breast pocket and withdraws the photograph.

You look, I'll navigate.

"I'm looking."

And what do you see?

"I see two men in front of the Opera House. The one guy looks an awful lot like Kalvos."

And the other?

"He looks familiar, but I can't place him."

You just saw him.

An alarm suddenly ululates in Ramzy's head. He looks again. Yes, he knows the man in the photo. But he can't believe it. "Inspector Nahas? But how is that possible? Nahas works for the force. Kalvos is…" He struggles to understand. "It doesn't make sense."

Yes, it does.

So much makes sense now. That conversation between himself and Nahas when they approached the murder scene. The parking lot.

It's starting to add up.

"What is?"

Nahas is in on it, and I think Deeb is, too.

"The brigadier?" Ramzy laughs alongside him. "Are you out of your mind?"

Just a hunch.

"You're going to need more than a hunch to prove that."

Wasem scans the street around them.

We're going to have company.

The inspector stops. Already, there, across the street, a black car pulls to the curb, and two men step from it. Thirty somethings, athletic, both moustached, dressed in jeans and windbreakers, one blue and one green. They are looking straight at him.

The inspector gestures to an upcoming intersection. There, pedestrian traffic is noticeably enhanced, even at this late hour.

There. We'll separate when we hit that crowd.

"And then what?"

Then you get on your phone and you call someone other than Deeb. Then you go into hiding.

He crosses the street, Ramzy attached at his hip. The men continue to follow unconcernedly.

I'll contact you when I get a chance.

Ramzy wants to say something else, but Wasem is suddenly turning and crossing back to the original side of the street, leaving him alone. It doesn't take the youngster long to realise what he needs to do. He runs.

At first, the pursuers are confused. Then they likewise separate, one tailing Wasem to the other side of the street, the other breaking into a jog, quickly morphing into a sprint, after the rapidly vanishing Ramzy.

Wasem watches as Ramzy fuses with the motley collection of pedestrians. He admires the youngster's agility, his athleticism. He quickens his own pace, but he knows his limitations, knows that the man behind him is closing the gap between them, will catch him eventually. Something tells him to keep walking. Plenty of people around; nothing will happen in public. There is safety in numbers. All he needs to do is endure.

At the southern edge of Gezira is the island's only subway stop, Gezira Station. Permanently congested, he might lose the man in there, buy a ticket to another part of the city where he can collect himself, lay low, plan his next move. Of course, his pursuer could attack him on the train; there is always that possibility. Regardless, for now, it's best not to give any opportunities. As long as he stays with a crowd, he decides, he is safe.

Therefore, the subway it is. Now all he has to do is walk the dozens of blocks south in order to get there. As long as his heart doesn't give out, he might make it.

He moves along the eastern edge of the island, past the awe-inspiring Marriot Hotel, the former Gezirah Palace. The hotel is just south of the first of the three major bridges that intersect the island and thus link Gezira with the rest of the city—the 15th May Bridge.

From a bird's eye view, Gezira is unusual: its northern tip is dominated by high rises and posh shopping districts; in its centre, lush greenery dominates. This area is part of the Gezira Sporting Club, a multi-use park which houses an 18-hole golf course, tennis facilities, a running track, swimming pools, and a soccer training field. The south end of the island, where the subway station is located, morphs once again into a collection of hotels and apartments.

A night on the streets of Zamalek is always an interesting experience: naturally, Egyptians en masse can be spotted strolling the avenues, but the tourists can also be seen. They arrive in droves to inhabit the bars, the restaurants, the shops. Dwindled drovers these days, unfortunately. This is the one part of the city, apart from the sights of Giza, where foreigners are substantially evident. The inspector listens to the collection of intermingling discussions that drift past like cigarette smoke: English, French, Italian, Greek, Russian, Japanese, Mandarin, Korean, Spanish, German.

He works his way along Mohammed Mazhar, then west onto El-Fardous, and finally south again on Aziz Abaza. Passing under the May 15 Bridge, the hulking Marriott levitates into view on his right. The road transforms to Mohammed Abd El-Wahab, then again to El-Khalig much further south. Here he knows it will bank sharply to the west and culminate with the intersection of Al Gezira and El Andalus. He will then continue south on Al Gezira until he comes to the roundabout known as Opera Square, just east of the famous Cairo Opera House. Finally, he will arc west onto El Tahrir as it emerges from the roundabout, and the station will be on his left across the street from the opera house. How long will this journey take? He doesn't want to guess.

Commotion ahead. A protest. More people voicing their support for the Muslim Brotherhood. This is old news; Morsi has been out of power for some time now. But his supporters remain. There has been disapproval of the new government, and of Morsi's ousting, and lately the violence has increased. Not like it was been before, and even that was overhyped in the West. Egypt is still a safe country. He would bank his reputation on it. Mistakes were been made during the Arab Spring: people died. That had been a mistake. In the country's fringe territories, admittedly, there has been more clashing between protesters and government. But here, in Cairo, where protests ensue, things are generally fine. There is nothing immoral about protests so long as they are peaceful. These people want Morsi back. With some protests, the military has intervened, and things have escalated. People need to be allowed to speak their mind, even if one doesn't agree with what they have to say. This, he believes, is what is at the heart of democracy. One cannot call in the military every time citizens congregate. Dissatisfaction continues, even with Mubarak long gone. Now Morsi is out, and still there is dissatisfaction. Had life been better before? No, certainly not. Is life perfect now? No, certainly not. This must also be what democracy feels like.

Bring them on, he breathes, sensing the diversion in the late night activists. Men and women are marching up and down the sidewalks, flags in hand. Tourists are stopping to take pictures. There are the police, standing at the ready. A difficult position to be in, with so many foreign observers. They hadn't acted quite this way during the Arab Spring in Tahrir Square.

He melts into the campaigners, crouching low and passing amongst them with surprising ease. He offers no resistance to their voices, and no one seems inclined to retaliate for his interruption. His gait brushes several onto the busy avenue, all the while cars speed past. Some honk. Some have their windows open, shouting obscenities. Words his mother would not have approved of. But he does. Cursing in Arabic is such fun. He listens to their individual pleas. They communicate independently, but they speak as one. He can remember when protests like these were unheard of. He likes what he sees.

He cannot discern his pursuer: flags and animated protesters block his vision. The man must be there, though. He forges on, and then, just like that, he is out of the crowd. The people are moving north; he is heading south. His cover blown, he turns and sees that the man is in fact there.

He can feel perspiration begin to drip down his face, his sides. First in droplets, then in torrents. He knows he is beginning to panic. His heart is pounding warnings in his chest. He needs to stop, to rest. He wonders amusingly, despite his inner fear, how much weight he stands to lose tonight if he keeps up this pace.

Gezira Station is one of 57 that comprise the Cairo Metro. The Metro itself has three lines that intersect the city —identified on maps by the colours red, yellow, and green—but there are plans for more. The oldest, the red, was opened in the late 1980s. The system itself is one of only two on the entire continent of Africa. The other is in Algiers. Gezira Station arises from the asphalt on the busy southern highway known as El Tahrir, a staircase descending into the bowels of the city fringed with a large sign in both Arabic and English. The red "M" on the sign indicates "subway."

Wasem reaches out and grips the station's handrail on the right hand side, clumsily clambers down the flight of steps. Artificial light from below screams out at him, and his eyes readjust from the lamp light that has guided him thus far.

He considers his options. For whatever reason, west appeals to him. His home is to the west, only a single stop away. But he cannot go home. Past home, then. Across the Nile, towards the pyramids. Plenty of desert out there, plenty of darkness to hide in at this hour.

He heads for the automated vendor line up, turns, and stares straight at the man behind him. Two women in burqas separate them. He smiles. The man does not return the gesture.

He sidles up to the machine, inserts his money, grabs the ticket. He steps away, strides casually past, assuming he is being watched all the way. The man will be able to see which boarding platform he is heading for—there is no avoiding that.

He waddles towards the western platform, joining a throng of domestic as well as foreign pedestrians. He considers the possibility of shaking off his pursuer right here and now: dart into one train, walk through, exit. Just like in the movies. He glances back. The man has not yet arrived. He stares down the tunnel, willing the train to arrive. The wait is inexorable.

And then the train is rolling into the station. Pneumatic breaks screech, releasing air and grinding it to a stop. He exhales thankfully, watches as several people rush towards the waiting transport. His assailant is among them.

The doors open, and the train's occupants emerge. He waits patiently in line behind several others, then steps in. He can sense his pursuer is several compressed people behind, a matter of a few metres at best. He listens for the warning bell, which will ring approximately five seconds before the doors close and seal automatically. This will be his opportunity.

People are still getting on. He listens. There, finally, he hears it. Five seconds. He leaps forward, bowling travellers out of his way, passes between the opposite doors. They close a second later. He turns, now on the other side of the tracks, realises his ruse has worked: his pursuer, hopelessly positioned behind several others, has not anticipated such a manoeuvre and is trapped on the train. There is nothing left for him to do but reach for his phone. Who is he calling? Nahas? Deeb? Someone else, perhaps? It doesn't immediately matter. His mistake has bought the inspector some time. That's all that counts.

The train is off, and the pursuer is sucked along with it, through the tunnel and out of range. Wasem begins to breath more slowly. He is still going west; that hasn't changed. He waits, and within a few minutes, amid a freshly-filled platform, he sees a new train barrelling through the tunnel. He waits for those occupants seeking the pleasures of Zamalek to exit, then boards.

Almost immediately, he settles into an empty seat and slumps back exhaustedly. His cell phone is ringing. Nahas. He decides to answer.

You bugged my phone, didn't you?

"We've been listening, yes."

Those two you had trailing us didn't do so well.

"You can't run forever."

It is obvious, he surmises with a slight and surprisingly positive heart palpitation, that Ramzy has not been apprehended either. He relishes the small victory.

I have an idea: why don't you turn yourself in at the nearest station of your convenience, and I'll drop by and see you there.

"I think we both know that's not going to happen, Hondo."

Think about your family. Have you considered them?

"That's exactly why I'm doing this."

Clearly they are on different wave lengths.

I have evidence. You and Kalvos, together in that photo. And your virtual admission to sending those two twits after us. That's plenty to start with.

"Oh, the photograph. So that's what it is. That's easy enough to explain. You don't really have anything there. A couple of Copts in their youth, that's about it. There is so much you don't understand."

I'm working on it.

"I just hope it won't be too late."

Silence.
The law is on my side, Nahas. I'll find you.
"You have no idea who you're dealing with."
I think I can handle Deeb.
"Deeb?" Nahas is laughing. "No, I don't think you get it."
Why'd you do it, Nahas?
"We're under attack, Hondo. Just like we were all those centuries ago. One person tried to change things. He paid for his actions."
Trent?
"No. Centuries ago, I said. I'm talking about someone else."
Who?
"The heretic."
What the hell are you on about?
"When his son came to the throne, he restored all. He gave my ancestors back their prominence."
Your ancestors?
"But it isn't so much Tutankhamun we appreciate. Unto Horemheb we bestow our loyalty. It was he, as a general and advisor, who suggested Tutankhamun restore my ancestors to their former greatness."
What ancestors? What are you on about? You're a Copt, Nahas.
"A useful cover all these years. In those days, we were known as the Hanuti."
The inspector scans his sense of history. It is a speedy probe.
You mean those idiots we passed on the street corner last week, on the way to the murder scene?
"They are far from that. We are their descendants."
And then the portly investigator remembers Nahas' lingering stare that day as they passed the oddly-adorned men on the corner. And he remembers Nahas defending their right to exist. Now it makes sense.
Maybe you should join them.
Maybe I should.
"The heretic banned the Hanuti. Because of Horemheb, we live again. And our powers are growing."
Maybe you haven't heard: Egypt's been a largely Muslim nation for several hundred years now. There isn't much of a market left for ancient priests.
"You're wrong, Hondo. We've been watching, listening, hiding in the shadows. Waiting. And now our time has come."
To do what, exactly?
"To rise up, to reassume control."

Wasem was apathetic.

And how do you plan on doing that?

"There is strength in numbers. We're everywhere."

You should hear yourself talk. You and Alexander Kalvos. Your old friend.

"An old friend, yes. He was homeless in his youth, and we met in our teens. He and I found purpose together. We were close at one time. But he drifted, became disenchanted with the Hanuti. He chose a different path. I'm glad to see he's resurfaced, glad to see someone else shares our concern for world safety."

World safety? You hired him to kill Trent.

"No. Someone else did that. But I applaud the effort nonetheless."

You're being ridiculous."

"Am I? First, it starts with an announcement on the news. A major historical discovery. Everything about our history is called into question. *We* are called into question. Then people stop coming to visit. And Egypt grows poor. Then the people here get angry, and the government has to act against its own people. And then Islam is questioned. Judaism. Christianity. And so on. The Arab Spring all over again, except that this time it won't be just Arabs fighting. It'll be everyone. We can't let that happen, Hondo. We won't let that happen.

Nahas, you need to come in. We need to talk.

"It's too late. Things have already been set in motion."

What things?

Nahas hangs up, and Wasem stares emptily out at the passengers on the subway. Then he scrolls through his contacts for the professor's telephone number.

The door to Yaghdjian's cell opens. An Egyptian is there, dressed casually. He wipes his recently shaved head with a white towel, smiles, notices the cufflinks, gestures for their removal. He offers his hand. "Inspector Fadil Nahas. Sorry about all this."

Inspector, can I ask what this is all about?

Nahas beckons him from the cell, into the narrow corridor.

Yaghdjian notices the warehouse, darkened before, is now torch lit. Torch lit, when modern electricity is available? Several men are present, all bald and bare-chested, sporting skirted white linen at the waist. *Shendyt*? Why? They surround what appears to be a gurney, stationed in the centre of the room. Along one of the walls is a collection of jars. Canopic jars? For what? He turns nervously to Nahas, who is suddenly stripping naked. But only momentarily: one of the other men hands him a *shendyt*, which he dons in the fashion of the others. Yaghdjian stares. He knows what this is. Every Egyptian knows. But this sort of thing hasn't been done for centuries.

Others are entering the room. Some Egyptian, some foreign. One limps slightly, the left leg dragging. He sports a navy blazer, khaki slacks and a white collared shirt unbuttoned near the neckline. His clavicle is clearly exposed. Freckled with sun spots, his weathered skin is deeply bronzed.

Yaghdjian mumbles almost incoherently, wiping at a bead of nervous sweat running down his face.

I was taken from my apartment without any explanation, and then brought here. I have already spoken to an inspector this past week.

"Yes, we know," Nahas replies. "I've some news for you regarding Hondo Wasem. He's been cooperating with an international terrorist group responsible for the death of David Trent. You knew him well, Trent, yes?"

He nods.

A very good man.

"He was that and more."

Yaghdjian's eyes boggle. This makes no sense.

Are you sure? About the inspector, I mean?

"Unfortunately, yes."

But he seemed so intent on finding Trent's killer. You're saying he was investigating his own murder?

"How do you think *I* feel? Hondo Wasem was my friend. His betrayal cuts deeply. And now he's gone missing. That's why we've brought you in."

You brought me all the way over here to ask me if I know where he is?

"In part."

I don't think I can be of any use to you, sir.

"I wondered if he might have contacted you this evening."

No, he hasn't.

"We were concerned for your safety."

My safety?

"Wasem is a trained killer. We brought you here to keep you safe."

Why me? And why Professor Trent?

Nahas runs a hand over his smooth cranium. "Wasem has gotten himself involved with a rather nasty international terrorist cell that views all foreigners as a threat. They are committed to mass murder."

I can't believe it.

"And when he came to you, snooping around, he was looking to see what you knew. He was hoping you might unknowingly suggest other necessary targets." He holds up a photo of a foreign man in his late fifties or early sixties. "Does this man look familiar?"

Certainly.

"Henry Booth may be in danger, too. So, you see, it's very important that you tell us everything you know so we can track Wasem down and catch him before he kills again. Where he might be hiding, for example."

Yaghdjian scrutinises the inspector. There is something wrong about all this. Not something—everything. It reeks of dishonesty.

Unfortunately, as I said, I don't have anything to tell you.

Nahas is clearly unimpressed. He glances at the elderly European, who looks away exhaustedly. "You're sure?" he says after several calculated seconds. "He hasn't called you tonight?"

Definitely not.

"I just want to ensure you're not holding out on us."

Yaghdjian stares at the warehouse floor. What is the inspector getting at? What culpability should he be feeling?

I don't understand.

"Abetting a criminal is a very serious charge."

Yes, but I don't know anything. I swear he hasn't contacted me.

"Then let's talk about the things you *do* know."

The things I know?

"We know about Trent's trips around the world—you told Wasem that much. But we are certain you know more."

I'm sorry. Can we back up here? I mean, why wasn't I brought to the police station? Wouldn't that be the safest place to take me?

The inspector suddenly slaps him hard across the face. He yelps, droops his head protectively. After several seconds, he looks up, wincing. But Nahas has turned his attention to the much older man in the suit. They are speaking in English.

"You wanted me to be pleasant. Look where that's getting us. It's late, and we need answers," Nahas is saying, waving a hand flippantly in Yaghdjian's direction. "From now on, we do it my way."

The older gentleman shrugs. "You do what you want."

Nahas makes for the entrance to the room, calling beyond to someone. Yaghdjian stares. Another door can be heard opening in the narrow corridor. Another cell, perhaps. Another prisoner.

The elderly European steps into his path of vision. "Come," he says. "Tell us something."

Someone is being brought out through the doorway. An Egyptian male, past middle age, white haired and moustached. Naked. Handcuffed. Struggling. Yaghdjian watches as he is unceremoniously dragged to the gurney, his legs collected below him, then dropped aggressively onto it. Two priests hold him down. Someone is chanting in Khemitian. He immediately recognises the passage from the Book of the Dead.

"They're animals," the old man says urgently, gesturing to the priests. "They'll tear you apart."

He shakes his head nervously.

I swear on my life I don't know what you're talking about! Please...

The prisoner screams in fear, and someone covers his mouth with a cloth. They are drugging him.

"Listen to me," the European says in accented English, jostling a horrified Yaghdjian back to reality. "What did he tell you about the trelleborgs?"

The what?

More strange places. A verbal onslaught spills from his mouth. Trelleborgs, Amarna, Delphi. Ley lines. Grids.

Ley lines? He has heard of this theory. The professor told him of it. Did he? No. No, he'd read about it. He can't remember! He must remember—but he can't, he can't! His entire body quivers in panic. Why does any of this matter? Why do these people think he knows these things? What do world grids and trelleborgs mean to him?

He needs to slow things down. In his nervous state, he suddenly reverts to Spanish. *Mas despacio, mas despacio.* Then he extends his hands, gesturing for patience, to which the man acquiesces. After several seconds, he speaks.

I don't remember anything about these places, this grid.

He realises as he says this, he is actually lying. He does know something— he and Trent did discuss them. But they have no relevance to him. He should have said that just now.

"What about the Americas—Mexico, perhaps?"

Mexico? Yes! He does know something about that. He wants to scream it out, cathartically, that it might quell his fear, his impending doom. Mexico, yes! He'd received a photograph from David Trent of a mountain in Mexico. Yes, yes! He knows all about it. Or does he? No, he doesn't know anything. A photo of a mountain. That's all he knows. Trent gave him a photo of a mountain. Or did he? Was it from someone else? He doesn't know!

In the end, all he says is one word. Nothing.

"Nothing comes from nothing," the European sneers. "Tell me. Biblical stories, perhaps. What about the Exodus?"

The Exodus?

"What did he say? *What did he say?*"

I don't know! Do you hear me? I said I don't know! We didn't talk about these things! Not that I can remember offhand, anyway! I don't know anything about ley lines, and Mexico, and about Israelites fleeing Egypt.

The old man nods dejectedly, throws a plaintive look at Nahas, then stares at the unmoving prisoner on the gurney. "Do what you think best." And with that, he and the other suited men depart the room.

A door swings closed behind them, its echo a terrifying terminal sound. Yaghdjian watches them go, begins to whimper.

"I want you to see something," a stoically hardened Nahas says to him. "This man here is named Charobim. He did something rather stupid this evening. He's come to repay his debt."

Two of the priests move towards the ledge where the canopic jars have been stored. There is also a box present, rectangular in shape, covered with linen. One of the them removes the cover.

Yaghdjian already knows what is in there, knows even before the first of the surgical devices is brought into view.

"I want you to pay attention," Nahas says. "I want you to understand how we reward dishonesty."

You're mummifying him?

A florid death mask of trepidation overcomes Yaghdjian.

I don't understand!

"You will."

Priests appear at both sides, bookmarking his view.

Nahas nods to the priest with the medical blade. The priest steps forward, and, one hand on the Charobim's abdomen, he begins to slice along the left flank. Blood pools immediately, dark and sickly. Charobim convulses for a brief second. He is not dead yet. Does he feel this? He must. Or perhaps it is a reflex action, spasms without understanding.

The priest who has committed the incision turns and flees the room, as is the ancient tradition, the verbaliser of the Book of the Dead incantations condemning him for his action.

Another gurney is being wheeled over, the canopic jars having been placed on it. The two other priests abruptly reach through the incision and into

Charobim. They are extracting organs, one at a grisly time. Charobim stares upward with almost lifeless eyes—he continues to convulse mildly.

One of the priests ventures towards his head, an instrument in hand. He works the utensil into the nose, wriggling it as he forces it up through and into the brain. Charobim spasms one final time and is finally stilled. The priest retracts the hook. A smallish piece of cerebral viscera is caught on it. Like a fish. The priest taps the instrument over a jar; the piece of brain falls in. He turns back to extract more.

Alongside the body, spilled blood is mounting, then dripping uncontrollably onto the floor. It tinkles as it impacts with the cold, hard surface.

They are placing the organs in the jars.

And Yaghdjian is screaming.

AMUN

Cairo's subway closes at two in the morning, and it is nearly that time when Wasem arrives at Giza Station. Normally teeming with tourists, the station is largely deserted at this hour.

He is still several kilometres east of where he wants to be. He climbs the stairs exhaustedly, one hand clasped reassuringly on the protruding hand rail. The air has cooled since he boarded the train, but his shirt is still completely soaked, even though he's been riding in the controlled air of the underground train for the past several minutes.

He emerges onto the normally active Al Ahram. He has tried several times to contact the professor, all to no avail. He verifies with his phone again. Still no reply to his texts. Best to concede defeat for now, perhaps until first light. That will give him a few hours to himself to rest. Where he can accomplish this is easy.

He hails the first toktok that passes by, quickly steps in.

Take me all the way west along Al Ahram until we hit the entrance to the pyramid complex.

The driver is puzzled. "At this hour? It's quite late. Nothing's open."

Perfect. Just drive.

The inspector slumps into the back seat.

The toktok speeds away, and the breeze gushes through its open sides. But Wasem is immune to it just now. Drained seemingly beyond repair, he watches through collapsing eyelids as passing buildings and lights fuse into a single continuous essence. After several seconds, he consents to the toktok's gentle coercion and sleeps.

He is awakened moments later. The toktok is slowing, then grinding to a halt. This is it.

It has been some time since Wasem last saw the pyramids up close. Here, at the gated entrance, he gapes as he always has at the monstrous structures rising out of the shadowed sand. And not barricaded, as the young woman Lauren had suggested. He remembers now raising the walkie talkie to his lips, then becoming distracted. Damn his memory.

He pays the driver and exits the toktok, stretching his weary legs. He makes his way across the sandy terrain. His phone is ringing. The professor at last? Excitedly, he reaches down to answer, without looking to see who the caller is. The voice he hears on the other end is unexpected.

"Wasem, what the hell's going on?"

Deeb.

"Do you know how many hours it's been since you organised that Zamalik raid without my approval?"

It wasn't a raid, sir. We brought a warrant. We searched the house legally.

"The hell you did. Who signed for it?"

The inspector withholds laughter.

"You acted without my authority. I'll have your badge for this."

That's the least of my concerns.

"Do you have any idea how much trouble you're in? How much trouble *I'm* in?"

Oh, I think I have some idea.

There is a confused pause on the other end. "What does that mean?"

He speaks more plainly.

Nahas indicated your involvement.

This is a lie. Wasem is bluffing. Nahas said nothing of the sort. But so much of the brigadier's enmity makes sense now: the personal attacks, the relieving him of duty. He has been a thorn in Deeb's side from the beginning. And now, he ponders, he understands why. Deeb has always had an agenda with which Wasem continuously conflicted.

"My involvement? In the raid? Is Nahas there with you right now? Put him on."

I'll find a way to get to you, Deeb. I'll make sure you don't go through with whatever it is you plan to do.

"Wasem, are you on something?"

Perhaps you can enlighten me on the disappearance of Mark Brydges.

"Drugs? Or have you been drinking?"

Has he been located?

"Damnit, Wasem!"

Brydges!

"Yes, the disappearance. I've got people looking into that."

He must give Deeb credit: the brigadier is trying to follow on the other end.

"Damn you, Wasem. I'll have your badge!"

Deeb, you're as good as dead. Do you understand what I'm saying? When they arrest you, they will gut you like a fish.

"Are you threatening me?"

Not a threat. A promise.

"I just want to be sure when I have you arrested."

Come and find me.

"I intend to."

He hangs up, replaces the phone in his pants pocket. Let Deeb seek him out. There is reason to believe the brigadier will be circulating his name to every police station in the city, and that soon enough, Cairo will swell with officers searching for him. While he rests, he will strategize. It will not be difficult to hide; until daylight, at any rate. But, then, of course, Nahas had intimated that arrest was not in the offering. No, when they come, they will come to liquidate.

His mind drifts to thoughts of Ramzy. He has, for the past several hours, neglected the only ally he likely has left. He scrolls through his contacts and dials the officer's number. There is a chance Ramzy, too, has still evaded his pursuers. But Ramzy is not answering. What can that mean?

He stands at the deserted gate to the complex. There should be TAPs here, but they have conveniently disappeared. He scans the area in front of him. There are plenty of places to lay low. Too many, perhaps. He crosses under the swinging gate, spies the nearest of the three pyramids. He's often heard people brag about spending the night out here, atop the Great Pyramid's flat summit. In his youth, it had been the thing to do. Friends had climbed to the top and camped out. But too many have been injured over the years, and now climbing is strictly off limits. Hence the TAPs, for safety reasons.

He trudges across the deserted parking lot, his eyes fixated on the illuminated stone megalith rising from the sand. Only its eastern side is lit, a face that looks down on Cairo. Beyond, all is cloaked in darkness. He eyes the visitor's centre, which is assuredly locked for the night. Its domain offers a more comfortable option, but the thought of breaking in and setting off the alarm begs for rationale. No, the Great Pyramid it is. A charming stone bed for a few hours.

Al Ahram, the road that ambles in and around the complex, procures its existence from the Cairo-Alex Road on the other side of the gate. It is here that Wasem largely staggers, longing for respite on legs ill-designed for such burden.

He remembers the light and information presentations at the Plateau every night. Visitors treated to lasers and massive hieroglyphic reflections. He'd gone in his youth. The show has likely modernised since then. Thankfully the third show, which starts at 10:30, is long over by this time, the tourists having faded away to their hotels.

The bottommost stones on the Great Pyramid are smooth and sparkle by day. These are casing stones, the last surviving remnants that confirm the original pyramid's appearance. It is a little known fact beyond the learned that Cairo of one thousand years ago was largely built using casing stones plundered from the pyramids, stones that either toppled during an earthquake or were simply stolen from the pyramids. Modern-day Cairo sports them still. The walls of mosques, mostly. The Great Pyramid is naked at its summit, clothed only here at its base, a base Wasem now caresses with his hand. The alluring smoothness of sanded Tura stone, still persuasively supple these many centuries later. At one time, all of the pyramids at Giza were completely smooth. It would have been impossible to climb any of them. They must have been radiant in the sun, these mathematically-precise, glistening colossi. Their splendour comes flooding back to him now. Why has he ignored them for so many years? Why has he not taken an afternoon to quietly soak in the majestic allure of this place?

He is going to hurt himself out here. If he doesn't fall trying to lumber up the massive stones, his heart will give out; either way, he's done for. He reconsiders his action. No, he'll be all right: the flight from his pursuers earlier should have already led to heart failure, and that hasn't happened. How hard can this be?

The key, then, is not to go too high. There are 203 rows of stones on the Great Pyramid, and the higher one goes, the cooler and windier it gets. Especially at night. No, he'll simply climb a few, find a comfortable-enough shadowed locale, and call it a night. Then he'll figure out what to do tomorrow.

He freezes, halfway up the first stone. Somewhere, up on the blackened north face, someone has called to him. He remembers who he is—he is the police.

What the hell are you doing up here? You can't be here!

"I don't speak Arabic," the other intones in English.

He instantly transfers to English.

Fine, then I'll speak your language.

You can't be here.

"You're here, aren't you?"

I'm the police.

At this, he notices, there is no response.

If you leave now, I won't report you.

"And what are *you* doing here?" the other calls again from the darkness.

He finishes climbing the first step. The other man must still be a few rows up. He gapes into glaring darkness.

That's none of your business.

"Then I'll make you a deal: if you don't tell anyone I'm up here, I won't tell anyone you were up here. Fair?"

No deal. You can't be here. I can.

"You really don't recognise my voice?"

He stops, thinks. Does he?

"We're five rows up. Come on."

Easier said than done. He fumbles for the stone in the next row, pulls himself upward. He sits, turns, gazes out on the myriad of differentiating light that is Cairo. He can hear the sound of intermittent vehicular horns, some muted, others much more distinct—klaxons in the night air. A gentle breeze engulfs him. A hand reaches out towards him, and instantly he begins to laugh.

Thought you might turn up at some point. You're well?

The summoned nods. "I am now. Came for the view. Heard it was exhilarating."

The inspector gestures to Seldon.

So, who's this, then?

"Someone with a change of heart."

I see.

There will be plenty of time before the day to understand Brydges' words. Does the professor know?

"I don't have a phone. Maybe you can contact him for me."

I've been trying. No answer.

He glances upwards.

It gets cold as well out here at night. You're not dressed for the occasion.

"Neither are you."

I'm insulated. Make yourself at home.

"This one looks good." The summoned pats a stone.

You know, when this thing was built, we wouldn't have been able to do this.

"I know." The summoned stares into the night sky. "There is something up there. Do you see that?"

Wasem studies the glowing object.

I've been seeing it the past few nights. It's been big news here.

"What do you think it is?"

I feel foolish for thinking what I do. I don't like to feel foolish.

"Care to listen to a story, then?"

Wasem studies his watch. Three a.m.

I've got all the time in the world.

"Inspector, do you believe in aliens?"

The professor steps out onto the villa's patio. He needs a breather: the house is still flush with police officers and other non-uniformed men. But Wasem is the one he truly needs, and Wasem is not here.

He tries the inspector once again. For some reason, he cannot call out. It is as if someone has tampered with his phone. Who could have done that? And when? Strange.

At this early hour, the carefully articulated patio stones no longer burn the his flesh. He remembers briefly the day-time sensation. He's spent many an uncomfortable day in the Egyptian heat to learn how to acclimatise. For him, heated stones are not the problem: the desert, after all, is nothing if not continuous discomfort. But he loves it nonetheless.

He watches as several Egyptians in black slacks, berets, and buttoned tops wade past. Gold insignia emblazoned across the heart of each. Egyptian Homeland Security, the former Egyptian secret police. The heavyweights.

One of the men stands out. He must have just arrived; Lauren is directing him over. His uniform displays star-studded epaulettes on rather broad shoulders. Little shoulder brushes. The professor has always found them fascinating to look at. Fox-silver hair protrudes from beneath the officer's beret, documenting age and experience beyond these others. A pair of pronounced cheekbones flank an unusually cumbersome nose. Below, rosy lips part like curtains to reveal an earnest, courteous smile.

"Professor, I'm General Kamal Abdalla." He offers his hand. "I have been apprised of the situation. We will find your friend."

Then I suggest we make our way to the Giza Plateau, General.

He nods. "We're on our way."

The general's phone is vibrating. He reaches for it, glances up at the professor. "I'm sorry. If you'll excuse me…"

The professor studies the general's professionalism as he shifts to Arabic. "Yes, fine, transfer the call." Then: "Yes. Yes, this is. And your name? Wasem. Why are you calling me at this hour?"

Both the professor and Lauren are elated.

"Is that so?" Abdalla turns their way, resuming English. "Your friend: he's with this Inspector Wasem." Then he returns to the conversation. "Now, wait—who is this? Mr. Seldon, whoever you are, you cannot simply call *me*." He pauses, unnerved. "Vannevar Denison. *He* had my number? He gave it to you? Then how—what? No, I—what? What?" And then muted nods and the occasional "I see." At one point he says, "Of course I've heard of it. Do I sound like a tourist? Stay where you are. We'll be there soon." He ends the conversation, begins ordering his men in Arabic. He glances at the professor. "It seems we've got ourselves a confession. A man wants to meet, says he has something to show me."

"Something? You mean some*one*."

"No, Professor. He said some*thing*. At a place called Lake Qarun."

Thursday morning. Pharaoh awakes, groggy and annoyed. He's only slept a little. He parts the curtains to his room, gazes out at the pyramids nudging the sky beyond clusters of sycamores and palms, apartments and hotels. There is still something completely surreal about the view. And these Cairenes go about their daily lives, indifferent to the breathtaking grandeur of these remarkable monuments. *Maybe like people who live around Niagara Falls*, he surmises. *It's nothing special if you're from there.* Except that this is not Niagara Falls. This is much, much more.

He showers quickly, dries off, gels his hair. There is a knock at his door. Clothed solely by towel about his waist, he opens it to reveal Sanderson. The minion appears jovial.

"Morning. I see you're already up."

He begins ruffling through his closet for a collared shirt.

How could I sleep? Get Brydges up. Let's get moving.

"Sir."

He views himself in the mirror: chiselled biceps through the folds of the shirt, shoulders protruding underneath, abs. Oh, those abs. He's proud of those. He pulls on a pair of khaki pants and makes for the hallway. He hears a commotion, and immediately he knows something is up. His eyes dart to Brydges' room, and his heart sinks.

He's gone, isn't he?

Sanderson lowers his eyes.

How?

"Not through the door."

What?

"You're not going to believe it."

Let me guess. He climbed.

It is ridiculous, laughably ridiculous, but it makes perfect sense. And since no one else is laughing, he knows it must be true. The wanted man, the superconductor, the energy pulse of the world himself, can scale hotel walls. He can probably fly, too. He's been genetically enhanced, after all. He's probably always had powers. Born with them, like that man from Krypton.

He steps past his gathered minions, in through the entrance to the summoned's room. He strides across the carpet, opens the sliding door, steps onto the balcony. The air is scented with car exhaust. He can see thousands of them far below, little insects speeding along thoroughfares, halted in jams, parked along shoulders. He looks up, gazes into a cloud-impersonating haze.

He places his hands on the railing, bends forward, gapes downward, retreats quickly. How could he have done it? It doesn't seem possible. He turns to Sanderson, ever at his side. Already he has another thought on his mind.

And Seldon?

"Also missing."

Also missing? Pharaoh wants to explode, but at the same time, he had already suspected as much. Hours ago, everything was perfect. Now, everything seems to be falling apart.

How could *he* get away?

"Maybe they left together, sir."

What—out through the balcony? Have you *seen* Seldon?

Sanderson reconsiders.

Find those two. I don't care what you need to do. I'm not leaving without the both of them.

Men scurry and disappear, but Sanderson remains. Pharaoh turns his attention to the man he had left to guard Brydges' room. He can contain his anger no longer.

"Sir, I don't understand it," Bowles is saying. "I was here at his door all night."

He didn't go out through the door, you idiot.

"But it makes no sense, sir. He couldn't have *climbed*."

Shut up.

Bowles closes his mouth, looks away.

Pharaoh regards his own hands, watches them clench with rage. He scrutinises Bowles. The minion begins to stammer again. He silences him with a wave of his hand.

Give me your sidearm.

"Sir?"

You won't need it anymore.

Bowles hands the pistol over, head bowed in submission. It is masked with a silencer. Excellent. Without pausing, Pharaoh raises it to the man's head, pulls the trigger. The sound is minimal.

He watches the body crumple, turns to Sanderson.

Understood?

Sanderson nods, staring down at Bowles' lifeless corpse. Two men move near to lug the guts away.

He hands the pistol over to Sanderson. When he speaks, the summoned is his only concern.

He can't get far. He's probably on his way to the Canadian embassy. I'll make a call. He's not getting out of this country.

He can feel his phone vibrating. It is a text message. He studies the words, and a smile begins to creep ever so tantalisingly across his face. That's interesting. He turns back to his subordinate.

Hang on. We make for Giza.

From where he is perched on the side of the pyramid, the summoned sees the first of the government vehicles enter the complex. Through an escalating cloud of dust that dirties the pinkish early morning sky, he distinguishes black Homeland Security SUVs. He scurries from his position along the north facing, raises his hands in the hopes of attracting attention. He hears the inspector nearby.

They're here.

The vehicles align themselves somewhat strategically in the visitor's parking lot, black on grey surrounded by the desert's golden powder. From the phalanx, Homeland Security personnel tumble like candy.

Beside him, Wasem breathes a sigh of relief. People they can trust—he assumes. The inspector gestures to Seldon.

Come. Time for redemption.

They descend, then trek across the sand-swept Al Ahram. Egyptian agents are already proceeding towards them. As well, above the milieu that is daily Cairo, the sound of propellers rage in the sky. The summoned scans the cloudless backdrop. Sure enough, two choppers are on their way. Beside him, he hears Wasem call to a man. The name is Kamal Abdalla. And Abdalla nods back, simultaneously growling at his men, who are busily opening tailgates and sporting barricades. They mean to block the entrance. Apparently, there isn't going to be any tourism today.

Then he sees familiar faces, and he rushes into the waiting arms of Lauren and the professor. Is her face wet, or is it simply perspiration? It is, after all, already unbearable out here in the desert. No, he surmises, it cannot be tears. They have not known each other long enough, and this is not Lauren Haaksma's style.

On this, he is wrong.

She tells him they didn't know if they'd ever see him again, and she stumbles over her own words somewhat awkwardly.

And he wants to say so many things to her, but there isn't the time. He envisions a day sometime soon when they can sit and talk and explore probable feelings, but for now, there are other matters at hand. He tells them the man who took him is Vannevar Denison, and how he escaped from Denison last night. But in the end, he was compelled to come here, to finish this. He gestures to the looming pyramid. He is going in there, and he'd very much appreciate their company.

He turns and sees Wasem and Seldon speaking with Abdalla. He hears Seldon refer to the uniformed Egyptian as "general." Abdalla glances up at the approaching choppers. The helicopters are here, he says in remarkably convincing English.

These are Aérospatiale Gazelles, designed in France but manufactured in Egypt. Built for five passengers, the Gazelle was and is a favourite of the

Egyptian army and Homeland Security; thus, the model is a regular a fixture in the Egyptian sky. These particular models, SA 342Ks, are specifically designed for hot, dry climates. Egypt fits the bill perfectly.

There is tension. The professor has approached Seldon, hand clenched. Before anyone can act, he has struck the New Zealander, knocking him onto his back.

Wasem makes a joke.

I see you and Mr. Seldon here have plenty to talk about, Professor.

The beaten man rises slowly, brushing away gathered sand.

I understand why you're angry. I'd be angry, too.

You represent the people who had David killed.

Seldon regroups, taking his time amid the din of propeller blades and blustering sand. Then he begins to spew. Even the summoned is unprepared for how much he is willing to divulge. It is a tsunami-like confession, powerful and tragic and painful and revealing all at once.

They met many months ago, Garrett Seldon and David Trent, when Trent was a devout non-believer of the astronaut theory. They needed someone like him, someone with a recognisable face and a presence to refute all. They sought Trent out, spoke by phone. They offered him the opportunity to search for the evidence that would disprove these theories once and for all. He would have an unlimited budget, unlimited resources at his disposal. And no interference.

The professor is sceptical. David was actually going to seek evidence to disprove him?

He was.

The professor shakes his head furiously. They were the best of friends. How could David have done something like that?

Perhaps the professor did not know Trent as well as he believed.

The professor clenches his fist a second time, and Seldon backs nervously away.

It is true. Trent was to be well compensated for betraying this friendship. His evidence was to be announced anonymously, and it was his express wish that the professor never find out it had been he who had finally proved him wrong.

How much? the professor wonders. How much was it going to take to buy David off?

Seven figures.

With that, there is momentary silence. Money always has the final word.

What sort of evidence could he have had?

He had theories. Plenty of theories. His best was the Hall of Records. Under the ground here, where secrets have been buried in the form of scrolls and hieroglyphics for centuries. The plan was to uncover it once and for all, and find uncontaminated evidence that the history books weren't lying after all: that men like Khufu built the pyramids with copper chisels and hammers. That the pyramids were in fact tombs. That the Khemitians believed in gods. That Khafre built the Sphinx. And more. The theories on the whereabouts of the Hall were well known to Trent, and so he would dig alone, at night, then somehow conceal his work to daytime tourists and TAPs.

And then a curious thing happened. Somehow, some way, even before he began excavating, Trent suddenly changed his mind. He'd had a revelation. His faith in ancient astronauts was born. He thought he was keeping this to himself, but they had been watching him, and they knew. How this revelation occurred was unclear; Trent never said. But something had happened. He'd been travelling much of late—perhaps something on these journeys? Thus, he became untrustworthy. They let him dig, but their minds had been made up: for this betrayal, David Trent would have to die.

As he listens, the summoned can only ferment one thought: that Trent, too, might have been contacted. Not in a forest, perhaps. Not at night. Perhaps in his own home back in Toronto, on the sunniest of days. Lounging by the pool. In a hammock. Reading on a couch. And while it all seems so ridiculous, what other explanation is there? What else could have turned a man so committed to his beliefs?

Money changes people, Seldon admits.

The helicopters alight nearby, stirring dust in all directions. Seldon raises his voice accordingly over the din of the propellers.

Trent was concerned for his reputation. And about his friendship with the professor. It was necessary to calm him. Then he was killed and the evidence he found confiscated. Naturally, what he found was never going to be made public.

Seldon is ashamed at what he's done. He knows he is going to jail. But these people he works for—they are incredibly powerful and dangerous. And the others who have been onto the summoned as well—he simply wants to do what he can to stop anyone else from getting hurt.

Abdalla puts an end to the discussion. It is time for he and Seldon to board a helicopter, to travel south to Golden Horn Island. To find what it was David Trent uncovered. He moves across the parking lot towards the helicopters, Seldon and two other men trailing behind. They board the pair of waiting birds, and in seconds are airborne, soaring across sand and towards the horizon, then disappearing into the blue of the southern sky.

But within seconds, as if on cue, Al Ahram spawns a new assortment of cars and SUVs. A horde of locusts, rapidly descending on the complex. A line of Homeland Security personnel form along the road and behind the hastily-erected barricades in a show of force. These visitors haven't been expected.

The summoned knows who it must be.

As the vehicles approach, however, their speed does not waver. The temporary roadblocks will not hold. Several agents shout ineffectually to the oncoming mass in a effort to control the situation. And there are people leaning out the windows of the vehicles, seeming to listen. Then, in the hands of these listeners, weapons materialise, pistols and machine guns. It is then that bullets begin to fly and agents begin to drop. The first vehicle, an SUV, smashes through the road block, stampeding onward like a Spanish bull. Others follow the lead, lurch sideways, finally halt, men oozing from them, firing madly.

Within seconds, something becomes clear: the Homeland Security officers who have stood their ground at the barricade, and now lie in puddles of blood, are not being reinforced: those who linger in the rear, instead of returning fire, seem appreciative to what is transpiring. It has all been planned.

As the dust settles and random screams from injured agents continue to fill the air, the summoned watches as a motley horde of occupants emerge from behind the newly-arrived cars. Egyptians, interspersed here and there with Europeans. A strange blend. Many of the Egyptians are dressed in the familiar uniforms of the Tourism and Antiquities Police.

Of course, Wasem mumbles beside him in English. Nahas. You son of a bitch.

The professor turns to the summoned. These are the people who took him?

No. He doesn't know who these people are. And as he peers at the oncoming strangers, his eyes linger on a certain elderly member of their party. Tall, limping slightly on his left side, overdressed for the heat in a blue blazer, khaki pants, a white collared shirt. He has seen this man before. Yes, he has seen him. The exposed clavicle, the weathered skin. And then he remembers. So long ago, it seems. Alumni Hall. The man reading Exodus, the man who had asked if he himself read the *Bible*. And where was that *Bible* now? No longer tucked into the gentleman's right armpit.

However, there is a third party sprinkled amongst the Europeans and Egyptian officers: clean-shaved locals, garbed unconventionally all in white.

Loin cloths and sandals. As if they have emerged from the past. Apparently the Hanuti have returned.

Wasem can distinguish Nahas amongst them, the other's newly smoothed head glimmering in the vivid sunshine. He says as much to the others.

The Hanuti? Lauren says.

This is what they are calling themselves. They have rather unrealistic aspirations.

Nahas and another man are striding his way purposely, and so the inspector steps forth, prepares for the confrontation. Nahas is ordering his men to detain these others. Such is easy: they are unarmed.

The elderly gentleman stares at the summoned but says nothing. It is not a look of anger or disdain. It is a look of relief. And the summoned now understands why: this is the man Denison alluded to, the one responsible for the exploding van in the parking lot and the chase down the 404. These events seem like years ago. He has lived a year in a week. And so the relief is for finding him. They don't want to know what all the fuss is regarding him; they don't care. He is a threat to world peace. To religion. He must be eliminated.

But how…? he wonders.

We've been aware of you for quite some time.

Why? Why me?

The response is the worst thing he has ever heard. It is hopelessly ambiguous and hopelessly logical all at once.

Ask your mother.

Two black and silver trimmed Gazelles flee across the desert wasteland. Below, their shadows pursue them like playful dolphins, lurching ahead at intervals, then uniformly falling back into formation.

Gazing out the viewport, Seldon, no longer handcuffed, watches as Cairo explodes in all directions, a mass of drab concrete amid a palette of rich north-south greenery. This greenery is the tiny swath of vegetation that has been retched up by the Nile. Or, perhaps, this is all that remains of a once tropical Egypt. Everywhere beyond this lush ribbon, far into the horizon, is desert. Endless desert. And something else. The higher they climb, he discerns a heavy pallor of smog clearly visible over the city, blanketing its millions of occupants. Its cause is the roads and highways into and throughout the city, endless tributaries all chocked full of vehicles.

To his right, the pyramids of Giza now far behind, he perceives the structures at Abusir. Rising like dunes out of the sand, 14 pyramids, though none of them equalling the grandeur of Giza. Saqqara will be next in line. He can't help but marvel.

Beside him, Abdalla speaks into a headset, similar to the one Seldon now has over his own ears. The conversation is in Arabic, presumably between the general and the two pilots, as well as to the men in the adjacent bird.

They proceed south at a speed of well over two hundred kilometres per hour; hence, Lake Qarun will materialise in a matter of moments. Seldon refocuses on the great sparkling river far below, how it meanders this way and that, slicing spasmodically like the tail of a crocodile. Or a snake. Are there snakes here in Egypt? Certainly. Asps, he remembers. Cleopatra died by an asp. This, then, he corrects himself, is what he sees: the asp of the Sahara amid a jungle of sand. A jungle of sand, or a sea? He wonders. Additional swatches of architecture approach far below. Towns, cities. Carved out of the lushness of the river banks like tiny nicks to the skin, a compendium of surgical incisions. And the overcrowding. How can so many people live in such an unbelievably cramped vicinity?

The glistening blue waters and green trimming suddenly fade to the west, replaced by a carpet of perpetual beige and brown and yellow. They are leaving the Nile behind, now turning southwest towards the lake. *The* lake. It sounds ridiculous. How many lakes does New Zealand have? He can't guess. But here, a lake in the middle of a desert is something miraculous.

Then he glimpses it, a bead of water on a sandy carpet. The lake forms the northern edge of a teardrop protruding from the Nile, linked by a single, slim, bridge-like patch of green. There are bits of settlements south of the water, in and amid a large expanse of vegetation. Faiyum and other smaller communities, pleated amid the vastness of the Faiyum Oasis. The Oasis, he realises, is much wider than the Nile and its banks. And there, below and far to the left, the Nile carries on, eventually lost amid its undulating green banks. He glances back down at the Oasis. There are fields down there. Fields everywhere. And trees. Or, rather, forests, set amongst the arable land. Who could guess how beautiful it all looks from the air?

He spots Faiyum, the largest settlement ahead, largely nondescript amongst the green belt of the Oasis. He can also see that there are two other lakes slightly south of Qarun—or perhaps one lake that appears like two, separated by a tiny discoloured patch in between. He can't tell from this distance, but the patch is a waterfall—the Rayan Falls that separate the North and South Lakes of the Rayan Wadi. He refocuses on the much larger emergence below.

General Abdalla understands what the prisoner is looking at. He gesticulates to the body of water rapidly approaching. That is Lake Qarun south of them.

It is amazing, Seldon breathes.

Over eighty million people living on less than five percent of land. That is amazing.

He points. There is Golden Horn Island. There they will land.

There should be a boat house on the island, Seldon tells him. He had ordered the artefact planted there. Does the general see? He is pointing to a tiny, dilapidated and solitary structure far below.

Abdalla peers. He can't make it out from this height. Within seconds, however, he reconfirms. There it is. And into his headset, he barks to lower the craft.

The Gazelles begin their descent. Within seconds, Seldon's boat house is plainly evident, the only thing on the island. But something is wrong.

The accompanying bird touches down first, and almost immediately, three black uniformed men with machine guns spring from it. They race to the building, which it is now clear to everyone has been tampered with, to say the least.

Seldon's headset explodes with various metallic voices. He can see the men scurrying around the site and reporting back. Indeed, someone has already been here. The cabin, if that is what it was, is now little more than rubble. They've been beaten to it. He cannot be completely surprised. It was a gamble all along. He wonders if the Scorpion ever brought the artefact here in the first place. He wonders, too, how long it has been since Pharaoh left. Since that is assuredly who has been here.

The general turns to him. Why would someone want to do this?

Denison must have come down here, he says. He was after the object that was taken from Trent. He had mentioned he would be coming to get it, but he hadn't specified when. There was the hope they'd beaten him to it.

Apparently not.

You haven't specified why this artefact is so important.

We will need more time for that.

Before Seldon can offer an explanation, something streaking through the sky catches his attention. He gasps. It is no bird. It is black, cylindrical, and moving rapidly towards the rubble on the ground. It collides with the dilapidated shack, and a sudden explosion erupts, rocking the Gazelle violently. Within seconds, amid the red-orange glow of the blast, a massive column of black smoke vomits upwards. The men on the ground are nowhere to be seen, all but vaporised.

And then a second streaking missile flashes across the expansive blue sky, targeting the grounded bird. It, too, detonates, and another blast reverberates the air. As its fuselage burns, its tail fin topples to the sandy floor. The main propeller, now split in two, sags on either side of the burning hulk. Other pieces of debris are being thrust dangerously upward.

A piece of the grounded chopper—part of the tail, perhaps, or a piece of the propeller—shoots upwards with such speed and force that it catches the two pilots in the encircling Gazelle completely by surprise. It crashes through the front viewport, slicing into them and imbedding itself beyond, into their chairs. One of the pilots is killed instantly. The other tries valiantly, through profuse bleeding, to steer the helicopter to safety.

Seldon reaches for the wall of the bird to steady himself. He can plainly see that they are spiralling uncontrollably, can feel his stomach screaming against the force. They swerve over water, then again over land, the uninhabited stretch of desert north of the tiny lake. He watches the weakened pilot fight with the controls, and he knows it is a battle that cannot be won. Blood rushes to his head. Abdalla is beside him and speaking emphatically in his headset, to whom it is not clear.

Finally, the pilot expires, releases his hands on the controls, slumps forwards. Jagged edges of the debris protrude clearly from his chest. The pain must have been unbearable; it is remarkable that he struggled for as long as he did.

Now completely out of control, Abdalla and Seldon scream in unison as the Gazelle careens, then plummets swiftly downwards. It impacts with the ground in a fury of sand and rotating blades. Seldon is thrown violently to one side, his seatbelt having been ripped away, then the other as the bird flips violently. Eventually, it comes to a rest on its starboard side. The propeller blades continue to spin, burrowing into the earth, ultimately splintering into pieces that pepper the landscape in all directions. Unimpeded, the rotating engine atop the vehicle maintains its rhythmic revolution.

Seldon reaches out, rights himself. There is pain in his shoulder where the belt had been. He sees that Abdalla has remained fastened, though he is slumped forward, hanging from what now constitutes the side of the cabin, his face hidden under a canvas of red. Seldon turns the lifeless general his way, and his hands come away thick with blood. He climbs past, towards the opposite viewport that is now the ceiling, wrenches his body through, stares down at the bits of glass still suctioned to the frame. Something is grabbing at him from behind. He turns and grasps that his right foot is caught, the lip of his shoe impaled. He ranges for it, begins to panic, jerks the shoe loose; it tumbles back into the helicopter. Now atop the fiery wreck, he leans over and collapses onto blistering sand. He remains there several seconds, then sits up, wiping his face and surveying the damage.

The Gazelle still hums with life. Oil leaks from its upturned side, and he staggers to get clear before another explosion rocks the Egyptian countryside. He makes it just in time. What is left of the bird goes up in smoke and flames, a fresh cloud comingling with that of the other two. He gazes into the black-blanketed sky.

He remains there in the hot sand, for how long he can't guess—seconds? Minutes?—until adrenaline causes him to react to its vicious heat. He writhes to his feet, searches for shade. There is nothing. Nothing at all.

Copious sweating obscures his vision, perspiration dripping into and stinging his eyes. He tears a strip of material from the bottom of his unbuttoned shirt, quickly ties it around his head. He must look ridiculous, but what does that matter now? What matters is that he is far out in the desert, the Gazelle having circled uncontrollably and drifting much further from the lake than he initially realised. It is going to be a long walk to anywhere.

But there is a silver lining. He is now free.

Travelling to Faiyum or any of the other oases towns will very likely provide him with aid, and he can't help but rationalise that he is now no longer a prisoner. And he isn't cuffed. What evidence would there be that he'd been a prisoner in the first place? Suddenly, all that earlier talk of surrender fades. He must take advantage of the situation.

Who has shot them down? And why? Who fires missiles at helicopters in the full morning sunshine?

He stares north, into impenetrable desert. Before he can logically deduce why, his legs begin to move. He can't go south after all; he needs to get away, escape before help arrives. He can't look like he has been a part of the disaster. He was a simple tourist who'd gone out wandering, gotten lost. He'd misplaced his shoe. Will it work? He wonders. He glances up at the teeming sun. It is only morning. It is going to get much hotter. And then he reconsiders. Why not stay at the crash site after all? Help is surely on its way; Abdalla was speaking to someone before he died. Yes, but then he'd be discovered. At least out here, if he can make it to somewhere nearby, he has a chance. *If* he can make it.

He begins to formulate a plan. He works at the New Zealand embassy in Washington. He's lost his identification. Yes, that is it. He will need help getting his I.D. back so that he can leave the country. Unbelievably, though he is covered in dirt and grime, he doesn't seem to be bleeding. Might that be useful? Perhaps. He certainly won't look like a disaster survivor. And how far is Lake Qarun from Cairo? What was it Abdalla had told him—eighty kilometres, perhaps? He could walk that. In the prime hours of daylight. He isn't that out of shape.

He pauses. What is he thinking? He will die out here. Then again, if Pharaoh finds him, he is dead anyway.

He surveys the surrounding terrain. Out here, the Sahara is unique: the sand is speckled sugar white. He expects to sink into it, but that is not so: the ground is hard and curvaceous. There are no gently rolling dunes: here, the land bellows upward into tiny ridges and even mountains. Boulders are everywhere.

He thinks of the Bedouins, the travelling nomads found across the Middle East. These tribes move in whispers, here one moment and gone the next. They can cover several kilometres in a day. They can help him. He reflects on Ondaatje's English patient, Count Almásy, who fell burning out of the sky. They took him in, loaded him onto a skid and garbed him in cloth. They breathed life back into him. A life saved on a Bedouin prayer.

There is always hope.

He notices a shadow emerging in the distance. A silhouetted man, face obscured, dressed in the traditional one-piece Egyptian *jellabiya*. Long, white, flowing. He has something large and black and cylindrical in his one hand, rising up and reposing on the shoulder. It is no telescope. And this is no Bedouin.

The figure speaks, and he is stunned by a voice he recognises. He feels the blood drain from his face, and he falls to his knees in helpless fear.

"Something wicked this way comes, yes? And already you have endured much. That I can plainly see. But the truth is, Seldon, your suffering has only just begun."

✻

Someone is shouting, and Nahas turns to gaze back at the entrance. Several vehicles are arriving, more SUVs interspersed with cars. They halt several metres from the barricaded entrance, discharging yet a new force of men. Caucasian, they sport drab desert military fatigues offset by dark bullet proof vests. They are armed, too: machine guns and pistols. And they are fanning out, across the road, some to the west, where a line of trees precedes the ticket centre; others remain, assuming a defensive position behind opened car doors.

The TAPs begin to form their own defensive posture, dropping to their knees and pointing their own rifles menacingly. But it is obvious they are too much in the open, easy targets for the most part.

The summoned watches Nahas shout orders, and the prisoners are corralled to the other side of the visitor's centre and beyond. All but himself. Evidently, he is to remain. He sees Nahas fiddling with a pistol, glancing his way, ordering that he be held. Is this his time? Here, in this desert wasteland, when he is so close? He cannot believe it, but he now begs for Denison and his Myrmidons to open fire on these men. To save him. Damn it all! He would gladly deal with those consequences in time.

Adjacent to the western edge of the Great Pyramid is the remnants of what is referred as the West Field, a collection of cemeteries of prominent Khemitians associated with the pharaohs. Here are the uncovered tombs of princes and princesses, priests, judges, building overseers, acquaintances, secretaries, attendants, and so on. These tombs are known as mastabas: flat-roofed structures, rectangular in dimension, and constructed of mud-brick or stone. There are varying sizes of mastabas in this field: some are rather small, others quite large. It is here that the professors and Wasem are ushered.

Then the metallic sound of a voice through a megaphone terminates all movement. The words are laced with surprising confidence.

"Throw down your weapons. If you open fire on us, I promise you we will shoot every one of you dead."

The Hanuti and their European counterparts glance nervously about, in search of leadership. The elderly man emerges at Nahas' side, walks into the open.

The summoned imagines Denison's eyes narrowing. Is he surprised by the sight of this aged man? Apparently not.

"I wondered if you might be behind this."

Apparently, it has been some time since they have spoken. At least, that is what the gentleman says. Denison responds that he obviously still harbours resentment. Resentment? For what? the summoned wonders. And it is as if he and the others are suddenly swept up amid a personal squabble between these two.

"Still meddling in the affairs of the world, I see," the elderly European says, the contour of lines on his forehead tightening uncertainly, like strings on a guitar. "Ruining lives must run in the family."

"I'm about to ruin yours unless you surrender. Besides, you aren't here to play hero. I know who you want dead."

The summoned knows. And from where he stands, despite the heat in the air, a chill caresses his innerved spine. These men mean to fight for him. In a twisted way, he should feel honoured. Of course, the reality of the situation is much less encouraging. He wipes at his forehead, glances about apprehensively. His eyes rest on Lauren, and he can see her mouthing a word to him over and over.

Run. Run.

Run to where? These men are armed; surely someone will shoot him dead if he tries. And he wants to be here, after all. He cannot run. He concentrates, and he can hear the voice inside his head again, the one he has heard before, most recently when climbing the Sofitel. The voice is telling him to stay. Stay and trust. Trust what? Trust who? He considers what he has been through these past days, he realises it is more than most could endure. He has endured to this point, and endure a little longer he must. He will trust the voice.

"One small death to prevent far greater disaster," the European is saying. "Isn't that how your grandfather used to think?"

"Do you really want to do this? Here, in front of all these people? We've been over this. It was war."

War? What are they on about? What war? The Second World War?

"They were on the same side!"

"Were they? Your father's actions were treasonous. My grandfather did what he had to. People were hurt, that much is true—"

"People were murdered! How many died in the death camps under your grandfather's supervision?"

Concentration camps? All the world knows the horror of those places. The summoned recoils at his thoughts of a moment ago, how he had wished for Denison's salvation.

But the conversation continues.

"Shall we tell these others here, Denison, what we are talking about, how you and I are connected? How my father and your grandfather were both German scientists? One respected, the other disgraced?"

"It was a different time and place. Things were done."

"Weren't they!"

And then the conversation gravitates to a time before that war. To a crash site in a Bavarian forest in the winter of 1936. How what was seen defied explanation. For this had been no ordinary crash site. And years later, now safely in America, Werner von Braun would famously claim that what was found on that chilly night provided the Nazis with the technology for his V-2 Rocket. How what was found had been tested on other new technological weaponry mercifully terminated with Hitler's suicide. How what was found was eventually supplied by Braun and other Nazis to the Americans in their never-ending quest to one-up the Soviets in the space race. How what was found eventually landed men on the moon.

And now Denison, like his grandfather, is looking to harness new technology all over again. How many people will suffer this time? the gentleman wonders. No. He will not let it happen again. He won't allow innocent people to die as others did so many years ago.

There is still more to this, the summoned reasons. So much more. And he would love to know the whole story. But his immediate concern is his own life, the value of which these two clearly have divergent views. To the gentleman, his death will benefit humankind; to Denison, his life.

Denison sneers. "Throw down your guns. We're coming in."

It is Nahas who responds. "You will not. Lay down *yours*."

"Over my dead body."

"If that's what it takes."

Someone crouched behind the protective wall of an SUV ascends slowly, aims.

Fires.

The summoned hears the bullet split the air, but he sees nothing. Then beside him, Nahas suddenly buckles, grunts awkwardly, and crumples. He does not move again. The summoned half turns, looks. Blood is running down Nahas' forehead, comingling with the soft sand. Lifeless eyes, glazed over, stare at the sky. He spies the pistol lying close by. Then he does the only thing that comes to mind: he runs.

The next several seconds unfold with pure tension. No one moves. And then someone, on who's side it is unclear, loses their nerve and begins firing. The single rifle is answered tenfold. And then everything descends into chaos. Those safely behind the protection of their vehicles discharge a deadly volley of bullets at the visible TAPs and Hanuti priests, many of whom make for easy targets. But Denison's attack does not stop there. Those in his company who had been ordered west under cover of the tree line now come into full view around and behind the information centre, attacking the flanks of Nahas' men.

Beyond the firefight, yards away to the east now, towards Cairo, the summoned sprints. He does not process what he is doing; all he knows is that he is afraid. What he will remember most about this day is this terror he now feels. Ahead, a wall separates the plateau from modern civilisation. Overhanging sycamores peer from above, representative of the perimeter of the Mena House golf course. He will make for there; the pyramid can wait.

As he races across the gently declining plateau, he notices that men are in pursuit. One of them is Sanderson, Denison's chief minion. In front of him, the wall carries on as far as he can see. Could he scale it? Doubtful, at least without necessary time. But he has no time. His thoughts turn to the professor, to Lauren. Where are they? Can he leave them? He looks to the pyramid.

There you must go.

No. He cannot. Not with these men on his tail. He races on, and suddenly, he isn't thinking about action. He is thinking about her. Doesn't she know he would have done anything for her? She is his mother, of course. Family is family, to the ends of the Earth. And then the anger begins to swell anew. *Ask your mother. Ask your mother.*

Climb.

Two of the men are gaining, manoeuvring themselves along the wall in the hopes of occluding his flight. It works: he is forced into altering his course, towards the Great Pyramid itself. Rows of uneven stone gawk at him. The men are fanning out across the landscape, a human partition between themselves and the pyramid. There is no other option: he will have to follow the voice. He will have to climb.

He moves along the eastern edge of the structure, glancing back at his pursuers. They seem to be falling behind. He looks up. What can he be thinking? His friends aren't up there; there is no one up there. Only destiny. He stares at the massive casing stones he's been told about. The last vestiges of antiquity. He turns. The men are closing in. He has to go now.

The entire first row is composed of casing stones. He pulls himself up. He is on the pyramid for the second time.

What strikes him almost immediately is just how rough these once-hidden stones are. In the darkness of last night, he could not discern how their imperfection nonetheless forms into rows. Some are taller than others. With others, pieces have fallen away, like shed skin, adding to the difficulty of the task. Regardless, he hasn't the time to dwell on the danger he is imposing on himself.

As he rises, he can see past his pursuers desperately climbing one stone after another in the hopes of catching him, can see all. The professor, Lauren, Wasem. Denison, who clearly has them. The firefight must have ended. He assumes he must end this, too. And part of him wants to, wants to be down there with the others, with her. So that he can enter this enormous engineering marvel, just as Denison wants him to, to breathe in whatever secrets it holds, to understand just who he is after all. But he cannot will himself to surrender. It is simply illogical at the moment. Call it human nature.

At first, he takes to traversing the pyramid horizontally, circumnavigating it in the hopes of eluding his pursuers. And as he nears its north-eastern edge, he perceives that his pursuers are also having difficulty; these stones were never meant for races.

They shout to one another, coordinating their attack by separating. They will attempt to seize him in his flank.

He abandons the horizontal scaling, turns instead and gazes upward. What is up there? He remembers something he'd read, something that suddenly makes sense to him. The top of the pyramid is flat. He will make that his final stand, then. Or he will offer terms: he will enter the pyramid alone and discover therein what awaits him.

Or, perhaps, he will die up there. There is always that possibility.

How long has he been climbing? With each row he conquers, the sun creeps ever higher into the sky, the city becomes less and less visible behind a thick hedge of pollution. Minutes have given way, he assumes, into hours. Or perhaps not. Perhaps time is passing sluggishly by.

At one point, the sound of breathing flourishes audibly behind him. He glances over his shoulder. One of the attackers is outdistancing the others, is gaining on him. He refocuses, slips on a broken stone, staggers awkwardly, hanging by his right arm only, his legs dangling over the pyramid's edge. The attacker sees this, and he slows in an effort not to arouse panic. The summoned fumbles with his loose arm, realises shards have been pried loose. Wait—shards can be weapons. He clutches one, revolves, throws it downward. It bounces harmlessly near the pursuer, who tosses back a hollered obscenity. He finds a larger broken piece, hurtles it down. This time, the projectile lands near enough to the attacker that the man loses his balance, and he topples backwards and down the face of the pyramid, row after row after row, until he lands in a heap far below on the desert floor. He does not stir.

A second attacker appears from around the side of the pyramid. The summoned searches for other loose shards, but there are none. A hand emerges on his left calf. The attacker has moved several metres in mere seconds, it seems, and now he has him. The summoned strains to free himself, but the minion is too large, too strong. And he is reaching ever higher, his hands now around the summoned's throat. He calls down to the others. A hand ranges down to a belt for something. The summoned can see the cold steel of a revolver. And then he can feel it, the muzzle against the ridge of his jawline. He glances up into the man's eyes.

He wriggles again, but his arms have been pinioned in such a way that they are immobile. He studies his position and sees how this is possible: the man is leaning forward, one forearm across his chest, elbow on one bicep, hand on the other. The man's second hand is holding the pistol. A very powerful man. And confident. But there is one weapon he has at his disposal, something the minion has not considered. It is what men consider a low blow, both figuratively and literally, but he has no option. He draws his knee backward and rifles it into the other's groin. The minion writhes, clutching at his genitals, rolling clear, pistol still in hand. The summoned lashes out, kicks the gun from the hand, amazed at his own agility. The man lunges for it, and it ricochets down the side of the pyramid. Then, seething and whispering obscenities, he turns back to face the summoned, who in turn kicks again, this time catching him squarely on the jaw. The minion loses his footing and follows the pistol, rolling like a snowball down the side of a mountain. At length, he must have smacked his head, for blood suddenly begins marking the stones he leaves in his wake. Then, like the first man, he topples onto the sandy bottom, and he moves no more.

203 rows. That is how many rows encircle the Great Pyramid. And that is how many the summoned climbs. He glances every now and again at his remaining pursuers, both of whom are falling behind, gazes out at the vast, murky city, traces the winding path of the Nile southward. He can see pyramids to the south, the architectural chain he has read about. The Band of Peace. Obscured in the heat, but rising just the same from the sand.

He realises that the air quality has changed. A fierce wind now pesters him, and despite the sun dominating high overhead, the temperature has dropped. At times, the wind is overpowering: he misplaces his grip at one point and falters mid climb, dropping down a row, dangling momentarily over the edge. He stabilises himself and moves on.

If only he had something to throw at his assailants. A pocket full of stones would do wonders. *A pocket full of shells.* But he has nothing, and they are still coming, even if they have fallen behind. At least he will have time to prepare for them when he reaches the top.

At length, helicopters float across the sky, touch down by the group of greatly diminished people now far below. A myriad of specks, like Leningen's ants, scurrying about. He can't make out their details, but he assumes Abdalla has returned with Seldon. Might that be awkward, Seldon and Denison face to face once again.

He stops. What is he climbing for, then? He can come down after all. Abdalla is an ally.

But he can't will himself to give up just yet. It is as if this is his Everest, and he must see it through. And then there is the summit at last. A single, solitary beam rises vertically above the vantage point of the stones still above him. A flagpole, perhaps. But there is no flag waving in this veritable breeze.

He propels himself over the final few stones, searches about. The summit is not as he has imagined it: it is not level: stones are clumsily elevated higher than others. A plethora of signatures are etched into these stones, evidence of past adventurers. The summit is several feet across in all directions. The flagpole is not a flagpole at all; rather, it is a tripod of sorts, intersected by a single rising beam. Beyond the confines of the summit, on three sides, is endless desert, shadowed and pock-marked. To the east is sprawling Cairo. Here he can fully grasp the sickening cloud of pollution, cancer for antiquities. He has heard stories of Greece's ancient sites crumbling to dust under the same oppressive stuff. He hears nothing of the city far below, a rhythm of eerie silence. Sees little, too, of the skyscrapers, hotels, and apartments, little of the mosques and churches. Cairo recedes into the horizon like a washed-out painting, far to the east, where it eventually merges with greyish clouds in the sky. And all the while, the great river, the life blood of this ancient land, flows on, ambling its way through the heart of the murky metropolis, passing beyond, where it, too, eventually vanishes into the vista.

He hears something. Dialogue. Down to his right, the men must be approaching. He hunts for something to use. Nothing, except for stone blocks. He cannot hope to heft them. What is he planning to do now, now that he has led them all the way up here, to this capstone-impaired peak? He glances at his fists. He will have to make due with these.

The first minion appears just then, clearly winded, breathing profusely, dragging himself over the top and reaching for a pistol. The summoned is unmoved. These men will not kill him now. The man stands, wiping a blanket of sweat from his forehead. He wrings the hand, and perspiration drips from it.

He positions himself to call down to the other still out of view, his eyes still very much fixated on the summoned, who now crouches and steps threateningly to his right, pacing the summit's perimeter, staring back with equal intent.

And then the summoned charges, head down, body bowed forward. He strikes the man, tackling him directly in his midsection. The pistol flies, and the assailant teeters backwards, onto hard stone. He gasps as his back makes contact with the rock, clearly injured. The summoned stands, grasps the pistol, steps away.

The second minion is now visible at the summit's parapet, and while the first rolls painfully onto his stomach, grasping at his back, the summoned makes for this other. There is no need to tackle here; his foot will supply all the force he needs. He lashes out, striking the man squarely on the jaw, then recoils and hits him again. The other, dazed, hastens to protect himself, arms flailing. He loses his grip, desperately reaches back, hopeful that his foot will find some sort of leverage with which to balance himself. But there is nothing, nothing but air. As the summoned watches, the man screams with awareness and tumbles backwards, down onto the next tier of stones, off which his head impacts. It is not altogether clear whether or not he is knocked unconscious; either way, his body goes slack, and he floats down, onto the next rung of stones. And then another and another, gaining speed, until he free falls several more rows and ricochets again. He continues to spiral towards the base of the pyramid. He must be long dead before he finally comes to rest amongst the casing stones far below.

He has just killed a man. The others he cannot be sure of, but this man positively. He pauses, reflecting. How does it feel? How should it? Is *kill* the right word? He has attacked the man, but ultimately his efforts were precipitated by self defense. And the man deserved it, after all. They all deserve this, Denison most of all. But Denison isn't up here. Just this man and the other—

The other man. Too late he remembers. The assailant has apparently regained his composure, crashing into him from behind. He falls, positions his arms to protect his head from colliding on the stone below. The pistol disappears over the edge, following in the wake of the others, revolving round and round as it cascades down and out of sight.

His hands fumble around the man's throat, but he is elbowed on the cheek. He recoils, screaming out in pain. He sees the man close his fist, tries unsuccessfully to deflect the blow. Again, he is struck in the face.

He retaliates, astonishing himself despite the pain, drilling a finger into the minion's eye, and the other screams and goes to his face. He punches the man twice down low, somewhere in the vulnerable midsection, and the minion collapses in agony. He stands, wiping at his bloodied face, and kicks the man twice more. Then he grabs the pursuer by the ankles, drags him precariously towards the edge of the summit. The man, blinded by pain, offers little resistance.

But there is another sound, incredibly loud and very much close by. The summoned turns. The Gazelle rises like a periscope over the partition. If this is Abdalla's chopper, he is not in it. Denison sits alongside the pilot, already reaching for a communicator. His voice resounds through an outside speaker, only too loud and clear.

There is no choice.

He submits.

Help did come to Seldon, then, in the form of a Bedouin. But the form was not the man. Bedouins did not carry bazookas. Seldon knew who this other was, then, and why he had come; he understood that this wasteland would be his tomb. The sand would desiccate and mummify him, preserve him for all time. Perhaps one day someone would dig him up, study his bones for tantalising clues of his existence. But no archaeologist would ever be able to comprehend his guilt. The guilty know no justice, nor would he now.

The Scorpion had had to come.

He tried his best not to whimper, threw off all attempts at gallantry. "So, you never did take the artefact there in the first place," he said as he stared hypnotically at the smoke from the burning Gazelle. "You've had it all this time."

All this time, the assassin replied, tossing the spent weapon aside. He had known others would eventually come for it. He had expected Seldon, but he had also expected Denison. Before he had launched the missile into the air and ended a half dozen dreams and aspirations, he had been plotting. But it was disheartening to see that his quarry had eluded him.

His quarry. So, he had always known who Denison was. Of course.

"How did you evade those men he sent after you?"

He was noncommittal, and he toyed with the terrified, round, little man. He gestured to one of Seldon's two feet, acknowledged a missing shoe. And yet, even as he said it, there it was again: the pain had returned. Almost expectantly now. Yet another aggressive bout, a mental *khamseen*. He closed his eyes, tried to blot it out. The headaches had been increasing the past few days, then they seemed to have subsided. Now, here was another. And more pronounced than before. He composed himself. Wave after tsunamic wave was gnawing unrelentingly at him. Head buried beneath a turban, sunglasses, and a moustache, he could at least conceal his discomfort from Seldon. He had come riding into Seldon's world like a Krueger nightmare, a deluge of darkness, yet he was not even in control of his own body.

You may want to go look for it, he continued. The shoe, he meant.

"Look for it?" Seldon mumbled. Bewildered, he eyed his naked foot, remembered. "No. I think it's gone." He turned and stared at the debris behind him.

The assassin followed his eyes. Perhaps it was. He breathed in the asphyxiating desert air, his mind seemingly elsewhere. But appearances are deceiving. He stepped forward, reached down, and, without pausing, grabbed Seldon by the collar and dragged him to his feet, all the while stalking across the sandy carpet towards a rocky hill.

"Are you going to kill me too?" Seldon's entire body quivered.

He had tried that already.

"I am not prepared to die."

That was a pity. The assassin had learned long ago that one should always be prepared, should always make peace with oneself. The police had no doubt discovered his address by this time, and so his time was soon at hand. We are all on borrowed time, he said. He was ready for the afterlife that awaited him. Nahas had referred to it as the weighing of the heart. Surely Ammit would take pleasure with his.

Seldon strained to keep pace, sagged at one point, dropped to one knee. The assassin simply tightened his grip on the collar, hauled him to his feet once again.

"Where are we going?"

He pointed to the rocky cliff, wincing unperceptively from the pain in his head. Why, over there, of course.

"To a hill?"

And over it.

Seldon ran his tongue across his lips, sampling the imbedded dryness of the desert. "I understand you're angry with me. I understand I owe you money."

Was he serious? Money? Was this what desperation looked like, *rashwah* at the opportune moment? As if he was after money now. Yes, payment was due, but that was hardly all. No, Seldon owed him much more than that. He owed him his soul. His *ib*, *sheut*, *ren*, *ba*, and *ka*. All of it.

"My soul?"

He turned to Seldon just then, blotting out an upsurge of pain. A single topic confused him: why was Denison not here just now?

"He's come and gone."

Certainly. But why send Seldon afterward?

"That's complicated. He didn't send me."

The assassin nodded without knowing. No matter; Denison was still alive. He would rectify that soon enough.

"Denison means to harm innocent people. I wasn't about to let that happen."

So you turned on him? Brought the government down here in the hopes of beating him to the artefact?

"Something like that."

Innocent people always became involved, the Egyptian told him. Someone in this line of work should have known that by now. David Trent had been innocent, in a way. He had knowingly discovered something, yes, but he had acted in good faith, for what he had considered the benefit of humankind. Trent had known the dangers of such an action.

And then he wondered what Seldon might have told the authorities about him. What little he knew, at any rate.

"I told them some things," Seldon mumbled anxiously. He closed his eyes, felt the hand on his collar suddenly tighten. He braced himself. But nothing came. He opened his eyes. The assassin was staring at him, a merciless gaze that tore through every fibre of his very being. And he understood finally what pure hatred looks like in a man's eyes, in his heart; what it feels like, in the form of a clenched hand on a shirt collar.

What did this pathetic creature take him for? That he'd unleash a beating out here? No, he reaffirmed, that would be too easy. There were some things left to do first. And he might need Seldon alive.

"You plan to escape?"

No, he had no intention of escape. His journey would end here, where it had begun. Egypt had birthed him; so, too, would it be his grave.

"You still plan on killing Denison."

He laughed a second time, then seized Seldon and began walking again.

"I would have loved to have seen the look on Denison's face when he discovered there was nothing hidden in the boat house after all. And it's ironic: I warned him of the possibility. Because you never did hide it here, did you?"

Denison came to dig in the sand. As with Trent.

"What was it like, the digging for it?"

Seldon, whatever do you mean?

"I mean, Trent and the artefact. I assume you accompanied him at least some of the time. What was it like, right under the pyramids and all? It must have been exciting."

Seldon, Trent was digging in the sand, but he was nowhere near Giza. You must have assumed, even with your bribing the MSA, that such an enterprise at Giza would have been monumental. And costly.

"But he was looking for the Hall of Records."

No, he was looking for evidence.

"But that's what the Hall of Records is—direct evidence."

Trent wanted you to think he was at Giza, assumed you were stupid enough to exclude logic. An excavation at Giza could never have been undertaken by one man—two, if you include me.

The assassin looked askance at him.

You did consider this, did you not, Seldon?

No answer.

Oh, Seldon. So naïve.

"Where, then?"

Far from there. His secret will die with me. That much I do for him.

Seldon gazed out onto the desert, wondered at the vastness of it all, hopelessly tried to understand what he was hearing, hopelessly tried to conceive where Trent must have gone. How could he have been so stupid?

"He could have been anywhere."

Not just anywhere.

Seldon relented. "I see. Let the secret die with you, then, as you say. But seeing as you plan on killing me anyway, perhaps you can divulge where you hid the artefact."

They began ascending the rocky dune. Seldon flinched, his feet impacting on a mixture of jagged stone and golden powder.

"You lied to me."

Yes, he had lied. He had betrayed Seldon, just as Seldon had betrayed him. Just as Denison had betrayed him.

Seldon forced a laugh. "Then we're even, yes?"

Not quite.

The remark was brief and ominous. Seldon sensed fresh sweat forming on his forehead, slowly weaving its way through his hairline, down the side of his face. "I won't tell anyone anything. I just want to get out of here."

They both knew that wasn't going to happen. The assassin calmly extended his left arm to balance himself as they continued to the crest of the hill.

There were many people interested in what he had in his possession, he explained. And, admittedly, he did not fully comprehend what this artefact represented. So, he was curious as well. Therefore—

He gestured ahead. They were almost there.

"Almost where?"

Within seconds, they had cleared the rise of the hill. A solitary and starkly white Rav4 awaited. He smiled, reassured. "We're not walking."

It would have been a rather long walk from here.

The Egyptian stepped to the rear of the vehicle, opened the back hatch, and Seldon could see him fumbling for something. He also saw several wooden cases, the lids of some bobbling, as if things within were trying to get free.

I cannot read ancient hieroglyphics, after all, so I am in need of a translator.

"Wonderful. Where are we headed, then?"

They would learn the secrets of Trent's artefact together.

"And how do you plan on doing that? I can't read hieroglyphics either."

A translator was no doubt there now.

"Where?"

Patience, Seldon.

"A translator?"

The assassin smiled once again.

Perhaps you've heard of him. His name is Henry Booth.

Sunlight stabbed Yaghdjian playfully in his one functional eye. He must have blacked out. They'd tied him up, while the embalming was still transpiring. Beaten him senseless. He was in utter agony. He knew his right eye was swollen closed. His mouth had been taped. There was some relief, however: they hadn't broken any of his appendages.

He saw the body on the gurney. Two priests were hovered nearby, carefully applying linen strips. Normally this didn't happen for several days, not until after the corpse had been dipped in natron to dry out. Nahas had mentioned speeding up the process. That had certainly been accomplished.

He spied the canopic jars. The intestines, kidneys, lungs, brain. Other organs of the body. But not the heart: he presumed it had no doubt been left in place. For the weighing in the afterlife.

And then came salvation.

There was the sound of something being wrenched. The door to the warehouse burst open, armed police officers racing through. The priests backed cautiously away. One of them moved to the table of jars, dove for a gun. An officer discharged a bullet into his back, and he fell at once. The second priest tried to run, but there was nowhere to go. Two other officers downed him with ease.

More and more uniformed men were entering. Two knelt down close by him. He closed his good eye, willing them away. They did not exist, this was not happening, he would soon be dead, all was lost. He waited. Nothing. He opened his eye. One of them was loosening the rope around his arms, his ankles; the other was removing the tape across his mouth.

He saw another man, a boiling tempest for an expression. The others snapped to when he entered. He looked down at Yaghdjian. "Get him up," he commanded. "And get him something to drink."

Yaghdjian felt his body being lifted from the floor. He was carried out of the room towards the office he'd once been locked in. Positioned into the desk chair, he collapsed in relief. He glanced up at the commander, who was towering over him now, staring straight into his terrified eyes. The words were exactly what he'd needed to hear.

"It's all over now. Do you hear me, son? It's over."

Another man approached. "Here's some water."

The commander grabbed the cup. "Thanks, Gamil." He turned to Yaghdjian. "Here. Drink this."

Yaghdjian downed the contents in between muted thanks.

The commander turned to an officer hovering close by. "Ramzy, is this the man Wasem spoke with?"

"I think so, sir," Ramzy nodded.

"Are you Nubar Yaw-Gin?"

Yaghdjian nodded vigorously.

"You spoke with Inspector Wasem."

He nodded a second time.

Yes, yes. I'm the one. Policemen kidnapped me and brought me here. For my protection. They said Inspector Wasem was a—a...some kind of terrorist, and he was responsible for the death of Professor Trent, and...

His voice trailed off amid the laughter emanating from the officers.

The commander forced back a smile. "We're not laughing at you."

He's not a terrorist?

"No, he's not a terrorist. He's an awful son of a bitch, but he's no terrorist."

Then who were these men?

"Good question. Someone's going to have some serious explaining to do."

They had their heads shaved, and they were dressed like Hanuti.

He could tell the officer didn't understand what he meant.

"What else can you tell us?"

The image of the elderly European focussed in his mind.

There were also some Europeans.

"Europeans?"

"Was there a man named Nahas here?" Ramzy wondered.

Yes. He seemed to be in charge. But there was an older man, one of the Europeans, and he seemed to have some clout as well.

"Nahas is the reason we found you, by the way. He blew his cover last night. Officer Ramzy tracked him here."

Yaghdjian stared through the door, his eye lingering on the form of Charobim. What kind of people would do that to a person?

Ramzy followed his gaze. "Sick people."

They had so many questions.

"Like what?"

They wanted to know about the conversations Professor Trent and I had. The older man with them. He started asking me all these strange things. About Denmark, Mexico, the Exodus.

"The Exodus?" Gamil wondered. "What the hell's that got to do with anything?"

I don't know. He was asking about ley lines, this thing called the World Grid.

He looked up and saw Ramzy and Gamil glance expectantly at each other. Then the commander asked him the question he had hoped to answer most of all.

"Where did Nahas go?"

I don't know. When I woke up, he was already gone.

Brigadier General Deeb straightened, looked at his men in turn. "Find him. And somebody get this young man looked after." And he turned and departed the scene with bravado.

The Great Pyramid—all of the pyramids at Giza, in fact—are largely devoid of writing. Largely, but not completely, since some hieroglyphics have been found, discovered more by accident than anything else. In the Great Pyramid, there is a single etching that reads "Khufu." It is high up in the ceiling of the King's Chamber. Historians largely attribute the pyramid to this pharaoh in part because of this etching. However, the Westcar Papyrus, discovered in the 1820s, does mention Khufu as the apparent pyramid's builder. On display at the Egyptian Museum in Berlin, scholars have debated its age, but many agree that it was likely copied from some source that predates it. Regardless, it tells stories from the 4th dynasty, the time of Khufu. In one, Khufu is contemplating building his own "horizon." By the term horizon, "pyramid" is assumed. Khufu wants his horizon to rival the monumental sanctuary of the god of wisdom, Thoth—*Djihauti*, as the Khemitians might have pronounced it. But no one knows how many chambers are in Thoth's sanctuary. Well, almost no one. There is a rumour that an old magician by the name of Djedi, 110 years old, has the answer. So the pharaoh commands Djedi brought before him. Djedi is extremely talented: he can reattach severed heads, can teach lions to walk tamely behind him, and, of course, knows all about Thoth's sanctuary. He also has quite an appetite: he supposedly eats five hundred loaves of bread a day, a whole shoulder of beef, and he washes it all down with five hundred beers.

Djedi arrives, and Khufu brings in a condemned criminal. In perfect Khufuan tradition, the malevolent ruler orders the magician to cut off and then reattach the man's head. Djedi refuses, offering instead to showcase his skills on a goose, some other unidentified type of bird, and a bull. Khufu agrees, and the animals are conveyed to the royal court. Djedi does as he says: he cuts off and then reattaches the animals' heads. But of course, this is not why he has been summoned. The fun over with, Khufu now demands the answer to his question: how many chambers are in the sanctuary? Djedi replies that he does not know, but he does know where the chambers are kept: in a flint box in the holy city of Heliopolis, the home of the Temple of Ra. Khufu is undeterred. He demands this flint box be brought to him. But Djedi again refuses the pharaoh, maintaining that only the eldest of three future kings will bring it to Khufu.

And so, perhaps there is evidence that the Great Pyramid belongs to Khufu.

Unless this was all written by generations long after the pyramid was built, generations politically intent on attributing the structure to this pharaoh.

Regardless, nowadays, only a handful of tourist tickets are issued daily to enter the pyramids at Giza. But there is always the *rashwah*. *Bakshish*, the TAPs would prefer. Yes, the *bakshish*. Regardless, most people never have the opportunity to see inside.

The summoned will have that chance. He will have it because Denison will force it on him, but also because he must go: the voice gently bids him enter. And he does so without fear; this is his destiny, after all.

A man approaches Denison. "Sir, no word from Abdalla."

Denison bites down hard on derision. "That's disconcerting."

The summoned stares at him.

"We're not the bad guys, remember?" Denison intimates to the entrance to the complex, where several Egyptians and Europeans alike have their hands raised hands in supplication. "They are."

You're all the same. You killed David Trent.

"Not true. I only ordered his death."

Somewhere under this plateau is the greatest discovery in the history of archaeology, and you really think you can keep it a secret?

He laughs, gestures downward. "You're mistaken. That's not the greatest discovery in the history of archaeology. You are." He then turns back to Sanderson. "Where did he go?"

By the frustration in his voice, it is evident that he must mean the old man, the one who once sat next to him at Alumni Hall, the one who Denison seems to know so intimately.

Sanderson shrugs. "He must have taken off when the shooting began."

"At least he wasn't successful." Denison nods to the summoned.

The professor points to a slightly obscured staircase, consisting of six short flights of steps, leading upwards. "We'll go up here." He smiles at the summoned, gestures again. "About seven rows up is the entrance Al Mamun ordered carved in 820."

The summoned spies the crude opening.

"And further up—" Lauren is pointing to a location higher yet—"That's where the original entrance is, sealed by the ancients."

He gazes, sees the angular stones above the ancient doorway.

Wasem stares at the daunting mountain in front of him. He had not gone so far last night. "How many rows of stones are there in total?"

"Two hundred and three," Lauren says. "The equivalent to a 48 story building."

The summoned regards the first row in front of him. Only so recently he'd touched them. Foundation stones, perfectly smooth. And to think the entire pyramid used to be covered by them. He can only imagine what it once looked like.

Denison is short on patience. "The sun will only get hotter, and I'm already warm enough as it is. Let's go."

The climb to Al Mamun's entrance comprises approximately one minute: six mini-staircases, then a slight step down onto a platform that leads to the entrance itself. The professor arrives first to the ancient caliph's tunnel. He waits for the others, then glances at the gash in the wall. Beyond the roughly carved outline is pure darkness.

"Pass the lights up," Denison commands to the minions behind him.

A few fumble in knapsacks slung over their shoulders. They are searching for something. Within seconds, it is clear: flashlights.

Denison offers one to the professor, who grabs it, turns abruptly and begins shining it along Al-Mamun's entranceway.

The entrance itself is crude: teeth-like dents of a dozen pitchforks indicate a hastily and likely desperate struggle to break through. Above, every so often, a beam has been inserted in modern times to stabilise the makeshift tunnel's ceiling. It is a tight space, and the procession instantly falls into single file. The professor, still in the lead, steps confidently into the darkness.

"It's dark, but when we hook up with the actual passageway the ancients dug, you'll see a difference." The professor glances past the summoned and the silhouettes of others. "We'll make for the King's Chamber."

And there it is again. The energy, pulsing through the summoned's body. Like before, at Tanis; but not like before: this force is far more powerful now, the most acute it has ever been. He is close, so close, to answers.

I suppose no one feels anything strange?

Lauren dips her head in his direction. "Such as…?"

I don't know—energy?

"People have commented on some sort of energy given off by the pyramids," she offers. "The same thing happens to some when in the presence of other historic structures around the world. All of these structures are connected."

Ley lines.

They continue for a few moments until the professor halts at what appears to be a modern flight of stairs angling slightly to the left, then upwards. All around is evidence of sophisticated masonry on display: the walls are gigantic solid stone blocks that have been carved and fitted together as if by machine precision.

The summoned stares. Petrie, Dunn. Yes, machines. He touches the seam between two such blocks, runs his hand along it. Astonishingly perfect. A hair will not pass between the stones, just as he has read.

They are now in a much more angled passageway that breaks into two parts: one hallway continues upwards, while another passes straight ahead.

"If we go straight, we hit the Queen's Chamber," the professor explains. "But we're not going that way: we're going up, to the King's Chamber."

Here, along the walls, the travellers notice handrails that have been inserted in modern times. As well, the floor seems to have been covered over with wooden planks resembling short steps. At one time, this passageway must have been arduous at best through which to manoeuvre.

The precipitously inclined hallway is changing again: while it lingers on the same proportionate slope, the close ceiling suddenly gives way, now angling upwards several metres. The walls grow in unison, and flashlights from the travellers dance along these unexpected towering partitions and beams, splaying the raised ceiling above in soft, pale hues. Regularly-spaced rectangular holes punctured in the walls are visible, as well as unusually roughly-hewn chisel marks further up and running along the shaft.

"This is the Grand Gallery," the professor calls down to those behind him. "It carries on for a few minutes until we reach the King's Chamber itself."

The ceiling is marvellously high, impossibly high. As one stares upward, one will notice how the walls seem to converge. It is known as a corbelled ceiling. This, Egyptologists have explained, was likely done to alleviate pressure from so many stones weighing on one another. It is yet another marvel of ancient engineering.

The summoned scans the sparse walls, the ceiling, with his light.

Just like you said. Nothing written anywhere. This place is bare.

A sound from beyond startles them. The armed minions in their company reach for their side arms. Flashlights pan back down the way they've ventured.

What was that?

"Something going on outside," the professor offers.

Denison hesitates for several seconds, unnerved but unwilling to stop. They cannot now. Not when they are so close. And yet, he has no idea what they are close to. "Forget it," he orders anxiously. "Lead on, Professor."

Deeb gapes out the front window of his police SUV. Someone has smashed through police barricades. Now there are helicopters visible on the premises, as well as dozens of other cars and SUVs. Aérospatiale Gazelles. But there are several foreigners as well, men dressed in military desert fatigues. These men look like American Navy Seals. What are they doing here? And where is Nahas and his merry band of priests? He asks Yaghdjian, nestled next to him, if he can see any one of the men who kidnapped him. Yaghdjian's response is discouraging: these are not the men.

He glances skyward. That's strange. Something is happening up there.

The first thing he notices is an armada of copious, darkening pillow-like cumulus clouds swiftly approaching, where heretofore there have been none. They are like a pack of ardent hunting dogs, and in a matter of seconds, they have obstructed the placid blue sky, staining the sun with fog. He studies them, these fast-moving apparitions, and his intuition tells him to be afraid of what is coming. For this is no ordinary storm: these clouds move of their own volition. Those in front are actually pausing, immobilising in the sky. As if pulled on with invisible reins. How is this possible? But stopping they are. They are hovering above the Giza Plateau.

Does anyone else see this? Young Yaghdjian, already gripped with fear, sees it. His driver sees it. Deeb radios the other cars. The men in there, too, see it. He looks ahead. The foreigners who have taken over the Plateau see it. All stare upward, transfixed, dreading.

And then there is a sudden reverberation throughout the complex, steadfastly increasing. The ground beneath, charged with life, begins to convulse, more and more vociferously with each passing moment.

Deeb watches as the military men, whoever they are, begin to wobble, as though trying to gain footing on a trampoline. The ground is heaving uncontrollably. Some of them are falling over outright, others spacing their legs to steady themselves. He looks to the dashboard of the SUV. A walkie-talkie has been left there, and it now bounces haphazardly, then slides off altogether.

He orders the driver to weave around the toppled barricades and enter the complex. Yes, he repeats, enter. The driver is disbelieving, and he wears a face of fear that he cannot mask. But he does as he is told, and as they pass through, new details begin to emerge of what has happened here in the moments before their arrival. Many of the vehicles have been racked with gunfire. As well, blood is unmistakably evident on the convulsing sandy floor and tarmac. Blood, but no bodies.

They halt, just as several of the foreigners who have regrouped are drawing on them, threatening to fire. Threatening but not intending. It is a purely natural reaction. Deeb orders Yaghdjian to stay put, stumbles clear of his vehicle. The trampoline flooring. A megaphone is in his trembling hand. He steadies himself, draws it to his lips, speaks in surprisingly efficient English. These men are to throw down their weapons and surrender at once.

He spots someone else. Someone he knows. Large, dirty, insufferable. Wasem. He relishes the conversation they are about to have.

One of the foreigners makes his way over to the brigadier. Deeb demands he identify himself, offer some sort of explanation.

The man's name is Sanderson. His superior is inside the Great Pyramid this very moment. This is a matter of national security, he says, of the highest order. General Abdalla of the Homeland Security had been here earlier, had apparently left, has not returned. In the meantime, a firefight ensued.

When this Sanderson speaks of Egyptians with shaved heads alongside TAP officers, Deeb cringes. He has many questions. Why are people inside the pyramid? What is happening in the sky? Why are these Americans—for that is who he assumes they are—running amuck with weapons and battle gear in his country? Why have they commandeered the Giza Plateau?

Sanderson makes like he wants to speak, but he instead directs the general to the pyramid, indicating he might want to have a look for himself.

He will have his look. But first he will secure the area. Secure the area—that's ironic. The area is completely not securable. In the distance, he can hear multitudes of horns honking, ambulance and police sirens droning. There must be widespread panic across the city at the moment.

He demands the bodies of those killed be shown to him. He wants to see one in particular, a former inspector whom he had at one time had some regard for.

But a massive, guttural emission from above drowns out anything Sanderson has to say, and the brigadier looks up once again. Something very bad is about to happen.

The Grand Gallery is a truly impressive piece of architecture, the summoned contemplates. Eight metres high, just over two metres wide, 48 metres long, an incline of 50%. He waves his flashlight. Above, he scans blocks, each weighing an estimated 60 tonnes. 60 tonnes. That is over 132 000 pounds. *Each.* Oh, to know Leedskalnin's secrets!

His body continues to pulsate. An electric charge, renewed, increasing rapidly in sensation. He regards his own hands, turning them over. He laughs.

The professor glimpses uncertainly at Denison. "Something tells me you're going to get plenty of answers today."

"Maybe so." The expedition's leader stares at the summoned with a maniacal look about him, a morbid fascination intermingled with jealousy.

The summoned regards him.

Satisfied?

"Are you?"

Not yet. This is only the beginning.

"How do you know?"

In the wan light, he stares at his hands a second time. He simply knows.

The further inside we travel, the stronger the charge gets.

"Ahead is the King's Chamber," the professor announces.

He remembers from his reading. For anyone who has never been inside the King's Chamber, suffice to say it is an engineering wonder. The room itself is expansive: ten and a half metres in width one way, and just over five metres the other. Like the Grand Gallery, the ceiling here towers overhead, almost six metres above. Here, one can view more masterful craftsmanship: red granite blocks translated into walls, so expertly fitted together that nothing can pass between any two of them at any one point; the ceiling is comprised of nine massive blocks, also cut from granite, collectively weighing hundreds of tonnes.

Furthermore, the acoustics in the King's Chamber are remarkable. This is immediately obvious as soon as the professor enters from underneath the low-slung antechamber leading into the room and breathes a sigh of relief: his exhalation is operatic in volume, and he relishes the chamber's power.

The others arrive en masse, speaking, unaware of the potency of their voices. An immediate, cacophonous wall of sound resonates within. It is beautiful and harmonic glossolalic mumble jumble.

Upon entering, the summoned laughs, a curious reaction he hadn't contemplated. Perhaps it is the anticlimactic appearance of the room, this surprisingly sparse, darkened chamber. Regardless, the guffaw immediately echoes off the walls and ceiling, is restored voluminously to him, like falconry. It is aggressive, overwhelming, yet delightful. He wonders what it must have been like to record musically in this space; others have in the past, and he is jealous. He listens to the reverberating voices of the others, varying pitches intertwining, pursuing a common tone. Such haunting beauty. He knows that musical pitch that now dominates the chamber. He's known it for years, from back when he had superstar aspirations with Stand Up for Bastards, back when he wrote and performed songs in this key. He's always loved that tone, has never understood why. Now he knows. They have instilled the love of F# into him, they who took him when he was twelve years old, from that blackened nightmare of a forest. But there is something else he now understands, something that makes perfect sense.

He'd felt the same tonal harmony at the crop circle.

He begins to hum. Slowly at first, uncertain, but gaining in momentum, confidence, tuned with the pitch of the voices.

"What are you doing?" Lauren wonders.

I'm humming. This room is tuned to the harmonic frequency of F#. And so was the crop circle.

"F#..."

Our conversation the other night in the pool. Remember?

Yes, she remembers. Water. DNA. Crop circles. The Great Pyramid. A single symbiotic relationship. F#. The key signature of the Earth.

"I remember," she says. "And I do feel something now." She seals her eyes and breaths in the surrounding acoustical energy. "The King's Chamber was built like this on purpose, to draw energy from the room, and, in this case, the people in it."

The professor is pointing his light far up into the terraced section of the ceiling. As the summoned draws closer, he can see far above a gabled ceiling of granite slabs. There is a sequence of graffiti evident on the walls.

"Lots of people have taken it upon themselves to autograph the pyramid," the professor says. "However, if you look there, you'll see some ancient writing. Do you see it?" His light passes over a smallish series of hieroglyphics.

I do.

"That's Khufu's name. When Howard Vyse came here in 1837, he discovered it. Zechariah Sitchin proclaimed it a fraud, that Vyse put the inscription there. Either way, the hieroglyphics read 'Khufu,' and scholars use that as more evidence the pyramid was indeed built during the pharaoh's time."

He stares at a large, oblong container, its corner torn. To most, it is a sarcophagus, apparent overwhelming evidence that this massive structure was in fact a tomb. Where Khufu's body was laid to rest. His hands gravitate to the empty container, probing its smooth outer walls. The energy is increasing again. Something is directing him to this abandoned box, just as it directed him at Tanis, at the Sofitel. The voice. Just as it likely directed him to Alumni Hall, to meet the professor in the first place. He raises one leg after another over its walls, steps into it. As he does so, there is a equalisation of sorts: the shockwaves in his body decrease. Equilibrium. He feels alive, though entirely composed. Absolute tranquility. It is difficult to describe just what he feels, except to say that he has never felt so good in all his life. He has found his place of calling. And in his mind, images of triangles and the number 42 drift towards him, but in a peaceful sense, not with the overwhelming surge as they'd once done. He's arrived. This has been where they have always wanted him to go, needed him to go.

He can hear lowered voices in the room, then nothing, a lull in the reverberating melody of their words. He knows they are staring at him. "What are you doing?" he hears one of them say finally, and he knows it must be Lauren.

I don't know exactly, he says. But I feel good.

He spreads his arms, revolves in a circle. This is it. This is where they wanted me to come. Ever since I was twelve years old, a terrified boy in a forest.

And then, he begins to radiate. Power is flowing through him. But not an overwhelming current, not an unwelcome sensation. No, he still feels fine. Feels *right*, is better. Feels, in a heightened sense, like everything has been set in order. He closes his eyes, envisions what it must look like inside of him, this current of energy gushing through his veins. He senses it in every extremity: pulsating in his toes, up his thighs, through his torso, into his chest and arms, his head. He clenches his fingers into fists, watches them quiver. He spreads them outward, away from himself, toward an unoccupied wall.

Almost immediately, the increased surge of energy is felt in everyone in the room, as if they'd all suddenly stepped onto an electrified floor. Several of the armed minions retreat nervously, grumbling tense words under their breath. Denison is visibly shaken as well, though he smiles like Dr. Frankenstein. At any moment, he might break into screams of "It's alive! Alive!" But this is not what he says. Instead, he says, "Can you feel that? That's power. Real power!"

They listen; or, rather, sense: a low hum, rising in crescendo, eventually morphing into a much more obvious drone. It is as if the entire chamber is beginning to convulse.

"What's happening?" Lauren shouts anxiously.

"It feels like the room's becoming unstable!" the professor hollers. "He needs to get out of there!"

"He doesn't need to go anywhere!" Denison retorts. He notices movement out of the corner of his eye, turns, watches to his amazement that several of his own men are scurrying to the chamber's entrance, back under the low-cut entrance, and disappearing beyond. "Where the hell are you going?" he calls after them.

But he will not leave. Not now. As terrifying as this has all become, he cannot leave. Mark Brydges has tapped into a source of energy beyond his wildest imagination. Mark Brydges *is* energy. He imagines the implications.

It takes them all a few seconds to realise, but something has happened to the summoned. Something has taken possession of him. He remains in the box, arms still erect, but his eyes are now closed. Something like he was at Tanis. He is gone again, off into some other universe, some other dimension.

Though this time, nothing can prepare him for what he is about to experience.

Around him, the others slow, then freeze, fixated on where he had been. Or is it he who has sped up, like Captain Kirk in that old Scalosian episode? It is impossible to know.

They are taking control of him in that ancient rectangular container, this he does know. He is departing, drifting upwards and out through the chamber's entrance, down through the gallery, out past Al Mamun's tunnelled entrance, into the open air. He glides out over the pyramid complex, and he sees in front of him, undisturbed as if for centuries, a solitary ovular object in the sand. Some sort of craft? A spaceship? From where? Is this real, this thing here and now? He peers beyond the ship, and he can no longer see Cairo. Instead, there is lush greenery fed by the waters of the Nile. But through the trees, he thinks he spied civilisation. Temples, pylons, pillars, all highlighted in dazzling reds and blues and greens and yellows. Memphis, known to the Khemitians as Inbu Hedj, *the White Walls. Thousands of years ago.*

His feet gravitate downward, and he is gently ushered towards the craft. It is solid silver, crafted to perfection, with no visible markings. A door opens, and he sees nothing but a single chair inside, and a viewport beyond that. He steps in and sits. The door closes, and his stomach lurches; he is ascending.

He gazes out the viewport. He is rising ever higher, and below him, spread out now like a worn map, is the Giza complex. Then Memphis. And then the Nile. Always the Nile. But like everything else, eventually it, too, diminishes, a simple blue streak, a curved line on a canvas of dull brown, off gold, and occasional green.

As he travels higher, he sees that the whole of the Mediterranean is unfolding before him, the dull brown and off-gold of North Africa terminating dramatically at the radiant blue of the ocean. And he sees Europe, an array of greens and browns and even whites—the mountains—and the leg that is Italy, her Sicilian boot drifting nearby. And then he is moving higher again, and Europe and Africa begin to recede. White clouds materialise, partially obscuring all below.

And then he is through the atmosphere, gliding through the blackness of space, the Earth now an orb, retreating into darkness. And there, too, is the pock-marked moon, squatting shyly, partially hidden from view. And then stars. Endless stars.

His little craft swims further into night, and he knows he should be afraid. The darkness is everywhere. But he is not afraid. Just as he should have been afraid on that ship when he was twelve but was not. Where is he going? He thinks he could make out constellations. Is that Orion he is heading for? It must be, can only be. The Duat. The realm of the gods. He cannot be sure but is altogether sure in unison. There is the belt, the three closely approximated stars that Giza so artfully represents. He is accelerating, and the stars unexpectedly distend, as if someone is toying with their elasticity. Stretching. Yes, they are actually stretching, elongating. How is this possible? The light is dazzling, and he closes his eyes.

He is hurtling through the cosmos. This is the reason for the altering stars—the speed warps and blurs them. There is Mars, god of war, a far more washed-out red than he had assumed, with dark forest-shadows across her facade. He flies past a cluster of asteroids, and thinks of Millennium Falcons and TIE fighters in hot pursuit. He flies past pale brown and orange Jupiter, king of the universe, studies the dull pastel hues of the giant planet, latitudinal bands of colour encircling her like a child's water colour. There is the Great Red Spot, south of the equator, the size of Earth all on her own, a perpetual anticyclonic storm. And her sundry moons, little multicultural children encircling her. Many small, four large. The Galilean Moons: Io, Europa, Ganymede, Callisto. Then Jupiter vanishes, and within minutes, he spies drab Saturn, god of plenty, and its harvested rings, or bands, composed of trillions of tiny ice and dust particles, endlessly gyrating. He flies past the pale blue Uranus, Greek god of the sky, a portion of her northern hemisphere a lightened sheen from the glare of the sun. Then Neptune, god of the sea, much darker in hue, more horizontal bands encircling her. He sees other planets, dwarfs, circling past, and he wonders if Nibiru is out here amongst these others? Then he is free of the Milky Way, careering into the undiscovered country of the universe.

Undiscovered—no, that is not true: satellites like Voyager have penetrated this far, beaming images back to Earth. But he is plunging beyond even these reaches, into the night-time eternity of beyond. And what he sees amazes him.

There are hordes of stars, irregularly spaced pin pricks on black. And each of these stars is its own solar system, and he passes through several of them. He *glimpses planets, gas giants and oxygen-generators, red and blue and brown and white and green, and sometimes all colours at once. He beholds Earth, or something like it, time and time again. Breathable worlds. Extraterrestrial homelands. He sees accompanying moons, singular or in clusters, and all in varying shades and pigments. And he sees the cores to these systems—suns, great yellowish orbs of fire.*

From time to time, he spots rectangular, winged birds of prey, spaceships gliding effortlessly through the blackness. Silver and grey. And there are other ships, too, smaller and larger of all configuration—round, square, wingless, antennae-dominant, cylindrical. Still others of bright orange and yellow and red streak past. Some of the ships float in space like frozen mummies, and he passes so close that he can see the viewports along their sides, thinks he can see beings moving to and fro within.

And then a single planet is before him, so much like Earth that at first he assumes he is home. But this is not Earth: the enlarged continents have shifted, and the oceans have receded. And there is not one moon, but two, neither resembling the lifeless bulb suspended in the Earth's pull; they are like the planet itself. Little mini planets. Like shabtis to their pharaoh.

For, indeed, this is the world of the pharaohs.

He ruptures through the atmosphere, zooms across a blue sky darkening on the horizon. Overhead, the sun moves in the opposite direction, away from him. A mass of continent spreads below, but it, too, quickly passes into the shadows of night. And he sees, pixelating the terrain, millions of lights. Civilisation. And then he is moving on, rounding the planet, ascending rapidly towards a new continent, a massive rectangular patch of land, dominated in the east by white-capped mountains, in the west by lush green fertility. The trees look eerily Earth-like: maples, pines, firs.

Through the summits of these snowy mountains he passes, makes for the west, where forming amongst the green he perceives clusters of grey, expanding and diffusing like spilled water. Cities and town and villages, cultivated upwards towards the sky, structures taller than anything he's known. Conical, cylindrical, rectangular skyscrapers, linked by sky bridges, intersected with viewing and landing platforms. Steeples, campaniles, and turrets for summits. Silver and grey and black and white and blue. And everywhere, windows. Many are taller than the 828 metre, 163-storie Burj Khalifa rising above the Dubai cityscape, a miniature pony in this land of stallions. Taller than the proposed Kingdom Tower of Jeddah, projected at 1000 metres. Taller, too, than the proposed 189-storie Azerbaijan Tower, anticipated to house over a million people, as well as schools and hospitals. These structures must be 200 stories, maybe even 300. He cannot comprehend how high this is, 300 stories. What are they made of? Concrete and steel? No, probably not. And so many of them: one commercial district after another. And he sees obelisks, also of unknown height, decorated in symbols he guesses at once must be hieroglyphs. Out here, millions of light years from Earth, hieroglyphs. How can that be? But then, how can any of this be? How can he even be here, in a world so much like Earth yet nothing like Earth?

The city skyscrapers give ground to much smaller structures. There, too, now discernible amongst the shorter buildings, are grid like patterns. Roads. But there is something else out there, too, far into the zenith of the horizon. Three large, triangular shapes, flanked by several smaller versions, offset by buildings like temples. And here, in the majesty of a morning sun, the pyramids are sheathed in radiant casing stones. Before the second-largest of them is a statue, seated on its haunches, forelegs for paws extended, sheathed, too, in dazzling casing stone. And a face, a face he knows he's seen before. The kohl encircling bulbous eyes, a shrivelled nose, drooping ears, corpulent lips, the head enclosed in a brilliant black and gold nemes, *extending backwards, obscuring a misshaped skull. Here is the genesis of Giza.*

He is slowing, sinking to the earth, by the same invisible hands that have led him across the cosmos to this place. Onto what appears to be a columned temple courtyard, enclosed by buildings. It is an ancient temple, a relic in the midst of a modern metropolis. The columns are Doric in design, spaced a distance of two intercolumniations. Between these can be seen the naos, *the inner chamber of each. There, a pediment exhibits representations of these beings' past: stories of wars and conquests, of an age when the chariot was the mode of travel, when shields and spears were thrown, before modern spaceflight was invented. These beings had an ancient past as well.*

There are people down there, a crowd staring up at his approach. People— can he call them that? Dolichocephalic skulls, snubbed noses, elongated ears and arms, stunted legs, bloated protruding stomachs, beady little black eyes, pale lips. Most wear dresses or flowing robes in an array of colours and patterns. From these, he recognises the style of the kalasiris, *white, colourfully garlanded about the neck, drawn together and broached at the waist. But some are bare chested, clad solely in the* shendyt. *All sport sandals.* Nemes *conceal some elongated skulls, diadems in corresponding two-tone hues. But there are other designs, too, ones that seem oddly incongruent to the ensemble. Rounded symbols, feathered. Brilliant colours. Mayan? Aztec? And the dresses and robes—from the Americas as well?*

As he lowers, the faces of the progenitors dissolve into view. Eyes offset by kohl; *black hair, shoulder length. Wigs. They must be. Like the Khemitians. Wigged so many centuries ago. Earrings dangle from extended ears like weights, mouths curve upwards, wrinkling at the sides. They are smiling at him. They have been expecting him.*

The door to the little ship sighs open, and he steps forward onto what feels like stone. His eyes waft to lines of trees encircling the pavilion. Sycamores. Cypresses.

They converge on him. One in particular, in a robe reminiscent of Mesoamerica: dominant brown counterbalanced with intricate motifs in red, green, and blue. Kohl-enfolded eyes, ears of dangling gold. Gold? Maybe so. He wears the double-crowned pschent *of ancient* Khemit, *and he is flanked by several similarly-clad beings in loincloths, crisscrossing chest leather straps, and* nemes. *Each grasps a long, slim spear. Guards? The one in the pschent seems to be addressing them, and they nod, but no words pass between them.*

At length, the crowd parts like waves, and he thinks he hears the sound of a horse whinnying. He stares, disbelieving what he is seeing. No, that can't be. But there it is. A beautiful dark stallion, in a splendidly-embroidered headdress, blanketed about its back. It pulls a wheeled chariot, wooden and golden all at once.

The one in the pschent, the master—the summoner, he decides—gestures to the chariot, and he steps onto it. And as the others look on, the summoner guides the horse towards one of the furthest buildings. A rectangular, pillared structure. An extraterrestrial Parthenon.

They abandon the chariot, ascend stairs, enter, bisecting sun light streaming in through intercolumniations. He sees the frieze on the naos *ahead. Vibrant images he strains to comprehend. Visions of space flights, first contacts, alien worlds. A representation, then, of the journeys these beings have taken, their first forays into the cosmos. Beings. There are the beings in their suits, just like the astronauts he saw in the forest, hands extended to unknown creatures. Lofty creatures, miniature, green and red and brown, armless, dolichocephalic, non-dolichocephalic, clothed, naked. He searches. Where is Earth, where the first contact with the primitive human? Nowhere. How many other worlds have the pharaohs visited, then, that Earth is not even represented here? Countless.*

He turns to the summoner, makes to speak. The other extends his arm towards the entrance to the naos *and an incredibly vacuous room—more a warehouse than anything else. But this is no warehouse: the walls are emblazoned in multitudinous Egyptian hieroglyphics. The main floor space is dominated by tables and stools and lined with rows upon rows of stone shelves in methodically and competently arranged rows. Passable light emanates from holstered torches fastened along the walls. He peers at the shelves. What is on them? Scrolls of paper? Yes. Thousands of them. Hundreds of thousands. Stacked with care, trolled up neatly, wound with wool or rope or something. A library. A hall of records.*

Just as he'd seen in his Tanis vision. There is, however, one major difference: the summoner at his side is not that pharaoh. How can any of this be real? But it feels real. Completely real. He touches the ramparts of the hall. The cold stone is real enough. And so he submits.

The summoner gestures to a specific shelf, reaches forward, takes a scroll in his hands, holds it aloft, unfastens its ribbon. The summoned stares down. Hieroglyphics. He shrugs. He cannot read hieroglyphics. The summoner makes a face, speaks without sound.

You can.

He studies the lines of pictographic text, and suddenly, inexplicably, it is true. He can.

It is not what he wants to read, of the pharaohs arriving thousands of years ago, and experimentation with primitive humanity; of the pharaohs instructing the resulting hybrids on the guiding principles of enlightened thought; of the origins of civilisation on Earth; of a terrible disaster befalling the new race of humans; the deluge, millions killed, civilisations vanquished, guiding principles forgotten, languages and traditions forgotten; how the descendants of the original Khemitians sought to reunify; how the Hanuti *sprang into being—.*

No. What he reads is much simpler. Yet so much more.

To my king, my lord, the restorer of all things; you, my king, who…

He skips ahead.

Oh, let us rejoice in this wondrous day, that Ra-Mesu, the one in the ear of the heretic, is hereby ordered from the lands of Bu Wizzer. *Ra-Mesu, who is of the* sesh, *but has striven to turn the people against one another, who preaches the blasphemous words of that true heretic. Ra-Mesu may go, to take with him his twelve tribes of blasphemers, to spread their heretic teachings to those who dwell in the darkness of foreign lands…*

He turns to the summoner. Ra-Mesu? Sesh?

Today we rejoice in the expulsion of Ra-Mesu, of the ear of the heretic whom we know was a gift from the birthplace of Ptah. The heretic, born of foreign woman; the heretic, who was tutored in the blasphemous teachings of his mother, that same woman who believed such wisdoms had been passed down to her and her descendants ever since the beginning. She who so abused the High House, and who taught her heretic to do likewise; he who corrupted Ra-Mesu, who banished the *Hanuti*, who forbade the worship of all neters but one, who forged the lie that Aten was not the sun. Such teachings sought to destroy all that is sacred. But the heretic has died, and now we celebrate the banishment of Ra-Mesu and his followers…

Heretic? Ptah? He searches his mind. Ptah was one of the creator gods. He was revered for creating the Khemitian world. The birthplace of Ptah was written Sa-Ptah *in Khemitian. Sa-Ptah. This is where he is now, then. Sa-Ptah. That is the name of this place, this world. And he knows that Sa-Ptah has been retranslated by modern scholars as Sirius. Sirius, then. The birthplace of the human race is Sirius. Sa-Ptah. He thought he had passed into Orion's Belt. He was wrong.*

Who is this heretic, the gift, as the letter says, born of a woman who taught forbidden words? Of course. Akhenaten, born of Tiye. Tiye, meaning "She is the One." Tiye, foreign-born. Akhenaten, a gift to the people from Sirius. Born of woman, but not technically of her.

Yes.

But this is interference! You impregnated a woman with the future Akhenaten. But the scroll says you returned merely to observe humanity.

Observation in the form of examination.

That was interference.

That was a necessity. The Hanuti *had evolved, had become too powerful. Akhenaten was sent to restore all things. He was sent to cleanse the* sesh.

The sesh*?*

The sesh *is all the people of* Bu Wizzer. *He was sent to purify the* sesh, *to banish the* Hanuti, *which he did. For a time. When he died, his successors undid all of his work.*

The king being written to in the letter—it must be Horemheb. Horemheb had been ruthless in erasing Akhenaten from existence.

Yes.

But who is Ra-Mesu? And who are these followers who were banished?

You know. You know.

Yes, he knows. Somehow.

Ra-Mesu was one of Akhenaten's chief advisers, a vizier, someone in Akhenaten's "ear." A very important man.

Yes.

He was eventually banished years after Akhenaten's death because he continued the teachings of Akhenaten. Horemheb exiled he and his followers.

But there is more. Ra-Mesu meant "The Second Reincarnation of Ra." A title, nothing more. The Greeks had mistranslated it as Ramose. And then, as time progressed, it had evolved again.

He pauses. It can't be.

Ramose.

Ra-Mose.

Mose
Moses.

But this makes no sense at all. Moses had not been alive during the reign of Akhenaten, and he most certainly had not been a vizier. He was a Hebrew, raised an Egyptian, who had then become aware of his true identity and had led his people to freedom. The Exodus.

No. He has forgotten something. He closes his eyes, concentrates. Yes, it is there. Like food between cushions, it has slipped through.

Moses the Hebrew. But herein lies the fiction. It is said that Moses is Hebrew for moshe, *which means to draw or take something from the water. The Hebrew baby was drawn from the water by pharaoh's daughter. But the irony is that he could not have been called Moshe by his people, simply because Hebrew was not yet a language, would not exist for hundreds of years. And so obviously, it could not have been spoken by Hebrews living in Egypt at the time of Akhenaten. Hebrews spoke Khemitian.*

And the time of Ra-Mesu's existence was also a modern falsehood, perpetrated by popular culture. It is believed by some that Ramses the Great was the pharaoh who granted Ra-Mesu and his people the freedom to leave Egypt, but there is no credible evidence to suggest such. Ramses lived from the approximate years of 1,303 to 1,213 B.C.E., but the truth is, he was not born until forty years after Akhenaten's death. Therefore, by the time he became pharaoh, in 1279, Moses/Ra-Mesu would already have been very old, not the young, robust ear to the king.

Ra-Mesu and his heretic followers—who refused to accept the dynastic religious teachings of the Hanuti, *who were stubbornly bound to the notion of monotheism—were banished. But they did not worship one god. They worshipped a principle. Enlightenment. Aten. And when they emigrated to the land that would one day be Israel, over time, the teachings of enlightenment slowly decayed. In the end, Aten became a god after all. They called Him Yahweh.*

Yahweh.
God.
Allah.

When Ra-Mesu was exiled, he took with him twelve tribes. Twelve of an original 42, the founding tribes comprising the Khemitian people, representatives of all the different peoples of the Earth. 42 tribal descendants who migrated to Khemit, where they formed a single, cohesive, multicultural whole.

42 tribes. 42 triangles on paper.

He stares at the summoner.

There had been 42 people on that ship. And he had counted in their number.

Yes.
There had been men, women, children.
Yes.
But you said you impregnated women.
Yes. What you witnessed that night on the ship were descendants. The first-born of first-born.
Descendants?
He considers the scroll. Tiye.
A descendant?
She was. Sprung from the original bloodline.
He freezes. His mother.
Yes. First-born of first-born. As were you.
As was I?
Come.

Ask your mother, *the man had said.* Ask your mother. *Ask her what? What did this all have to do with that aged man?*

The summoner gestures for him to follow. He does so, his mind swirling. They are leaving the hall, it appears, descending the stairs and passing between columns, towards another somewhat smaller temple. A crowd of beings are with them, curious onlookers ever.

The second temple's naos *is vastly different. It is a room of mirrors. Mirrors for walls, for a ceiling, for a floor. Individual but secreted as one, like the stones of the King's Chamber.*

But these are not really mirrors. They are devices of some sort, machines. He counts the devices. 42 in all. 42 comprising the walls, ceiling, the floor. And suddenly, each springs to life, and the room is flooded with the colour of 42 distinct images of babies, over and over again, throughout the ages.

The original 42 hybrid offspring? And their descendants?
Yes. Always a perfect balance. 21 males, 21 females.
He tries to recall the people on the ship. A perfect number—21 of each? He can only guess.
Those I saw on the ship—do they know?
Some will come to know, just as you have come to know. Most will not.
Why?
There is no need.
And why the examinations?
Humanity must evolve.
Evolve?

Upgrades. Enhancements. Each descendant has a gift. Some will use this gift, some will not. You have been enhanced.

Me?

The summoner gesticulates to one of the mirrors.

There. Your birth.

He sees himself. He sees his mother, jubilant, hugging his newborn body close to hers. He sees joy on her face. Joy. She had been happy once, he remembers. Baseball games, trips to the zoo, to museums. Joy.

And no father. Now he understands why. His mother lied; none of these descendants had had fathers. Immaculate conception of the third kind. His mother was destined to have a child, a single child. And in time, when she understood the true implications of who she was, who he was, understood that at some point they would take him and experiment with him, she had lost the will to be happy. She had shrivelled up, become a shadow and nothing more.

He wants to laugh. How he hated the darkness, how she hated it, too. The examinations. They'd come to her, too, over the years. How often? When? At night, when he was in the room next door, sleeping through everything as youngsters often do? Had they entered through her open window, like the breeze, between faintly ruffling curtains? Had they stood over her bed, and had she sat up, terrified but unable to scream? Had they examined her there, or had they taken her away, as they had taken him, onto their ship?

There are people who have been trying to kill me.

Yes.

One of them told me to ask my mother why. Why would he say that?

That is for you to discover.

He wants to hate the summoner now, wants to hate them all. Why not this one last answer? And what of his supposed enhancement? The ability to scale hotels, to emit energy? This is a gift? What gift is there in this? They have destroyed his relationship with his mother. How many other relationships have they destroyed? How many other sons and daughters have grown up in the joyless confines of a broken home? What fortune is there in this? What is he supposed to do with the knowledge that he was an embryo implanted into the unwilling womb of a woman, herself once an unknowing implant? And then he thinks of his grandparents. Of course. He's never had a grandfather; his mother had never known him, she had said. She'd had a terribly distant and strained relationship with her own mother, his grandmother. In fact, he now concedes, he has never really known his grandmother at all. So many lies, efforts to conceal shame. What did she have to be ashamed of? She had been raped by the pharaohs. Rape. They all had.

This was wrong, he tells the stranger. With me, with all the others throughout time. You have forced yourselves onto people. This has always been wrong.

All things have a place, a purpose, in this universe. Collectively, all things bring balance. You are our creation. Were it not for us, you would not exist. We took advantage of inferior beings. We did do this, yes. But you must remember, you humans have forced yourselves upon others, have you not? Animals in zoos and aquariums, animals hunted to extinction, your planet harvested and damaged beyond repair. And what of your wars? Wars fought over vengeance, over religion? How often has your race imposed its way on itself and its planet?

He wants to say it is not the same, but he knows he cannot justify such a response. Yes, humans had raped and pillaged just as effectively.

We have had good teachers.

The summoner seems content with the response.

He has another question.

How often did you come to see me?

Only that once. But we will come again.

When?

Soon.

Now the mirrors morph with the faces of the 42 modern descendants. Above him, beside him, below on the floor. Faces he knows. As they are today. They are naked, and their bodies are revolving, as if on display, and he sees their birthmarks.

And then the mirror projecting his own image dissolves into something completely different. Of a scene at night, where a man digs by lamplight in the sand. A man discovering a doorway, opening this door, descending a flight of stairs, emerging into what can only be the Hall of Records. And the man falls to his knees and weeps. Then he collects himself, and he peruses the shelves. He unravels scroll after scroll. And then one gives him pause. Transfixed, he gapes in awe. And then he rolls this one back up, gently places it in the breast pocket of his jacket. Then he travels back up the stairs, closes the door and tosses mounds of sand onto it.

David Trent.

Yes.

And this is the Hall of Records.

No, it is not.

But this must be the Hall! The doorway down, the shelves, the scrolls. A vast repository of knowledge. You summoned me there in my vision.

I did. But this you see now is not that place.

But he had to have found it. He had been digging at Giza, under the Sphinx.

No, he had not.

The summoned gapes. There is no logic to this.
Where, then?
Somewhere else.
He never looked at Giza?
No.
Then he wasn't looking for the Hall?
In the beginning, perhaps. But he found his own path. As will you.
Where?
And then he knows.
Amarna—Akhetaten? He went there?
Perhaps.
Tell me!
In time.
He yields.
That scroll. He took it with him.
What he found had been meant for the world.
Of course. And he was killed for it, for the secrets it contained.
Yes.
And then it was hidden.
Yes.
We need to see this place.
In due time, it will present itself to all of humanity.
What was on that artefact?
You know. You have just seen it.
He knows. Ra-Mesu, the Exodus, Akhenaten. The descendants.
But on his computer, he had written 2958450631080309. I am 2958450631080309.
You are.
But those coordinates are the Great Pyramid! The pyramid is the key! It must be! The Hall of Records—
The pyramid was but the doorway. The Hall is someplace else.
His head is spinning.
You brought me to Egypt to learn all of this. To Giza, to Tanis and the crop circle.
Yes.
The break-in at the Cairo Museum. It was you.
You will come to understand why. Egypt is only the beginning.
That statue from the museum—why did you take it?

No answer.

Where did you take it?

And then a mirror's image is dissolving again, from his face to a single mountain, its top sheared as if by some giant unseen hand. A mountain in the midst of a barren land. He knows this mountain; he saw it in that vision in the museum.

He turns.

Is this Egypt?

No. This is not Egypt.

I've seen it before.

Yes.

Where is it?

That, too, is for you to discover.

And the others, too? The others from the ship?

No. Only you.

Only me? Why?

Because you are different.

How?

You will come to know.

But I—

In time, all will be revealed. I have faith in you. You will discover these things. And when you do, we will come to you.

You will come to me?

We will come. And all the world will know the truth.

There are many who will not be convinced. They will not believe.

Then we will give them something to believe in.

When?

Now.

And then he was back, back from the cosmos, back to where he'd begun. How long had he been gone? It had felt like hours.

He saw that the others—there were fewer; apparently many of Denison's men had either abandoned him or had been ordered out—were staring at him. Concern, he read on their faces. Some of their faces. Denison was panting like a dog.

I have so much to tell you, but we have to go, he told them, and it was only then that he realised the room was shaking ominously. He dropped his arms, raw with strain, stepped clear of the container.

Denison waved a finger resolutely. "No!" he hollered over the din of the vibration. "Where did you go? What do you know?"

I know that we have to go *now*!

"Tell me!"

This was no longer the man who had been his captor. Gone was the composed confidence from the limousine, the hotel. Denison had become possessed, frantic, desperate. As if he realised finally that he was no longer in control of the situation. As if he realised now who was.

He lunged forward, and the summoned felt a hand tighten around his shoulder blade. And it should have hurt, Denison's grasp. But it did not. At least, not as he had expected. He freed himself of the grip, swung at Denison, caught him on the cheek with his fist. Denison staggered backward, rubbing at his swiftly swelling face.

The next time you touch me, I'll kill you.

Strange he should say this; he'd never been a fighter. But Denison was not calling his bluff, consigning himself instead to motionless silence.

The summoned turned to Lauren, to the professor.

We need to leave.

"Then let's go," she replied, spinning on her heel and turning towards the darkened entrance.

Something was blocking the way. Not something. Someone.

That wasn't quite accurate either. There were two figures, one guided by the other, pistol in hand. A pistol suddenly pointing directly at the head of Denison.

The few minions who had chosen to remain waited for Denison to say something, anything. But he was speechless, unarmed, defenseless.

The stranger gazed at each of these men in turn, three in all, shaking his head slowly. "I do not recommend it."

And then one of them panicked, glancing apprehensively at the others and reaching far too obviously for his own side arm. A single shot rang out, rumbling along the stone walls. Wounded on the side of the head, the minion reached up, an effort to stem the flow of blood emanating from the porous wound, then slumped to his knees, toppled sideways, writhing uncontrollably. Within seconds, he was still.

The stranger turned and fired on the other two in turn. The first was struck in the forehead, and he was dead before his body hit the ground.

The other, however, was able to draw and squeeze off a single shot, which ricocheted uselessly some distance from the attacker. A bullet found his own shoulder, and he grimaced in agony, but a second shot to his forehead silenced him, too.

The pistol refocused on Denison, who extended a pair of defensive hands. The figure stepped into the wan light. "You have no one to hide behind now."

"You've made your point."

"I have been waiting some time for this."

"I have no quarrel with you. But this other—" Denison's eyes fell indignantly on the form of Seldon. He seethed. "And to think I took you in. I gave you a purpose. And this is how you thank me."

Seldon gestured to the other, eyes trained on his former master. "You know why he's come."

The assassin dropped a backpack he was carrying to the stone floor. Things rattled within. Little wooden boxes, it sounded like. He reached into the folds of his *jellabiya*, eyes trained on the others scattered throughout. He scanned them more acutely, like a buyer at a car lot. The older one, further back. He extracted something covered all in cloth. "Professor Booth. A pleasure to make your acquaintance."

The professor said nothing.

"I will need your assistance. I have something here I cannot read."

The professor's eyes graduated from the face of the killer to the object held tenderly in his hands. An object now exposed. A clay tablet.

The summoned stepped forward.

I can save you the time. But not here. We need to get clear.

Something in the summoned's eyes caused the Egyptian to hesitate. He knew this man. Of course he did: it was Mark Brydges. But that wasn't it. He knew him from another time and place, long before he had met Fadil Nahas and had embraced, then parted from, the ways of the *Hanuti*. And certainly before he had learned how to kill. He and this young man before him now had met years ago—something was telling him this. But how could that be?

And then the pain began again inside his head. He reached up with his armed hand, rested a palm on his forehead, closed his eyes, winced. It was then he noticed Denison stepping menacingly towards him, and he lowered his arm again. "I don't think so."

The summoned was struggling with recognition, too. Strange, he thought, how he should know this man. Yes, he was the assassin who had killed Trent, who had planned to kill him. But he was more than that. He poured through the volumes of details in his mind. There, the temple, the mirrors of faces of descendants. Asians, Caucasians, Africans. And then he was twelve years old again, back in the alien craft, staring at others on gurneys. One stood out. In his early twenties, staring lifelessly upwards in submission. He had turned, and the face had become clear. A face of fear when there was nothing to fear. It was the face that was staring at him now.

He breathed.

I know you. You were there. But it can't be.

He gazed at the suddenly cowering Egyptian.

But it is. You were there. You were there, too.

The assassin shook his head amid spasms of pain.

They took you, too.

He reached for his shirt, turned.

Here—does this look familiar?

The assassin stared at the birth mark, and he instantly recognised it. He had one impossibly the same on his own back.

The summoned gazed around the grumbling room at the others.

He was there with me, on the ship. With me and the others.

The assassin broke his silence, though his voice, much restrained from the unremitting pain in his head, was a shadow of its previous authority. "I don't know what you're talking about," he moaned, waving the tablet in the air, but esoterically he knew full well that what the summoned was telling him was perfectly true. Repressed memories, images, suddenly invaded him: a desert night, a conflagration of bright lights in the sky, something lowering itself towards the ground. A hatch. Opening…

You never had a father, did you? Only a mother.

And then the plane crash, and his miraculous sparing. Debris vomited forward across the landscape, death everywhere. It had defied explanation at the time, and he had pretended he had been there with a little boy in rags, had pretended that he hadn't been the only survivor, that it wasn't so astonishing after all. But there had been only one survivor that day. He, the wretched little boy. Only now did it make sense. He had been born different. He should have died that day in the desert when the plane had dropped out of the sky. But he hadn't.

"No!" he shouted at length, flinging the artefact uselessly to the ground. But it was true. And with this sudden admission, the incessant pain in his skull abruptly evaporated. Vanished, as if it had never been there. He flexed his eyelids downward, impeding all light, opened them again. Yes, it was gone.

And he thought he had been in control of his actions! That was impossible now. He had *had* to come here.

But what was he supposed to do with this information? Rejoice? Is this what *they* wanted? To rejoice in the knowledge of who he really was, what had happened to him all those years ago? His mind was spinning uncontrollably: his youth again. The incident in more detail. The uncontained desert at night, portentous shadows on dunes. The lights in the night sky. The unfamiliar hands on him, the ship, the gurney, the others around him. And he remembered that he had felt no pain, and that the fear he had initially experienced had evaporated.

Was this reason to rejoice? He felt no happiness now. All he could feel was shame. Unadulterated shame. It had been a lifetime since he'd been ashamed about anything, and he hated it now, hated it more than anything.

He reached far down, under his flowing *jellabiya*, and probed his lower back with a sudden certainty. There, the birthmark upon which he had always wondered, had always concealed, had never spoken of. There. And now the summoned was exposing this enigma.

It was implausible, yet it was all that made sense.

The summoned was advancing on him, arm extended, hand curled and pointing.

You're just like me.

"I am nothing like you!" He was trembling now, hysterically, afraid for the first time in years.

They gave you a gift. And this is how you choose to use it?

"I have no gift!"

You lie. You were there. You know.

"I know? What can I possibly know?"

The summoned fumbled with his words. What did the Egyptian know, really? That he'd been taken aboard a spacecraft years before, that he had been one of many, that he'd been examined by a race of benign beings, that he had been returned to a life of homeless misery, of unknown identity. The memory had been repressed, just as his own had. And so, how could the Egyptian now know anything?

The assassin struggled for control of the pistol, fumbled to point it at him. There was no time. He leaped forward, knocked the weapon away, and it went off. The assassin lashed out, smacking him across the face, and the two of them tumbled to the stone floor in a mass of desperation.

Then they were rising to their feet, arms flailing for supremacy. They backed against the stone container, and the summoned was swinging wildly with his fists in the direction of the other's face. The assassin ducked, turned him over, and forced him into a headlock. But the summoned kicked backward, his foot impacting somewhere in the assassin's groin. The arms around his shoulders and neck relaxed, but the pair of hands were racing upwards toward him, curling deliciously around his neck. He fumbled, fell sideways awkwardly, the Egyptian on top of him. He felt a pain along his side.

Then he saw Seldon emerging from nowhere, pistol raised high. The man was swinging with all his might, and the gun crashed destructively into the back of the assassin's head. Dazed, the Egyptian fell away, grasping at his head, crawled for the nearest wall, offered no further resistance. As if a suddenly caged animal, a snivelling, pathetic creature, prostrate on the floor near the far wall, face buried in hands, moaning harmoniously with the trembling walls around him.

Then he crawled towards the backpack he had brought in with him. Loosed the strings, extracted the boxes. Opened them. Black orbs began to dance across the floor. They slithered past, through the entrance to the chamber.

The summoned stared at the floor, suddenly writhing all around them. What were those things? And then one of them was crawling up his leg, up his thigh, his chest, toward his face, and it was all too clear. He swashed away, and the scorpion toppled uselessly downward, scuttled past. But another was on his back, and he shook himself violently, hoping to lodge it free. Nearby, he could hear Lauren screaming, then the professor ordering them out. He saw Denison dash past, then Seldon, pistol still in hand. Then the professor, grabbing at Lauren and helping her along. Something was crawling through her hair, but the professor was swatting at it.

And then another was on his leg, crawling more rapidly than he had anticipated. He reached down, and in the faded light, something stabbed his palm. Cold, hard, moist. Searing pain raged within him all at once. The scorpion scuttled away, and he staggered backwards, against the wall, lost his balance, stumbled towards the sarcophagus.

The convulsions began to increase, far more severe now. A horrifying sound accompanied the seizures.

He screamed, or at least tried to, and he felt hands reaching around him. The professor, helping him to his feet. They stumbled from the antechamber, beyond and into the Grand Gallery, past someone, prostate against the wall, head buried in his hands, *jellabiya* spilled about him like water. The Egyptian had not escaped after all. Why? Why was he still here? He seemed inclined to remain. They left him then, gladly, faltered through the Gallery, towards Al Mamun's entrance.

And freedom.

Deeb stared as one individual after another trickled from the pyramid, itself clothed in shadow under the night-like sky. It was afternoon, yet it was midnight. Egypt had been thrown into virtual darkness. A new plague.

Amid the confusion, Wasem ogled the unfolding spectacle. He saw people exiting the pyramid, scrambling down its face. A force greater than any was at work here.

"I didn't notice you."

He turned, saw Deeb gazing at him. He noticed the brigadier's tone. Deeb was no longer angry. Then, again, there were other matters at hand. "What is happening?" he wondered, to which his superior shrugged.

"Who can know."

"Listen, General. About everything—"

"It's alright, Wasem." Deeb chose not to look at him, winced as he spoke, as though the conciliatory tone in his voice was hurting him physically. He pointed ahead. "I have a horrible feeling about this."

"We need to clear this area."

"Good idea."

And then Cairo itself began to convulse. Within seconds, whole sections of chosen walls, roofs, minarets, turrets, sidewalks, road—all were instantly and violently torn free with explosively destructive force. As if specifically targeted. All with one thing in common.

Remnants of pyramidal casing stones.

High into the portentous sky above from these select structures, a torrent of limestone, thousands and thousands of tonnes, was being thrust, then hurtled by some unseen catapult, towards the Plateau. Hurtling and then magnetizing, for they did not bombard Giza: they affixed themselves to it. To the Great Pyramid specifically. One after another, after another, after another, recalled with meticulous precision. Giza was quaking with new life.

A squall generated by the movement was born, gained momentum. Police cruisers buckled, onlookers were toppled, debris mingled with surrounding sand and was thrown about haphazardly. Anything not possessing of significant weight became airborne. Book shelves, paint cans, toktoks, pots and pans, ox carts, garbage cans, umbrellas, couches, chairs, glass, street and collapsible sidewalk signs, wrappers, boxes, cartons, food items, electronics, tables, clothing, canes, motorcycles, car parts. Even the stones along the Plateau itself, which had long since fallen from the earthquake that had ravaged the area. People and animals were bowling down streets, crashing into one another, into walls, into vehicles, tumbling from bridges into the Nile, careening towards the Plateau, some pulled to safety, others abandoned where they fell.

When the final stone passed overhead and found its place on the pyramid, the earthquake-like rumblings instantly ceased. The squall died, bringing to a halt the horde of city possessions which had been dragged across streets, through or over fences, and onto the Plateau. Several seconds passed. Seconds of deafening silence.

And then the complex spoke once more. A shriek. And those who could turned and watched, saw an explosion of dust emanate from the pyramid. When the particles settled, they left in their wake a completely smooth pyramid, unbelievably, as it must have been thousands of years ago. Sanded by some unseen hand.

The clouds parted, retreated from sight, and brilliant sunshine once again reigned over Cairo. But nothing was as it had been. For now, a new pyramid, encased in faded casing stones, punctiliously smoothed along its walls, stood where a battered old remnant had once been. Beyond, Cairo was a monumental mess. Whole buildings had been decimated or obliterated completely; others, no longer able to stand on their own, could be heard crashing to the ground, into a mountain of dust.

The summoned stood, wiped himself clean. He remembered the scorpion bite. He gazed down at his hand, at the gaping wound inflicted by the arthropod. But there was no longer any pain. He should be dead by now. Or at least dying. But he was alive. Alive and well.

His eyes passed merely over the catastrophe, to the lioness in the sand. He could feel a shadow across his face. Denison.

Well?

"Well?"

Well, what now?

"What now? Now you go home. I don't think it would be right to make a scene just now."

Good thinking.

"Stay safe. And wait for the day when I call on you again. Because I will call on you."

I look forward to it.

With that, Denison turned and began traipsing towards a now-battered squadron of SUVs, his men clamouring to keep up with him.

The summoned called after him.

Was it what you thought it would be?

He stopped, glanced back. "Everything. And more."

Everything has changed.

But Denison had nothing more to say. The summoned watched him retreat to his vehicle, turned, saw Wasem speaking somewhat cordially with someone important. It must be Deeb, the one Wasem told him about the night previous. The conversation began with bravado, then the two seemed to calm, even share in a joke. He moved on. Seldon in custody. And there, the professor grinning at him. He nodded, gazed up into the sky.

She was beside him now, and he could feel her arm enfolding in his. The touch was warm and pleasing all at once, and he smiled.

"What?" she said in his ear. "What are you thinking?"

His eyes traveled from the heavens, settled on her heavenly face.

I think I need to call my mother.

From where he reposed on the hillside, a lone observer stared down at the evolving scene, a photo in his hands. A woman, once attractive and now pale and withered with depression. *Ask your mother*, he had said to her son, sensing bewilderment beyond words. And although she was not here to respond, she was here all the same. She, he—they were all connected. Connected to this architectural impossibility that now dominated the landscape. Linked. From a crash in a Bavarian forest on a cold, lonely winter night, to this marvel here and now. And he had been watching her for years, just as he had been watching the boy, the boy that was now a man. Just as he would continue watching.

He'd made how many attempts on the boy? Two? Three? He had begun to lose count. But the boy's luck would run out one day soon. And then the world would be safe again.

Nahas was dead, as were many of his followers. They had barely begun before they had been cut down. But they would regroup. They were hundreds, perhaps thousands, strong. And one day very soon, they would unleash themselves. Not like this pitiful display here. The shopkeeper they'd embalmed. What of that? This misguided attempt at killing Brydges. A pittance of their capabilities.

Below was mass confusion. A horde of new witnesses were entering the Plateau. There was the sound of sirens and horns. Helicopters dominated the sky. And he saw, with little musing, Denison and his men pile into their vehicles and navigate through the crowd, unmolested of the police. How things never changed. He saw, too, that some of his own men, those who had survived the gunfight, were retreating towards him, up the sandy hill. The cowards who had not taken the initiative to escape, as he had. Feeble old he. But he could not blame them. He was the veteran, not they. He had been fighting the good fight since before they were babies. And he would continue that fight.

His eyes alighted on the summoned. There, embracing the professor, the assistant, the Egyptologist, the inspector. The hero. The hero of what? Had he any idea who he was, what he was? Who *she* was?

One of the men dropped exhaustedly beside him, wiping at the sweat on his forehead. One of the elders among the group, middle-aged and Danish, too. Behind him, others congregated, speaking incoherently.

"We did not accomplish our goal."

"No," he said, "we did not."

"And the *Hanuti*?"

"They will surface again. But I think it safe to assume we are no longer partners."

The man pointed to the summoned. "He is down there. Free to go."

"As are we. The artefact that Trent uncovered is buried again."

"How do you know?"

He gestured with an aged and confident finger, to the pyramid. "It's in there."

"The assassin?"

"He entered with it. But he did not leave."

"You're sure it was him?

He was sure. He knew the man well enough. Marseilles, Barcelona, Leningrad, Dubai, Lima, Paris, Rome, Mexico City. Al Aqrab had been the best.

"What will you do now?"

He fumbled in his blazer pocket for something, extracted a folded photograph. Laid it down on the desert floor beside the image of the woman.

It was a mountain, flattened at its peak. He studied it for several seconds, ran a finger up one side of it, down the other. Then he delved into his blazer again, and this time beheld a cell phone.

"We have work to do."

EPILOGUE

The Ranger frenzies along a dirt road that dissects the landscape, depositing a trail of dust in its wake. Like shadowing waves from a speedboat. Within, Maná's gently-soothing "Mariposa Traicionera" fills the otherwise vacant air. *Mariposa traicionera, todo se lleva el viento/Traitorous Butterfly, gone with the wind.*

Gone, but not lost. He knows something is out here, in this grimy, disorienting wasteland. But he is not lost. He knows exactly where he is going.

He decided to cross the border at Laredo-Nuevo/Laredo, and sweep west through the states of Tamaulipas, Nuevo León, Coahuila, and then into the northeast corner of Durango. This has taken him through the bleak though beautiful Sierra Madre Oriental Mountain Range.

He glances into the rear-view mirror, sand-soaked dark locks a gable over weary brown eyes. His face is caked in sand, too. In fact, everything is: the dashboard, the wheel, the radio, the seats. Even the floor is bronzed from the stuff. That tends to happen here when one drives with the windows down. He steadies the wheel with one hand, reaches up with the other, wipes at his face. What a discovery: there is skin under that grime. He applies more pressure. Some of it gives way. Now he is playing archaeologist.

And then there it is. Rising conspicuously amidst the austere backdrop that is desert: Cerro San Ignacio. He'd been here only recently with David Trent, before all that unpleasant business. And now he is back again. For the last time? That depends on whether or not he finds what he has come for.

He has crossed into the infamous Mapimí Silent Zone, the Zona del Silencio, or Zone of Silence—whichever name one prefers. He knows all the stories: deadened radio signals, the sightings of strange beings, suddenly useless compasses. In truth, there is precious little evidence to presume the Zone of Silence is anything but ordinary. But it is fun to dream.

He angles along the dusty road, arcing north and then west of the hill, where he eventually parks. He does so just off the main road. It is early enough in the morning that there are no other cars parked; the afternoons sometimes bring adventure-seeking tourists.

The heat is overwhelming. He wipes at his brow, already the seal broken and the sweat leaking down. He gazes up into the sky. Winged creatures overhead. Vultures? Eagles? They are far away, and it is difficult to be sure.

He studies San Ignacio. At just over 1430 metres where it levels off so dramatically, it is no easy trek. He knows how to hike, however. What's better, he's hiked here before.

He exits his truck, fumbles in his pocket for the reminder: a photograph taken while in David's company. He stares down at it now. Taken from the opposite side of the hill, the specs are the same: the upward surging of the earth and then the sudden levelling-off that forms the table top peak is distinguishable. How many months ago had that been? Three, perhaps. Four? No, more likely four.

He reaches into the truck for his backpack. Plenty of water, small snacks inside. He is wearing khaki shorts and a navy-buttoned short sleeve top. Hiking boots. Hiking hat. And sunglasses, naturally. He closes the door, locks the truck, sets off to San Ignacio.

He is suddenly bombarded by an avalanche of thoughts. All concerning David. Good memories. David had come to him a doubter, left firmly convinced. And it had been himself, Brent Hammond, who had accomplished the feat. They'd travelled the world together. They'd both learned so much.

And soon it will all come out.

Ahead, the rising sun vibrantly drenches the hill in light, exposing an unnaturalness contrasting with the drab terrain. Here and there, shadowy swaths of darkness amid grey and green. Then the blatantly dark brown table top. Beautiful, majestic, awe-inspiring. He glances to the sky, a canvas of pale blue dabbled unintentionally with intermittent flecks of white. He can already feel the potency of the sun on his neck. Better not to doddle.

His balance shifts ever so slightly: he has officially begun his ascent. He will switchback along already carved trails between the flora that dot the hill. Though San Ignacio is not steep, he'll get his work in nonetheless.

He perspires rapidly, and he stops to drink several times. Is there any rush? He glances around, suddenly aware that he might have been followed. Dust trails would expose anyone on his tail. But there are none. Nor are there, as he rises higher and higher into the air, any other parked vehicles he might have failed to notice before. There is his once-green Ranger, rapidly diminishing with gained altitude. The sunlight glints off the windshield as it would a pair of sunglasses.

He exhales more emphatically the higher he moves, and he conjunctively regulates his breathing. He wipes his brow under his hat, replaces it atop his head, lets immediately congregated sweat once again trickle down the sides of his face. Soon it will run like rivers, down recently-shaven cheeks, a minor irritant to smooth skin.

Then he has done it. When he reaches the hill's summit, he turns immediately, stares out at the vast panorama sprawled before him. Pale grey desert interspersed with clumps of greenish fauna. And smooth, flat as southern Saskatchewan. The sun radiates down on him, but his sunglasses do a passable job in redirecting its beams. He continues to stare. There is his truck: a darkened blemish against the pale desert.

There is a slight breeze atop the shaved peak, warm and pleasant. He rubs his brow again, replaces his hat, extracts his phone, studies a code of geographic coordinates contained therein. A hunch, but a confident one. Straight ahead, where the ground is more level. The anticipation is a killer. Cautiously he moves. And then he halts. This is it. This spot. He captures several photos of the terrain with his phone, then bends down to inspect the ground. Runs his hand over the smooth sand, the tiny stones. And then he sinks the same hand into the earth, buries it up to the wrist. There. He is touching something. Large, hard.

He reaches in with his second hand, pulls, pauses, dabs at sweat in his eyes. He regroups and pulls a second time. Part of the object is freed; with renewed vigour, he wrenches the rest into the open. He sits back, studies what he has found, what he has come all this way for. A bust of an Egyptian pharaoh, still vibrantly coloured beneath partially obscuring sand. He studies the protruding lips, the recessed cheeks, the rear-sloping skull beneath the pschent, the little abdomen protruding below sunken breasts. He raises the bust, gently shakes it, watches sand spill from it as from an upturned hourglass. He laughs. It is unmistakable. A bust of an Egyptian pharaoh. Not of the saint-seducing gold; no, this little statue is wooden. It should be in a glass case on display in Cairo, but greater forces have brought it here.

He straightens, glancing skywards at the sea of blue gaping back at him. He eagerly licks his lips. He wants to call out.

What's next, Pharaoh?

Something out of the corner of his eye motivates him to turn. There, from the west, far in the distance, a dust trail. A vehicle. He knows who they are, why they have come. Knows he must leave. Now.

Quickly, he places the statue in the backpack. Then he is off. Back down the hillside, faster and faster. They will not catch him, *cannot* catch him.

So he hopes, in any event.

ACKNOWLEDGEMENTS

When I first began this odyssey in early August 2011, I did not know how long it would take to arrive at this stage. Along the way, I learned not only about the art of writing, but about myself. This has truly been my own adventure for the ages.

First of all, I must thank several life-long friends, many of whom appear in this work in one form or another: Brent Hammond, Mike Brydges, Mark Glanzmann, Kyle McKenzie, Jimmy DosSantos, and Rob Bobinac. Rob's London, Ontario company, Red Iron Design, has been reincarnated with all due respect.

To my work colleagues, Susan Legge and Bill Havercroft, for their support and suggestions. I appreciate their comments and concerns, in particular, the recommendation that Mark be more prominent. I listened, and I believe his character is stronger today for it.

My mother-in-law, Julie Jamieson, has been a faithful supporter of this venture since the beginning. It was her suggestion of the birthmark that helped steer the novel in a new and ultimately superior direction.

To the television program *Ancient Aliens*, the genesis of this novel, I offer my utmost thanks. If it wasn't for that Thursday night in early August 2011 when I discovered Christopher Dunn talking about the pyramids, there is no way this novel would have ever been written. I have been an avid supporter of *Ancient Aliens* ever since.

There are many authors who have inspired me along the way. The aforementioned Christopher Dunn, Robert Bauval, Ahmed Osman, Adrian Gilbert, David Hatcher Childress, Stephen Mehler, Andrew Malkowski, Philip

Coppens, Robert Temple, Michael J. Behe, Robert Wright, Robert Schoch, Carl Sagan, Zecharia Sitchin, D.S. Allan, J.B. Delair, Graham Hancock, Toby Wilkinson, Sigmund Freud, Erich von Däniken. As well, countless hours of documentaries and interviews introduced me to many others, John Anthony West and Steven M. Greer chief among them. Thanks to all for the motivation.

iUniverse has been tireless in its efforts to educate me in the world of publishing, and there are several people there, past and present, who I would like to thank. In as chronological order as I can remember, they are Sarah Rancouret, Amy Flaherty, Eddie Wright, James Berry, James Marquis, Robin Sawyer, Kathi Wittkamper, Dianne Lee, and Nolan Estes.

And, finally, my wife has read more versions of this novel than anyone else. She has seen characters and settings change or vanish, and she has patiently offered to read it all again and again. Juggling our busy lives with two little ones has not made things easier, but she has persevered. To her, I owe so much.

CPSIA information can be obtained at www.ICGtesting.com
Printed in the USA
LVOW11s1506080316

478281LV00002B/442/P